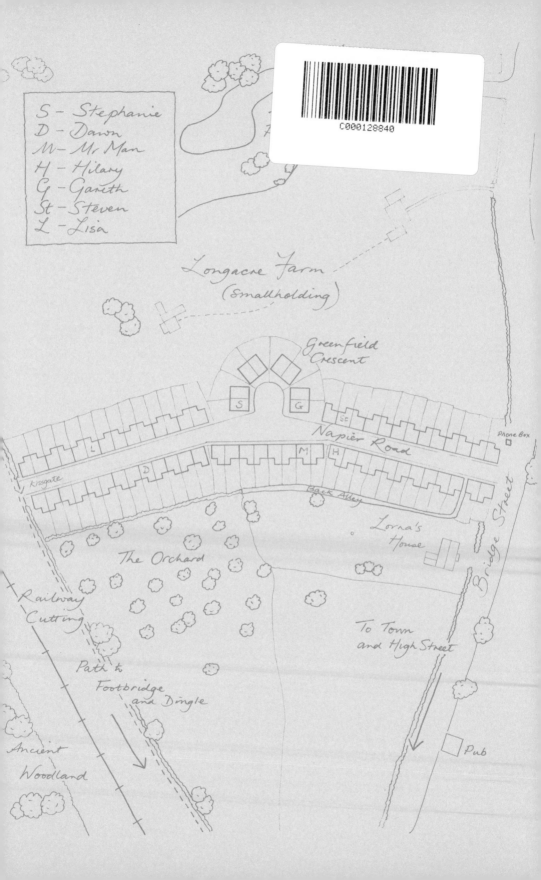

S – Stephanie
D – Dawn
M – Mr Man
H – Hilary
G – Gareth
St – Steven
L – Lisa

Longacre Farm
(Smallholding)

Greenfield Crescent

Napier Road

Back Alley

Lorna's House

The Orchard

Kissgate

Railway Cutting

Path to Footbridge and Dingle

Ancient Woodland

To Town and High Street

Bridge Street

Phone Box

Pub

Praise for *Sorry Isn't Good Enough*

'Told from the perspective of a nine-year-old embroiled in tragedy that shapes her whole life, childhood memories carried with her that resonate on so many levels, it evokes the past in glorious technicolour. I absolutely loved it and cannot do justice to the goldenness it contains, bittersweet and touching'

Amanda Reynolds

'Wonderful. Literally (literally!) couldn't put it down, to me it reads like Joanna Cannon/Maggie O'Farrell with a slice of *Stand by Me* era Stephen King'

Hayley Hoskins

'*Sorry Isn't Good Enough* was gripping and surprising, and at turns chilling and heartbreaking. Stephanie's story will stay with me for a long time'

Melanie Golding

'What a wonderful book; it swept me back to the sixties and my own childhood. Touching and gripping – a story that will stay with me'

Jackie Kabler

'The heart of this emotionally-literate coming-of-age story is Stephanie who, with her eccentric take on the world, yearning for love and unexpected bursts of wit, is as believable as she is sympathetic. What seems like a gentle story on first glance soon reveals itself to be much more: full of life's sorrow, joy, and misunderstanding. I always love Jane Bailey's books, and this is her best yet'

Kate Riordan

Jane Bailey was born and brought up in Gloucestershire, where she now lives. She has written seven novels, including *Lark Song*, *What Was Rescued* and *Tommy Glover's Sketch of Heaven*, and has been shortlisted for the Dillons Fiction prize and the RNA award. She has edited four anthologies of work by young people as Writer-in-Residence for Cheltenham Festivals, First Story and Gloucestershire Hospitals Education Service.

www.jane-bailey.co.uk
Twitter: @JaneBailey15
#SorryIsn'tGoodEnough

SORRY ISN'T GOOD ENOUGH

JANE BAILEY

ORION

First published in Great Britain in 2022 by Orion Fiction,
an imprint of The Orion Publishing Group Ltd,
Carmelite House, 50 Victoria Embankment
London EC4Y ODZ

An Hachette UK Company

1 3 5 7 9 10 8 6 4 2

A CIP catalogue record for this book is
available from the British Library.

ISBN (Hardback) 978 1 3987 0493 0
ISBN (Trade Paperback) 978 1 3987 0494 7
ISBN (eBook) 978 1 3987 0496 1

Typeset by Input Data Services Ltd, Somerset

Printed and Bound in Great Britain by Clays Ltd, Elcograf S.p.A.

MIX
Paper from
responsible sources
FSC® C104740

www.orionbooks.co.uk

To Anna and Lucy
and your wonderful laughter

The characters in this novel are fictional
(although my lovely mum's DIY skills were legendary:
she could make anything – except, perhaps, a decision)

Chapter One

The Man on the Station
May 1997

I have never told anyone what happened that summer.

I find myself trailing back to those woods over and over. Back, back along the paths that led me there. I was nine years old, and the prospect of telling anyone was unthinkable. I thought I'd successfully blocked it out for thirty years. But something has just happened to jolt me out of this delusion. And now I'm running. I'm running down the platform on Paddington station in my stockinged feet.

Less than an hour ago I was the headline speaker at The Dolphin Project conference in a smart London hotel. Everything had gone better than I'd expected, and I was taking questions when a woman at the back asked me a question I had hoped never to hear. She took me completely by surprise.

'Do you think your development of this project is in any way connected to your own traumatic childhood?' I went over suddenly on my right heel. I knew I couldn't wear stilettos. What a fool I'd been to imagine I could pull off the look. I had no doubt that the question had been intended to trip me up. 'I mean, as I understand it, you were implicated in a notorious murder when you were nine. Is that right?'

The words I had prepared to say at the end of my talk seemed to pile up at the roadblock of her question. They formed a tailback down my throat. All the clever things I had imagined saying, choking me into silence.

The woman who had introduced me sprang into action. 'I think that may be a question for another time. Now, we can fit in just one more question . . . Yes, man at the back in the blue jacket.'

It was another unexpected topic, and I thought it suggested he knew something about my children, but I fumbled my way through an answer. I was so shaken up that I didn't hang around afterwards, although lots of kind people came up to me to discuss ideas. I darted for the exit and got in the first taxi I could flag down for Paddington.

As soon as I was at the station I allowed myself to relax a little. The truth is, I'm something of a hick from the sticks, and I was feeling quite cosmopolitan standing there looking at the board for train departures, hundreds of people of all nationalities milling around me. I'd been to the conference in my new role as leader of The Dolphin Project for young people. I thought, I'm one of them. I belong to this bunch of busy, worldly individuals. I felt anonymous rather than invisible.

And it was while I was immersed in this special glow that I spotted a man staring at me from about twenty metres away by the warm baguette stall. I ignored him at first, telling myself he must have mistaken me for someone else. The next time I looked he was still eyeing me, and I wondered if this was how it happened, this was how you got 'picked up' by a stranger, how love stories started. But of course I knew that wasn't going to happen to me. This was some weirdo. Or perhaps he was the man standing next to that journalist who'd asked me the last question. It was. It was him. I looked back at the screen. Platform Five. Good.

I started to make my way to the gate when he leant in front of me, almost standing in my path. 'Stephanie Townsend?'

I looked directly at him, and wondered if there might be something familiar about the eyes. I was about to speak when I remembered another man leaning against a wall once, saying my name with that exact questioning tone, and it sent a ripple of terror through me. I said nothing.

'I thought it was you,' he said.

He followed me through the ticket gate, feeding his ticket in like me. I could feel the pulse in my temples.

'We should talk.' He took hold of my arm and I yanked it away, panicking now.

'I'm sorry,' I said, turning myself away, heading down the platform.

I walked briskly and painfully in my unfamiliar heels, passing the first carriage, and the second. He followed.

'I know what happened. I'm—'

The tannoy cut in with a loud, grating announcement: 'The train now standing at Platform Five . . .'

That's when I took off my shoes and started to run.

Chapter Two

Poppet

My earliest memories of Dawn Webster must be from reception class, in 1961. I have a vivid memory of her mother bending down to hug her at the school gates and calling her 'poppet'. My own mother lets go of my hand and tells me she'll be there to pick me up later. To the amazement of our mothers, we start to seek each other out in the playground, and we are inseparable for years.

Dawn wants my loyalty; I want her mother.

Dawn is short, spiteful and smart. She is spoilt and prone to tantrums. I think I know this straight away, from the way she arches her back when she stands. She is tightly sprung. 'Whatever do you see in Dawn?' Mummy asks, bewildered. I want to tell her – because it's simple – but I can't articulate it. Dawn gives me the time of day; she seeks me out. I am flattered. I want to please her, because when I please Dawn, the world is a better place for a short while. 'You let her walk all over you,' says Mummy. 'You can't say "no" to her. You're like someone half-baked.' But Dawn likes me, I think. Which is more than can be said for Mummy. Nothing I do seems to please her. Also, seeing a lot of Dawn means I get to see more of her mother, who calls me poppet.

We are different to other people. It's possible that my father, lay preacher and Bible class teacher for the Church of the Three in One, has made up this church himself, because no one else I know goes to it. Dawn, for example, goes to a different Sunday school sometimes, at the end of Plum Lane. So does everyone else. Or else they don't go anywhere and have a free Sunday. In any case, it makes us different. Every week we press our knees into the hard prayer cushions that Mummy puts out with some other women in hats, then I go to Sunday school.

We don't have a television. Daddy thinks they 'brainwash' you. And Mummy agrees. Dawn watches television, and saves milk bottle tops for *Blue Peter* and gets to help choose a dog's name. So does everyone else. I see Blue Peter as a fairly tall boy, painted in the same pale blue as the Websters' front door, who organises things in a good cause. It's not until Dawn lets me watch her television in secret (her mother says best not tell Daddy she let me watch it) that I realise it's a cheery children's television show, with pets, news and, best of all, instructions on how to make wonderful things from bits and bobs. Later, I make a tie rack for Daddy out of a cornflake packet, and he says I have a good imagination. Of course, my creation is not as good as the one made on the television, because I have no sticky-backed plastic to cover it with. It has a cockerel on the side, though, and half a bowl of cornflakes, which look quite nice.

Dawn has three teddy bears to my one. Mine is called Trevor, after next door's rabbit who died, and he is threadbare with cuddling. Hers are called Teddy Stroud, Teddy Gloucester and Teddy Hackney, after the places they came from. All their fur is intact.

I know very early on that Dawn has a cruel side. From the way she steps on ants and caterpillars for fun, to the way she happily blames me for stealing apples from the orchard. Her father, who is a short, angry man, is so furious about the owner of the orchard abutting his garden making complaints about stealing, that he cannot let the matter go. He bawls at Dawn until she's red and shaking and tells him it was my idea.

'You!' he shouts, pointing a finger with wide, stumpy nails, just like Dawn's, but larger. 'You, of all people! I expected more from you, Stephanie Townsend. You wait until your father hears about this!' I'm sure I detect a look of satisfaction on his face when he says this. It's useless to protest. I've learnt this. I look at Dawn, but she looks wronged, for all the world like someone who didn't call me a wimp for not wanting to join her in scrabbling through the hedge at the bottom of her garden and gathering apples in our skirts. I have the measure of Dawn, but still I am loyal to her.

Dawn says she's a 'Cockney', which sounds like something you would keep in a hen coop, but she says it with such pride that it makes me wish I was one too. I don't know what I am, apart from a freak. She plays with me even though I have a wonky walk caused by a disease when I was little. This is because Daddy didn't believe in vaccination because God said it wasn't okay. And Mummy agreed. God decides what diseases we get. So I got a disease and I 'drag' my foot. Daddy *does* believe in vaccination now, and Mummy does too. So Jonathan got vaccinated and he walks like a normal person.

Daddy is always happy to sing me to sleep with hymns and he always has hugs for me. It's not that I don't want them – I need them – it's that I need Mummy's hugs more. I have to hang onto what I have, though. Mummy hugs Jonathan. Daddy hugs me. I know it's fair, but it doesn't feel like it. I watch Mummy carefully, and she takes her lead from Daddy when it comes to things like God and so on. So I try to be like her. I find church a bit like school, full of rules it seems impossible to make sense of. Not being worthy to gather up the crumbs under God's table makes as much sense as our teacher telling us not to stand with our hands in our pockets. But I try to learn everything I'm taught anyway, and I can parrot the parables to impress Daddy. I need his approval, because it's all there is. I don't see that the more he praises me, the less she wants to. Or if I see it, I make no connection. I just keep on digging myself in deeper.

When Daddy accosts me about stealing apples from the orchard (Mr Webster has been treacherous and told him), I speak honestly.

'It was Dawn's idea. I didn't know there was an orchard there. She told me the owner didn't mind and she'd done it before.'

'Why doesn't *that* surprise me?' says Daddy. He is still cross with me, and gives me a slap on the leg for stealing.

I say I'm sorry, but Mummy says, 'Sorry isn't good enough.' She wheels that phrase out every time I apologise, but I've never been brave enough to ask her what *would* be good enough. The worst thing, though, is that Daddy forbids me from playing with Dawn again, as she is 'a bad influence'. And Mummy agrees.

Well, he can't stop me from playing with her at school, where I'm endlessly delighted by her mischief and daring. One playtime, she spots that Miss Worth has popped into the infants' toilets when there's no one in them. She wears flat brown lace-up shoes and has a furry face.

'Bet she's taking a piss!' says Dawn, nudging me. 'Let's go and look.'

I follow her into the toilets, which are in a block in the play-ground. There is a row of four cubicles, and one is in use. Dawn widens her eyes at me, then kneels down and bends her head to floor level, taking a peek under the toilet door. She turns back to me, grinning. 'Go on!' she mouths. I do the same.

There is our elderly teacher, her flesh-coloured knickers around her knees, suspenders exposed, her skirt gathered in her lap. I can only assume that she must have had her eyes closed in concentration when Dawn looked, because now her pinprick pupils focus on me, and her purse-string mouth tightens bitterly. I get up quickly, and we run out into the playground, where we hoot and giggle. I don't believe we've got away with it, and we haven't. For whatever reason, Miss Worth only picks on me, for being 'rude and disgusting at playtime'. I am invited out to the front of class after break and given the ruler ten times across my palms and ten times across my knuckles. I set my mouth in a rigid line. I don't cry. Mummy says crying is weak and manipulative. I am four years old, and I have already taught myself not to cry.

7

If Dawn thinks it's not fair that I got punished when she didn't, she doesn't say so. When I show her my sore hands and say I wish Miss Worth would die, she says, 'Fuck her.'

'Miss Worth is a stupid kant,' says Dawn, and I agree. We don't know what this word means, or even that we both have one, we just know that it's something like a person who is really horrible. I also know it's French, because when Dawn's dad was talking about how he called his boss at work a stupid kant, he said, 'Excuse my French.' Speaking a foreign language comes in handy when people annoy us.

I suppose it shouldn't surprise me when I overhear Miss Worth talking to my mother after school. I'm tidying the folders when she says in a low voice:

'Stephanie is a very strange child, Mrs Townsend. There is something very odd about her. Very, *very* odd.'

Do they think I'm deaf as well as odd? I'm just on the other side of the classroom with my back to them. Grown-ups can be so dense. The turned back is such an easy trick.

'What's she done?'

'Well, I'm sorry to say, she looked under the door while I was . . . spending a penny.'

'Really? I'm so sorry! That's shocking.'

Mummy yanks me by the hand and walks me home in silence. 'I'm sorry,' I say, but it isn't good enough, because she still seems cross. Because I am odd and shocking.

Our house, with its 1950s bay window and garage, is the first one in the crescent, and so at an angle to Napier Road, appearing to face up the road as we walk down it. Whenever I see it there, waiting for me at the end of a school day, I feel a sense of relief. It has different moods, though. Sometimes it seems to welcome me as I come through the door; other times it sighs, 'Not you again.' Either way, I like the familiarity of it. The smell of the floor polish on the hall tiles, the shoes that stand in pairs or on their sides or piled up, high heels and fluffy slippers, offering different possibilities, different roles I can try out. I like the dining room with the toy cupboard that Mummy made, the red carpet she fitted, the black china horse on the mantelpiece – Mummy's pride and joy – and the wireless on the sideboard with its two knobs like eyes and its wide smiley tuning dial mouth. I don't like the cruel drawers of the sideboard that contain scratchy hairbrushes and fearsome elastic bands to tie back my hair. I don't go in the 'front room' much, except to read comics, unless it's the weekend and that's the room where the fire is made. The bathroom is far and above the most troublesome room in the house. The sink, of course, is where I can wash myself clean. But the curtains are white with spiteful green spots that make them look diseased, like they have a rash. Or else they're watching me, staring with hundreds of tiny eyes. My own room is the best, because that's where Trevor lies: my bear, waiting for a cuddle. Trevor always loves me, no matter what. A bit like Jesus, really, only I prefer Trevor. Jesus doesn't have fur, and I suspect he's a bit of a clever Dick. He may be a bit smug, too. I feel bad even thinking that, but he does sometimes look smug in pictures. Trevor isn't smug. He doesn't expect anything from me, except cuddles.

Sometimes at the weekend, when we are all in the front room because of the fire, I feel as if we've all been glued into place: Daddy and Mummy on the sofa, me and Jonathan in the chairs or on the floor. I wonder if we're really all made of wood or plasticine, and just being moved around by a giant child, who seems to have forgotten about us today.

Chapter Three

Germs

Things don't get much better in the class after reception. I'm determined to make an impression on Miss Maddison, who is dark and squat with a line of fur over her top lip. Which I like. I like fur. Although her hair is dark, she has pale, bloodless skin and her forehead looks like a lined parsnip. However, after finding out that we're going to do Tens and Units this year, I promptly go down with measles, and I miss how to do them. When I come back, she makes no allowances.

'What is the difference between eleven and twenty-two?' she asks the class. Nobody says anything. Clearly this is a hard question. Then she writes the numbers on the board in squeaky chalk. We're asked to work it out in our books. But I don't need to. I look at the ones, I look at the twos. I know! *I know* the answer! I put my hand up, tentatively.

'Stephanie?'

I take in a big breath.

'Stephanie? Do you or *don't* you know the difference between eleven and twenty-two?'

'Yes.'

'What is it, then?'

I prepare myself for her congratulations. 'Twenty-two is more curly,' I say, trying to control my satisfaction.

There is silence. Someone stifles a giggle. Someone else guffaws, and tries to hide it in a sneeze, as Miss Maddison's face becomes darker and darker. Her eyebrows knit, her mouth purses up.

'*Mock* me, would you, Stephanie Townsend?'

I have no idea what 'mock' means, and conjure up images of Mummy's mock cream, which is made of custard and icing sugar. I don't think I'd like to cover Miss Maddison in mock cream.

I shake my head, but it's no use. I'm rapped over the knuckles ten times with the wooden ruler and sent to stand in the corner. I should have known it was too easy. I will always be wrong. With my back to the class, I allow the tears to well up. No one can see. One spills over treacherously and makes my cheek sore. I hear her tell the class they can find the difference by doing a subtraction using tens and units. She's showing them the secret. I revise the image of mock cream. I'd like to squash a plate of it in Miss Maddison's face like a custard pie.

Miss Maddison is delighted to be able to tell my mother that I'm 'not the full shilling', but still I feel she was hoping for something more, something to better the reception class teacher in terms of my weirdness. Even Daddy thinks the curly twenty-twos is funny. When Mummy tells him, he roars with laughter. 'You have to hand it to her, Kath, twenty-two *is* curly!' He chortles and slaps his knee, and I'm pleased because I'm funny.

I don't feel so funny later in the term when Miss Maddison manages to trump even Miss Worth. We've been doing very simple 'verbal reasoning'. We aren't very good at full sentences yet, so most of the questions need just one-word answers. The one that I don't see coming, the trap I fall into like a baby elephant, involves some rubbish or other about a boy called Brian who is very mean and doesn't share. The question is, 'Why doesn't Brian share his toys?' and the answer goes in a space after, 'Because Brian is . . .'

It's not until I am kept behind after school and Mummy is brought in that I suspect something is up. Even then, I'm not expecting the word my teacher uses about me – 'depraved' (which means nothing to me) – to mean so much to my mother. She is shown what I have written. Miss Maddison's look is definitely one of spiteful glee as my mother silently views the answer in my neat handwriting. After slapping a hand over her mouth, Mummy exclaims that we never use words like that at home, that she can't think where I could have picked it up. I now know it must be to do with dirt, or women's bits, which are the same thing. Of course, Mummy knows exactly where I picked it up, although she probably doesn't know it's French.

Not long after that, I find out something important about Mummy and why I don't please her. Dawn is allowed to play with me to help out her mummy, who has had a baby called Karen. I feel sorry for Dawn because she's no longer the centre of attention. Karen is instead, and Dawn has to make do with a few crumbs of poppety-ness. I think Mummy must feel a tiny bit sorry for her too, because she lets her come over a lot, and gives us both jelly babies. So Dawn and I are unstoppable.

We get bored with playing on the swing, so we try to climb up the sloping swing poles instead, pretending we're on a climbing frame. When we get our feet off the ground we stop and look at each other. 'It's a funny feeling, isn't it?' she says.

'Yes. Funny but nice.'

We stay there for a while, perched just above the ground and enjoying this new discovery of the pole between our legs, when Mummy comes out.

'What on earth do you think you're doing?'

I scramble down and try to explain so that she won't be cross. 'We were just doing funny-but-nice,' I say.

'You what?'

'Funny-but-nice.' I touch myself where it feels nice by way of explanation. 'When we climb up the pole it feels nice here.'

'Stop that! Stop it! Don't be so filthy!'

The look of disgust on her face makes my throat ache. I swallow hard. So, I am filthy. This is a clue. This is why Mummy doesn't love me as much as Jonathan. She sends Dawn packing and rushes into the kitchen to clean down some surfaces with her antiseptic Dettol. I go to the bathroom and wash my hands, without being asked, and tell Mummy.

'Good,' she says, her mouth a tight seam as she puts the potatoes on to boil, and I know then that I'm still dirty.

While all this is going on, Mummy continues to attack germs wherever they might be hiding, and it's amazing where they are. One day, when we have a neighbour round, she lifts me onto her hip and I find myself squishing her breasts to see how spongy they are.

'Don't be so *dirty!*' she snaps, and I'm left bewildered, and when I get down, I go and wash my hands, and tell her that I've done it.

Another time, there's a picture of an actress on the front page of Daddy's newspaper. The woman has a low-necked dress which shows off her bosom. She grabs the paper and tears it out. 'Filthy slut!' she hisses. 'Filthy!'

There it is again, that word. Filthy. Like me.

'Am I a slut?' I ask.

Mummy screws the offending picture into a ball, which she throws into the wastepaper bin. 'Not if I can help it,' she says.

I only half realise, then, that germs are a complex mix of sex (women's bits) and dirt. I am learning to associate the two.

Germs are invisible, Mummy says, and can spread easily by 'catamination'. I pull up something to stand on by the sink so that I can carefully turn on the taps. Then, with my newly washed hands, I feel close to tears as I realise I have to turn the taps off again, which means I could pick up the germs that I left on the taps when I turned them on. Sometimes, when I come home from school, I hold my thumbs folded inside closed fists. When my parents ask me what's wrong, I can't look at them. There's a blur across my eyes, but I mustn't cry.

I become ever more skilled at washing my hands. I learn to turn the taps on with my elbows so that I won't pass the germs onto the taps. But there are new horrors in store. The germs, the 'filth' I am guilty of, clearly has something to do with 'naughty bits'. I try hard to avoid them, but a boy in our class, Steven Willis, decides to show me and Dawn his willy one playtime. After that, I feel certain he's cataminated. This means that if I ever touch him, or he touches me, I will be too, with new germs. It seems easy enough to avoid him, but no. Not so simple. Everything he touches becomes cataminated: the desk, his chair, the crayons, and so on. There is no end to the terror.

Things sometimes become so intense and frustrating that I have to find a way out of the horror in my head. There are two ways I have. The first is to rock my head from side to side when I go to bed. If I keep this up long enough, I can almost empty my head of thoughts. It makes me dizzy, but it doesn't really work for long. It's too exhausting. The other way I invented out of pure desperation. If my mother comes to say goodnight to me (it's usually Daddy, but it has to be Mummy for this to work), then I ask her to smooth her hands, back and front, on the white candlewick bedspread. After this laying on of hands, I do the same, in the same spot, thus absorbing her cleanliness and purity. *Hey presto!* I am clean. This little magic trick only works if Mummy is willing. She certainly finds it daft, but I think she goes along with it because it seems to have a positive effect on me.

Round about this time I start having 'dreams', which I somehow know are bad. They take place, interestingly, in the building used for the Church of the Three in One Sunday school (a long, thin room next to the small church hall). Basically, I enter the building and I'm put on a conveyor belt. Every now and then there are 'stops' on the conveyor belt, and something is done to me. For example, Steven Willis or the grocery delivery boy might touch me in my funny-but-nice place. Eventually I am taken to one of several rooms off the main room, where a man in a white coat does something to me. This usually involves me being completely passive.

Guilt is never far from my thoughts. One night, when I'm in bed, Mummy wonders why I look so miserable. I can't explain. So she tells me in her kindest Mummy voice that I can always talk to Jesus. She assures me that this is very easy, because Jesus knows everything in my head already, so I won't need to explain everything. This is terrifying news. I'm filthy and disgusting and *Jesus knows*. He knows *everything* in my head. Now I'm in real trouble.

There's a picture of Jesus at the top of our stairs, carrying a lantern and looking holy and a bit sad. I keep checking on him to see if his expression has changed, staying awake as long as I can, trying to think what I can do about the germs in my thoughts. The next morning after breakfast, when Daddy is in the bathroom, I ask Mummy for help.

'Can we have a television?'

'No. All they do is brainwash you.'

She brushes my hair firmly. I knew she would say this.

'But I think I would like my brain to be washed.'

She yanks my head back with the brushstrokes.

'Wouldn't you like me to have a clean brain, Mummy?'

'Don't be cheeky.'

The words cut into the soft flesh of my hope.

I don't know how not to be a disappointment to her. I have never stopped hoping for signs of my mother's love. My heavy, blundering hope. Sometimes this wretched hopefulness pulls me along like a giant dog on a lead, and other times it stops at a lamp post and holds me back just as I've got into my stride. I don't want to have the responsibility for it, but it keeps on pestering, eager and panting, until I take it out again.

'Mummy . . .'

'Get your coat on.'

'You look really pretty in that dress, Mummy.'

She goes to retrieve Jonathan from the kitchen and puts him in the pram. 'Come on, we'll be late for school.'

Napier Road has rows of terraced houses with tiny front gardens just big enough to house a dustbin, a pram and a bicycle. They lead down to the old railway cutting, which is covered in long grass and full of coppery slow-worms and adders. The railway track threads through the grassy banks, joining one small, forgotten town to the next, through hills of tatty, smiling sheep, slowly hiding itself in undergrowth like a snake in the grass. Trains used to go up and down the track but they don't any more. I miss the sound of their *chuh-chuh-chuh-chuh* when I'm sitting quietly at home. Off Napier Road, with its ragged terraces curling down to the old railway, is the recently built Greenfield Crescent, with farmland behind it. The crescent is where I live, in a semi-detached house with a proper front garden and a proper back garden. There is even a garage, although Daddy doesn't believe in cars, because they're dangerous. Mummy doesn't believe in them either because Daddy doesn't believe in them, but also because they cost a ruddy fortune. There are a lot of rich people in the country led by someone called Muck Melon, who is the Prime Minister.

'Bloody Muck Melon!' says Daddy over his newspaper.

'Mind your language!' hisses Mummy. I assume this is because Daddy says the word 'muck', which is clearly full of germs.

The people who live in Napier Road are envious of the people who live in Greenfield Crescent. I don't see this when I'm five, so when Dawn tells me her Daddy owns a *huge* factory that makes aeroplanes, I believe her.

'What does your daddy do?'

I have to think about this very hard, because I'm not sure. 'He works in a shorance.'

'What's a shorance?'

'I'm not sure. I think it's a big building – a *huge* building – where he keeps people out of danger.'

'What sort of danger?'

'Accidents – where people get run over and crushed, and fires

16

where people get all burnt and their skin falls off. That sort of thing.'

Dawn looks suitably impressed. 'How does he do that?'

'I'm not sure. I'll ask him.'

First, Daddy tells me that Mr Webster does not own a factory at all. He's only a 'four man' at a factory. There is something about the slight contempt with which my father says this that makes me embarrassed for Mr Webster and for Dawn.

'How many men work at that factory, then?'

'I don't know. Not that many. Twenty or thirty, perhaps.'

This is terrible. Poor Mr Webster is only a four man. He's not even a five or six man. It will probably take him for ever to be at the top.

'Oh, well. At least he invented the telephone.'

'What? Did Dawn tell you that?' There's a weird smile on his face, which makes me uncomfortable. 'Geoff Webster did *not* invent the telephone.'

This is bad news. I won't tell Dawn.

'And what do you do? In your job? In shorance?'

'I make sure people are safe if danger strikes. Obviously, I can't keep everyone out of danger, but I can help in times of need. For example, if someone's house catches fire, our company helps to pay for it to be rebuilt.'

I nod. This seems like the sort of good thing my father would do, and I imagine it's all tied up with the Church of the Three in One. He omits to tell me that people have to pay. Instead he takes the opportunity to tell me about all the dangers there are in life. There are threats around every corner: deadly accidents, cars that drive too fast, little children who set fire to themselves with matches, who fall out of trees or run across the road without looking or who play on the big grass rollers on the sports field. Life is scary, and don't I know it.

The trouble is, we don't recognise every danger when we see it. And that's how Mr Man manages to creep into our lives.

Chapter Four

*Item: **Koala bear pen (and 46 defunct biros)**. Chuck.*

I should've bought one of those warm baguettes on Paddington station, because as soon as my nerves settle, somewhere near Reading, I feel hungry. Returning from the buffet carriage, I'm convinced I spot the man I've been avoiding, sitting further up my carriage. He wasn't sitting there before, and I'm pretty certain it's him, although I look away quickly and sit down at my table seat. Did he see me? Of course he did. Why else is he sitting there? I have to stop obsessing. If he wanted to speak to me again, after my rebuff, he would have done. He's facing away from me now that I'm in my seat. It's probably not him.

I unwrap my egg and cress sandwich and look at it critically. Matt has strong feelings about plastic packaging. Out of its synthetic swaddling the sandwich is soft and floppy. I take a bite, as much to make it easier to hold as to satisfy my hunger. I miss Matt. I wish I could speak to him more often, but whenever I sit down to ring him, the time in Australia is never quite convenient for a phone conversation. When I get back this evening at about seven thirty, it will be four thirty in the morning over there, and if I ring him at my bedtime, it might be a nuisance while he's getting ready for work in the morning. Midday UK time is best, but I'm rarely at home at midday, except at weekends, and I always feel a little intrusive ringing him on his weekend evenings. I don't want to interrupt his relationship with his girlfriend. Alex seems to be the real thing, The One, and I struggle between being thrilled for him and sorry for myself. I always feared, from the moment he told me he was heading off to Australia 'for a bit', that he would fall in love with someone out there and want to stay. All he said, earlier this year, when he was due to come home, was that he was going to stay on another year to give his relationship with Alex 'a chance', as it was going so well. Already I pictured her accidentally getting herself pregnant and having to marry him, and me never getting to see my grandchildren, let alone my son, except for once in a blue moon when I would have to stay with them claustro-phobically for three weeks at a time to make the airfare worth it, and outstay my welcome. How to become a reviled mother and mother-in-law in one easy step.

'I just need to spread my wings a bit, before making any decisions.'

I had imagined he would earn some money in a factory or on a building site, and then go interrailing around Europe, sending me postcards from vineyards and ancient remains. And then perhaps university. But no.

'*Australia?* Do you need to spread your wings quite that far? What about Rome? And Florence? And the Greek Islands? *Norway* – you've always wanted to see the Northern Lights.'

'*Mum.* I want to explore the world a bit.' He had perched his ankle over his opposite knee and stared down at it, as if what he was about to say was written on his sock. 'I just need to get away. It's not personal.'

I looked at his sock too, hoping to read an appropriate response on it. But there was just sock. I thought, if you fall in love and have babies in Australia then the *impact* could be very personal. Had he even considered the cost of an airfare? And coming back? And me visiting him if he settled there? *Oh God oh God.* I knew I had to let go. Of course, I supported him, with every sinew of my body I supported him.

He turned the television on and there was football. A player sank to his knees and put his head in his hands. I thought I would like to do that now. I also wanted to skid along the grass on my knees first. Then the camera was on another player jogging along all cool and swanky, spitting onto the grass. I wanted to do that, too. Spit. When I was little my grandad used to spit in the street and I copied him once. He yanked my arm and told me off. I said that when I grew up I was going to spit in the street like him.

'Ladies don't spit in the street,' he'd said.

'Well, I will. When I grow up I will spit in the street whenever I like. Just like you.'

I wanted to leave Matt watching the footy and go for a walk. I wanted to work up a good mouthful of saliva like the football player (how do they do that?) and gob on the pavement near the Co-op. But I didn't.

Instead I became ridiculously encouraging and jolly, and started buying him books about the Australian outback, t-shirts with kangaroos on and a koala bear pen. I hated the sound of my own pathetic enthusiasm. (He forgot to take the koala bear pen. It's still on his bedside table with the aloe vera gel I bought him for sunburn.)

We're pulling in to Reading station now. I can't believe I feel like this, so achingly desperate. He is lugging my heart around with him wherever he goes. As if he packed it in the bottom of his suitcase when he went to Australia, transferred it to a bottom drawer in every place he's stayed along with other bits and pieces and – just like the special super-strength insect repellent I gave him to use – he probably doesn't even know he has it.

There were so many things I needed to tell Matt before he left. I have never told him what happened that summer when I was nine. I couldn't bear him to hear it from anyone else. Thinking about it makes me feel sick.

My first experience of counselling was with a woman called Paula. I saw her on the National Health, so it was free. It wasn't my idea; it was my doctor who recommended her. Reckoned I needed some support. Good of my doctor, really. So I sat with Paula every week and she asked about me, and left long silences for me to fill. She asked a lot about my parents. I couldn't tell her much. Or maybe I didn't want to. To me, my parents were just normal. Or could pass for normal. Everyone thinks that, don't they? After all, as a child, what else do you know? I was more interested in talking about Simon, and finding out why he didn't stay with me, why he'd betrayed me, why I was so . . . so not worth staying with. I didn't want to talk about my childhood. I didn't tell her anything about what happened. But I didn't see the roots she saw, reaching far out and down and under the firm earth of my past.

Chapter Five

Mr Man and His Dog

The first time we come across Mr Man, I think Dawn and I are about eight years old, although time is all whisked up now, since the thing that happened. But one day there is a long-haired golden dog who drifts into our lives and trots up and down the road and around the fields. The only other dog in the road is Mr Hewlett's dachshund, who wears a tartan coat with a hole in it for his tail, and is too nervous to be stroked. This new dog is called Goldie, and is happy to be stroked. We don't know anything about Mr Man, but obviously he has little imagination. (Dawn would have called the dog Ringo, and I would have called it George – until we find out that it is actually a girl dog.) We could ask him his own name, of course, when we're bending down to stroke Goldie, but we don't care about his name, and he never offers it. He asks ours, though. He has a bit of a stutter and a slight lisp, so Dawn says she's called Priscilla, or 'Cilla' for short. I say I'm called Stephanie, because I'm bad enough without being a liar too.

Mr Man lives further up Napier Road from Dawn, almost opposite our crescent. He often sets off for a walk with Goldie about home time, so we get to stroke Goldie on the way back from school. Once, he asks us if we'd like to come back to his house for some ice cream, but we say no. Even Dawn knows you're not supposed to speak to strange men. We're pretty sure you can stroke their dogs, though. Of course, Mr Man isn't a kidnapper or anything, because he is sad and gawky and wears scuffed shoes.

He looks like he needs someone to look after him. Sometimes we imagine what it would be like to go back to his house.

'I bet he has a big fat chamber pot in his bedroom full of wee,' says Dawn.

'I bet he has a smelly sofa with newspaper to sit on,' I say.

'I bet his carpet is brown.'

'I bet he doesn't have a carpet – just sticky lino.'

'Yuck. I bet he doesn't have any ice cream. I bet he doesn't have a fridge.'

'Poor Mr Man. I bet he sleeps with Goldie,' I say.

'That would be *nice*.'

'That's what I'd do, if I had Goldie.'

'Me too.'

I get to know Goldie better than Dawn, because on Saturday mornings she goes to ballet with Lisa Warwick and Nina Elliott, and most of the other children do something: Church Lads' Brigade, Venture Scouts, or other forms of fun activity. I'm not allowed to do ballet, because I drag my foot. But I heard Dawn's mum say to my mother: 'Miss Dukes, the ballet teacher, says Stephanie would be more than welcome, you know, Kath. There have been other children who've gone to her lessons with posture problems. It does them the world of good. And Stephanie would love all the pretty costumes. It's such a shame for her to miss out!' My mother mutters something and says she'll think about it, but she doesn't think about it. When I ask her, she says no. When I beg her, she says no more firmly. When I leave a note on her pillow saying all I want to do in the whole world ever is to be a ballerina (which is not actually true, as I want to be a steamroller driver), she takes me aside the next day and says I must stop asking, because it costs too much and we can't afford it. This seems unfair, because Dawn's father is only a four man and they can afford it, and Daddy puts five shillings every week into the collection plate at the church. Ballet lessons only cost two shillings. It's not fair at all.

Anyway, the upshot of not going to ballet is that I play in the road with the older girls who have stopped ballet, and I get to hold the rope while they skip, because my jump is too slow for their skipping games. They have all sorts of chants, like:

I'm a little Girl Guide dressed in blue,
Here are the actions I can do:
Stand to attention, stand at ease,
Bend my elbows, bend my knees;
Salute to the officers, bow to the Queen,
Show my knickers to the football team.

Sometimes, with a long rope, they get three of them all in together, doing the actions in unison. I feel awkward in case someone sees us. Sometimes they think it's funny to make me do the actions on the pavement, without jumping, when I'm not holding the rope. I do them because I'm scared, but I hope to God that Mum won't see me lift my skirt, because she would go mental.

When they're not skipping or French-skipping or playing Dusty Bluebells, they're swapping private stories and tell me to go away. So, what I usually do is wander over to Mr Man's house, where Goldie is always in the little garden, poking her nose through the front gate. I stroke her head every Saturday and she gets to know me better than anyone. Sometimes Mr Man gives me a dog biscuit to feed her. Sometimes he offers me a digestive biscuit for me to eat, but I always say no. When I tell Dawn, she is jealous, and I'm a bit glad, because I'm jealous of her mauve tutu and her apricot chiffon skirt and her pink ballet shoes ('nude', she tells me, which sounds very rude and exciting). She advises me to accept any further biscuits from him, and to go in his house if invited and report back. It seems I need to be careful, though, because if he is a kidnapper, he will try to have his Wicked Way with me.

'Do you mean . . .?' I do a cut-throat sign.

'That, and ... his Wicked Way.'

'What's that, then?'

'I heard Aunty Ruby telling Mummy about it. There was a kidnapper up her way, and he killed this girl, but first he had his Wicked Way, and it's ever so rude.'

'*What?*'

She puts a hand up to shelter her mouth, although there is no one passing her garden wall who is interested in our secret. Then she whispers: 'Sex!'

'What?'

'Katrina Pearson told me. Her sister's had it. It's when a man puts his willy in your hole.'

I am alarmed. 'What hole?'

'The hole between your legs.'

I think about this, looking down at the skirt of my dress. 'I don't think I have a hole,' I say, relieved.

'Me neither. But Katrina says we do. I *think* it's ...' she beckons me close to her and guards her mouth with her hand again, and pronounces solemnly, 'your bottom.'

The stakes are suddenly very high. Sex just sounded a bit like chickenpox a minute ago, and Katrina's sister has had it and survived; but now there is danger and horror surrounding it, and I am certainly not going into Mr Man's house – even if he does seem sad and has a lisp – to report back on anything without Dawn by my side.

My parents have given up trying to stop me playing with Dawn, although they wouldn't be happy if they knew what we talked about. Perhaps they are just happy that I have *someone* to play with. I know I am. Our parents don't tell us to stop hanging around Mr Man, because they don't realise we do. All the children like Goldie. But increasingly, we do hang around Mr Man, and he hangs around us. We have no idea how this will change our lives.

*

Mum does make attempts to get me playing with other children. One day she breaks a necklace and gathers all the glass beads together in a saucer. She can see me playing with them, intrigued by the way the cut glass catches the light. She fetches an old toffee tin and puts them in. 'Here,' she says. 'You can have them. When I was a girl, we used to collect beads and swap them. Maybe you could show these to your friends, and see if they have any beads they can swap.' She knows I don't have 'friends', but it's a clever move. Dawn copies me straight away, and before long all the girls in the street have a tin of beads and bead-swapping becomes hugely popular. Instead of having to watch girls jump about, I can sit on the kerb and open my tin with the best of them. When I perch on the wall after school, I am no longer a sad cripple sitting alone waiting for someone to play with me; I am a girl with a tin of beads, waiting for someone to do 'swapsies'.

But someone else notices me sitting on the wall, and that's the lady opposite. Because we don't have a car, another family often asks me and Jonathan on outings with them as we get older. When I'm eight years old and Jonathan is six, the Hoopers, whose house faces ours in the crescent, always say there's plenty of room to squeeze in another two when they take their boys to the Forest of Dean, for example. Our parents let us go (despite the fact that we are taking our lives in our hands riding in a car).

The Hoopers have a son called Gareth, who is in my class at school, and a smaller son called Paul, who is the same age as Jonathan. We pile into the back seat of their car, the four of us in a row. Every time we turn a corner, a little orange plastic arm signal sticks out of the car. Sometimes Mr Hooper puts his own arm out through the window. Sometimes Mrs Hooper cranes her neck out of the passenger window and says, 'Nothing coming this way, darling.' *Darling.* I like it when she says that.

We love it in the Forest of Dean. We love the soft pathways of ancient beechnut shells and brown leaves rotted down to make our footfall easy. We love the secret paths that go off in all directions, the soft bracken leaves and the coiled fern, the velvety moss, the smell of damp earth, the risk of getting lost, the promise of adventure. Gareth and I assume the responsibility of the elders. (I've no idea where Mr and Mrs Hooper are on these day trips. I think they must go off somewhere for a cup of tea. We seem to be always completely alone.) We hoist the ends of branches onto the crooks of beech trees to make dens, and weave them with cool fern fronds. We clear spaces for rooms no bigger than a child can crouch in, build pretend fires with sticks, fight off imaginary enemies. We see rabbits, squirrels, ragged wandering sheep and sometimes fallow deer. Gareth tends to take the boys off to hunt deer and rabbits for supper, while I stay at home and make stews. They come back with their kill, and Gareth hands me a dried-up piece of log. 'Here, wife,' he says, 'skin this rabbit and cook it.' I carefully peel off the bark, pleased to be able to extend his imaginary bunny idea, and then shove it in my upturned sun hat, which is the stewing pot. I settle unquestioningly into the role of mummy, and Gareth is daddy.

I like Gareth. I like his dark floppy hair and freckles, and I like that he points out butterflies called 'grizzled skippers', 'purple hairstreaks' and 'silver-washed fritillaries'. Sometimes I imagine what it would be like if we played proper mummies and daddies, like other children do at school, at the bottom of the field.

As we get back into the car at the end of our trip one day, I stumble and hurt my knee. Mrs Hooper rushes at me and envelops me in her arms.

'Are you all right, sweetheart? Does it hurt, darling?' She inspects my knee with its tiny specks of blood and kisses it. She looks me in the eyes and holds my gaze, mirroring my slightly bewildered expression. 'Is that better, sweetheart? Oh, you're being so brave!'

Then she smiles broadly at me and hugs me again. 'What you need, poppet, is an ice cream. Who wants an ice cream?'

Everyone does. She helps me into the car and strokes my head. I am a Sweetheart; I am a Darling. I am a Poppet. I feel as though two very broken pieces inside me have come together, just slotted into place. As we drive off, she turns round from the front seat and winks at me.

This is the summer I forget about germs. They simply evaporate.

Chapter Six

Walks

The thing about having a funny walk is that you become very interested in other people's walks. On Sunday mornings, after church but before we have had our Sunday roast, I like to sit on the wall of our front garden and watch people coming and going. Because we are on the corner of the crescent, and our house looks up Napier Road, I see people coming down, and they see me, but people walking up the road, towards the town, don't know I'm watching.

On Sundays I always feel like an alien. Not everyone goes to church like we do, and most people have their Sunday roast much later than us. The men seem to walk up the road to the pub, and stay there until about two o'clock, when the pubs close. It's no good watching them walk home then, because they are all over the place, wonky-walking worse than me, back home to their roast potatoes and Yorkshire pudding. There are fewer children out on Sundays. Dawn isn't allowed to play in her Sunday clothes, and she has to keep them on until her dad comes home and they've finished eating.

I like to sit on the wall and watch people go up the road towards Bridge Street, which leads into town if you turn right. Dawn's dad, Mr Webster, is usually the first to go up. He walks with his arms wide like a gorilla and his legs spaced apart, as if he is straddling a small horse. I call this Gorilla Walk.

Mr Willis, who is Steven Willis's dad, swings his arms with

such force he looks like he is parading for the Queen. In fact, I think he was a sergeant major in the war or something. I call this Moustache March. Sometimes he has a sturdy dog called Furrow with him, who looks dangerous and stern. Lisa Warwick says that when his wife was ill in hospital her mum made him pies for her sister to take round to him, and he chased her round the kitchen trying to grab her bum. I can't see it myself. What would he want with her bottom (unless it's the Wicked Way . . .)? I always think of it when I see him, though. He has a big blond moustache, but you only see that when he's walking home.

Then there is Mr Man, who comes out of his front gate quietly with his golden dog trotting merrily on silent paw. He has no colours to him – just ones like earth and stone – as if he is trying to merge into the background. He treads softly, up the road or down, with his dog in front of him. His brown, scuffed shoes stick out at an angle as he walks, like the penguins in Birdland at Bourton-on-the-Water, which we visited with the school last year. He doesn't swing his arms widely and his shoulders are a little drooped, almost as if he is apologising for being out at all. As if he hopes he isn't disturbing anyone or anything – not even the paving stones. I call this Lonely Walk.

I wouldn't want to be any of these people, but what wouldn't I give to have their legs instead of mine. Mum says I mustn't let it hold me back, so I try to join in with everything, even climbing the new ropes that have been installed in the school hall. We have this game our teacher invented called 'Pirates'. Two people are made pirates and chase everyone else, who have to escape. You can climb the climbing frame or the ropes or the horse, you can bound between floor mats, but if you touch the hall floorboards (the sea), you're out. You're also out if you get tagged by a pirate. Shinning up a rope is ideal, but it's much harder than it looks. What people don't tell you, when you climb a rope, is that it's your feet that do the holding on far more than your arms. If your feet work properly, you can push yourself up. And if your feet work properly, they can hold you up. I tried it once, but it was a disaster. I got about a third of the way up, but it was just my arms holding me. I really, really wanted to get up as far as Dawn, who had scooted to the top and was touching the ceiling. But all I could do was cling on. My feet wouldn't grip the rope any more. I was just hanging there, arms rigid with strain, willing myself not to lose my grip. I could feel the blood in my face and I thought I would burst. In the end, Gareth came and stood underneath me and helped me down. The other children were making too much noise to notice, thank goodness. We were both tagged out because of it, though. Because of me.

And he didn't seem at all cross about it. There's something solid and certain about Gareth, like a beech tree in the Forest of Dean. Times like that I imagine myself curling up with him in one of our dens on a soft bed of rotted beechnut shells.

Country dancing is another challenge. I really like country dancing, and thankfully we don't have to wait to get picked by a partner because we're just lined up in rows. Last week, Steven Willis was my partner and he swung me round so fast I forgot about my legs altogether. At the end of the dance he kissed me on the cheek. I don't fancy Steven Willis or anything, but I did feel excited that he'd kissed me. But then he spoilt it all. He leant in towards me, as we all trooped back to the cloakrooms to change our plimsolls, and said:

'I was thinking of marrying you.'

'Oh.' I was a bit taken aback, because no one has ever wanted to marry me before – or kiss me.

'Yes. But I was wondering . . . do you think you'll *always* walk like that? I mean, can you get it fixed?' He looked at me anxiously, and I was just trying to digest what this actually meant, when he added: 'I could marry you then.'

It reminded me of a song we sing in Folk Singing on Fridays. There's this man who asks a maiden where she's off to, and she says milking, and then he asks what her fortune is and when she says it's her face, and he realises she doesn't have anything else going for her, he says, *Then I can't marry you, my pretty maid*, and it's really cheeky because she didn't even *ask* him. And I wish I'd replied to Steven Willis what she'd replied to the man: *Nobody asked you, sir, she said.*

But I hate myself, because I was so ridiculously flattered and happy when he asked me to marry him. I felt like I was walking on air, like I did when he swung me round. When I told Dawn that he'd kissed me, she said he'd kissed her ages ago and he does it to all the girls. I wish I hadn't told her. It was like watching her foot step on a caterpillar and twisting it round. Hard. She can be quite harsh.

Sometimes, after I've had Sunday roast, I sit on the wall again and see her mum, Mrs Webster, go up the road. She walks with her shoulders hunched forward and her cardigan loose around her shoulders. She wraps her arms around herself as if she's holding her cardigan on, or holding herself together. I know she's going up to the pub to tell Mr Webster that the spuds are burnt, and if he doesn't come home soon the whole lot will be burnt. I know, from the way she stoops and hugs herself, that she isn't looking forward to telling him. I wonder if she knows that her walk gives her away. *Do you think you'll always walk like that?*

Chapter Seven

The Amazing Gift

The autumn term of 1965 is when everything starts to go horribly wrong.

Mum decides that I should have a ponytail. This means brushing my hair completely off my face and tying it up almost on top of my head. I frown in the mirror. My face looks like an egg, harshly exposed.

'It looks lovely from the back,' says Mum.

Dawn decides shortly afterwards that she too should have a ponytail. It takes me a while for it to sink in that she is copying me. Her hair is so thin I can see her pink scalp through it, and even though she's mean to me, this makes me feel an ache for her. My hair is thick, although I don't place any store by it, and cascades in a foam of chestnut curls from my crown. Mrs Hooper admires it, saying it's 'glorious'. Dawn's ponytail is a slim, mousy thing, and looks more like the pointy little tail of Mr Hewlett's dachshund than that of a pony. It doesn't occur to me to exploit this small advantage over her. Maybe at some subliminal level I keep it tucked away in case I need it one day, or maybe I think I can build on it, like the savings stamps I stick in my post office savings book. I see no advantage in saying to Dawn, ever, 'Let's face it, my ponytail is better than yours, which is a sad little thing.' But the knowledge that, in this small way at least, she wants to be like me, gives me a complicated feeling of pleasure and sadness.

*

At Christmas, my grandad gives me crisp ten-shilling note. I stroke the creamy-pink note between my fingers.

'Would you like me to take that for you?' says Dad. 'Put it in the bank and invest it for you?'

'No, thank you. I want to look at it for a bit.' This meets with a slight frown, so I add: 'And keep it in my money box.'

Dad nods, understanding. 'Well, just remember, it's safer in the bank. Anything could happen to it here.'

My parents give me a Sindy doll. (I know it's not Father Christmas any more, by the way. I recognise the fake fur on the trim of Sindy's coat. It comes from Mum's Astraka coat, which she shortened.) It's such a huge step forward for our household. Sindy is the 'free, swinging girl that every little girl longs to be'. A 'teenage' doll is a symbol of life gone mad for my father, and my mother is worried about some of the outfits being 'tarty', and also the existence of a 'boyfriend' doll, which seems to be encouraging bad habits. She told me I didn't need a doll as I already had one (a baby doll with a cretinous grin), and a teddy bear. So I'm thrilled to unwrap the Sindy doll. At least a year after all the girls at school, but there it is.

A few weeks after Christmas, it's Dawn's ninth birthday. She has a party where girls mime to Marianne Faithfull singing 'As Tears Go By' and dance to 'Barbara Ann' by the Beach Boys. It's very grown up. Very teenage. Dawn tells everyone that in four years she will be a teenager. This is particularly exciting, because my birthday is soon and that means I will be, too. In four years, we will be *thirteen*! And three years after that we'll be *sixteen*! We'll be able to wear black patent high heels with tight black skirts and black polo-necked jumpers. We'll wear our hair flicked up at the ends, like film stars. And we'll have boyfriends! Well, Dawn will, or so she says. I can't see me being allowed to wear any of that, or to have a boyfriend, but I let myself be carried along on the dream. We call our parents 'Mum' and 'Dad' now – although

I often forget – but in my head they are still sometimes Mummy and Daddy.

Dawn is a Capricorn, which means she craves success and never gives up. (I'm a Pisces, which means I am emotional and passionate and one of the most misunderstood signs of the zodiac.) She gets a Paul doll to go out with her Sindy doll. (I have longed for a Paul, but we're both disappointed when she pulls his jeans down and discovers he has no willy.) We spend the whole weekend making clothes for them out of rectangles of material from my mum's material box. She has chiffon and corduroy and fur and lace. The Sindy doll outfits are expensive to buy, and we long for the shoes the most. Skates and sneakers and knee-high boots – you have to buy the outfits to get these cherished moulded plastic items. We make do with gluing bits of felt onto tiny cardboard soles. Cindy and Paul have a lot of slippers.

For my ninth birthday in early March, I get a Sindy wardrobe made out of plywood by Mum. She has painted it and stencilled it with roses. Two weeks after my birthday is Mum's birthday. I know it's coming, because it's always nearly Mum's birthday after mine, when Dad always says, 'What do you want for *your* birthday, then, Kath darling?'

Mum always shrugs and says, 'A happy family is all I want. I don't need anything else.' Dad smiles, pleased with this answer, because he doesn't have to buy her anything except a card. He never buys her anything.

'But what would you *really* like?' I ask.

She parts her lips to say something, but Dad says: 'She doesn't want anything.'

I feel shut out.

'I'm painting you a picture,' says Jonathan.

Mum smiles at him. I want her to smile at me. 'But what little thing would you like, Mum?'

'Don't go wasting your money on me,' she says firmly. 'I'm quite happy as I am.'

I want to give her something. If I draw her a picture, it'll just look like I'm copying my brother now. I try to think of anything I've seen on *Blue Peter*, but the present for Mother's Day I made – a set of egg cosies – has been put in the drawer and never used. To be fair, they were too big for anything but ostrich eggs.

I have to up my game.

The next Saturday I go to play with Dawn and persuade her to come to the shops with me. By this time, when we are nine, our parents just assume we're playing in the road with the other children and rarely check up on us. Shepford is a small town and we walk to the shops, making up scary stories about the neighbours whose houses we pass along the way, mostly involving kidnapping and murder.

It's exciting wandering around the centre on our own. She stops in front of a shop window and points to a transistor radio. 'I'm having one of those when I'm a teenager.' There are three, at different angles, on a stand, and we're busy choosing which one we will have in our glorious teenage years when a man appears behind them. His face is familiar and ordinary. It's Mr Man, and I remember Mum saying something about him having an electrical shop where she got her new twin-tub washing machine. It's not usually open on Saturdays, though, because he mostly does repairs. His eyes meet mine, and his mouth curves into the shyest smile. I start to smile back, but Dawn, who has excited herself with tales of him kidnapping girls and keeping them in his garden shed, bursts into a fit of giggles. We run away and I'm ashamed.

'Why did you laugh at him?'

'Did you *see* him? Creeping up to us with that creepy smile!'

I give a half-smile of agreement and follow her down the High Street. He'll think I laughed at him now, too, and I don't want him to think that. It's as if Dawn decided our reaction for both of us, and now it's too late to change it.

We don't get any good ideas for presents. Even in the little Woolworths store there is nothing that will really bowl my mother over. I want her to be awestruck. I want her to hug me, to cover me in kisses and call me poppet. Dawn keeps picking up silly things like a bottle of shampoo or a bracelet made of plastic or a dress that costs far too much and saying, 'What about this?'

I'm about to give up and buy her a bar of soap or some bath cubes (*don't go wasting your money*) when we spot the Saturday market, which is just closing up.

A man is heaving great rolls of fabric into the back of a van, but on his stall, there is still plenty of fabric folded into squares with a price tag on. I pick up a pretty bundle of fabric in pink with red flowers on it and read: '7/6 – 3 YDS'. As I look at it, he stops what he's doing and comes over. He pulls the tag off and shakes out the fabric, as if I've asked to look at it.

'That's pretty,' says Dawn.

'Three yards you've got there, ladies. And all for seven shillings and sixpence.'

Dawn nudges me. It's enough to make a dress. But I can't make a dress. Even as I look at it, though, beautifully draped over the market stall, I can see that a shift dress would be easy. Like making dresses for our dolls. Just two rectangles sewn together, basically.

'Tell you what, ladies. Just for you, and as I'm packing up, I'll throw in some matching thread.' He rifles about in a box and then holds some cherry-red thread against the fabric. It's as if the deal is done. I reach into my pocket and hand him the ten-shilling note. He gives me a half-crown change and shoves the folded material into a paper bag. 'An excellent choice, lady. That'll make you a pretty dress, that will.'

In the week that follows I use every moment that I can on the dressmaking. I fold the material in half on the bedroom floor and cut a hole for the neck. Then I slip it over my head. It really is nearly a dress already. I borrow one of my mother's new shift dresses and measure the width in slipper lengths, then I cut off

37

the sides to make it about the same. Next, I tack it together as I've seen my mother do, with pins and long, rough stitches. When I try it on again, I'm pleased. It needs to be a bit too long and too wide for me in order to fit my mother, and the dress is both of these things. Then I realise I've made a mistake. To hide the stitching, when I eventually do the final sewing, it needs to be inside out. I undo the tacking stitches and start again.

Over the following days, I stitch a close line all along both sides. When I come to the neck, I fold the material inside, but it's too tight. I refer to my mother's dresses again, and see that there's another band of material stitched inside the neck, with a tiny seam attaching it. I have just enough material from the bits I've snipped off to make a curved neckband, but when I attempt to try it on again to admire my work, I realise I have stitched up the armholes.

Close to tears, I open up the neat stitches again, with just two days to go before her birthday. I hide under my bedcovers at night with a torch, and fold a tiny hem around the sleeves, snipping it to get it to stretch and lie flat inside the curves. The material starts to fray a little, but it looks okay from the outside. I notice I haven't taken up the hem, but tell myself that Mum will probably prefer to choose her own length.

I don't have any wrapping paper, so I draw flowers on the paper bag, and little boxes with ribbons on to show that it's birthday paper, and then I fold the dress and place it carefully inside.

On the morning of Mum's birthday, Dad gives her a card at breakfast and a kiss on the cheek. Last of the big spenders. She seems pleased. Jonathan gives her a drawing he's done of a double-decker bus, and she beams. He is so talented. I wait with the present on my lap, beside myself with excitement, and after she pours some more tea for everyone, I make my grand presentation. Ta da!

Mum looks surprised. She admires the wrapping paper, maybe imagining there are a few egg-cosy-type presents inside and preparing herself to be unexcited. But when she lifts out the dress, her face is a picture of awe.

'What's this?' she says, as she shakes it out beside the table.

'A dress.'

'A dress? But how could you afford . . .?'

'I made it!'

My father looks confused. So does Mum. She holds it out by the shoulders.

'Try it on!' I say. 'Please, Mummy! Try it on!'

She chews her lip. 'After breakfast.'

'Do you like it?'

'Of course.'

There is none of the thrill I was expecting.

'Where did you get the material?'

'I bought it. With my own money.'

She narrows her eyes. 'Oh, Stephanie. You've been wasting your money. I don't want you wasting your money.'

'It isn't wasted. It's a dress for you.'

It's not until after breakfast that I realise she can't get it over her head, because I forgot to put a zip in it. I could get it over my head, because I'm smaller.

'We can put a zip in it together,' I suggest.

Mum looks dubious. She takes a big breath in. 'It was a nice idea,' she says. 'But in future, don't go wasting your money. It doesn't grow on trees, you know.'

I walk to school with a stiff throat, Jonathan tagging along behind with Gareth's little brother.

'Your mum like the present?' asks Dawn.

'Not sure,' I say. My face is aching, and I want to cry more than ever, but crying is manipulative, so I don't.

'Didn't she say anything?'

'Not really.'

'What, after all that?'

I look down at the pavement, chewing my lip. I have refused

39

to play with Dawn a couple of times because I've been doing the dress, even though I still want Dawn to like me. I don't want her to think badly about my mum, though. I say nothing.

'Fuck her,' she says.

Just before we reach school, we see a dead fox at the side of the road, almost certainly hit by a car. While all the other children stop to stare at it and examine its entrails, I march ahead. My throat is leaden, my face is suddenly sore, and I realise there are streams of hot tears running down my cheeks. I turn aside and place my forehead against the cold school railings so no one can see, and I cry and cry and cry. It is like a storm bursting. My shoulders must be shaking, too, because Dawn catches up and says, 'It won't have felt anything.' When I don't turn round, she pulls at my arm, exposing me and my gasping, blotchy face. 'Don't be such a crybaby.'

Since the new year, there has been a new girl in school, Hilary Gibson. Hilary is the colour of violins and has hair that is gathered up in a huge, springy black pom-pom. She is made to sit next to me, on the other side of the class to Dawn, because Dawn has been separated from me. I like Hilary Gibson straight away. She smiles at me and makes me laugh. She's not afraid to know the answers to things, although she never shows off. She tells me to put my hand up when I'm too shy, and she lifts it up for me, linking her hand around mine. When Hilary comes into our lives, things change. When she is with us, she interrupts the power circuit of Dawn's hold on me. Our interactions are more measured, because Dawn can no longer reveal the true extent of her manipulation. Hilary is far too clever not to notice it.

I love Hilary Gibson, and Dawn likes her too. To start with. And then she hates her. Then it's too late to stop her.

Chapter Eight

Item: ***Tartan holdall bag****. Chuck.*

The train has come to a halt. It appears to be the middle of the countryside. I crane my neck at the window, but there is no sign of a station ahead.

What now?

As I brush some sandwich crumbs off me, I notice that I'm still wearing my lanyard. Feeling self-conscious in front of the couple opposite, I remove it discreetly. Then I realise it has my name on it, in large black letters. How stupid of me. Hardly surprising that the man who stopped me knew my name. Maybe he just looked a bit like the man at the conference, and was just a stranger, trying it on.

Eventually, a voice comes on the tannoy apologising for the delay. This is caused by an obstacle on the track: a sheep. The buffet is still open with a variety of hot and cold beverages and snacks. That man further up the carriage, facing away from me: it *could* be him. He's getting up, and I see he's wearing a blue jacket and jeans, like the man at the station. Shit. Oh, it's okay, he's making his way to the buffet car. Maybe it's not him. There must be loads of men with navy-blue jackets and jeans. But he knows I'm on the train. And then a thought hits me: he didn't just know my name; he knew what happened. *I know what happened.* I close my eyes in horror. He's going to bide his time. He'll grab me when I get off. Oh God.

*

41

Paula, the counsellor, kept harking back to my parents. She barely seemed interested in Simon, or my children. She had this notion, after a few weeks of sessions, that I had an *emotionally absent* mother. I didn't want to be mean about my mother. I remember all those psychological surveys, the questions with barely concealed subtexts, like 'Is or was your mother a good woman?' I wasn't going to run her down so that Paula could suspect me of being a head-case. But all the questions she asked (What was the relationship like between my parents? Was my mother unhappy?) threw me into a turmoil. I realised I hadn't questioned my childhood version of the past. I had failed to update it.

My mother was a frustrated design engineer. Among all her other chores she was always making things or planning to make things. She built fitted cupboards for all three bedrooms; she made two chests of drawers with dovetail joints. In the garden she built a shed, laying a rectangle of sub-base and concrete foundation first, which she mixed herself in an old tin bath. No one had taught her how to do these things. She watched builders and carpenters with a gimlet eye, and when she came back from the library, there was always a book about joinery or tiling slipped in between her Mills & Boons. She fitted carpets, laid linoleum, changed washers, and later, when we eventually had electric fires and no longer needed coal, she plumbed in a downstairs toilet where the coal cupboard had been. She only ever hired a workman begrudgingly, if she was completely stumped, and then she would shadow him and watch every detail of his work, challenging him if she wasn't happy, so that he became exasperated. No workman ever cheated her.

My father had a good deal when he married my mother, as he was afraid of heights and totally impractical. He would come home from work and find her on the roof fixing a tile or painting the eaves. 'Careful, Kath,' he would say, holding the ladder as if he was helping. 'Careful, now.'

My mother is a mystery to me. In many ways she was so

competent and skilled and in control of things. In other ways she was a total doormat.

Something came to me then, though, when Paula was asking those questions. I was looking at her bag perched beside her chair. It was standing next to her like a little dog, its handles flopped down like ears. And I remembered sitting on Dad's knee, with Jonathan perched on the other. He was reading us a comic, and Mum came in saying, 'Where's my bag? I can't find it anywhere.' Dad must've carried on reading because she became a bit frantic, and shouted, 'Has anyone seen my bag?' Then I remembered this quite vividly: Dad said, 'You've got plenty of bags under your eyes.' I don't know if he winked at us, or what. Maybe he smirked. Either way, Jonathan and I fell about laughing, in that way small children do when they first understand a grown-up joke and want to emphasise that they've got it. And I remembered, equally vividly, that Mum didn't laugh. She didn't laugh at all, but went out of the room. I think it was the first time I understood that grown-ups could feel hurt too.

My grown-up self likes to reinvent this scene. In it, I slip off Dad's knee and find the bag that Mum is looking for. It's a shopping bag with a sturdy base made of a stiffened tartan – maybe it has a rubberised backing – that stands up on its own. It has a big zip across the top. It's just like the holdall that Mr Man brought with him to the Dingle, on the last evening that summer. The evening it happened.

I run to the front door and hand it to Mum as she's going out. 'I don't think you have bags under your eyes, Mummy. I think you're very pretty.'

It's always the next bit I have a problem with. She looks at me, pink-eyed, and takes the bag. 'Thank you, poppet.' But I know she found the bag herself. I didn't help her look for it because it didn't occur to me to help her. I was far too self-centred. Sensitive, maybe, but it was all about me. And if I *had* been thoughtful enough to try to reassure her, I would've hesitated over the words.

And I know she would've looked at me and said, 'What? What *now?*'

Now when I think of a tartan holdall, it makes me shudder. Not that one, of course, but the one Mr Man brought with him on that day.

Chapter Nine

Crushed

Hilary and I play together quite a lot on Saturday mornings, when Dawn and the other girls are at ballet. These feel to me like secret encounters, because I know I wouldn't be able to play with her if Dawn was around. My parents welcome Hilary, which makes me feel proud of them. Mum likes to talk to Mrs Gibson about dressmaking, and Dad is pleased that we have a black family in our neighbourhood. He likes to talk to Mr Gibson about football and the World Cup, which is coming up. Playing with Hilary is so easy, so relaxed, that I can hardly believe my luck. We laugh a lot, make up adventures, and when we discuss things, I feel that my opinion matters as much as hers.

'What do you like about Dawn?' asks Hilary one day.

I am completely thrown. I open my mouth to say something, but can't find anything at all to say.

'I mean,' says Hilary, 'I wouldn't put you two together at all. You're not at all alike.'

I'm shocked at how pleased I am by that final sentence. I don't want to be like Dawn. I've never wanted to be like Dawn, I've just wanted Dawn to like me. And that's because I envy her mother's love. But Dawn is suffering a bit. Now that her mother is busy with her little sister, Karen, who seems to be ill a lot, she doesn't have as much time to spread around; her poppet is having to share with a new, much needier poppet, and I feel a bit sorry for her.

'I'm probably going to break up with Dawn soon,' I say, with treacherous abandon. 'But I just feel a bit sorry for her, what with a little sister like that.'

Mrs Gibson calls us in for some biscuits. She also shows us a selection of little glass beads that we can have for our bead collections. They are all different colours, and she offers them to us in an upturned jam lid. 'You can have six each.'

'Thank you, Mrs Gibson. They're beautiful.'

'And I do have two brooches I don't wear as well.'

'We don't collect brooches,' says Hilary.

'I like brooches, though,' I say, in case Mrs Gibson feels hurt. 'I have three golliwog brooches from saving the Robertson jam labels.' Mr Gibson lowers his newspaper and looks at me from the sofa, as if he is interested. 'You can collect them,' I add, helpfully. 'And then they send you a golliwog badge, but it's a brooch really.' Mr Gibson is frowning at me now. 'I like golliwogs,' I add, just so they know I like black people.

He takes in a deep breath and says, loudly, 'We do not like golliwogs, Stephanie. Golliwogs are a caricature ... they are making fun of—'

'Eli ...' Mrs Gibson puts her hand gently on her husband's arm. 'Won't you have a biscuit, girls? They're custard creams!'

I thank Mrs Gibson profusely, but the biscuit is hard to swallow in my thick, swollen throat. I think I've upset Mr Gibson, but I don't know why. My face is hot and my scalp is tight, as if I'm wearing a hat that's too small. I just want to go home now. I vow to ask Hilary about it as soon as we're on our own. Even she looks shifty now. I always say the wrong thing. This is why Dawn is my friend. She is the only person who can put up with me. I wish I could disappear.

'They make fun of black people,' explains Hilary. 'Golliwogs in general. But don't worry. You weren't to know.'

We are standing outside her front gate. 'I'll throw them all away!' I am decisive. I want her to be my friend. 'Tell your parents. I'm going to throw them all away.'

In fact, I give them to Jonathan. My little brother has always squabbled with me over whose turn it is to get a badge, and now I offer him all three. He's amazed at my apparent generosity. I might as well get some advantage out of their disposal, I consider, selfishly. Now he owes me.

A few things start to make me feel uncomfortable about Dawn. For a start, I stupidly tell her that I like Gareth. Instantly, she likes him too. I suppose, after the ponytail, I shouldn't be surprised that she copies me, but Gareth is my secret dream. I don't want to share him. Now, every time we see him, she nudges me. Now she starts to imagine what it would be like to kiss Gareth or to hold his hand or to marry him. One day she goes too far.

'When I grow up, I'm going to marry Gareth. We're going to have four children – all boys, and they're going to be called Kevin, Ringo, Dave and Paul.'

'You can't,' I say, bereft. 'I'm going to marry him and have two girls: Carol and Linda.'

'We're going to live in a house by the seaside and he's going to be a policeman.'

'No, he isn't. He's going to be a zookeeper!' (I actually know he's going to be a zookeeper because he told me.)

'That's what you think,' she says, totally undaunted by my superior information. 'We're getting married in Rome and I'm going to wear pink chiffon and sunglasses.'

She is so exasperating.

It never occurs to us, in our imaginings, that we should not get married, and it never occurs to us that we should be anything but wives when our husbands are zookeepers or policemen. It also never occurs to us not to want to be something earnestly when we grow up: steamroller drivers, ballerinas or, now, in my case, a zookeeper, an architect or a wildlife photographer. Quite how we expect to marry these two expectations together doesn't enter our heads. We are perfectly capable of imagining ourselves on an African plain with lions while being simultaneously a zookeeper's wife with umpteen children. Our mothers never had this problem. They always knew they would be housewives, and they drill the idea of this happy ending into us with a smile, because if they don't, they will have to admit they've been duped. We accept the idea lovingly, at the same time as listening to our fathers or *Blue Peter* saying we could be brain surgeons.

Anyway, I would like to be a wildlife photographer/architect/zookeeper *and* marry Gareth, be a housewife and have his children, but Dawn has other plans for him that completely exclude me. She goes on like this all the way to school. I let her because she's having a tough time lately. Dawn hates her sister Karen with a vengeance. Karen is four now, and gets loads of attention, and is poppeted to death. Dawn is feeling totally excluded from her mother's love – and I can feel for her there – although I notice that Mrs Webster still calls her poppet, and sometimes she caresses Dawn's hair or her shoulders while she's standing in the hall. What I wouldn't give for that. Still, it's hard for Dawn, having to get less love, so she's feeling pretty pissed off.

I know Dawn is as desperate to please her dad as I am to please my mum. She boasts about him whenever she can. So it should come as no surprise when she suddenly takes against Hilary – especially as I have been seeing more of Hilary, and she probably feels excluded.

'Dad says people like her are taking our jobs,' she announces one day. We're on our way to school and the pavement is puddled, drying out in patches from heavy rain the night before.

'People like Hilary?'

'Like the Gibsons. They come over here and they take *our* jobs.' She points at her own chest when she says this, for emphasis.

'But we don't have jobs.'

'No, our parents' jobs.'

I don't think Mr Webster or my dad want to be bus drivers, but I keep quiet.

'*And*, they're taking our houses.'

I think about the 'For Rent' sign that was in the front of the Gibsons' house in Napier Road for ages, and the way the weeds took over the garden and crawled out under the gate and along the pavement. Since the Gibsons have moved in, the garden is neat and there are pots of herbs lining the windowsill. There are pretty curtains at the window and the front door has been painted red.

'Dad says they should go back where they came from and I should stop playing with her. And you should stop playing with her too.'

'But she's nice.'

'Dad'll go bonkers if he catches me playing with her.'

'But my dad likes her.'

'Look, *I'm* telling you, okay? You should stop playing with her.'

I know better than to contradict Dawn when she's in this mood. I can just see Mr Webster jabbing his finger at her about the Gibsons. He's always angry about something. I think she's probably just afraid of him, because she'll do anything he says.

'Anyway,' she says, 'it's no wonder Hilary's picked on you to be her friend.'

'What do you mean?'

'You're weak. You just agree with everything. You'll do anything she says.'

I stare at the pavement moving along beneath our feet as this comment seeps through the thick layer of my ignorance. She probably doesn't know what she's told me here, about us. I say nothing, because I am not going to agree with her, even if it's true.

The following day, when I'm looking sulkily down at the cracked paving stones and trying not to listen to her about her married

49

bliss with Gareth, I spot the most beautiful peacock butterfly by the side of the pavement, underneath a beech tree.

'It must have fallen from the tree,' I say, as we watch it click its wings open and shut. 'Perhaps it was startled by a predator.' I know these things because me and Jonathan read the *Treasure* comic. It's the only comic Dad allows. It's full of sensible information. If I'm honest, I'm a little scared of the butterfly, which has big blue eyes on its wings and seems to be watching me, but Dawn is fascinated. We crouch down and watch. Looking back down the road, I see Hilary Gibson coming. She is still some way off, but I'm afraid, if she catches up, that Dawn will be rude to her. Too late. She's seen her.

'Oh, here comes the new girl. *Hilary*.' She says it with such sarcasm that I stand up quickly and sigh.

'She's okay,' I say, monitoring the space between us and her, as it shortens.

'*Okay?* No, she's not. She smells.'

I brace myself. 'She doesn't smell.' I am not agreeing with her.

Dawn raises herself slowly and speaks slowly, as if I'm an idiot. 'She smells, and she thinks she's clever.'

Hilary *is* clever, and she's approaching fast. *She is clever*, I think, standing my ground, dangerously, but only in my head.

Hilary is just yards off now, waving and smiling, running towards us.

'Fuck her,' says Dawn, bitterly. 'She's nothing. I could squash her flat.'

'Hello,' says Hilary, breathlessly.

'Hi, Hilary,' I say, smiling. 'Look what we've found!' Distraction, I always find, is the best way to deal with Jonathan when he's in a mood. It seems to work with Dawn, too. She smiles at Hilary as well.

As if I'm not there, Dawn says, 'It was probably in a tree and got startled by a predator. It's a peacock.' I'm relieved. We all look down at the butterfly, Hilary bending to get a closer look. As we gaze, Dawn puts her brown lace-up shoe over the creature. Then, before either of us can do anything but gasp, she presses down hard. Then she screws her foot from side to side, watching our faces. A whoosh of horror scuttles through me. I think I'm going to throw up. I can barely hear Hilary asking, 'What did you do that for?' And anyway, I know why she did it, and it still makes me feel sick.

Chapter Ten

The Candidates

There is to be a general election. This is a competition between different men who want to be the winner.

'Who knows who the Prime Minister is?' asks Mr Spruce.

I never dare to put my hand up, but I know this answer. I lift my hand tentatively in the air, and he points to me, eyebrows raised.

'Muck Melon,' I say.

Mr Spruce ignores me. It is as if I haven't spoken, even though he chose me to answer. He asks someone else. It seems Muck Melon is long gone, and now, in 1966, the Prime Minister is Harold Wilson, who smokes a pipe. But he wants another election to see if he can win even more votes and make more changes. Our teacher, Mr Spruce, thinks it will be fun for us to have a pretend election in class, so that we can understand better what is going on. There are forty of us in his class, and everyone wants to be a candidate. In the end he asks people to put their hand up and explain why they would make a good candidate, and which party they will represent. This reduces the number of hopefuls considerably.

Mr Spruce is torn between Hilary and Gareth for the Labour candidate, and eventually selects Hilary, and Gareth says he doesn't mind being the Liberal candidate, and Steven Willis is chosen as his deputy. Hilary asks me to be her deputy, and I agree, because I'm sitting next to her and I don't want to disappoint. I'm also thrilled that she thinks I'm good enough. This leaves the

Conservative candidate, and by now, Dawn, whose family probably don't vote Conservative, is wetting herself to stand against Hilary Gibson in open combat. She is duly appointed as the Conservative candidate and selects Lisa Warwick as her deputy, while squinting meanly across the classroom at me.

The pretend election will take place on Thursday, the day of the actual election. The candidates have a couple of days to prepare.

Hilary and I go round her house and her mother shows us how to make rosettes. She has a whole room full of material and lace and ribbons, as she makes a living as a seamstress. Hilary has an older brother called Abe, who is very tall. He plays music loudly in his bedroom, and he lets us come in and watch him dance. I love to watch him move. Hilary copies him, and I wish more than anything that I didn't drag my foot, but she pulls me in to join her, and teaches me all her fluid movements. Then Mrs Gibson makes us chicken and peas and rice. Before I leave, we have two magnificent red rosettes, and I try hard not to feel as though I am betraying Dawn. I already feel sorry for her, and wonder whether I should tip her off about the rosettes, so that at least she has a chance to compete on the image front.

On the day, Mr Spruce takes us all into the hall so that the candidates can stand on stage. I stand next to Hilary, as Mr Spruce introduces the three parties, starting with Hilary, the Labour candidate for Plum Road Primary School.

'We in the Labour party are fed up with thirteen years of Tory rule. In the two years we have been in power, we have built more houses, hospitals and schools than the Conservatives. We have got rid of prescription charges and increased pensions . . .' She goes on like this, for all the world like a proper grown-up. Children watch her with their mouths open in awe. My knees feel wobbly and I can hear the blood pumping in my head, because I know what's coming. At the end, she turns to me and says: 'If you vote for me, we will . . .' I take over and say: 'Modernise, modernise, *modernise!*'

(I badly want to impress Mr Spruce. I can hear the tremor in my voice, but I carry on, louder.) 'We are going to take this country forward! Vote Hilary Gibson for a better future!' (This is what Hilary has told me to say, and we have been practising at her house.) There is a pause, then everyone claps.

Next up is Gareth, and I sit enchanted as he makes his plea for the Liberals: 'We are going to give new life to the poor regions. We will also give more power to Scotland and Wales, so that they can have a say in how to run their own countries. We'll put an end to war. We'll make school holidays longer. We will make sure that everyone gets a holiday, whatever they do for a living, and, ladies and gentlemen, we will make sure that there is equal pay for men and women!' (A cheer goes up among the girls.) His deputy, Steve, is a bit of a show-off, and he wiggles his hips and makes the girls laugh before saying in a fake American accent that he can recommend his friend Gareth Hooper because he's never let him down yet, and he's kind to animals. (He's not even Gareth's friend. He just lives in Napier Road.)

By the time Dawn is called to the stage, I feel physically sick. She stands there with a rosette made from a cereal packet, coloured in blue crayon on the grey side of the cardboard. It is a small, sad thing. I am embarrassed for her. And that's before she starts.

'If you elect me, I will get rid of taxes. Everyone will be paid more, so there won't be any more strikes. We'll stop immigration, so people won't come in from other countries and take our jobs . . .' here she looks pointedly at Hilary, 'or come to our schools and our hospitals when we don't have room. There will be no more semolina pudding or liver for school meals.' (Here there is a cheer.) Her deputy, Lisa Warwick, shouts: 'Britain for the British! Vote Dawn Webster if you want to back Britain!' There is applause among the girls here, because Lisa Warwick is fairly popular.

Mr Spruce is on the stage, rubbing his hands together. I cringe. I can't look at Dawn.

We all have a piece of paper with three names on it, and we

have to put a cross by one name. Then we fold it and put it in a cardboard box with a slit in the top. When we get back to the classroom, Mr Spruce gives the papers to three children to count out. Then he gives them to three different children. This is how it works in a real election. Votes have to be checked and checked again.

Mr Spruce is amazed by the results: 'Nineteen votes for Labour, led by Hilary! That's almost fifty per cent! It could well be what the real Labour party will poll today. And sixteen votes for the Liberals, led by Gareth, with five votes for the Conservatives, led by Dawn. That's almost exactly what the other two parties are expected to get, only reversed. In the real election the Conservatives are likely to get the bigger vote, and the Liberals the smaller vote, like Dawn. But we'll know the real results on Friday. Let's see! Well done, everyone!'

We walk home in a clump, everyone from Napier Road and the crescent heading off on the same stretch of pavement. Dawn is up ahead, talking to Lisa Warwick about Sindy dolls. I scurry up to her.

'I thought you did very well in your speech, Dawn.'

Dawn and Lisa continue talking.

'And you, Lisa.'

Lisa smiles briefly at me, or she might be smiling at Dawn's offer to lend her some Sindy outfits. Gareth is behind me. I want to tell him he was really good, but then Dawn will think I was fibbing about her, which I was. I walk next to Dawn all the way home, my cheeks hot with shame, not knowing where I belong on the pavement.

There are a couple of incidents that lead to my walk alone with Mr Man. This is the first one.

Chapter Eleven

Bye Bye Baby

Mum is washing some clothes in the sink, and looks worn out.

'Would you like me to help you?' I ask.

'Roy!' she calls to my father. 'We must get that washing machine fixed! I've had it apart but it needs a new motor. Honestly, I can't cope.'

'I can wash some clothes,' I say.

'Roy? Are you listening?'

My father's voice comes from the living room, telling her to go ahead and get a man to fix it.

'We had an election today, and I won. Well, not me, but Hilary, and I was her deputy.'

'Make yourself useful, then, and lay the table.'

At teatime I tell Dad about the election and he is pleased. 'You should play more with Hilary Gibson. That's a nice family.'

'Mrs Gibson's got a whole room for her haberdashery,' says Mum. 'I wish I had that.'

'Me too,' says Dad, 'then maybe this place wouldn't be such a tip all the time.'

Mum looks hurt. 'Well, I'm doing a grand spring clean tomorrow, just so you all know.'

'Can I help you?' I ask. 'When I get home from school?'

'Anything that's lying around goes in the bin.'

'I'd better not be lying around then,' laughs Dad. 'Good job I'm at work. But if there's anything half-decent, Kath, it can go to the church jumble sale. We're raising money for Oxfam.'

'Fine by me,' she says, pouring tea defiantly, and spilling some on the tablecloth.

'And me,' I say, watching Mum carefully.

'Do either of you children have any toys you no longer play with that can go to the sale?' Dad asks.

Jonathan says they can have his tricycle, but that's not really his to give away, because it used to be mine.

'Well done, Jonathan. What about you, Stephanie?'

I don't want to give any of my toys away. I look around my bedroom with my mind's eye. They are all precious, even the broken glass swan on my shelf and the snow-shaker that doesn't work because it leaked. Then I have an idea.

'You can have Golly if you like.'

'The one Father Christmas gave you?' He looks almost disapproving.

'Yes, but golliwogs make fun of black people.'

Dad frowns. Jonathan – clearly remembering my gift of golliwog badges – narrows his eyes at me.

'Anyway, I've grown too old for that sort of thing,' I say, reassuringly. 'Now I have Sindy and everything.'

'That's very kind.'

There is no Dawn to play with after tea. She usually meets me in the street, but she's not there, and I feel too churned up to tag along with the other girls. Hilary isn't there yet, and I'm almost relieved. I go to my room and play with my dolls. I go down for a cup of Ovaltine before bedtime, then make sure my room is tidy before I go to sleep. I don't want anything put in the dustbin. Seeing Sindy still on the floor, I tuck her in next to me. 'Night night, Sindy,' I say. Then I turn to my trusty old teddy bear, Trevor, in case he feels jealous and thinks he's about to be replaced. 'Night

night, Trevor.' I pull him into my chest, as I do every night, and he makes everything all right.

We return home from school the next day to see a television set in the corner of the living room. It is perched on a little table that has been in the shed for years. For some strange reason, Dad has decided that the evil that is television is now allowed in our house. Until this day he has refused even to consider it. Until this day it has been the cause of monstrous brainwashing, and unthinkable that Dad would allow such a tool of Satan into our home. We are all somewhat bewildered, including Mum, who let the TV man into the house and made him a cup of tea. But none of us challenge Dad, in case he takes a notion to change his mind, but it is a mystery. A bit like God, really. It being 1966, though, it does come in remarkably handy for the World Cup.

The washing machine is also fixed (Mum did it herself), and the house is spotless. True to her word, Mum has done an impressive spring clean. By the door is a cardboard box full of things for the jumble sale. I do a quick rummage through, to check she hasn't taken anything I still want, and I see Golly there. That's fine with me. He was never very cuddly.

We are all so busy watching the new television that it's bedtime before I notice that Trevor is not in my bed.

'Where's Trevor?' I call from the top of the stairs. There is no answer. I run down and burst into the living room. My parents are watching *Z-Cars*, and Dad turns round and tells me to be quiet.

'But where's Trevor? Where's my teddy?'

'Let's worry about that tomorrow,' he says.

I smell a rat. 'Where is he? Mum? You didn't throw him out, did you?'

I expect her to tell me not to be so silly, that she's put him in the toy cupboard or something.

'Honestly, Stephanie! You said you'd grown out of that sort of thing.'

I feel a sharp pain across my chest. 'Of Golly! Grown out of *Golly*! And only because he makes fun of black people and Hilary is black. I *love* Trevor! I've had him for ever and I . . . I . . . *love* him, Mummy! You haven't thrown him out, have you?'

I'm almost sobbing now. Mum looks at Dad, and Dad sighs and gets up to turn the television down, but he keeps watching it.

'He was pretty much *bald*, Stephie. You haven't played with him for years!'

'He's my *bear*! You've thrown out my bear!' I am practically screaming. 'Where is he? In the dustbin? I'm going out to get him!'

I make for the door, but Mum gets up and says the dustbin men came mid-morning, and he was already in the bin. I put my arms over my head and wail.

'That's enough!' says Dad. Then, more gently he says, 'You're far too grown up for teddy bears now, anyway. Look at how grown up you are. Even standing as a deputy Labour leader. Goodness, I doubt Harold Wilson has a teddy bear.'

I'm dizzy and sick. He was bald, but he was my friend. He was my shield. I choke as I think of him being tipped out of a dustbin somewhere I can never find him, buried in carrot and potato peelings.

'Well, I never had a teddy bear,' says Mum. 'We couldn't afford it.'

Chapter Twelve

Special

All at sea the next morning, a Saturday, I wander up and down Napier Road in the hope of finding someone to play with, or at least the possibility of walking further on to the railway cutting and disappearing for a bit. No one will miss me. I try to imagine how my mother will feel when I don't go home at midday, and, as my fish fingers and peas go cold on the plate, whether she will regret her heartless act and worry a little about me. I am so riled up with emotion – anger, self-pity and an immense sadness – that I can barely swallow. My chest is tight, my throat swollen and my lips are trembling in a way I have no control over.

The houses outside are like small creatures, alive and warm with beating hearts, but feeding quietly now. I can smell other people's mealtimes coming together as I walk down Napier Road. From chip fat at one house, pie pastry at another, on through onion, gravy, cabbage, to stewed apple, with accompanying sounds of plate clatter, sharp remarks or laughing. The scent of other people's lives, the strange half-heard notes of them, all seem better than mine.

And then I hear a bark. Turning, I see Goldie's big friendly head sticking out of Mr Man's front gate and I speed up my pace to go back and stroke her. I get down on my knees and let her lick me through the bars and push her head against mine as I stroke her soft ears. 'Goldie, Goldie,' I whisper as the tears spill over into her fur. 'I love you, Goldie. I love you so much.' I hide my face quite successfully like this for some time, and Goldie lets me cry secretly into her neck, occasionally poking a paw through the gate as if she wants to comfort me. It is such a relief to spill some sorrow, because I don't think I could have waited until the railway bank.

Eventually, secure in the knowledge that the worst is past for now, I stand up and wave Goldie goodbye. There's a motorbike parked opposite the Gibsons' and Abe and a couple of other boys are out taking a look at it, as if some marvellous spaceship has landed in Napier Road. I pretend not to have seen them, discreetly taking my hanky out of my dress pocket when no one is looking and wiping my snot. I make my way down towards the railway. Well, there was no Mum running out onto the pavement to call me back in, to say she'd buy me another bear, to wrap me in her arms and hold me tight and say *Sorry, my dear little poppet*, just for a few moments. And Dad, where's he when you need him? Fat lot of good he is to anyone when he's writing his sermons. If Jesus really exists, he would turn his donkey into my teddy bear, Trevor. Like to see Dad's face if he did. A skittering noise on the pavement makes me turn, and Goldie is jumping up at me, panting.

'Goldie!'

I can see Mr Man at a distance behind me, carrying the dog lead. I wonder if I can continue walking, but Goldie keeps jumping up at me. It would be far too embarrassing to walk to the railway cutting and have to talk with Mr Man. I start to walk quickly but the dog shadows me.

'She likes you!' shouts Mr Man, fast approaching now. 'I saw you playing with her at the gate, and I realised it was time for her walk.' He has caught up with me now and matched his pace with mine. 'Yes, Goldie always gets excited when she sees you and your friend Cilla.' He looks sideways at me with a nervous smile. 'But she likes you the b-best.'

'How do you know?' I say, flattered.

'Oh, you get to know these things when you have a dog like Goldie. I can always tell what she's thinking.' He is quiet for a moment, as if he's embarrassed, as if he's said too much and has startled himself. 'Um. I mean, she came in just now, whining for a walk. I think it was because of you.'

I feel instantly lighter. I allow myself to feel a little special. Relaxed by this compliment, I start to ask about Goldie's routine: how many times a day she has to be walked (twice) and what she likes to eat best ('lights', which are giblets and things, and I have to work hard inside my head to forgive Goldie for this disgusting habit). In this way, we pass the time until we get to the railway cutting.

'You have the most b-beautiful hair,' he says suddenly.

I put my hand up to feel it, as if to check he really means mine. I don't know what to do with all these compliments, so I bat them away. 'Oh, no. My hair's awful. It's always such a mess. Mum can never get a comb through it.'

He looks over at me coyly, and closes his eyes briefly like a cat. He doesn't mention my dragging foot or my wonky walk. He just notices my hair. He says it is the colour of chestnuts and it is free-raffle-light. I don't know what that is, but he seems pleased about it, so I am too.

'We usually catch slow-worms here,' I say, by way of conversation.

'We usually turn left down here and go over the little bridge. Know the one?'

I shake my head. We've never been down to any bridge.

'There's a beautiful wood – with bluebells in soon. Oh, you must see the wood!' He turns to his dog. 'Mustn't she, Goldie?' But Goldie is already bounding on ahead, to the left like he said, and so I go with them.

The footbridge is a good ten-minute walk down along the top of the bank, but he is right about the woods over the bridge. It's enchanting, and I keep thinking how I must show this to Dawn, and how impressed Dawn will be that I came here with Mr Man. *All alone* with Mr Man. That's if she ever speaks to me again.

We walk in single file along the woodland paths, although Goldie bounds around both of us, constantly distracted by things in the bracken, which is unfurling in curious fiddle-heads of green. I follow Mr Man, noticing how he barely swings his arms, but how the dog lead's metal clip swings and glints in the dappled light, how his old leather shoes need a polish, how his trousers don't fit him very well. When Goldie darts off suddenly, in pursuit of a pheasant or something, Mr Man runs after her in a panic. He grabs hold of her collar for the next bit of the path, and seems out of breath. Eventually we come to a small clearing by a stream. There are trees on the far side of the stream, but here the ground is bathed in sunlight and grassy enough for a picnic.

'This is the Dingle,' he says. 'Haven't you been here?'

'No.'

There is a delicious sound of babbling water. Goldie slumps down next to the water's edge in the sunshine, as if this is what she always does. Mr Man sits a little way back from the stream, on a big flat stone. He lights a cigarette, takes in a deep breath and wheezes a little. There is plenty of room for me to sit there too, and I'm afraid he's going to pat the place next to him, so I make a beeline for Goldie and sit down with her. Although there are lots of blown twigs and old leaves on the grass, it is warm. The only sounds are birdsong, the water running over the stones and Goldie panting heavily. The dog lies down, wagging her tail, and I lie with her, facing her back and the stream. Her fur is thick and soft, and I put my arms around her, not looking at Mr Man. 'It's lovely here,' I say.

'Yes,' he says, his voice still reassuringly coming from a few yards away, on the stone. Good. I lie listening to the birds and the stream. Wait until I tell Dawn about this. She's going to be bowled over. She won't believe me. She'll say I made it up, but then I'll bring her down here and she'll see for herself. Maybe we'll even call on Mr Man together and ask if we can take Goldie for a walk. I listen to a blackbird fluting merrily away. There are wood pigeons, too, cooing their insistent love songs. Dawn and I have worked out that the rhythm is the same as 'I *love* you, darling! I *love* you, darling!', and I whisper it now into Goldie's fur. The sun is warming my skin, and I swing a bare leg over Goldie's body, and she lets me. This is so lovely. I almost forget about Trevor being thrown away. The sound of the birds singing, the babble of the stream, Goldie panting. But there is other panting. I turn my head and see Mr Man is breathing heavily.

'You okay?' I ask. He doesn't seem okay.

'Yes, yes,' he gasps. 'I'm okay.' He is taking in great gulps of air as if he's just run a race, his eyes are wide and fixed and I don't like looking at him. I turn back to Goldie. I think I might like to go home now.

I get to my feet, and Goldie gets up too.

'I'm afraid I have to get back,' I say, chewing on a nail and trying not to look at him.

'Yes!' he pants.

'So, I'm . . . going to . . .' I slowly make my way past him and try to look as normal as possible. When I reach the bushes, I turn to see his shoulders going jaggedly up and down, and by the time I dare look round again, he has lain back in the grass, and Goldie is standing next to him, licking his face.

I walk fast. I run. I run back up through the woods, across the footbridge and all the way home. Mum is just putting dinner on the table when I get in, and I am panting like Mr Man.

Chapter Thirteen

Don't Tell Anyone

Dawn does speak to me again. Not of her own choosing, but because we are forced into each other's company. A couple of weeks later, something happens with her younger sister, Karen, and Mrs Webster has to go into hospital with her. So, my mother agrees to give Dawn tea after school each day. She is being spoilt rotten by everyone. Her mum has even bought her some new socks with red hearts on them. She is sulky to start with, making it clear that I will have to try extremely hard if I want her to like me again. I am desperate to please her, and I hate myself for it.

It's like offering food to a horse. I have to hold my hand out perfectly flat and still, so she can nibble it off me in her own good time. She won't take suggestions from me any other way.

'I've seen Mr Man on my own!' I whisper, while we sit on the warm pavement with our bead boxes, waiting for tea and hoping that Lisa Warwick will come out and swap some beads from a new broken necklace. Dawn opens her bead tin and starts to count her 'diamonds'. Diamonds are high currency, and she has them in a variety of colours, which I envy.

'One, two, three, four ...'

'He showed me his secret place.'

'... eight, nine, ten ...'

'And he did something really weird.'

She gives me a withering, bored look. I know she wants to know more, but she heaves a great sigh. 'What, then?'

Lisa Warwick comes over and shows us a whole tin of green glass beads. They are beautiful.

'Swapsies,' she says. 'Got anything you want to swap?' She quickly pinpoints two or three of Dawn's best diamonds, and hands over six glass beads in return. She looks in my box and can see nothing of much interest. 'I suppose I could give you one bead for those four,' she says, selecting my best amber-coloured beads.

'I'm collecting amber,' I say.

She plonks them in her tin and gives me the green bead. 'Well, now you're collecting green!'

I close my tin and walk over to Mr Man's gate. Goldie has just scuttled up to it and Mr Man is at the door, preparing to go out.

'We'll take Goldie for a walk,' I say.

'Oh.' He looks over at Dawn, who is watching us now. I'm pleased, because she can see Goldie is licking me, and that I am chatting casually with Mr Man. 'Well, you can come with me if you like.'

'Oh, we have to have tea soon. We could take her after, though.'

Dawn comes over and stands next to me, stroking Goldie through the gate.

'That would be helpful. I'll just let her out now to do her business.' He opens the gate and the dog jumps up at me. She trots down the pavement of Napier Road, sniffing, then lifts her leg against a lamp post. Mr Man calls her back, and she bounds up to him. 'Good girl! Good girl!' He closes the gate. 'Would you two girls like to come in for a biscuit and see my cat?'

I tense, and I feel Dawn's excitement beside me.

'A cat?' she asks.

He lowers his head towards us: 'Yes. And I'm pretty sure she's expecting kittens.'

Mum and Dad warned me about men like this. Men who offered you sweeties or to see their kittens or puppies. Dawn knows this too.

'Oooh!' she says. 'Can we have one when they're born?'

66

'Of course!' He opens his front door and beckons us in. Dawn makes to go, but I hold her back.

'No.'

'What?'

'We can't. We're not allowed in people's houses.'

Mr Man overhears me saying this, and says, 'Oh, of course. I quite understand. You can't be too careful.'

'But we're *nine* now!' Dawn shakes me off, disdainfully, as if she is prepared to go in alone, but I know she's not. 'Can't you bring her out?' she asks.

'She has to do that of her own accord. Cats aren't like dogs. Never mind. Perhaps when she's had her kittens you can come with a parent.'

He's about to close the door, so I say, 'Later, then? Can we take Goldie out?'

'Of course. Just pop round when you're ready.'

The door closes. We turn away from the gate.

'What, then?'

'What do you mean?'

'What weird thing?'

So I tell her. And after tea I take her, with Goldie, to the secret Dingle over the railway footbridge. I have no fear, because I have no idea what will happen here before the summer is out.

The mid-April evening is golden. We lie back on the sun-warmed grass by the stream and look up at the bright green leaves beginning to unfurl. The new, swaggering spring foliage dapples us in light. Everything seems right with the world – at least, to me. We put our sunlit arms in the air and run our nails up and down over their insides, marvelling at the feeling.

'Where did it happen?' she asks, propping herself up on her elbows.

'Over there. He was sitting on the stone. I was lying here with Goldie, and he was panting worse than her.'

She smiles and nods slowly. 'We're going to have to watch him. He was probably playing with his willy.'

'No! Do you think so?' I don't really believe her. She's just making it up to scare us.

'Yes. And I know where he was thinking of putting it.'

I take in a huge breath of horror. 'Yuck! Yuck, yuck, *yuck*! No!'

We squeal in revulsion and collapse into giggles. None of it feels like a real possibility. We are enjoying the shock of fear that Dawn has conjured up, so we begin to elaborate. Soon he is dragging one or other of us through the woods and trying to kiss us, and Dawn has him slobbering over us, pulling down our knickers and saying rude things in our ears. I do feel a bit wobbly inside, though. It's almost as if I'm betraying him, because he would never do anything so ridiculous, but I suppose that's why we're laughing, because it would be so unlike him. And I always like Dawn best when she's laughing. After five minutes or so we're exhausted, and roll onto our backs again, out of breath from snorting with laughter.

When the hilarity has subsided, and our breath is steady again, Dawn says, 'I've got a secret too.'

'What is it?' I know Dawn. She probably hasn't got a secret at all; she's just trying to compete with me. It has to be better than mine, so she will invent something hideous now.

'You have to promise not to tell anyone.'

'Of course.'

'No.' She turns and looks at me with a seriousness that makes her look stupidly unlike Dawn Webster. It makes her look like a normal person, who is afraid sometimes. 'I mean, you have to promise not to tell *anyone*.'

Chapter Fourteen

Item: **Singer sewing machine.** *Keep.*

The train screeches and lurches forward. We're off again. What a palaver. How can it take half an hour to get a sheep off a track? Still, I can't help enjoying the idea that one sheep, in search of a bit of adventure and new grass, should have caused such glorious chaos.

'Emotionally absent?' I'd said to Paula, as if I'd never come across those words together in my studies. Nevertheless, 'absent' still conjured up a school register, and I pictured a cross being drawn against my mother's name. If she'd been absent, where had she been all those years? All those emotions, where did they go? I used to think Jonathan had all her love, but he didn't have such an easy time of it either. My mother used to brandish a slim, pliable garden cane when we wouldn't get to sleep, and if we chatted beyond a certain time, running back and forward to each other's bedrooms to tell stories or play-fight, she would stomp up the stairs and whip it through the air. I forgot about that. I forgot about it because she never caned me, just scared me witless. She caned Jonathan, though. A few times, he tells me now.

It was as if she'd longed for her life to begin, and when it did, she made a gift of it to my father, and then spent the rest of her life waiting for something vague, huge and romantic to happen in it. But it never did. It was all a con. I suppose what happened that summer was a drama of sorts. Not one to be wished for, but it put her at the centre of things for a while.

I remember her so vividly sometimes. I remember the smell of her, flowery and musky as she bent over me, occasionally, for a brisk goodnight hug. I remember her dark china horse leaping across the mantelpiece, a strange, one-off purchase for herself. I remember how she once took my hands on the coldest, snow-filled winter's day and rubbed them between her own. I remember all the pretty dresses and coats she made for me on her little Singer sewing machine. I remember her being proud of me for the way I cleaned the dirt from around a tap on one occasion. I remember her saying once, just once, to Mr Webster, 'Leave my daughter alone. She's only a child, and she's been through enough.'

And I remember, too, a recurring dream I used to have as a child. In it, I am in a boat at sea, and suddenly there is Mummy in the water, her arms outstretched to me. I know she can't swim, so I reach out to her, and I know I can save her. But just as my arms go around her, I hear a shout, and there's another woman in the water who looks just like Mummy. 'Help me, Stephanie!' I know it's her, so I let go of the mummy I'm helping and reach out for my real mummy. But wait, there's another scream: 'It's not her, Stephanie, it's me! *I'm* Mummy! Help me!' And so I do help her, and just as I have my arms about her, ready to haul her over the side, another voice, even more convincing: 'Don't listen to any of them! They're all pretending! Look at me, Steph, I'm Mummy! Over here!' And so it goes on. I only remember it because I had a version of this dream after Matt was born. In it, she was trying to save *me*, only I didn't know which mum on which boat to grab onto. There were endless versions of her.

The only thing I have of my mother's – apart from photographs – is her sewing machine. I have an electric one myself now, but I still keep her old one, black with gold filigree, displayed on a small table, and I marvel that she managed to create so much with that one-stitch machine. Somehow it represents her beautifully: its practicality, its creativity and its promise of pretty things, of

70

dreams fulfilled. It seems to me now that my mother, in the elegant outfits she made for herself, managed to wrest some idea of the glamorous life she had imagined from a marriage to my father, who clung onto the safety of a small, restricted life. It was as if our house was a pole onto which she was tethered, and could go only as far as her rope would let her in any direction. A perfect circle. At its periphery were her dreams. At its epicentre her sewing machine, her drill, her ladder, her shed, her children. At its very centre, her husband.

We were oblivious to what I see clearly now, through the lens of my training, as his mental health issues. A natural hypochondriac, he scoured the home doctor's book for illnesses to accompany his symptoms. He naturally tended towards anxiety, and at times of gentle crisis he was highly anxious, suffering from an upset stomach and 'guts ache'. Whenever things became too much for him, he opted out, complaining, 'My stomach ulcer is playing me up again.' In a bamboozling act of loyalty, my mother bought into this self-diagnosis, so we had to as well. Whenever, as teenagers, we challenged him (staying out later than our curfew of ten o'clock or accepting a lift on a motorbike or smelling remotely of someone else's cigarette smoke), he would go into a meltdown of anxiety, saying we'd kicked off his stomach ulcer again, and my mother would say, 'Look what you've done now!'

If I had to list my mother's favourite sayings, or at least the ones that I have struggled most to forget and not to use myself, they would be, 'Sorry isn't good enough', 'Look what you've done now' and 'Don't be so filthy'. Even her compliments were smudged with criticism. With my psychologist's hat on, I am filled with a terrible sadness, because I think someone must have used these phrases on her. She spoke them with such assurance. They tripped off her tongue with such ease. Like her confidence that crying was manipulative and parts of a woman's body were dirty. Someone had got to her as a child, and that makes me overwhelmingly sad.

Even though she is now dead and in the ground (Dad insisted on a proper burial, after what happened), she seems more present than ever she did when she was alive. I see her now not so much as an absence, but as a hoard of Roman coins hidden beneath the earth, waiting to be discovered, each coin to be turned over in my palm, polished and examined.

Chapter Fifteen

Nowhere Man

I'm excited now. 'Of course. I promise.'

Dawn lies back and looks up at the leaves. 'I've got a big brother.'

She waits for this information to sink in. It's obviously made up, but I humour her.

'Where is he, then?'

'It's a secret.'

I wait for more. 'Do *you* know where he is?'

'No. Not yet.'

I lean on my elbow and pick at some grass, trying to look like I believe her. 'So ... how do you know about him?'

'I heard Dad shouting at Mum. He shouts at her quite a bit, but this was really loud. She screamed back at him, "How dare you look at ...!" something or other, and he shouted, "It's a good job I ruddy well did!" and then she started crying and then he shouted some more, and I didn't hear all of it but he said, "When were you going to tell Dawn that she has a sixteen-year-old brother?"'

'*Sixteen*-year-old?'

'Yep.'

'So ...' I don't understand. This is too complicated for one of Dawn's lies. She doesn't go in for this sort of detail, and I have a sharp twist in my stomach that spreads up to my throat. 'So, they've been keeping him a secret from you?'

She nods. 'Looks like it.'

73

'I wonder why he doesn't live with you.'

'Perhaps he ran away before I can remember.'

'Do you know his name?'

'Yes. He's called Neil.'

'Neil,' I say, fascinated.

'Neil.'

'Neil.'

We savour the new name for a bit.

'How do you know his name?'

She explains how she has been looking in drawers and being a detective. There's a key under the front doormat, and she's been in the house when her dad is still out at work.

'Mum went away with Karen and I found a letter.' Dawn has a little purse-bag that she wears over her shoulder. She keeps dinner money and handkerchiefs in it. Now she opens the popper and shows me a letter. It's in grown-up writing, but it's a bit childish, so it's easy to read. 'It's from my gran to my mum. Here's the bit: "I know you'll be thinking of Neil today on his 16th birthday. Big hugs, darling. Remember you did the right thing. And you have two lovely girls now." See? We don't know any Neils.'

I have the curious, exciting feeling that Dawn is telling the truth.

'We have to find him,' I say.

'Exactly.'

'I wonder what he's like?'

'I expect he wears jeans and a donkey jacket like Sindy's Paul.'

'I bet he likes the Rolling Stones!'

'And he has hair down over his ears – and a polo-neck jumper – and Chelsea boots!'

'And I bet he has a girlfriend . . .'

'Called Tracey or Linda . . .'

'And I bet he snogs her!'

We are off again, imagining whole new worlds for this new brother. But then Dawn gets serious again.

'You absolutely mustn't tell anyone – not even your mum. Especially your mum.'

'Why especially her?'

'Because Mum isn't in hospital.'

I look stupidly at her.

'She's gone to my gran's with Karen. She's escaped Dad because he was so shouty. He got really shouty and he grabbed her neck. He told her to get out and never come back. She only left me with him because she didn't want me to miss school. But she whispered to me that she'll be back soon, and not to worry. I mustn't tell *anybody*.'

I'm sorry for Dawn then, and I feel a little stab of sympathy for my mum, because she's been lied to, and she believes the lie. I don't like to think that she has this weakness, that she can be fooled.

We make our way back along the footpaths with Goldie, and Mum gives us tea with jelly and ice cream for afters. I know this is especially for Dawn, because she says, 'Don't worry, Dawn. Your mum has to stay with Karen because it's frightening being in hospital all alone when you're little. I'm sure she'll be home soon. She told me a week at most.' Then she offers Dawn a Fox's glacier mint before she goes home to her dad. I try to forgive her.

Chapter Sixteen

Don't Take this the Wrong Way

Someone – maybe Mrs Webster or maybe my mother – has clearly told Mr Spruce that things are tricky for Dawn at the moment, because she gets put back on my table in class. We have four two-seater desks arranged facing inwards to form a long table, so there are eight children at each table. We have five of these long tables in the classroom, seating the forty pupils. I wouldn't mind, but Hilary is moved away from my table and put on Gareth's. Now I will never get Hilary back as my friend. Now I am Dawn's for ever. I see that straight away, and so does Dawn.

Sadly, Hilary doesn't help herself, because she puts her hand up so much, and often gets a question right after Dawn gets it wrong. Also, Mr Spruce tells Dawn off a lot for talking to me when she should be listening, and he includes me in the telling-off. The worst mistake Hilary makes, though, is to put her hand up while she is sitting next to Gareth – who also has his hand up – and to link hands with him in the air, like she used to do with me. I cast a sideways glance at Dawn, but she has seen it. She spits out insults under her breath. I fear for Hilary.

'I'm going to kill her,' says Dawn, in the playground.

'I don't think she meant anything by it,' I try. 'She used to do the same with me.'

'I don't care. She's not having Gareth. Gareth is mine.'

Well, obviously he isn't, I want to say. In fact, I doubt he's even interested in girls, but I say nothing. To be honest, I'm a bit hacked off with him, letting himself look all soppy next to Hilary. I know she's easy with touching people, and it's nice, really, but she ought to be a bit more careful.

There's a giant snail making its way slowly along the edge of the playground, and I look away from it. But I can see Dawn watching it, assessing its crushability; can see her savouring in advance the deep crunch underfoot and the sense of power at ending a life. I walk away and sit on a wall so as not to be a spectator for her, and this is enough to change her mind. Dawn likes to be seen.

'Hello,' says Hilary, coming over to us. We are perched on the wall behind the climbing frame. 'Who'd like to play dancing?'

Dawn flares her nostrils and says nothing.

'What sort of dancing?' I ask, just to ease the atmosphere.

'Pop dancing. My brother taught me some new moves. Want to see them?'

'Why would we?' says Dawn, sullenly. (I don't like this 'we' she's using.)

'He's fourteen,' she says, smiling. 'He's a teenager. He knows lots of cool moves.'

I can't bear to see her smile pitted against Dawn's bitterness. I feel weak not protecting her, because she's being so brave.

'Okay,' I say.

'Well, my brother's *sixteen*!' says Dawn, venomously.

I look at her, shocked. So does Hilary.

'I didn't know you had a brother,' she says.

'Well, that just shows how little you know, doesn't it?'

I watch to see how Hilary will receive this flesh wound, whether she will go or stay. I almost hope she will wander off to play with someone else, to protect herself, but I don't see why Dawn's cruelty should win over. She looks down at her shoes for a while, then asks, 'Does he live away?'

'Yes.'

I wonder if Dawn is going to invent a flat for Neil and a job to go with it, both of which would be pushing it. But living away is quite plausible, since Hilary only moved here recently and has no idea that Dawn has never had a brother living at home.

'I can't wait to be a teenager,' I offer, hoping to move the conversation on. 'I'd like to have a flat of my own so I can play records and have parties.'

'Me too,' says Hilary.

'I'm going to have a boyfriend as soon as I'm a teenager,' says Dawn, narrowing her eyes at Hilary, as if she has already stolen her chosen man.

'And me,' I say quickly. 'He'd be a bit shy, but kind and handsome.'

'You'll never have a boyfriend!' Dawn scoffs at me.

'Why ever not?' asks Hilary. 'Of course she will.'

Dawn behaves as if Hilary hasn't spoken. She looks at me painfully and lets rip: 'Look at you, Steph. Don't take this the wrong way, but I mean, who's going to want you with that funny leg? I mean, no one wants to go out with a girl who hobbles, do they? And imagine going to a dance with a girl who drags her foot. Honestly. I don't mean to be unkind, Stephie, but you really shouldn't get your hopes up.'

My scalp prickles, and there is something hard pressing on my throat. Harder and harder until I can barely breathe. I think for a moment I might faint, but I know I probably won't, because it is not an unfamiliar feeling. All I have to do is walk away from my head, leave my body for a bit and look at us all from the air, or from over the other side of the playground. I can hear Hilary saying that her brother thinks I'm pretty, but I'm too far away from myself to absorb it.

'. . . and anyway, thirteen is far too young to have a boyfriend. My mum didn't start dating until she was eighteen.'

'Eighteen?' Dawn responds to Hilary now, because I am barely listening. 'My mum was dating when she was fourteen or fifteen. And my parents met when they were eighteen and married when they were nineteen.'

'Mine were twenty-two.'

'That's why your mum is so old.'

'She's only thirty-six. That's not old for a mum.'

'Well, mine is thirty-one.'

'Thirty-one?' Hilary frowns. I'm watching her now, back with them. The pain has been successfully held at bay. I've put it away to pick over later, and if I keep busy, I might even manage to forget to do that. That's a way I know to make things disappear. It doesn't always work. But Hilary's frown has caught my attention. 'If your mum is thirty-one and you have a sixteen-year-old brother, then that means she was ...' you can see her doing the sums in her head, 'fifteen when she had him.'

'No ...'

'Yes, it does. She was fifteen, and she must have had him with a different man to your dad.'

I close my eyes so that I don't have to see Dawn's reaction.

Of all the times Mrs Arch, the dinner lady, rings the handbell in 1966, she has no idea how significant this one is. It marks the end of playtime.

Chapter Seventeen

He Whispers to Me

Who's going to want you with that funny leg? I thought I could do my trick and push it aside until I forgot about it, but it's like some monster that keeps breaking the surface of the water, rearing up with a big, gaping mouth. I'm going to the railway bank. I have to be alone as quickly as possible before something bursts out of me, like violent sobbing I can't do at home. There *is* something bubbling in me, but it won't quite come out yet. I wouldn't mind so much, but she always introduces her spiteful stuff with *I don't mean to be unkind or anything, but* . . . Or else it's *Don't take this the wrong way* . . . What would the wrong way be?

I have just entered the gate to the railway cutting when I see Goldie tied up to a hawthorn tree along the path to the left. There is no sign of Mr Man, so I approach her and give her a stroke. She's so happy to see me, and it makes me feel special. I breathe in the warm, damp air. There's a tree stump by the path with wood sorrel and herb Robert, and I make a mental note to tell Mr Spruce, who tells us about the wild flowers he's seen. He'll be impressed.

Then I see Mr Man coming up the bank. His head appears first. He's panting slightly, like his dog. He sees me and puts a finger to his lips, as though to tell me to keep quiet. He's right up on the path now, and I look into his face. His eyes are a muddy green and his hair is the colour of wet sand. He is built for camouflage. I look around. There's no one about, and I feel a surge of panic.

'Would you like to see something very special?' he whispers. He can see me swallow air as I hesitate. I don't feel confident enough to say no because I'm only half-baked, so I stand there, wondering how embarrassing it would be to run away. I close my eyes in horror at the thought. I couldn't do that. What would he think if he's just being friendly and doesn't want his wicked way or anything? I'm stuck. 'Just here – come.' He's still whispering, pointing beneath him. I lean over the edge of the path, down the bank. I can't see anything, but where he's pointing is just a few yards away, beyond some gorse bushes, so I follow him, keeping a distance between us.

I know I'm doing everything you're not supposed to do with a strange man. I think he counts as strange. I'm not sure. But I'm following him I don't know where, and I can't run away fast like other children, not with my foot. Perhaps he knows that. Perhaps he was lying in wait for me – and that's why he tied Goldie up: so she can't save me, and no one will know where we are. He crouches down ahead of me, and stretches an arm back to beckon silently. I am dizzy with fear, but there seems to be no choice except to keep going. I wish I was more fully baked. I tread as noiselessly as I can over the long grass, edging diagonally down on the sides of my feet, and trying to lift my right one as high as I can off the ground so that it doesn't drag.

He's right. There is something special. One, two, three, four little fox cubs with their mother, about twenty feet away. They are gambolling and joshing and topsy-turvy-ing. I try not to let out a yelp of joy, but he sees my expression and smiles at me. The mother fox looks like she's having a well-earned nap in the sun, her head on her paws. The cubs start to fall asleep, one by one, in a little heap. We stay crouching for some time, and then he raises himself and comes towards me, back up the slope. I get up too, and try to keep ahead of him, pulling my foot as hard as I can so that he doesn't come up beside me and offer me a hand. I get up to the path just before him.

'I tied Goldie up as soon as I caught a glimpse,' he explains. 'Come on, old girl. Let's untie you.'

I watch him as his slender fingers grapple with the lead around the spiky branch. His shirt is creased, as though he hasn't ironed it, and his trousers look a little tatty. There is nothing to him. He's all skin and bone. 'Would Goldie have chased them?' I ask, for something to say.

'Probably not, but the vixen would've hidden them straight away if Goldie got too close.'

I stroke Goldie again. There is an awkward silence, apart from Goldie panting. Neither of us starts to walk in either direction.

'I've never seen fox cubs before,' I say, looking up at his awkward-man face. 'They're lovely . . . thank you.' He nods and smiles.

I don't know what else to say. The cotton of his shirt is so worn that there is a fluffy edge down the front beside the buttons. I almost want to touch it. His sleeves are rolled up, and beneath them his thin brown arms are corded with strong veins and covered in dark brown hair with glints of sun-bleached gold. The hair looks velvety, like Goldie's fur, and I know that if I were to reach out and stroke it, it would feel soft. I have to say something.

'Has your cat had her kittens yet?'

'No, but any day now.' He says that his cat is called Dumpling and she is definitely about to have them. He knows this because she is shaped like a barrel and she has been looking for places to hide around the house. Her favourite place is behind the sofa, and he's got a cardboard box ready for her with a soft towel in it.

I shuffle my feet awkwardly.

'Listen,' he says, suddenly. I think he might ask me to do something else, invite me back to his house or something, or on a walk with him. I prepare to make a dash for it with an excuse. 'Did you hear that?'

I wait. I listen. I'm not sure what I'm listening for.

'There!' he says, pointing up into a tree beside the path. 'Can you see? Perched on that top branch on the left – just there!' I follow his pointed finger and see a small greenish bird, tweeting away. 'It's a chiffchaff,' he says. 'The first one I've seen this year.'

We both watch and listen. I'm impressed by his knowledge of birds. 'How do you know?'

'Well, its song is a sort of "chiff-chaff, chiff-chaff", and it's that pale green. There's a willow warbler that looks much the same, but has pinkish legs. Our chiffchaff has b-black legs, can you see? And shorter wings, because it doesn't fly as far as the willow warbler. And the willow warbler has a descending trill.' He doesn't demonstrate. I know he's not the sort of person to demonstrate. He's far too timid to make any sort of fool of himself. Not unlike me, really. But he looks so happy that I think if he were a dog he would be wagging his tail. Actually, if I were a dog I think I might be wagging mine, too.

'It sounds a bit like a squeaky toy.'

'Ah, that's its alarm call, now. Yes, you're right. It does.' We both listen again. He turns and smiles at me, as if we share a secret. And I feel that in a strange way, we do. We share something, anyway. Something gentle and delicate, like the bird. Like the foxes. Something too good to tell Dawn.

Chapter Eighteen

Sifting

I lie in bed and think about the chiffchaff and the foxes and Mr Man, and how he is lonely and doesn't fit in, a bit like me. My bedtime is eight o'clock, so for most of the spring and summer, it's still light outside. I can hear the older children playing, hear their shrieks of laughter, their shouts and giggles and fake screams. I hear the neighbour call her cat in: 'Flora! Flo-ra!' My curtains are a big rectangle of glowing pink. Behind them, beyond the garden, Longacre Farm sends its evening noises: the gentle hoot of a tawny owl, the double croak of the raven as it does its solitary dusk patrol, its slow, flapping wings, which sound like when Mum shakes out a pillow to hang on the line. Then there are the last bleats of the sheep on the hill: the shrill bleater, the deep-throated bleater, and the one Dad calls 'smoker's cough bleater'. In the morning I'm woken up by the cockerel from Longacre and the clatter of the farmhand's buckets.

When I can't sleep, I sit in the window and look out at the sheep on the hill. I used to talk to my bear, Trevor, and he would talk back to me. Or else we would sing together, and Trev would dance on the windowsill:

In and out the dusty bluebells,
In and out the dusty bluebells,
In and out the dusty bluebells,
Who will be my master?

84

We play a game sometimes in the road or at school and we all make a big circle and sing this, while one person skips in and out of the arches made by everyone else. Then we sing 'Tippity-tappety on my shoulder . . . Who will be my master', and the person skipping chooses the next person to join them until there is a whole snake of children and only one arch left. Mr Man says this game is very old, and is about the magic of bluebells. It's unlucky for a child to pick bluebells alone, because they can be magicked away by a sort of Pied Piper spirit in the woods, and dance away with all the other children under his spell. I like that story. He also says that bluebells used to be used to starch ruffle collars in olden days, and to bind books. And if you hang a bunch of bluebells over your bed they will stop you having nightmares. Mr Man knows loads of interesting things.

So I still sing 'The Dusty Bluebells' when I can't sleep, even if I have to make do with Sindy now. When my parents hear me, they shout up and tell me to get to sleep. Sometimes, there are footsteps on the stairs, and although I long for it to be Mum, I know from the *stamp, stamp, stamp* if it's her, and that she won't be pleased and won't stay. Dad is nimble of foot on the stairs, and the keys jingle in his pocket. I am relieved when he comes in, as he most often does, and puts his arms around me. He'll sing me a song – usually a hymn – and I get to breathe in his sweaty jacket, which I like.

What a friend we have in Jesus
All our sins and griefs to bear
What a privilege to carry
Everything to God in prayer.

Please God, make my mummy love me. Please God, heal my wonky foot. I wish more than anything that Mum would put her arms around me, that she would read to me sometimes, that she would speak to me softly. At least with the girls in the street I know why I'm excluded. But with Mum I just don't know. All that washing didn't work. So, I just don't know. But Dad loves me. And Jesus loves me. *Jesus loves me, this I know, For the Bible tells me so. Little ones to him belong, They are weak and he is strong.*

A couple of days ago Jonathan was distraught. He had been playing in the flower beds earlier with his plastic animals, and lost his favourite, a stag called Nate. Jonathan can't sleep without Stag Nate beside his pillow. Mum was on her knees with a garden sieve (her 'riddle', as she calls it), sieving through the soil all along both flower beds which line the driveway. It took her all evening, shaking the riddle and disposing of the lumps, until at last she found him. Jonathan was already in bed. She washed the stag, soaked him in a bowl of Dettol, and in the morning, Stag Nate stood beside Jonathan's bowl of Rice Krispies. The look of joy on my brother's face was reflected in a smile on Mum's. He had no idea how long she was out there on her knees for him.

I don't understand Mum. It's strange, we know Dad's family but we don't really know Mum's at all. Grandad Townsend is old, in his sixties, and his wife died so we don't have a Gran Townsend. There's my Aunty Babs who is his daughter, but she's quite quiet and we don't see her much. Grandad comes up on the train from Cornwall about once a month and brings with him a small brown suitcase, which we watch hungrily until he opens it. Always there is a bag of humbugs for Mum and a bag of jelly babies for me and Jonathan. Grandad takes us out for walks and in the evening, he babysits while Mum and Dad go out. Dad has no time for 'the pictures', but Mum says if he doesn't take her, she'll pack her bags and go. She uses this phrase so often that we know she doesn't mean it. Once, when Mum tried to make Jonathan eat Brussels sprouts, he said, 'If you make me eat these, I'm going to pack my bags and go.' Everyone laughed, so we know it's just a thing she says.

Anyway, Grandad tells us stories in his deep, Cornish voice, and they are exciting and about pirates and things and have nothing to do with God. Or else he tells us funny stories about the pigs that he keeps. Sometimes he sings us hymns with a twist, like:

'Now the day is over,
Night is drawing nigh,
Grandad's little piggies
Are sleeping in their sty.'

Or:

'There is a happy land
Far, far away,
Where little piggies run
Three times a day.
You would laugh to see them run
When they see the butcher come.
Three slices off their bum,
Three times a day.'

Of course, we laugh our heads off, but we never let on to Dad, and he knows we won't. He also drinks a bottle of beer or two from his suitcase, which he knows Dad would disapprove of, because drinking is evil. But he knows we won't tell on him for that either.

Mum's family, though, are a bit of a mystery. We've seen Aunty Wendy a few times, but Mum doesn't like her much. Dad doesn't like her husband, Terry, but I don't know why. He always cracks jokes and makes us laugh. But we never see the rest of them. I remember a train journey and a bus journey when we went to see Gran and Grandad Wilden. Mum knocked on the door and nobody came. Me and Jonathan started knocking too, and we looked through the letter box. Then Mum shouted through the letter box, but nobody came. We knew they were in, because Mum saw the curtains move upstairs. I can't remember how long we were there, banging on the windows, going round the back, and Dad saying, 'This is a waste of time.' Then a neighbour came round with a key, and they were in, and Granny Wilden (Mum's mum) said, 'Oh, we didn't hear you!' which Dad said later was a fib.

All I remember is a smelly parlour and a lack of welcome. Granny Wilden didn't put her arms around us, which I thought a gran might do, like Dawn's two grannies. She didn't even take the newspaper covering off the chairs for us. There were much older children there who must have been Uncle Ken and Aunty Valerie, Mum's brother and other sister. Grandad Wilden looked like a kind old man, and I went to sit on his knee. I think I was quite small, but I remember it because everyone was shocked. Even he was surprised. To me, grandads' knees were for sitting on. I always sat on Grandad Townsend's knee, and here was another grandad, with two free knees. After his surprise, he looked down at me and smiled, and I snuggled into him. He smelt of cigarette smoke. He didn't read to me or tell me stories or anything, but I felt quite happy there by the fire. I remember seeing everyone smiling about it, except for Mum. She didn't look pleased at all.

Chapter Nineteen

Item: **Dansette record player.** ~~Chuck~~. *Donate.*

A young woman is walking down the aisle of our carriage with headphones on, listening to her Walkman. I can hear the tinny sound of her music as she goes by. How wonderful to be able to take music around with you. It used to be the radio or the record player, and that was it.

It was only a bit of a wrench to give that old Dansette away. Mainly because it was the only gift my dad had ever bought my mum (although it came in surprisingly handy for Bible class parties), and that gave it a special status somehow. But I also have a bad memory associated with it.

It was a wet Sunday afternoon, and Jonathan was fiddling with the record player. He had found a single record still on the turntable, left over from when Hilary had come round to play. Her brother had lots of records, and she sometimes brought one or two round for us to dance to. It was 'Stop! In The Name Of Love' by the Supremes. We decided to play it, and Jonathan started jigging around to it, but I had some dance moves, which Hilary had taught me. He started to copy me, and we fell about laughing.

'Play it again! I can do it! I can!'

So I put it on again, and he copied me again. By the third time of playing, we were not bad. He ran into the dining room where Dad was reading the newspaper. 'Come and watch us, Daddy! Come and watch us dance!'

89

Mum must've been in the kitchen, because I remember that only Dad came. He sat down in the armchair under the window to be our audience. The needle came down on the vinyl, and we were off.

'STOP . . .!' We stretched out our right arms, palms up, then swung our arms over to the right, wiggling our left hips. Then we pointed over to the left, wiggling our right hips. We placed our hands over our hearts, we wiggled down and up. As we came up, we placed our hands on our bodies and smoothed them along the lengths of our thighs and sides, wiggling our hips all the while. Jonathan giggled at this and so did I. He looked daft doing it, but he kept in time. Dad smiled and rolled his eyes, but I was certain he was impressed. We relaxed into it now and re-peated the sequence. At the words 'Haven't I been good to you?' we wriggled down and up, drawing our hands up our thighs and sides, and my shift dress rose up a bit, just like Hilary had shown me.

I don't know how long Mum had been standing in the doorway watching when she let out a scream: 'STOP! What *on earth* do you think you're doing? You little *slut*!' The music was still going, but drawing to its close as she said, 'Where did you learn that *filth*?'

I could feel my pulse pounding in my head. I swallowed hard. I had to get this right.

'The playground,' I lied. If I said Hilary she would stop me playing with her, and I didn't want to lose Hilary.

'Well, I'm going up to that school and having a word with your teacher!'

'Kath . . .'

'Although I can guess who's behind it.' I knew she thought it was Dawn. She marched over to the record player and dragged the record off it. 'Don't let me *ever* catch you dancing like that again.' She clutched the record at arm's length like a piece of rubbish, and pointed the finger of her other hand at me, jabbing it. 'Do you hear me?'

'What about me?' said Jonathan, but she ignored him.

'DO YOU HEAR ME?' she shouted at me. I nodded, unable to speak.

'Making those *crude* gestures in front of your father! Your own father!'

'Kath—'

'Only SLUTS dance like that!'

I remember trying to make sense of this, trying to decode what she was saying, but I held onto my own arm at the elbow and felt powerless.

'Am I a slut?' asked Jonathan.

She ignored him, her mouth pursed into a tight knot.

'Am I? Am I a slut?'

'Don't be silly. Only girls are sluts!'

I could feel the tears backing up behind my eyes, but I willed them to stop, and folded my lips tightly to keep them from trembling. She grabbed hold of me roughly by the arm and dragged me out of the room. 'Get out! Get *out*! Get up to your room and don't come back down until you're sorry.'

I remember I lay down on my bed and cried and cried. Strong, hot tears that scorched my cheeks and made my face swell up. I couldn't go back down with a face that betrayed my tears. That would have been manipulative. So I went to the bathroom to splash my face and threw up in the sink. I pushed the bits down the plughole, feeling as disgusted with myself as she did. I washed my face in cold water and waited for it to return to normal. Then I went and apologised, but Mum didn't seem at all pleased. Clearly it wasn't good enough, as I had known all along it wouldn't be. I kept on trying, though.

It's the hardest thing in the world for a pleaser. Not being able to please.

We're pulling into a station, and I wonder if I ever once

managed to please my mother. That was the big attraction with Dawn, being able to please her, and her encouraging me to do so. That was the attraction and the problem. I nearly always did what she wanted me to do.

Chapter Twenty

Binned

I don't think my mother ever does complain about the dance moves I learnt 'in the playground', which is a huge relief, as I would curl up with shame if she ever spoke to our teacher about it. I adore Mr Spruce. He wears polo-neck jumpers, and when it's hot he puts his jacket on the back of the chair. Sometimes, when it's playtime, I sneak into the classroom and go over to his desk. The jacket's arms hang forward, and it can look a bit like him, sitting there casually. I like to stroke the tweedy material and the suede patches on the elbows. I bend into the collar and breathe in slowly, smelling the warm scent of him. *Old Spice*, I imagine, like the adverts. Dad doesn't use aftershave, just 'Old Sweat', as Mum says.

One day Mr Spruce says we can help to brighten up the class-room by bringing in flowers from our gardens. I bring in a bunch of early roses and give them to him at his desk. *They're red, for love*, I want to say. They are wrapped in paper I've decorated with little hearts all over. I've coloured in the hearts in blue, so that it doesn't look too soppy, but so that he can see I care. I've also added some birds because I know he likes birds.

Mr Spruce says, 'How magnificent!' and asks me to fill a jar with water. He throws the paper in the bin. But the roses are on his desk. Red roses from me. He tells everyone that I have brought roses in and that I've added 'a splash of colour' to the classroom.

The next day, Lisa Warwick and Dawn bring in flowers, and the day after that, so does Hilary. My roses share a jar with some clashing orange marigolds. Poor Mr Spruce has no idea about colour matching. A couple of days later, when I'm sharpening my pencil, I spot my roses in the bottom of the bin. The petals are as good as new. In their place on the desk is a jar stuffed full of sweet peas.

On the warmest days of May, Mr Spruce takes advantage of the weather to get us out of the classroom and walk us through the surrounding meadows in search of wild flowers. He knows all their names, and he stops every now and then to get us to gather round.

'Lady's smock,' he says, pointing at the palest of violet-pink flowers with his long stick. Or 'Bugle', 'Honesty' or 'Lady's bed-straw'. He never bothers with the common ones, cowslips and forget-me-nots and buttercups, because our knowledge of those is a given. Similarly, in the woods, he'll tell us all to stop and 'breathe in that wild garlic', but he doesn't point it out to anyone cretinous enough not to know it by sight. He does point out the poisonous flowers if we come across them. He shows us a woody nightshade, and says how similar it is to deadly nightshade, although the berries, when they appear, are darker. At the moment there are just violet star-shaped flowers, which are also very similar to deadly nightshade, and Dawn says, rather too loudly, that the golden cone stamen looks like a willy, and Mr Spruce is cross with her.

Later, in June, he will show us more flowers with more wonderful names: viper's bugloss, which is purple, and our particular favourite, great hairy willowherb, which becomes a term of mild abuse in the playground for at least a week.

Back in the classroom he shows us how to press the flowers we have gathered. We're allowed no more than five each, so that we don't deplete the meadows and woodland. ('Imagine, Class Four, forty of you times five – four fives are twenty – add a nought – that's *two hundred* flowers in one outing!') While we're busy

94

adding them to our nature books, he circulates two wild flower books to each table. He expects us to investigate our chosen flowers, and to write something about each of them. I love Mr Spruce for this. Both for taking us through the meadows and for trusting us to find stuff out all by ourselves, and choosing what we want to write.

'Look!' whispers Dawn. I ignore her, because Mr Spruce has told us to keep the noise down once already. I don't like it when he tells me off. I'm still feeling hurt about my roses in the waste bin. 'Psst! Look at this!'

I glance across at the page she is holding open in the *Book of Gloucestershire Wild Flowers*. 'What?'

'Look. Hemlock.'

'What about it?'

She points with her finger so I read, '"It grows in ditches and riverbanks and in disturbed areas such as waste ground and rubbish tips". So what?'

'*And*...' she jabs her finger at the text underneath. *If it is eaten, hemlock causes sickness and in severe cases it can kill by paralysing the lungs.*

I stare at her. 'What about it?'

She nudges me conspiratorially, and lowers her voice even more: 'We could kill someone with it.'

Her mum has been back for a while, and my mother made a big display of concern about Karen's health and the hospital stay when she came to pick Dawn up.

'How was it, Dot? How's Karen? You must've been worried sick!'

'Oh, she's fine now, thanks, Kath. And thank you for looking after Dawn. I expect she's had a whale of a time.'

'What was it, exactly? It must've been serious. We've all been so worried.'

There was something about the way my mother said this, and

something about the sheepish look Dawn's mum gave her, that alerted our attention.

'Oh, I'd rather not say, I ... it was, it was quite serious, but ... well, all's okay, thank goodness.'

When we met the next day, Dawn said, 'Your mum *knew*! She knew Mum was fibbing about hospital.'

'I didn't say anything, I swear.'

'Mum said I didn't keep a secret. She demanded to know who I'd told.'

I felt sick. 'Did you say you told me?'

'No. I said I hadn't told *anyone*.' Her voice was whiny, as if she believed her own lie.

It's not until a week or so later, when my mother seems to be distinctly cooler to Dawn's mum, that Dawn announces, '*She* told! Hilary Gibson! It must've been her. She told her mum about my secret brother!'

I want to remind Dawn that she never told Hilary not to tell anyone, that the rigmarole of sworn secrecy she made me go through had been entirely dispensed with in the face of getting one up on Hilary, that the secret had just slipped out of her lips like a slow-worm from the grass on the banks of the railway.

'I'm going to kill her,' she says.

'That's a bit extreme,' I say, trying to be funny, and failing. This is after the hemlock idea but I know she doesn't mean it. 'Let's go and see Goldie.'

I start walking to Mr Man's house, determined to distract her. She follows reluctantly, but Goldie isn't by the gate. We debate whether to knock. I don't want to, but Dawn seems recklessly keen. Then, as if by magic, the front door opens and Goldie comes bounding out, followed by Mr Man. Goldie snaffles and licks us, jumping up at the gate.

'Can we take Goldie for a walk?' I say.

'Oh, well, I was just about to take her for a walk myself.' He waves the dog lead in his hand. 'Why don't you come with us?'

'Okay,' says Dawn.

I glare at her. She's thinking about the panting. She's thinking about danger. I can tell by the way she juts out her jaw that she's looking for trouble. As we walk along the pavement towards the railway, with Goldie jumping up and snuffling at our heels, I am more afraid of Dawn than I am of Mr Man.

When we get to the stream, Goldie rushes in and makes such a splash that we both scream. Mr Man smiles and sits on his slab of stone. 'Go on,' he says. 'Why not join her? It's hot.'

Dawn looks at Mr Man and then at me. She takes off her shoes and socks and follows Goldie into the water. But the dog becomes so excited that Dawn runs back out, squealing, afraid of being drenched. 'Come on,' she says to me. 'Take your shoes and socks off. It's lovely and cold.' I shake my head. I don't want to get my socks wet. These are my new summer shoes. They are red, and Mum went shopping with me specially to get them. I don't want to put them back on with wet feet. 'Come *on!*' she says, as if she won't take no for an answer. Then she turns round to Mr Man. 'Why don't you come in? It's lovely in the water.'

We both look at him then. He smiles, reaches in his pocket and takes out a cigarette, which he lights slowly. We are mesmerised. He shakes his head. 'I'll just watch.'

Dawn gives me a look then. I know something is coming, and I'm scared. Dawn is angry with the world, and when she's angry she's unpredictable. Or rather, she's predictably wild and danger-ous. I watch her now as she takes the hem of her dress and tucks it up into her knickers. She turns, eyes Mr Man provocatively with a lowered head, and tucks it up further and tighter, so that all her leg is exposed and if she bends over, her knickers too. Then she turns back to the water and lowers her feet over the edge. Goldie bounds up and she steps into the stream, bending to take Goldie around her sodden neck. She shrieks again at the wetness, her underpants glowing towards us in a blaze of red and white stripes from beneath the puff of her pale blue tucked-up dress. The dog

97

is really excited now and can't leave her alone. She falls and saves herself in a crouch position. I try not to look at Mr Man. Then Dawn does something terrible.

She gets to her feet, giggling and screaming, and she slowly takes her dress off over her head. Then she throws it onto the bank, standing naked but for her red and white knickers, which are now so wet you can see right through them. Just for a fraction of a second, she looks at Mr Man again. I can't help but cast him a sidelong glance. He is puffing frantically on his cigarette.

I look at my watch. It's a quarter to seven. We'll be in trouble if we're home after seven. 'Come on,' I say. 'It's time to go.'

Goldie bounds out and shakes water all over me. I wipe my red shoes quickly with my hanky, hoping Mr Man and Dawn don't notice. I feel slightly sick, to be honest. I can't quite explain it, but it feels to me like Dawn has spoilt something with Mr Man. Something that belonged to me. I don't mean all that stuff about his willy. I don't believe any of that. I only laughed with her about that because it seemed funny at the time.

I have no idea how Dawn is going to explain away her dampness, but it's a warm evening, so by the time we get to the end of Napier Road, she may well be fairly dry. We have run out of conversation, and I can't bear the silence, the panting of Goldie, the click of Mr Man's dog lead as it swishes back and forth.

Chapter Twenty-One

Smell Heaven

Mr Man lets me tag along with him and Goldie any time I like. Saturday mornings are best, because I know Dawn is at ballet, and I get to be a whole person instead of a half of one. I feel easier around Mr Man when she's not there, and somehow, he seems easier around me. For one thing, he doesn't stutter. He still reaches for words a little, but you'd hardly notice.

'Why does Goldie always have her nose down when we're walking in the woods?' I ask.

Mr Man says that Goldie keeps her head down, like many animals, because she is in smell heaven. Animals on all fours smell the best because their noses are close to the ground, close to all the heady, fragrant scents that come up from leaves and soil and even the soles of our shoes.

'They have two hundred and twenty *million* olfactory cells (that's smell cells to you and me). A human only has five million. Imagine that. And our noses are nowhere near the ground. Think what we're missing out on!'

'Smell heaven,' I say.

'Exactly.'

I love the smell in the woods. The damp leaves, the earth, the moss, the ferns and the garlic. I breathe it all in deeply, and he sees me.

'It's smell that takes us right back to our beginnings – before vision and language. Right back to the scent of our mother's breasts.' I look at the path, embarrassed by the word, and suddenly so is he. We wait for it to pass, like a gust of cold air. 'Do you ever get that feeling that you've been transported back in time by a smell? Like something triggers a memory and you kind of time-travel?'

'Yes!' I'm grateful to move on from breasts. 'When I smell tar I always think of my grandad, because they were laying a road outside his house when I was little and he took me out to watch.'

'And when I smell carbolic soap I think of my mother, because she always used it. It has a nice association for me. And vanilla reminds me of my father – he smoked a pipe with vanilla tobacco.'

'And woodsmoke always makes me think of Bonfire Night and baked potatoes.'

'Baking potatoes make me think of my grandmother's house.'

'Damp wool – you know that smell? I love it. It reminds me of wet playtimes when we don't have to go out and we get to play inside.'

'Don't you like playing outside?'

'Not in the playground.'

He waits. Goldie pants ahead of us. Blackbirds sing.

'I don't get picked for anything much. I can't skip very well or anything. Sometimes it's okay. Just ...'

Goldie pants. Wood pigeons start up. We can hear the sound of the stream before we see it. It rained heavily in the night and it's flowing fast today.

'Well, Goldie and I won't be p-picking any teams. Or skipping. So you can relax today.'

I turn and smile at him. I do like Mr Man.

I am determined to see more of Mr Man and Goldie on my own, without Dawn tagging along and taking over, like she always does. So, the next few Saturdays in May, when she's at her ballet classes, I'm out at his gate, stroking Goldie, just as he comes out of his door with the lead.

'Can I walk Goldie with you?'

'Of course!'

This is what I like about Mr Man. He is always pleased to see me. We walk down Napier Road together in the direction of the railway bank, and he always checks with me that my parents know where I am.

Usually, when we've crossed over the little footbridge and entered the woods, he starts to tell me about the things around us: how the shiny leaves along the path we saw last time smell of garlic if you rub them between your fingers; how the bluebells are shooting up, and if we look carefully we can see a sheen of blue already; how the leaves in the trees have uncurled since last week and are sending a faint green light across the canopies above us. By our third walk together the woods are covered with a haze of the bluest blue. The flowers are everywhere, just beginning to open, and there is a reek of wild garlic, too, whose snowy flowers billow in soft clouds around the woodland floor to compete with the bluebells. I will always associate the overwhelming smell of wild garlic with the beginning of that summer. Although it only lasted for a few weeks, it is the scent that accompanies my most treasured compliments.

He points out a plant with four large leaves and an upright stem with spidery yellow-green petals. Right in the middle is a purple berry. 'Herb Paris,' he says. 'Or true lover's knot. It means this is ancient woodland.'

'Ancient?'

He nods and smiles shyly.

I am thrilled to think that we're in ancient woodland. I imagine people with animal skins walking on these paths before us. When we reach the Dingle, I sit on the warm stone slab with Goldie, and he sits further away on his own slab.

'Why are these slabs here?' I ask. 'It seems a strange place for them.'

He tells me that this part of the woods, and a little way along the bank, used to be in the grounds of a big house nearby, but that when the railway came, back in Victorian times, the house sold off some of its land. 'This would have been a stream that people in the big house used to sit by in the summer, or maybe bathe in. It would have been all muddy and slippery without these stone slabs, although they've eroded a bit now, because they're limestone. If you go that way,' he says, pointing over the stream and away from the railway track, 'there are all sorts of relics. It's a ruined garden. There's even a cast iron chair – all rusted up now, of course, but it must've been quite something in its day.'

A ruined garden. I lie back on the stone. It's still a little damp from rain earlier, but it's beginning to warm up in the sun. 'Why is the stone here so yellow?'

He gets up and comes to sit next to me, with Goldie trying to squeeze in between us. He has brought with him a large stone, the size of his hand. 'See this? This yellow colour is caused by the presence of iron oxide. The stone here is quite pale – Goldie's colour, really. But if you go up to the north Cotswolds, the stone gets darker and yellower. That's because there's more iron oxide in it.' He hands me the stone and I turn it over in my palm, examining it.

'There are tiny little shells in it,' I say.

'That's because all of this was underneath the sea once upon a time.'

'No! Really? What, all of England?'

'All of this bit, anyway. Look . . .' He touches a tiny fossilised shell in the stone, and I notice that his fingertips are yellow. I touch them, and he draws away slightly.

'Are your fingers yellow because of iron ox-hide?'

He laughs. 'No. That's because I smoke too much.'

'Can't you give it up?'

'If only I could. You get addicted. No one tells you that when you start. Or that it wrecks your lungs. I get out of breath sometimes now. I get asthma, too, sometimes.'

I don't know what asthma is, but I nod as if I do.

'I was twelve when I started, thought I was being really grown up.'

'Twelve?'

'Yes. I was showing off with friends. I tell you what, Stephanie, don't you ever start to smoke. You'll spoil all your p-pretty looks, and you'll never be able to stop.'

I look bashfully at the stone. 'What pretty looks?'

He looks at me, and I catch his eye. He puts his hand over mine suddenly. 'Stephanie, you must know that you're beautiful.'

I swallow. I am stunned. No one has ever called me beautiful. Not ever. I open my mouth to speak, but can do nothing except shake my head for a bit.

'No,' I say eventually. 'No, I have a wonky leg. I'm a freak.'

He takes his hand away and looks at me in earnest. 'Who says you're a freak?'

'Everyone. Dawn says no one will ever marry me with a leg like this, and the boys at school never—'

'Pah! You mustn't listen to any of these stupid people!' I wonder if he thinks Dawn is stupid, but remind myself that he thinks she's called Cilla. 'One of these days you're going to wake up and realise that none of these people matter. Young men will be fighting over you. Believe you me, Stephanie, you're going to knock their socks off!'

I let out a little laugh, relieved to be able to change the serious tone. 'Their socks?'

He smiles, showing teeth that must also contain iron ox-hide. 'Whoosh! Right off! Men will be wandering around Shepford with bare feet – and all because of you!'

I giggle, but the truth is I want to store up all the words he has said in the right order, pack them up like playing cards, so that I can spread them out later and study them. It's so much nicer when Dawn isn't here. When it's just me and Mr Man, he is a different person altogether.

'You won't want to hear this now,' he says, 'but the person who will love you best won't care about any of that. The person who will love you most of all will love you for your good company.'

'My good company?'

'Yes!' He laughs a little. 'Yours. Your very good company.'

When I play with Dawn in the afternoon, I don't mention Mr Man. If she brings him up, I try to change the subject. In bed at night I take out all the words and try to put them back together. *You must know that you're beautiful . . . You're going to knock their socks off . . . Whoosh!*

I remember the time – before Dawn made fun of his panting – that he said I had beautiful hair. He was probably only panting because he was smoking and his lungs are wrecked. And I think of the way he looked at me today with his sad green eyes, the way he placed his hand over mine, and the seriousness of that look makes me choke a little. I'm never going to tell Dawn any of this, because if I tell Dawn, she will grab hold of it all and make it seem ridiculous. Dawn will spoil everything.

The truth is, I think I may be in love with Mr Man.

Chapter Twenty-Two

*Item: **Red leatherette bag**. Keep.*

It's Didcot Parkway. A few people get off. No one seems to get on. I can't settle to my novel, I feel too agitated, and people keep moving up and down the gangway to the buffet carriage. One of them looks a bit like my brother. I remember the last time I saw Jonathan. It's funny how we became so close. I used to think he was distant, but really that was all in my head. Older sibling jealousy I hadn't dealt with.

It was when I was feeling a bit desperate about Matt last year. I just couldn't get my head around his having gone away – so *far*. And I knew it was nothing personal and all that, but it was the way he'd said it. *I just need a bit of freedom, you know, Mum. Just need to spread my wings a bit.* As if I was holding him back, as if I had him in a cage. Oh, I know, I know, it's what we all want when we're young – no one more than me. It's just that . . .

I had been crying so much my face was permanently blotchy, but when Jonathan visited, I made an effort. I'd washed my hair and put on some decent clothes and done all the washing-up. When the doorbell rang, I glanced in the mirror. I didn't look too bad.

Jonathan came in with four bottles of my favourite local cider and a bunch of carnations. He smiled and hugged me, then followed me into the kitchen. He watched quietly as I grabbed two mugs for the cider, and gave up on finding a vase for the flowers, putting them instead in the sink for the time being. I took him into the living room and hastily cleared a space for him on the sofa.

Then he stood back. His face was stricken.

'What?'

He was staring around him.

'Oh, Steph ...' He took in a great, sad breath and looked directly at me. 'Oh, Stephie!'

'What?' I felt a rising panic. Had Matt spoken to him? Did he know something I didn't?

He came towards me and put his arms around me. I let myself melt into him. It had been so long since I'd been held by anyone. 'Stephie, I had no idea.'

I surfaced. 'No idea of what?'

'About ... this.' He gestured around him. 'Look at it. How do you live like this?'

I followed his eyes around the room, and I saw what he saw. I could see how it might look to him. Heaps of newspapers in every corner, the overspill from the bookcase piled up in stacks all over the floor like the remains of a Roman central heating system, carrier bags stuffed with old cardboard models and pictures from Matt's primary school days, or bits of material that would at some stage come in handy for a patchwork (but hadn't yet); empty cider bottles I was going to recycle, piles of old clothes I would one day take to the Red Cross charity shop, a windowsill covered in useless objects (a broken snow globe, several chipped clay pots made by the children at preschool, glass animals from our own childhood with missing limbs, a penguin egg timer from Bourton-on-the-Water with no sand in it, a dish with a pile of dull coins in it that spilled over, broken sunglasses, some faded photographs curling on alligator clip blocks, piles of photograph envelopes stacked precariously in a wonky tower which leant against the window jamb). It looked a bit disorganised.

'I'm sorry,' I said. 'It is a bit messy, I'm afraid.'

'A bit *messy*? Stephanie, this is ... *clutter*. How do you move around in here? Where do you sit? Where do you eat?'

I felt under attack, and I started to throw things off the sofa in a desperate attempt to prove that there was room. I didn't want him to go. I needed him not to be appalled by me.

He sat down and opened two bottles of cider, handing one to me.

'I'm sorry,' he said. 'I had no idea it had got this bad.'

I looked around the room. 'I can tidy it.'

He took a few quiet sips from his bottle. 'Stephie, I think you need help.'

The tears came then, running down my cheeks before I had a chance to stop them. 'I just . . . I just wish Matt wasn't so far away!'

He stared gently at me. 'Actually, Steph, I don't think that's it. Matt told me things were getting a bit cluttered and he was beginning to feel a bit . . . claustrophobic here, and—'

'Matt said that?' I felt a sudden pain in my chest, as if he had thumped me there, right over my heart.

'Yes. He told me that before he went, but I had no idea it was this bad. He said it had been going on for years, but had started to get really bad.'

I was too stunned to speak. All I could hear was Matt saying it was claustrophobic living here, and all I could see was my brother sitting opposite me saying I needed help.

'He thought it may have started when Katie . . .' he said gently. 'Do you think that could be it?'

I could feel my mouth doing strange things, distorting itself. I tried to right it but it felt out of control. 'I . . . that might be . . . I couldn't bear to throw any of their things out. I couldn't . . . Please don't make me!'

'I won't.'

'But it's not so bad, is it? I mean, I can sort it.'

'I think it's a hoarding disorder. I don't know. You'd know more about it than me. But I'm sure I can get someone to help you – if you'll let me.'

'No! Please!' I felt my head rock forward into my hands and I grabbed onto my hair. The thought of someone coming in and making me throw out any of Katie or Matt's stuff caused so much distress I could barely think straight.

He reached out and took my hand. To do this, he had to kneel on an undergrowth of dominoes, loose pens and crayons and plastic dinosaurs. I sensed him wince at the pain. 'It's okay,' he said. 'We can have a go together, if you like. And we won't touch their stuff.' He spoke the words so kindly that I started to nod. 'How about that? I could come back tomorrow and we can make a start.'

I looked up, startled at the thought of him leaving me. 'Can't you stay? Can't we start now? Do you think Matt will come back then, if . . .?'

He sat for a long time just stroking my hand while I cried. Then he said that he was going down the shops to buy some bin liners and get some boxes. We could make a start now, he said, and if it went well, he could stay over until it was done.

We started in the kitchen. He made three piles: 'keep', 'chuck', 'charity shop'. Everything I put in 'keep' he would pick up and say, 'Are you sure? Why do you need this?' Perhaps it was a whisk when I already had one, or packets of flour that were out of date five years before, or a badly cracked plate, a threadbare tea towel or a heap of unworn aprons. He let me keep some baby spoons and a Winnie-the-Pooh mug. By the time we'd finished, the cupboards were almost bare. While I cleaned the surfaces, he got going on the living room. I cleaned as fast as I could because I was afraid of his zeal.

I was ashamed at how many newspapers I'd kept ('for the fire', although I hadn't lit it in years), amazed at how many irrelevant books were taking up room on the shelves ('A level Maths, Steph, *really*?'), shocked at the hair clips, biros, plastic toys, catalogues, expired phone directories and dead woodlice that had been lying under my sofa and along the skirting boards. I wasn't going to let go of any children's picture books, or any of Matt's toys without asking Matt. I rummaged through the 'charity shop' pile to retrieve items Jonathan had deemed unnecessary to me, and he would talk me down, gently.

'You really don't need this tat,' he said, holding up a creased red shoulder bag with a teddy embroidered on it. 'This wasn't Katie's. It was yours.'

'No! Don't throw that out!' I snatched it off him. I traced the embroidery with my thumb. Some things are hard to let go of. The thought of it is like falling, like losing a foothold on a rock face. Losing a grip.

Chapter Twenty-Three

Gathering Hemlock

I can't help telling Dawn that Mr Man's cat had kittens at the beginning of June, but of course she says she already knows this, because her mum told her. I feel crushed under the weight of her. I'm determined to see them before she does, to have some special treatment because I am Mr Man's special girl with the raffle-light hair who can make socks disappear with a *whoosh*. But she makes us chase after him on the cutting when he is on the way back from a walk with Goldie.

'How are your kittens?' she asks.

'Oh, they're fine. They're just starting to crawl now. Getting to be quite a nuisance. Under my feet half the time.'

'Does Goldie like them?'

'She seems to. It's not the first litter Dumpling has had.'

'Dumpling!' says Dawn, taking the opportunity to laugh.

'Yes.' He smiles. He likes it when Dawn laughs, I think.

'What colour are they?'

'There's two grey, one grey and white and one black and white.'

'I'm going to have one of the grey ones!' she announces. 'What about you, Stephanie?'

I know I won't be allowed a kitten. Mum and Dad don't like pets in the house. I've asked before. Hundreds of times. 'Mum and Dad won't let me have a pet.'

'I'll have both the grey ones, then, and you can share at my house. When did you say they'd be ready?' She smiles winsomely at Mr Man again.

'In a few weeks. About five or six weeks, I'd say. But, um . . .'

'Five weeks!' Dawn looks excited. 'We can play with them all through the summer holidays!'

'But . . . um . . . the thing is, the grey ones are spoken for.'

'*Spoken* for?'

'The Gibsons have already asked for the two grey ones, and I've said yes.'

'The Gibsons?' Dawn looks as though she can't tally the surname with the girl she knows. There must be a mistake.

'Yes, the two children from the new family – Hilary and Abe, I think.'

'But how did they . . .?'

'They came to see them with their mother. They were looking for a pet.'

I can't even look at Dawn. I study the pavement as we approach his front gate. I suppose it's no surprise, really. The Gibsons do only live about two doors up from Mr Man, so they're practically neighbours.

'But don't worry, the other two are just as sweet. The little grey and white one is really friendly, and quite mischievous.'

Dawn says nothing. Goldie rubs up against her and I tickle Goldie's head.

'Well, thank you for the walk,' he says, nervously. 'And please don't worry, Cilla. The other two are just as lovely. You'll see.'

'Thank you,' I say, to cover for Dawn's rude silence. He calls Goldie inside and closes the front door behind him.

Dawn stares intently at her hands, which are gripping the bars of his shabby, paint-peeling gate.

'I'll kill her.'

I still don't really think Dawn is serious when we gather hemlock from down by the stream. She has borrowed her mum's rubber gloves and is snipping it up into small pieces to fit into the Tupperware tub I'm holding.

'What exactly are you going to do with this?' I ask.

'We're going to heat it up in water, like tea, then leave it to soak. Then, hey presto! We have our poison.'

'And then what? No one is going to want to drink that disgusting stuff, are they?'

'Of course not,' she says airily, as though she has it all worked out. 'We put it in a drink, like orange squash or something, and we get her to drink it.'

'You mean Hilary?'

'Of course.'

'And why would she want to drink orange squash that you gave her if you weren't drinking it yourself?'

'We invite her on a picnic with us, in our secret place, and we each have a drink of orange squash, except yours and mine are normal.'

'I see.'

I don't tell her that I object to being her assumed assistant, that I don't want Hilary dead, although she probably knows I'm not keen. I marvel at her certainty that I am prepared to help kill someone at her command. Fortunately, I can afford to say nothing, because I know that what she is snipping up so carefully into the Tupperware container is nothing but common hogweed. I know my common hogweed from my trips out to the Forest of Dean with Gareth's family. I don't enlighten her. They do look similar. But what is disturbing is that she's completely convinced that it's hemlock.

We go straight back to her house and put the dastardly stalks and flowers into a saucepan. (Naturally, she's satisfied that a simple rinse will make the pan usable again afterwards.) When her mum comes in and asks what on earth we're doing, Dawn says sweetly that we're just making perfume.

'And you lit the gas on your own? Dawn, you know that's dangerous.'

'I'm *nine!*'

'I've told you, no. Turn it off now, and take that awful-smelling stuff outside while it soaks.' She softens then. 'You can collect a few rose petals if you like. But only from the roses that need deadheading.'

'Thank you, Mrs Webster,' I say.

She smiles and strokes my ponytail. 'That's okay, poppet.'

We take the pan outside, and wait until it's cool. There don't seem to be any roses that need deadheading yet, but I pretend to search. I'm still glowing from the tender touch of her mother. Then Dawn fetches a sieve and a large beaker of orange squash from the kitchen. We strain off the green liquid, add it to the squash and look at it.

'Yuck, it's brown!'

'It looks disgusting! She'll never drink it.'

'We've got some blackcurrant cordial,' I suggest, prepared to be helpful in her futile attempt at murder. 'I don't reckon you'd notice with blackcurrant.'

'Good idea!' says Dawn, with remarkable generosity. Plans move on to what food we can possibly filch from our respective tea tables the following day.

I lie in bed and worry about Dawn. I hope her plan is fully scuppered by Hilary just saying no, she doesn't want to come on a picnic with us or see our secret place, but I have an awful feeling that Hilary will say yes, because we have both been distant from her lately. Dawn because she loathes her, and me because I have to support Dawn. I heave a sigh of relief as I assure myself that, whatever happens, she won't die of poisoning.

Chapter Twenty-Four

Inside Mr Man's House

The next day Dawn says she's going to see the kittens straight after school with her mum, and do I want to come?

We enter Mr Man's house with excitement, feeling perfectly safe because Mrs Webster and Karen are with us. The hallway smells of gas and dog and earth, and the smell becomes earthier as we go into his kitchen. Goldie barrels into us as we try to squeeze into the cramped room, and Mr Man shoos her away. There is a piece of grimy lace curtain nailed up to the window, a flypaper coils down from the ceiling, and the veined ceramic sink stands alone next to a low wooden table covered in vegetables. There are shelves all over the walls, full of neatly ranged jars and tins. A string of onions hangs from one, alongside pots and pans.

Mr Man crouches down and pulls out a box from underneath the table. He places it gently on the tabletop, elbowing some carrots and beetroot out of the way. We can hear a slight mewling. Leaning over the box, we see Dumpling, a long black cat with a white tummy. All along this tummy lie four little balls of soft fur.

'I can't see!' Karen whines, and Mrs Webster lifts her up.

'You can hold one if you like,' he says kindly.

'Me too! Me, me!' says Dawn.

He lifts the box and takes it into his living room, where he places it on the floor. The room stinks of dog and has hairy blankets on the sofa. We kneel or sit around on the floor, which is mapped with biscuit-coloured patches where moths have eaten out the carpet wool. The overall colour scheme seems to be brown, but on closer inspection the sofa and chairs are a dark khaki green, and the carpet was once dark red. A grey kitten starts to clamber out of the box and he grabs it and hands it gently to Karen. Mrs Webster helps her with it. Then he lifts out the grey and white kitten and places it on Dawn's lap. She is immediately in love with it. She picks it up and looks into its big kitten eyes, and I am sick with longing. He must notice, because he lifts out the black and white kitten and raises his eyebrows at me. I nod, and he places it on my gingham skirt. So, so carefully, I cup it in my hands.

'He's very gentle, that one.'

I have already called him Trevor, like my lost bear. I hold him up and he looks at me sleepily, making a little squeak. I kiss his head tenderly and hold him against my beating heart. I love him. I love him, I love him.

Karen shrieks as the grey one climbs up her shoulder. 'He's scratching me!' Mrs Webster picks him up, and explains that he was just holding on. 'I want that one!' says Karen, pointing into the box at the other grey one, who is clambering over the side. Mr Man hands him to her. 'This is mine,' she says. 'Mummy, this is the one I want.'

Karen is four, and I see that to her they are just toys, nothing more than that, and she and her sister have always had what they wanted in the way of toys. Mrs Webster is clearly in the mood to spoil them both after the family upset, and she asks Mr Man if that is okay.

'I'm afraid the grey ones are both spoken for,' he says. 'But the other two are available in a couple of weeks.'

'I'm having this one,' says Dawn.

Karen immediately looks over to the kitten I'm holding. 'I'll have that one, then.' She almost sighs, as if she's doing everyone a favour.

'We can't have two, poppet. I said we could have a kitten, but only one.'

This sets off a tirade of wails, and Mrs Webster apologises and says it's time to go. Mr Man gathers the kittens, and as he takes mine, he says, 'I think Stephanie has her heart set on the black and white one anyway.' He looks at me and winks. I feel bereft that the kitten has been taken from my arms, but his acknowledgement that he was in some way mine makes me grateful. I nod.

It is two days after we make the potion and twenty-four hours after we have gathered our food that we have the secret picnic with Hilary. My stomach turns at the thought of it, not just because all we have to offer is a squashed and sweaty fairy cake that has spent far too long up Dawn's jumper, and two fish paste sandwiches that have been under my bed and now smell slightly 'off', but because Hilary is being so lovely. She has brought along a box of three little butterfly cakes, one for each of us. I imagine Hilary's mother making the cakes with her, and Hilary, excited, tilting the butterfly wings carefully into the butter icing. I can see her mother's face, round and smiling, pleased that her daughter has made friends so quickly, and I feel terrible. To make things worse, Hilary is enchanted by the picnic spot, and swears not to tell anyone about it.

'We're the Secret Three,' says Dawn, with such treachery I can barely believe her capable of it. Hilary beams, and offers round her cakes. My stomach churns again as Dawn snaffles one, and then asks if she can have mine, since I'm not hungry. I see her watching as Hilary sips the cordial and makes a slight face. We all sip our cordial. I can't imagine what Hilary's tastes like by now.

Nothing happens, of course, and it is all so dull that I wish Hilary didn't look so pleased to be with us. I feel we should enter-tain her. The way Dawn is scrutinising her for signs of imminent death is unsettling. We play twenty questions and I'm it and they have to guess who I've chosen. *Is it male or female? Is he sexy? Does he wear red pants? Would you like to snog him?* We all roll around laughing when I say it's Mr Spruce, especially as I said 'probably' to red pants and 'yes' to snogging him. I'm surprised to see Dawn laughing, but then she is hideously excited about what she thinks is about to happen, so probably a bit high. Hilary chooses someone and says 'yes' to female and to blonde hair and has us stumped for ages, but it turns out to be Goldie. Maybe Dawn is frustrated by her cleverness, because she stands up, strips down to her pants and gets in the stream, telling us to join her. Hilary takes off her shoes and socks and wades in after her, carefully negotiating the slimy stones and mud underfoot. I know I'll fall over if I try to walk in that.

'I'll hold you,' says Hilary, thinking about my foot straight away, and her kindness makes me take off my red shoes and my socks and dip my toes in the water, and then tentatively stand in it, supported by Hilary. I giggle stupidly at the thrill of it.

Dawn narrows her eyes at me. Nobody is showing any signs of dying. Not today, at least.

Chapter Twenty-Five

A Sorry

Mum has been beavering away at some embroidery for ages. I haven't asked about it, because she's always busy with some project or other. Although I have no idea at the time, this particular project will have two very significant impacts. One concerning my mother, and the other the power Dawn will have over me in the dreadful weeks to come.

It's Sunday, after bath time, when Mum presents her gift to me. It is a red leatherette shoulder bag (like the one Dawn has, which I've so often envied). I recognise the material as the leatherette with which Mum covered the dining room chairs. It is thinner and limper than Dawn's, which is pale yellow and real leather, but I push this thought away. Mum is studying me coyly. This is unusual. There is something on the front which I look at carefully. It's an embroidered animal – a teddy bear. Yes, I see that now, with muffled horror. It's far too babyish. She has embroidered the bear onto cotton material, and then machine-stitched it onto the leatherette flap. There is the most gorgeous sparkly red button to do up the loop of the flap. I take in a breath to thank her.

'Trevor,' she says, pointing at the teddy bear. 'It's Trevor.' She smiles at me, and in her smile, I see all her hopefulness and her sorrow and a glimpse of the tenderness I have longed for all my life. All of her *Sorry isn't good enough* is stitched into this gift. The hours of embroidery, of sacrifice, have been her penance. I feel, but I can't be certain, that she is apologising for throwing away my bear.

'Thank you, Mum,' I struggle out of a rock-hard throat. I want to put my arms around her, but I know that is a step too far.

'You can keep your bits and bobs in it,' she says. 'Just like Dawn.' She shows me a secret pocket inside as well.

As soon as I'm upstairs in my room, I lie down on my bed and cry. I cry and cry and cry and cry. Hot, desperate tears that make my cheeks sore. I cry for my mother, and I cry for myself, because I will have to wear this embarrassing object to school, and people will laugh at me. And that thought makes me sob for my mum, who has devoted her evenings to this little bag, has thought to please me, has shown me that she loves me, maybe, or at least that she has thought about me, and looked forward to making me happy. She has tried so hard, and I hate myself for not cherishing it. A stark, complex emotion wrenches me this way and that. I have to pretend to be pleased, delighted. The awful thing is, in order to compensate for all the work she's put into something for me, she has bought Jonathan a toy World Cup Willie – the lion wearing England's colours, perched on a little ball bearing so that it can move around. So, he gets a proper toy, and I get this ... object. I hate myself for thinking this way. Tomorrow I will put little things in the bag and wear it to school. I love what it stands for. I love what it means. I have to pretend that I love it, and that it doesn't make me cringe having to loop it across my body. I feel wretched at the prospect, but I know what I have to do. I have to show Mum that I'm glad she loves me. This is my big chance.

Dawn doesn't miss a trick. Even on the way to school, even with my cardigan wrapped carefully to hide it, she sees the strap and takes a good look. 'What,' she says, grinning with wide eyes, 'is *that*?'

'My new bag.'

'Really? But it looks like ...' She feels the flap between thumb and forefinger. 'It's cheap plastic. Where did you get it from? Woolworths?'

'Mum made it for me.' I feel my face flush.

'Whoops! Sorry. But ... what on earth ...? What's that thing on the front?'

'I think it's meant to be a bear,' I say, treacherously. I hate myself. It's actually a brilliant bear. Mum can do wonders with her embroidery. There's nothing she can't do.

'That's a bit babyish, isn't it? Does your mum think you're two, or something? Fuck it. I wouldn't be seen dead with that.' Then she does the worst thing imaginable. She laughs, and turns to Gareth and Steven and Hilary who are walking behind us now. 'Look what Stephanie's wearing! A plastic bag her mum made with a babyish teddy on it!'

Hilary catches up and looks at the bear. 'Nice embroidery,' she says, kindly. 'Did your mum really do that herself?'

I nod, appalled that it takes Hilary to make me feel proud of my mother instead of ashamed. Thank goodness Jonathan is way back, faffing around with marbles and the younger boys. I couldn't bear it if he told Mum Dawn's reaction. Or my 'It's meant to be a bear'.

But that's not the end of it. I can already picture how Dawn will display it to everyone in class and in the playground, how she will taunt me and encourage other people to laugh. So I leave the bag on my coat hook, hidden underneath my cardigan. It means I have to go around feeling slightly chilly all day, but it's worth it. Of course, I have to wear it again to go home, but after a few days, Dawn gets bored with it. There are only so many people she can humiliate me in front of on the way home, and she exhausts them all fairly quickly. No, what Dawn does is worse than any humiliation.

When I refuse to be part of her most fiendish of all plans to kill Hilary, she threatens me.

'I'll tell your mum you hide your bag on your coat hook every day, because you're ashamed of it.'

'I'm not!'

'Yes, you are. I'll tell her you think it's too babyish to wear, and that you only pretend to like it.'

'That's not true!'

She gives me a sly smile. 'Stephanie, you're so pathetic. You know you think it's embarrassing. And she'll know too, when I tell her.'

Chapter Twenty-Six

*Item: **Photograph album**. ~~Chuck~~. ~~Keep~~. Chuck one photo.*

What is a good mother, then? I ask myself this over and over. I should know. I've written papers on it. But it's easy to theorise.

I fell in love with Matt when he was born: his smell, his softness, the sweet, hopeful looks he gave me. I didn't have to worry about sleepless nights because I wrapped him in my arms all night long, and he slept contentedly, spooned between my breasts. I would wake only at his first sleepy squeak, to sit up and feed him.

I had no one to tell me to give rigid feeds or timetabled naps. He fed and slept when he needed to, and I got to learn the language of his little sighs and grunts, and he mine. We were a good team, me and Matt. Even in his teens we didn't have too much conflict. He rarely went out late, although when he did, he always got very drunk, and I worried about him and who was offering him what.

There was one time, I remember, when I caught the bus back from town and there were some schoolgirls on it, sitting behind me and wearing the uniform from Matt's school. I thought nothing of it, except that they seemed to be bunking off early, and then I heard my son's name.

'What about Matt Townsend?'

'Yeah, I suppose. We need more boys. Don't really know him that well. He's the one with curly brown hair, yeah? Bit quiet and swotty?'

'Yeah. But he's okay. Just had a tough time, that's all.'

'How come?'

'Oh, you know. Stuff. He doesn't get out much.'

'Why not?'

'Mum's a bit needy, you know?'

(*Needy? NEEDY?* Me? As if!)

'Oh ... Has he got a girlfriend?'

'No. Not as far as I know.'

'Okay then. He can come. What *stuff*, anyway?'

'There's lots of heavy stuff. Apparently ...'

Then someone got on the bus and interrupted them. They started giggling and flirting, and I will never know what the heavy stuff was. I thought about it for a long time afterwards. I watched Matthew more attentively around the house.

'Is everything okay?' I would ask.

'S'okay.'

'Are you happy at school?'

'I'm fine, Mum.'

'Is anything stressing you out?'

'I'm good.'

It felt like twenty questions. But I had to get it, so I kept trying. I knocked on his bedroom door. He sat at his desk in his bedroom, and I stood hopefully in the doorway.

'You're not being ... bullied or anything?'

'Why would I be being bullied?'

'I don't know. You were bullied when you were little, remember?'

'Yeah, when I was little. I'm fifteen now, in case you hadn't noticed.'

What did he mean by that? Had I not noticed? Perhaps I hadn't. I thought he hid himself in his room to get away from me, because that's what teenage boys did. But of course, he wanted me to notice. I looked at the pearly whorls of his ears under his chestnut curls, the hands that had grown ten times in size since they first gripped onto my finger.

'Actually, I was wondering if you'd like some new clothes. You know, more trendy stuff, now you're getting older? We could go shopping on Saturday, get you some cool gear.'

He frowned at me in horror. 'Cool gear?'

'Well, you know, you could have some money and go with friends.'

'Maybe.'

It was just like a quiz game. The word 'friends' seemed to sting him, though. Or maybe it was me who flinched at it. He just never seemed to have friends round, and he spent a lot less time with me. I realised I didn't really know him at all.

'How about we have a pizza night in front of the telly? Hire a good film?'

He took in a long, patient breath, as if I really didn't get it. But I wanted to get it. I wanted to know what the *stuff* was. The *heavy stuff*.

'I know. Would you like to invite some friends round?'

'Christ, no.'

'I can go out. You can have the place to yourself. Have a party! If you like.'

'*Mum*. I don't want anyone round here. I'm okay.'

I didn't pursue it in case I seemed needy. I kept wondering if that was his word, or someone else's.

I should've told Matthew. But when? I had imagined telling him round about the time he started secondary school, but that idea was trumped by something else happening – something far worse. And then, eventually, I thought maybe when he was eighteen, after A levels. And then there was the announcement about Australia, and I didn't like the idea of him disappearing before I could explain it all properly. And maybe I don't need to tell him at all. Maybe a good mother wouldn't. In fact, I'm sure that's true. But then he might come across it somewhere, might hear something terrible or read something that isn't true.

We often used to look through old photo albums at my parents' house when Matt was a child. He was always interested to see photos of me as a little girl. And once, when he was about nine, he pointed at a picture taken at a school sports day when I was the same age.

'Who's that?' he said, pointing at Hilary.

'That's Hilary. She lived in our street.'

'And who's that?'

'Dawn. That's Dawn. She lived in our street too. And that's Gareth, and that's our teacher, Mr Spruce. He was nice.'

He studied the photograph for a while, holding out a hand to stop me from turning the page. 'She looks a bit of a madam,' he said.

'Who?' Although I knew straight away who he meant.

'Her. Dawn.'

He looked long and hard at her, and she looked long and hard back at him. It made me shudder that she should be staring at my nine-year-old son like that.

Chapter Twenty-Seven

The Sinners' Seats

'I don't usually see you on your own on a weekday,' says Mr Man.

It's true, I'm always shadowed by Dawn on weekdays. Although that makes it sound as if she follows me around, whereas even if I don't really ask to play with her, it's always me who does the following, dragging my foot along after the brisk pace of her sandals.

'I know. Dawn's usually . . .' I don't want to explain that Dawn is avoiding me, but then I realise what I've said. 'She's not really called Cilla. She just . . . she's called Dawn.'

He smiles awkwardly. 'I know. Her mum called her Dawn when you were at my house.' He sees how embarrassed I am. 'It's okay. So, today she's not here.'

'No, but it's Wednesday, and sometimes nice things happen on Wednesdays, because they're yellow.'

'Wednesdays are yellow?'

'Yes. And yellow's a happy, sunny colour, isn't it?'

'I've always thought so.'

We enter the rickety old kissing gate, and I hang back until he's through so he doesn't have to kiss me. Not that he would, but I don't want him to feel obliged. It would be difficult. Goldie rushes on ahead, panting and jogging joyously along the path. We walk along in companionable silence, since most of this walk is single file. He offers to let me go first, but I don't want him to watch my silly walk, so I shake my head and stay back. I watch him do his strange, droopy walk in front of me as the path burrows down through the woods. It's already July. Swords of sunlight reveal basking flies gliding back and forth across the footpath all the way to the Dingle.

'So,' he says, when we're sitting by the stream. 'Do you see all the days of the week as colours?'

'Yes. Thursday's grey, Friday's black, Saturday is a sort of pale blue-grey, like morning sky in summer, Sunday's amber, Monday's blue—'

'No! My Sunday is amber too! Just that colour: amber. Fancy that. I'm afraid Friday is dark red, though. More of a maroon. And Saturday is white.'

I laugh. Dawn doesn't see the days of the week in colour, nor does Jonathan.

'How about numbers?' he asks, turning excitedly to look at me.

'Oh, yes. One is cream, two is blue, three is green, four is red, five is yellow . . .'

'That's amazing! My four is also red *and* my five is yellow!'

'Like Wednesday!'

'Yes. Do you see months of the year in colour, too? And names?'

'Oh, yes.'

'That's really interesting. Do you know, Stephanie, it's called "synaesthesia", this ability we have to see abstract things in colour? And I don't think I've ever met another synaesthete.'

'What is that?'

'People like us. We are synaesthetes.'

'We are sinners' seats!' I repeat.

'What colour is your July?'

'Oh, red. Definitely. Flaming red.'

He nods, thrilled. 'An orangey red. Crumbs! Extraordinary! This is wonderful, Stephanie!'

He lies back and folds his arms behind his head, smiling. I do the same. Every now and then he tests me on a number or a letter or a month, and we exchange colours. The water in the stream is burbling fast today, and the wood pigeons are going mad for each other. Somewhere on a nearby hill comes the bleating of sheep and lambs.

'The lambs are being taken from their mummies now,' I say. 'That's why they bleat so much.'

'They're chunky boys now, and they have to go off to market.'

'It's sad. I like lambs a lot. And sheep.'

We continue to listen to the bleating.

'When he was little, Jonathan used to think that lamination meant turning into a lamb. When Dad came home and said he'd had some things laminated at work, Jonathan wanted to be laminated, too!'

We laugh. (It isn't true: it was me who thought this, not Jonathan, but I don't want to sound babyish.)

'He used to think "contaminated" was "cataminated" as well, and that meant being turned into a cat.' Again, it was me who thought this, until I learnt about germs.

'Which would you prefer, Stephanie?'

'I'd like to be lamb-inated,' I say. I love cats, but I can't tell him that I've had enough catamination to last a lifetime, thank you.

'You'd make a good lamb.'

This feels like a compliment. I feel a rush of excitement run through me. *Oh, lamb of God, that taketh away the sins of the world* . . . No, no . . . there's something lovely somewhere . . . *Mary had a little* . . . No. I chase it like trying to catch a fish with my hands . . . Something lovely . . .

'*Little lamb, who made thee?*' I realise I've said it out loud.

He turns to look at me, and props himself up on one elbow. 'Dost thou know who made thee?'

'Yes!' I cry. 'Yes! That's it, that's what Mummy . . . that's what my mum used to say . . . said once to me. We were standing by the back door, and it was a snowy, snowy cold winter, the coldest ever . . . and the snow was up to my shoulders and . . . I'd been out all morning and my hands were blue with cold and she took my hands between her hands, and she said, *Little lamb, who made thee? Dost thou know who made thee?* How do you know it?'

'It's by a poet called William Blake. We learnt some poems off by heart at school. I expect your mum did too.'

'William Blake.' I lie back and listen to the stream burbling and the wood pigeons and the bleating and the sound of my mother's voice loving me. Loving me, warming my hands in hers. This is heaven. We may be sinners' seats, but Mr Man and me are in heaven.

Chapter Twenty-Eight

Broken

Two things happen before Dawn comes up with her truly sinister plan.

Dad is doing the sermon at a family service. I try to concentrate, because then I can make him happy afterwards by commenting on it, but it's not very interesting. It's about trusting in Jesus. I've heard it all before, and it's gobbledygook to me. People get healed because they believe in him, which doesn't seem fair, because I believe in him and he's never healed me. Anyway, Dad decides to make a bit of a thing about including all the children, so he says, 'Now, I wonder if any of you young people have a question you'd like to ask about Jesus?'

Nobody puts their hand up. I can see Dad looking around, eyeing all the children in the pews, raising his eyebrows hopefully. Nobody speaks. I feel desperately sorry for him. I should ask a question, to help him out, but then people would look at me, and I'd die of embarrassment. The silence is awful. He should just keep talking. 'Anyone?' Someone drops a hymn book. I can see his forehead glistening with sweat, his eyes still casting around hopelessly. I can't bear it. I put my hand a little in the air.

'Ah! Yes?'

'Um. Why did Jesus use his magic to turn water into wine?' I squidge my mouth over to one side and look down at my prayer cushion.

'Uh, well ... Jesus didn't do *magic*. He performed *miracles*.

They're different. Miracles are … miracles are … the difference is …'

I see him struggling, so I rescue him with: 'But why did he turn water into wine when wine isn't good for you?'

I know Dad hates alcohol. He sees it as evil. And Mum agrees. He frowns. 'It was at a wedding feast, and there was nothing to drink. In those days, people drank wine a lot.'

'But he must have known it was bad for them?'

Mum nudges me hard. His mouth widens into a sort of stiff smile. I know he must have a good answer ready because my dad knows everything about Jesus. I can't bear for him to be stuck like this, stuck with this odd, stiff grin. He rubs his chin. The boy in front of me picks his nose and wipes it on the Book of Common Prayer; his mum clips his ear. Someone coughs. This is a disaster.

'In those days, it was more like grape juice. Everyone drank it.'

I almost give a sigh of relief. I still don't see why Jesus didn't just leave it as water, but I say, 'I see. Thank you.'

This is awful. I don't have to look at Mum to feel the anger coming off her. It's worse than when we played charades one Christmas and I put a sheet over my head so I could be 'the Holy Ghost'. At least Jonathan laughed at that.

Anyway, a couple of weeks later, Dad is organising the Bible Class Summer Party, which is to be held in the garden outside the church hall. I ask him if I can be in the Bible Class and not the silly Sunday school, which is full of little kids. He says I have to be confirmed to be in Bible Class. Which isn't fair, because I'm far too old for Sunday school and drawing donkeys, and the Bible Class gets to dance to pop music.

Mum and Jonathan and I all help him to carry the food and lemonade up to the hall, and we arrive exhausted, with red grooves on our palms from the bag handles. As I'm helping him carry some tables outside, I say, 'It's a pity Jesus couldn't do some of his magic for us and set it all up.'

Dad puts down his end of the table and looks sternly at me. 'Jesus does *not* do magic.'

I put my end of the table down too, and we stand on the path leading to the tatty bit of lawn outside the hall. 'What about the loaves and the fishes, then? How come he turns five loaves and two fishes into enough to feed five thousand people?'

'Not magic. A *miracle*.'

'So, what's the difference?'

'A miracle is ...' I can see he is stumped all over again, and I feel suddenly sorry for him, and a bit fearful, as if I've just pulled off a plaster without warning. 'Okay, let's move this table and I'll tell you.'

I want him to be able to explain it to me. I want my father to be right. I can't bear him to be utterly wrong-footed and weak. Although I shoved him, I didn't expect him to stumble. Mum looks as though I'm quibbling about nothing. But that's the thing. She doesn't care as much as he does about God. She just kind of fits in.

'Okay. So, a miracle ... a miracle is when Jesus does something to help people – to really help people and save lives. A magic trick is ... well, it's to entertain people. Jesus didn't go in for entertainment, he didn't do *magic*. He never did miracles lightly. Okay?' He smiles, pleased with his definition.

'What about that changing water into wine?' I know it's wrong to remind him of this, even as the words come out of my mouth. 'I mean, how does turning water into wine *help* anyone?'

He frowns. 'It was at a wedding feast. It helped the host because he had nothing to offer. I grant you, it isn't the best of his miracles. Not an important one. Try to think about all the great miracles he did, all the healing.'

I take in a deep breath. There is something I've been wanting to ask for ages. 'What about my foot, then? Why can't Jesus fix that? That really *would* help me, and it wouldn't hurt anyone else. If the lepers and the blind and the *lame* get cured, why doesn't he make my foot better?'

'You can't ask God for *favours.*'

'Well, they did. You said last week, Jairus went and asked Jesus to heal his little girl, and Jesus went—'

'Stephanie, sweetheart, it doesn't work like that. You're like this for a reason. God is testing you, you see.'

Please don't say God works in mysterious . . .

'The thing is, God works in mysterious ways.' He looks help-less, and I realise he may well have asked God to cure me, and it hasn't worked.

'Don't roll your eyes like that, young lady.' Mum comes to his rescue and tells me to stop bothering my father. *Look what you've done now.* There is work to do.

It just doesn't wash, though. Jesus, if he existed – and Dad says he did, so I believe him – seems a decent sort, who helped the poor and the lowly. And we're expected to be like him. You'd think being kind to people would be enough. No chance. You have to praise him. But the thing is, if you get a bit cocky and seek a bit of praise in our house, you're told off for your pride and lack of modesty. And yet God in the Bible demands praise, he's always on at us to praise him. Praise him, praise him. Has he forgotten about being modest? And what sort of father organises the slow torture of his only son? If he was after a bit more praise, you'd think doing some amazing miracles would do the trick. I just don't get it. I reckon God's got a really mean streak in him.

Dad is gloomy for the rest of the afternoon, and I know he's troubled by the idea of magic, and it's my fault. He plays some old 'Twist And Shout' and 'Hippy Hippy Shakes', and Jonathan is the only one dancing. When the Rolling Stones come on the record player (the teenagers have brought their own records), me and Jonathan join in when everyone gets up to dance, and he doesn't stop us. They think Dad's very trendy, and say so, loud enough for him to hear, and I watch him trying to soak up this compliment. But between his smiles I think he looks defeated.

*

The second thing that happens, hard on the heels of the first, is a visit from Dad's Aunty Vera. Great-Aunty Vera is Dad's mother's sister, only his mother died when he was eleven. Dad rarely talks about his mum, but we know some interesting things about his childhood.

We always get a thrill, safe in our living room, trying to imagine what it was like in the olden days to have bombs falling out of the sky, night after night. Jonathan likes to supply the sound effects, as Dad recounts the story: 'When the war came my father worked as an auxiliary fireman, which means he helped the proper firemen put out fires, but without being paid. There were lots of fires to put out because we lived in Plymouth, which was blitzed several times.' (*Boom*.) 'So, when your Grandad Townsend was out help-ing put out burning buildings and rescuing people, I was all alone at home apart from my sister, your Aunty Babs, who was two years older than me. She cooked my meals, ironed my clothes and went to school like other girls. Imagine that.'

The idea of being alone in the house without parents is like something out of a book. 'Tell us about the bombs and the camping!'

'Well, one night, when the bombs came, Babs took me on a train to Saltash and walked me out into the countryside carrying a tent and bedding. I was scared stiff. We slept on the edge of a cow field for three nights, until we were sure the bombing had finished.'

'Could you hear them?'

BOOM!

'Yes, all night long. And the sky was all lit up on the horizon. Babs went to the farm and asked for food and everything, and when I got frightened of all the booming, she told me stories.'

Dad tells these stories so vividly, that a part of me thinks it has all actually happened to me: that I took Jonathan on the train to Saltash, trekked across fields carrying bedding and set up a tent for me and my brother to escape the bombs; I have always washed and ironed Jonathan's clothes, cooked for him and told him comforting stories to stop him from being afraid; I single-handedly saved my brother from being mown down by enemy warplanes. He has a lot to thank me for.

Grandad comes to see us quite often, but I have only met my Aunty Babs a few times, and she always looks a bit frowny to me. Dad told me that not long after a great big blitz they were both evacuated to Gloucestershire, but to different families. He had a great time on a sheep farm with a kind family, but she didn't have such a good time. Her family treated her badly, and she was unhappy.

'What did they do to her?'

He always shakes his head and says he doesn't know. We imagine her being given gruel to eat.

Anyway, now Great-Aunty Vera and Dad go into the front room and Mum goes to put the kettle on before joining them. She closes the door behind her, which is odd. After a few minutes she comes out and makes the tea, and tells me and Jonathan to 'go out and play' before returning to the front room. Jonathan is happy to go out, but I'm not going to be fobbed off like that. Something is going on, and I want to know what it is.

Fortunately, Great-Aunty Vera has a fairly loud voice, so I can hear her side of the conversation.

'I reckon it all started after that wretched family she was with. Happy as Larry before that, she was. Of course, she might've been able to tell her mother those things, if she'd been alive, but we'll never know. We'll never know. Any road, it's a tragic business, tragic . . .' I can hear her voice wobble.

I lose interest after a while because the other voices are so low, and my neck starts to hurt with my ear pressed to the door. Great-Aunty Vera seems to stay for ages but says she has to catch a train at teatime. Dad goes up to the phone box at the top of the road to ring for a taxi, and I watch him coming back down the road, his shoulders hunched, not like Dad at all.

Mum tells us both after tea that Dad's sister Babs has died. We aren't sad because we didn't really know her, and Mum and Dad seem fine too. But later on, when I see Dad in the hallway polishing our shoes, I spot that his face is all screwed up and his mouth is distorted. When I get closer, I see that his cheeks are wet. I feel a stab of embarrassment because I've caught him in the act of doing something you are not supposed to do. *Is* he being manipulative? It doesn't seem that way. He's trying to look away.

'Dad?'

A fearful stranger looks out of his face and he bursts into sobs. I'm so startled that at first, I think he is laughing. When I realise my mistake, I go to put my arms around his neck, but before he can have the comfort of my hug Mum arrives and shoos me away. I can't help feeling that Mum thinks he has let her down badly.

The upshot of these two events is that I don't have to go to Sunday school any more, and neither does Jonathan. Shortly after, Dad stops being a lay preacher at the Three in One, passing over to another man. Mum seems to agree with him about this. Dad has lost all his holiness lately. We still go to church, but his heart doesn't seem to be in it. He is very sad about his sister. When I ask how she died he tells me, 'She was ill for a long time.' When I ask if we are going to a funeral, he looks tearful. I will find out many years later that his sister took her own life, and that, because of this, the church refused to bury her.

Dad is never quite the same after that, and I don't know if it's his sister dying, or what happens later, down by the Dingle, that changes him. I do everything I can to make him and Mum happy, to make up for my contribution to the sadness. I help Mum make tea and I beg to be allowed to help her clean the house. She is reluctant to relinquish her bottle of Dettol, but she gives me a duster and I'm allowed to dust all the surfaces. It's while I'm doing this that something terrible happens.

I'm busy wiping the duster over the mantelpiece, and I very carefully wipe around Mum's horse (now in the front room). Then I pick it up, dust it tenderly, and replace it. I understand suddenly why she loves this creature. It's beautiful, striding out across the tiles, wild and free, its mane flowing in an imaginary breeze. There's a little spot of coal dust by its back foot that I hadn't noticed, and as I push the tip of the duster around it, I catch the horse's hoof. It slides swiftly like something on ice, and there's a terrible clatter as it hits the hearth stone. I look down in horror. There are several pieces of horse, and sorry will never be good enough.

Mum's rage is a strange thing. It doesn't show itself like other people's anger, but lies muffled, like a prisoner with bound hands and feet, with a gagged mouth. The screams and shouts that don't escape are terrifying.

She orders me to pick up the pieces and throw them in the bin. 'And watch you don't go cutting yourself and getting blood everywhere.'

I gather the fragments delicately, but instead of binning them I place them on the dining room table and try to fix them with glue. Eventually she joins me, but with an obvious reluctance. Even so, there seems to be a silent understanding between us that this is worth a try. She points out a little crumb of china that is missing on his chest, and I go and scrabble on the hearth rug to find it. She holds pieces for me as I apply glue. But although it's Mum's horse, there is something about it that feels like Dad, as though we are trying to assemble all the bits of him that have fallen apart. And despite the intricate job we do, we both know he will never be quite the same again.

Chapter Twenty-Nine

A Mind to Kill

Steven Willis brings in a page from one of his dad's magazines and passes it round the class. I know it's interesting because people are smirking or frowning. When it reaches me I see it is two photographs of a woman – a very young woman, a teenager perhaps – sitting on the edge of a bed. In the first one she is naked but for her knickers, and she is pulling these away from her and looking into them. In the photograph beside it, the same woman has pulled her knickers right out and down with one hand, and has the other hand touching herself. You can't see anything except a shadow of woman-fur. It's ever so rude. But the thing about the second picture is the woman's face. Instead of looking down her knickers like in the first picture, she has her head tilted slightly down, and her eyes raised up, looking directly at you. It's a very, very flirty look. Underneath the photos is a big heading saying, 'TRACY LIKES TO GO EXPLORING'. I pass it on to the person next to me. Eventually Mr Spruce notices something and challenges Lisa Warwick.

'Is there something you'd like to share with us, Lisa? Whatever it is seems to be making you smile.' Poor Lisa. The page is passed hurriedly back to Steven Willis, who pockets it before Mr Spruce has wandered over to inspect Lisa's lap.

I'm relieved it's back in Steven's pocket. But it worries me. So grown-ups have comics, too. But not like the *Beano* or *Treasure*. I always thought you could trust grown-ups to be sensible, but it seems you can't. This is worse than my 'dreams' about the conveyor belt in the Sunday school. But then I was contaminated. I can't believe Mr Willis, with his important Moustache March walk, would read comics with rude pictures like this. What's going on? The world suddenly seems very unsafe and strange. Everyone is wearing masks. Grown-ups can't be trusted to be what they pretend to be. So who can?

On sports day things take a terrible turn for the worse.

First of all, we are sitting out on the field waiting for our year's events to begin. It's actually quite warm and sunny, and we all lounge about on the grass. Mr Spruce is sitting with us too, although he occasionally gets up to chat to one of the other teachers. We're all in a good mood.

Suddenly, I notice Steven Willis raise his eyebrows and then grin. I follow his gaze. It isn't me he's looking at; it's Dawn.

Dawn is sitting upright with her legs splayed. She's wearing shorts, but as I glance over at her I see she is pulling her shorts and knickers out, like Tracy who liked to go exploring, and she is looking inside them. I try to look away, but all I can see is Steven Willis nudging another boy, and they both ogle Dawn. She has their attention now. In full view of anyone who cares to look, she pulls her shorts right down at the front to touch the grass, exposing her navy-blue knickers. There's more excitement among the boys, and Steven prods Gareth just as Dawn pulls her knickers down at the front as well to expose all she has, and then she gently tilts her head forward and looks up at them, with the exact same look as the woman in the magazine. It makes me shudder. She is in total control.

Most of the girls still haven't noticed, but all of the boys have. I glance over at Mr Spruce, and I'm shocked to see that he sees it too. But what he does surprises me most of all. He blushes and looks away, and picks at a blade of grass.

*

Dawn's anger at Hilary gets another boost that day. Dawn, short and wiry and fast, has always been the queen of the sprint. No one has beaten her at sports day. It's her thing. I always cheer her on from the sidelines, as I've never won anything. I am happy that Dawn has this skill, because it makes her easier to be with when she's a winner. But, of course, this summer the sprint is won by Hilary. Hilary also wins the high jump, the long jump and the hurdles, and the team she is in wins the relay race as well. She really is amazing, and I can't help admiring her lithe limbs as she moves through the air so gracefully and powerfully, a bit as I imagine Mum's horse on our mantelpiece would do if it could really gallop. Hilary is picked up by the boys and carried around the field like a trophy. I have to limp around after Dawn, trying to console her.

And there's another thing that week. Dawn decides she is in love with Steven Willis after all, and not Gareth. 'She's welcome to him,' says Dawn. 'Steve kissed me – on the lips – and he's going to take me down the field for mating. It was a proper snog.' She seems to have forgotten that she said Steven Willis kissed all the girls, and I don't remind her. 'Mating' is what we call going down the bottom of the school field and buttoning up your coat with someone else's and lying under it. The dinner ladies don't like it, and they're always trying to stop it. They don't know what goes on underneath the coats, and neither do I. Soon, I think, Dawn will be able to tell me.

But the next day, when I am probably at least as excited as Dawn for the dinner hour and her 'mating' experience with Steven, something terrible happens. I can hardly believe it, to be honest, and neither can she. She's waiting outside the school hall, barely tolerating my company, but accepting that it's better than looking like she's waiting on her own, when Steven comes ambling round the corner, hands in his pockets. He looks up and smiles, then spots a bunch of girls coming from the opposite direction.

'Hi, Hilary!'

'Hi!'

'Hey, you coming down the field?'

'Maybe, in a bit.'

'I'm going now. Come on.' And he walks up to Hilary and takes her hand. They head cheerfully towards the bottom of the field together like lovers, and join a row of buttoned coats by the side of the allotments. I can't bear to look at Dawn. I study a daisy poking up through the tarmac of the playground until she melts away, choking with rage and hurt. Leaving behind her words spat out in the air like exhaust fumes:

'I know how we can *really* kill her.'

It's all my fault, of course. I should never have agreed to go along with Dawn's plan, even though I intend to sabotage it. It's such a stupid plan. I know it won't work. I don't really believe that Dawn wants it to work either. I know she hates Hilary, but she 'hates' a lot of people, like her sister, Karen. It isn't real. It's in her nature, all this animal anger. She's like a caged tiger sometimes. I know how to go along with things until the anger subsides. Usually.

Chapter Thirty

Into the Bushes He Leads Me

I go for a walk on my own after the end of term. I don't want to be part of her plan, but I can't think how to get out of it. I'm startled by the level of Dawn's spite. Hilary was even modest about her own sporting success, saying it was only because she had long legs but Dawn had a far better technique. I want to burst with shame at my complicity with Dawn, because this is Hilary, who shows no one any malice, who stood up for me in front of Dawn and who taught me to dance. I imagine it must be jealousy that has sparked this rage in Dawn, because Hilary is so popular and successful. But what I don't see is that it isn't just about losing control of her position as top sprinter – or even losing her attractiveness to Steven – it is about losing control over me.

I shudder at the way she lured Hilary in with a promise of a surprise. A surprise all right. A trick. It's a cruel, vile plan. And all set for next Saturday. Helping Dawn feels like placing a fledgling in front of a cat. I've tried to talk her out of it, but she won't listen. She needs me to be her accomplice, and I need to stand up to her, but I know I can't. I imagine all the things I could say and do.

'This time, Dawn, you've gone too far. You can count me out.'

'That's just because you're a wimp.'

'Call me a wimp if you like, Dawn. But it seems to me you're being the coward here.'

'I'll tell your mum you think her bag is pathetic.'

'Go ahead.'

Except I would never say any of these things. I really am too scared of her. I imagine seeing her on a clifftop, mocking me, and I give her a great big shove. Then I watch her body spreadeagled in the air as she falls to her death. This scene is strangely satisfying, and I replay it a few times, before shoving her in front of a bus, strangling her with a skipping rope or hitting her over the head with a mallet.

I cross the bridge and go into the woods. I like it here. The trees are non-judgemental. They carry on regardless, living their secret lives, hiding wildlife from each other, feeding them with berries and nuts and insects, giving them twigs for their nests and trunks for their homes. They are far too busy growing and providing to care about my wicked thoughts.

There is a crisp, damp smell of earth and leaves, a sweet waft of decay. The wild garlic is all gone, as are the bluebells. It is deep summer, and the flowers have thinned out on the woodland floor. There are patches of milkwort and white bedstraw, and some pinkish clusters of marjoram. Then I spot wild strawberries, their little red globes poking out here and there in the grasses and too tempting to resist. I start to gather them and nibble them fast.

When I look up, there is someone observing me. I stand, motionless, unable to move. There on the path is the sweetest face I have ever seen: that of a deer. Her melting black eyes and large, soft nose give her a gentleness I don't want to disturb. She gazes at me with interest, lending me a sense of importance to her. What can be so intriguing about me? Still she stares, transfixed. I will always remember this exchange of looks; it's as if we recognise something in each other. The moment seems timeless and intense. Neither of us moves, and then suddenly she is off, silently, with barely a crack of a twig, and I hear – after she does – the sound that has made her turn tail. Goldie comes up behind me.

'A roe deer,' says Mr Man, standing now at my shoulder.

'How do you know?'

'Red coat at this time of year. Very dainty. The fallow deer have white spots. The males also have very different horns. And then you have the muntjac deer as well. They're much smaller. This was a roe deer. A beauty.'

I nod. I feel a little overwhelmed by the presence of the roe deer, so intimate and magical, followed by Mr Man so close to my elbow, with his own gentleness and his list of new, wonderful words. I make a mental note to remember them.

'I was picking strawberries,' I say. 'Look, wild strawberries. They're sweet.' I hold out my hand and offer him a couple that have sat in my palm for the last minute or two. He takes one and puts it in his mouth.

'The other one is yours,' he says, and I long for him to take it and put it in my mouth, but he doesn't.

'They're good,' he says. 'Let me show you something else, while you're here.'

He walks a little way off the path and I follow. Goldie comes too, excited at this change of plan. Mr Man pauses, he squints left and right, then heads off to the right. I continue to follow, unquestioning, certain he will have something interesting to show me. At last he comes to a halt. He stands in some green leafy bushes and beckons me over. I am flushed with anticipation.

Chapter Thirty-One

The Trick

He turns away from me into the bushes, and reaches down in front of him with his hand. I wait, breathless, wondering what it is he is going to show me, or if he might be going to kiss me or something.

'Here,' he says, lifting a stem from the bush. 'See this flower?' I nod. 'This is deadly nightshade. If you like eating wild berries, promise me you will never eat this one.'

'No,' I say. 'Our teacher, Mr Spruce, showed us woody nightshade. I've never seen deadly nightshade.'

'Well, this is what it looks like – the flower, at least. It's past its best now. Whenever you see this dark purple bell-shaped flower, beware.' He rifles around in the bush. 'Here's the berry ripening in this one.' He shows me a large green berry in the middle of a flower whose petals have shrunk back. 'This will turn a shiny black very soon, in a couple of weeks.'

'Like wimberries.'

'Not unlike them, only blacker and shinier. It's very poisonous. It can make you dizzy, make you hallucinate – that means imagine things that aren't real – and make your lungs stop working. It's lethal. It's also called belladonna, which means "beautiful woman". Beautiful, but the fruit is deadly.' I think he's going to go all biblical with me, and start talking about the Garden of Eden, but he says, 'It makes your pupils dilate, which is meant to look attractive, so women used to take it in small doses.'

'I see.'

'But don't you ever try it, Stephanie. You don't need to look any more beautiful.'

I try to bank this compliment to unwrap and savour later. He is being far too serious about my safety for me to enjoy it now. *You don't need to look any more beautiful.*

'Ah, look at this!' He holds up another stem. 'Well, this is a bit early. A ripe berry! And another one! There are quite a few already. See how black they are.'

They are the blackest, shiniest berries I have ever seen. I can see why children want to eat them. I won't tell Dawn about them. She'll just want to poison Hilary again. At least her new plan doesn't involve that.

'What do they taste like?'

'I've never eaten one, but they are supposed to be quite sweet.' He drops the stem and it folds back into the bush, hidden from view. 'Well, there we are. Warning over. You'll know now: one berry never to pick.'

'Thank you,' I say, and follow him back to the path.

I have to go now, as it's teatime soon, and I don't want Mum asking me where I've been. But I don't really want to say good-bye to Mr Man and Goldie as they head off to the Dingle. I badly want to go with them. I want to warn him about Dawn and her wretched plan, because she's going to get him involved.

'I have to go now,' I say, back on the main woodland path.

'Okay,' he smiles. 'It was good seeing you. And the magical roe deer.'

'Yes. The magical roe deer.'

I feel corny, just repeating what he's said. I don't move. I open my mouth to speak, to tell him about Dawn's plot, but nothing comes out. Nothing that will lead to an adequate explanation.

'Is everything okay, Stephanie?'

I find my breathing speeding up. 'I . . . if you . . . if Dawn . . .'

His look says, *Go on* . . . but he says nothing. He looks shy, and a little anxious.

'Um. Nothing. I've got to go.'

And that is the chance I miss. I could just say to him what I said to Hilary, but he would want to know why. If only I could share this terrible secret with him. Then, maybe . . . But how can I ever tell him such things? I would die of shame. He is Mr Man and I love him, and he may just love me too. *You don't need to look any more beautiful.* And he wants me to be safe.

When Dawn is late, she traps me. By not being at the Dingle when I expect her, she knows I'm thinking about her, wondering what's happened. She knows I'm picturing her leaving her house, walking at a certain pace, maybe stopping to tie her shoe or talk to someone. She knows that all the time she has made me wait, she has successfully made me fill the time with wondering about her. And it's always just at that point when anxiety for her could turn to anger that she appears. I can hear how needy my voice is at that point. She is an arch manipulator.

It's the day of the World Cup final: the day allocated to put an end to Hilary Gibson.

I'm intrigued to see how Dawn behaves when someone keeps her waiting for a change. She has no patience at all. 'Where *is* Hilary? She'd better come soon, or *he* will be here, and then it'll seem like we've arranged it.' She paces around irritably, kicking at stones. 'He's going to arrive before she's taken her clothes off.'

'Maybe she's been held up by tea – maybe her dad was late coming home and she's not allowed to leave the table until he has.'

'That's not helping.' She sighs and looks at her watch. 'Let's strip off now. Come on.' She pulls her dress over her head and slips off her shoes and socks. 'Come *on*, Stephanie. Let's at least look like we're doing it, so she'll get a move on when she arrives.'

'I'd rather not.'

'For God's sake, Stephanie! What are you afraid of? No one's going to be interested in *your* naked body, not with your gammy leg, for crying out loud. No one's going to be looking at *you*! Can't you get that into your thick head?'

'Then why do I have to?' I can feel my throat swelling up, hard and painful. I pick up her discarded socks and fold them together nervously.

'It's for Hilary, you dumbo. So that she'll join in. She's hardly going to undress on her own, is she?'

I disappear into the bushes as if I intend to strip off, but I delay. When I come out still dressed she gets mean, grabbing at the bag round my shoulder. I try to distract her.

'Maybe I should go and get her,' I say at last, treacherously, for she doesn't know what I said to Hilary yesterday, when Dawn had gone in after playing in the street. I enjoy watching Dawn being kept waiting herself for once, I enjoy knowing that Hilary won't come. Hilary won't come because I told her not to. I warned her that it was a trick.

'Stay here! Take your dress off!'

I don't know it at the time, but these are the last words she will ever speak to me. Even as I head to the bushes again at the side of the clearing, too shy to take my dress off in such an open space, I hear a familiar sound. Dawn doesn't hear the snap of a twig on the path, or see the golden head of a Labrador emerge into the clearing, because she has turned her back on me and is angrily sploshing through the stream. By the time she sees Goldie I have retreated behind a curtain of ivy hanging from an elder bush, and her pants are wet and see-through.

I will remember her wet pants, her mouth open, the way she climbs out of the stream in slow motion. I will remember every moment of what happens next, when the kitten pokes its head out of the bag. I will remember it for the rest of my life.

Chapter Thirty-Two

*Item: **Psychology textbook circa 1975**. Chuck.*

There is evidence to suggest that our brains don't develop fully until our mid-twenties. Even teenagers have a poorly developed sense of consequences, and children less so.

The prefrontal cortex, the part of the brain that deals with planning and thinking things through, the part that can predict consequences to certain actions, develops last of all. Most children's decisions are influenced mainly by their amygdala, that part of the brain associated with instinctive behaviour: emotions, aggression, impulses. This is why so many of us working in psychology are hostile to the British law that still says a child as young as ten can be convicted of a crime. We would argue that a child may well be old enough to know the difference between 'right' and 'wrong', but not necessarily developed enough in the frontal cortex to control impulses.

I think Dawn had almost no control over hers. She was all impulse.

I find myself trailing back to those woods over and over, and back, back along the paths that led me there. If only I hadn't agreed to Dawn's stupid plan, vainly convinced that I could scupper it all by myself; if only we hadn't befriended Mr Man at all, if I had never been for that special walk with him because Mum had thrown out my bear; if only I'd been allowed to go to ballet lessons, I wouldn't have been alone and wandering the street; if only I hadn't met Hilary, if only she hadn't won all the prizes, won the boys' admiration, won my friendship. You could go on for ever, if-only-ing, and it would all lead back to one tiny decision, one tiny event like the opening of a butterfly's wings.

I remember the day as if it were yesterday.

'I know how we can *really* kill her,' she'd said. 'We could drown her.'

I had let her elaborate with fancy ideas about pushing poor Hilary in the stream at the Dingle, tripping her into it with invisible wire, taking her to a nearby ornamental lake in a park, all sorts of rubbish. Then I said, 'Hilary can swim.'

She sighed heavily, kicking back at the wall we were sitting on in front of her house and digging out bits of mortar from the bricks with a stick. 'We could kidnap her!'

'Right.'

'We lure her down to the Dingle and we tie her up, then leave her.' I said nothing, but watched her face as she came up with more details and pitched them to me excitedly. I raised my eyebrows. It was meant to be sarcastic, but I probably looked earnest.

'Until Mr Man finds her dead and wasted body, out walking Goldie.' She was pleased with herself.

'Oh, oh, oh, wait! *Wait* a minute,' I said, pretending to enter into the idea, hoping to smash it to pieces, 'we get *Mr Man* to kidnap her.'

'And how are we going to do that?'

I knew for certain that Mr Man was not going to be coming out at his usual time because of the World Cup. I had seen the World Cup Willie sticker on Goldie's collar. So, I felt on safe territory with this one.

'Did you *see* the way he looked at you in your pants? When you took your dress off?'

It had been like offering a banana to a monkey. She'd snatched it up greedily.

'Yes. Yes, that's good. We get her to come and play in the stream with us, and—'

'We get Mr Man to bring his kittens to show us. We tell her there will be kittens.'

'He wouldn't bring them.' I knew she was right. Why would he? But again, this felt like safe territory. He wouldn't bring them, he'd be watching the World Cup. 'Although ...' She looked sly. 'He will if I ask him *nicely*.' She pulled a scarily seductive face. I had to reel this idea back in quickly.

'I don't think we can get Hilary to take her clothes off. And anyway—'

'That's easy,' she said, leaping off the wall. 'We *all* take them off. We take off all our clothes, *together*, and as soon as he arrives, we run away.'

'What about Hilary? She'd run away too.'

She was literally skipping on the spot then. I remember that. 'We take her clothes, stupid! We run away with her clothes, and she is left naked with Mr Man, and bingo! He just won't be able to resist!'

Dawn's pleasure at such a horror was sickening. I would have to remind myself of that later, the next day and the next. Maybe she really did, finally, mean to do some harm. Maybe after all—

I must've looked pretty hangdog as I trudged back from Dawn's front wall to our house. Gareth was kicking a ball in the crescent, in the road between his house and ours. He was skilful, launching the ball in the air with one foot and catching it with the other, like the players in the England team. I should've told him he was good, but I couldn't think of anything but Dawn. To my surprise he stopped as I approached and came towards me, holding the ball.

'You shouldn't let her bully you, Steph.'

'Who?'

He raised his eyebrows as if to say, *We both know who*. His eyes were so blue and his skin so brown under his floppy dark fringe that I wanted to throw my arms around him. I wanted to kiss him and smell his cheeks and his chin and his neck.

'Dawn.'

'She doesn't bully me.' For some reason I saw a bully as a hefty older boy who kicks smaller kids and duffs them up.

'She bullies everyone. Especially you.'

I swallowed. Did he mean I was weak? He must have seen me staring at the stitching on his football, because he put his hand on my arm.

'You're too nice. She picks on you because she knows she can trust you.'

I was reeling from being nice and trustworthy in Gareth's eyes; I was reeling from his hand on my skin, his nails so pink against his tanned fingers. It was almost as if he was looking after me, as if we were back in our den in the Forest of Dean and he was protecting me from danger. Only this time it was for real. It wasn't wild boar or wolves we needed to watch out for. It was Dawn Webster.

He removed his hand but put it on our gate, as if he wasn't finished with his role as my guardian. He looked me steadily in the eye. Briefly, I imagined licking his skin. 'Seriously, Stephanie. Stay away from her. She's bad news.'

I half expected him to say, 'If you ever want anyone to stand up for you, I'm your man', but he threw his ball into the air and started to kick it again. The rapid, rhythmic sound of his canvas shoes against the leather matched my beating heart.

I should never have pretended to go along with her plan. I should've tried to talk her down, make her see sense. I was good at waiting out her anger. She was always angry about something. She could work herself up into a violent frenzy, but it would fizzle out eventually. I didn't see that this time was different: this time she had felt provoked once too often. She was out of control. Whichever way you look at it, it was my fault.

I should never have run away like I did.

Chapter Thirty-Three

A Girl is Missing

When the police come to the house the next day, Dad is out. Mum offers to make them tea, but the burly man with a bloated face says, 'No, thank you, Mrs Townsend,' and a slim policewoman with short brown hair, who is with him, smiles at my mother and doesn't get a say in the matter. The four of us sit down in the front room, Mum on the settee with me.

'Now,' says the policeman, 'you've done nothing wrong, Stephanie' (that's what he thinks), 'but you were one of the last people to see Dawn, and we need to gather as much information as we can about what happened. Okay?'

I've been expecting this, because yesterday evening, after the World Cup match, there were a lot of people down the end of Napier Road. At first Mum thought it was a celebration, but there was an ambulance and a police car parked outside Dawn's house. After a while the ambulance drove away. I asked Mum what had happened, as if I didn't know. I couldn't sleep because there was a three-quarter moon and it filled my room with white light, and even though I rocked my head from side to side, I couldn't empty it of what I'd seen. I didn't know how to fill that trembling no-where time between Dawn's last words and the rest of the world knowing they were her last-ever words. I also couldn't forget what I'd put under my bed.

After about an hour there was a ring on the doorbell. No one comes to our house at night. I heard low voices rumbling in the hallway. There was a gentle knocking on my door, and Mum came in. She sat by my bed and explained that she just needed to ask me a question. Dawn hadn't come home. When did I last see her? I pretended to be surprised – and horrified. I didn't have to pretend to be shaken. Mum stroked my hair and told me not to worry. It should have been wonderful, that moment; I had only ever dreamt of Mum stroking my hair like that. But all I could feel was the pounding in my chest. She told me again not to worry. Mrs Webster was downstairs and she was quite sure Dawn would turn up soon, but they just needed to know when and where I last saw her. I said it was some time during the match and it was down near the railway cutting.

'Do you know why she didn't come home?'

'No.' I tried to sound really sleepy. Then I realised I needed to say something true, otherwise I'd be a suspect. 'I think she was waiting for someone.'

'Who?'

'Hilary, I think.' Hilary's mum would know she was at home yesterday.

'Okay.'

'Mum?' I looked distraught. 'Is she going to be all right?' I hated myself for my treachery, but my shaking voice was genuine.

'I'm sure she will be. You get back to sleep now. You can tell us more in the morning.'

The policeman stinks of cigarette smoke, and I know Mum can smell it too, and she won't like it. Neither do I. It's just after breakfast, and they are here already, in our living room. I fix my eyes on the arm of the settee. Its dark green piping is starting to fray. Mum has been measuring up the three-piece suite so that she can cover it herself, and she let me look at the swatches. I liked the velvet but she said it wouldn't wear. She favoured a coarse nylon-cotton mix, which I thought was horrible. I nod.

'Yesterday, you and Dawn arranged to play after tea, is that right?'

I freeze. I don't know what to say. I want to say I didn't see Dawn after all, that I changed my mind, but someone might have seen us go down Napier Road together. Even though the road was empty yesterday, with everyone watching the footy, someone might have seen us from a bedroom window or something. Have they spoken to Hilary? What if Hilary told them that I had warned her not to come? And if they haven't spoken to Hilary, they might, and I can't make her lie for me. I take a breath, but nothing comes out.

'It's all right, sweetheart,' says the lady. 'We know this is difficult for you. Take your time.'

I can sense my mother looking at me in expectation. She is bewildered that I don't speak, bewildered in the same way she always is about me generally. 'Stephanie?'

I nod. 'Yes.'

'And where did you go, when you met?' asks the policeman.

'We went down Napier Road.'

'To the railway cutting?'

I chew the inside of my lip. 'Yes.'

'And did you cross the bridge further down the track?'

'She's not allowed that far,' says Mum. 'She only goes as far as the Hadleys' house in one direction and the Drews' in the other. She's not allowed to lose sight of Napier Road.'

The policeman looks at Mum and smiles. The sort of smile you give to a child who says they're going to be an astronaut when they grow up. 'I think we'll have that cup of tea now, if that's okay, Mrs Townsend? I'm feeling a bit parched.'

As soon as she's gone, he looks at me. 'So, you crossed the bridge and went through the woods and down to the stream?'

I look round at the door to check Mum has gone. I nod.

'And what did you do?'

I can hear the metallic sound of the kettle being parked on the stove. I have minutes to tell my story, and seconds to decide what it will be. I stroke the piping on the armrest, feeling my heart gallop. It misses a beat – or adds a beat – *catung!* And then again. *Catung-tung-tung-catung-catung-catung-tung*.

'She wanted to paddle in the stream.'

'And did she?'

'Yes.'

'Did you?'

'No.'

'Why was that?'

I stroke the fraying piping almost tenderly. 'Because I have new red shoes and I didn't want to get them wet. We didn't have a towel or anything. And because I drag my foot, and I don't find it easy on the stones in the water.'

They both look down at my feet. Fortunately, I'm wearing my red shoes, and they look quite shiny, although they're hardly new any more.

'You've been in before?'

'Yes. I didn't like it. I found it difficult to balance.'

He notes something down. 'And did Dawn take her clothes off to get in the stream?'

'Yes.'

He scribbles something, and without looking up he asks, 'And why was that?'

I feel this is an important question. It feels like a trick. Then I remember another trick.

'She . . . she wanted to play a trick on our friend, Hilary.'

'Hilary?'

'Yes, Hilary Gibson.'

'What trick?'

I know I don't have long, and I can't say this in front of Mum, so I rush at it. 'Dawn thought it would be funny to get her to take her clothes off too, and then we could run away and take her clothes with us.'

'That doesn't sound like a very kind thing to do. Did Dawn often play tricks on people?'

'She was a bit ... upset with Hilary. She was jealous. Hilary won the sports day and the boys like her and she's clever and also I like her.' He looks at me. They both do, wondering what corner of this information to pick up. 'But I told Hilary beforehand. I told her there was going to be a trick and not to come.'

'So ... this Hilary was invited?'

'Yes.'

'Let's see. Dawn took off all her clothes and got into the stream?'

'Yes.'

'And you didn't?'

'No.'

'What did Dawn think about that?'

'She told me to take my dress off.'

'But you didn't?'

'No.'

He scribbles again, and again without looking up, he asks, 'So what happened next?'

I can hear the clatter of cups and saucers. 'I heard someone coming.'

'Who?'

I remember Goldie bursting into the little clearing. 'I don't know.'

'How did you know someone was coming? Did you hear voices?'

'No, just a twig snap, rustling, the sound of someone coming down the path.'

'And then what happened?'

'I shouted at Dawn to go. I said, "Quick! Let's go! There's someone coming!" and I ran.'

'But Dawn didn't?'

I hesitate. 'No. I don't think she can have.'

'Why do you think that was? Who do you think she saw?'

157

I shrug. 'Maybe she thought it was going to be Hilary. I didn't tell her she wasn't coming. She was waiting for her.'

He nods. 'So, you ran away, and she stayed, as far as you know.'

'Yes.'

'Do you have any idea who it might have been?'

I shake my head. He's already asked that.

'Think carefully. Any idea at all.'

I shake my head again.

'What did you hear?' I say nothing. 'Take your time. I know this is hard. Think back.'

I don't want to think back. I hear the kitten. I hear the mewling. I don't want to say that what I did was hide in the bushes, behind the elder covered in ivy. I saw everything. I want to unsee it. I hid in the bushes on the side of the clearing. I hid and stayed as still as I could. I won't see it again. I won't. However much they ask me, I can't tell them, and now Mum has opened the door with her hip and is manoeuvring herself into the room with a tray.

I waited until Mr Man had gone, having hardly dared to look at him leaning over her, oddly close, with his strange movements. I waited a long time to be sure he had gone, and Goldie too. I waited until the sound of mewling and the kitten – trembling through the bushes, sniffing at leaves with shaking whiskers, crying like a baby at the sight of me – forced me to make a movement. I picked it up. I wanted to hush it, in case it gave my position away, but there was no one there. Then I heard a shuffling sound. I was so certain of it. I crouched low and still, the kitten whining in my lap, and then I tucked the creature in my cardigan and made a run for it.

I didn't go back by way of the path. I couldn't go where he had been. I ran in the opposite direction, through the bit of the woods we had never explored. I ran and stumbled and ran and hobbled. Brambles reached out and scratched my arms, twigs popped out and clawed at my shoulders. I just kept running. I could hear panting. It took me until I reached the edge of the woods, when

I stopped, bent from the shoulders and heaved, clinging onto my precious bundle, for me to realise that the panting was mine. Turning round and about, I knew I was completely lost. I headed for the nearest slope. If I went down, then I might find the railway track, and if I found the track, I could go back up the other side.

I don't know how long it took me. I was in such a state of panic and exhaustion when I reached the top of the cutting in a place that was entirely strange to me, that all I remember is a temporary relief. Then suddenly a dog was coming towards me along the path: the Willis's dog, Furrow, I was sure of it. I ducked right down behind a gorse bush and closed my eyes tight, praying that the horrid dog wouldn't bound around and sniff me out. But he wasn't to be distracted from his pathway of smell heaven, and he forged ahead, catching the more important whiff of other dogs. I waited until I heard his owner go by, and I thought it was Steven's voice I heard call out to him. What was he doing there? In any case, I let out a sigh, but there could be no relaxing with that horror behind me. Over my shoulder, the sky was wounded, bleeding itself out. I pulled the kitten tightly to me and bent between two strands of a wire fence, scoring the flesh on my back and tearing at the threads of my cardigan.

I wandered to the end of this road, which was so similar to Napier Road but wasn't. It was like being in a nightmare. Nothing was quite as I remembered it. Strange, shocked-looking trees lined the street. There were Union Jack flags hanging from windows and music and voices seemed to come from behind every front door. When I reached the end of the road, I saw a sign that said it was Drinkwater Road, and I was about to sit down and cry when I saw the street it led into. There was the post office. This was the beginning of the High Street. I turned left and kept on walking. I walked, heaving with terror and relief and a strange joy, until it became Bridge Street and I saw Napier Road. I turned down it and went home, creeping up to my room while the others were watching television. I fished a large shoebox from under my bed and put my Trevor in. He was my kitten, the black and white one, and I was calling him Trevor. I had him at last. I fetched an old cot blanket from the airing cupboard, and when Mum called up to see if I was back, I shouted that I was, and I'd be right down.

I couldn't believe what I'd witnessed less than an hour before. I went downstairs for some milk from the fridge. The kitchen looked unmoved; the flying birds on the staircase wall hadn't noticed that a single thing was different, and Jesus still looked calm and holy on the landing. For a moment I was convinced that I'd come back to the wrong life. But, sitting on the bedroom floor, listening to the muffled sounds of the television below, the house was already reeling me back in to its normality.

Trevor made a tour of my bedroom, lapped up the milk I had put in a saucer, then seemed happy to get in the box. He fell asleep while he was in the middle of inspecting it, closing his eyes, nodding and melting into a soft heap. Luckily for me, kittens like to sleep a lot. In the morning I took him out and hid him in the shed.

'Sugar, Officer? Miss . . .?'

'Thank you.' He doesn't check with the policewoman. He helps himself to two spoonfuls from a posh china sugar bowl I have never seen used before. I am oddly moved that Mum feels the need to impress these people who are questioning me. 'Anything at all, Stephanie. Take your time.'

'I just ran.'

'Back up the path?'

'No. I . . .' I look at Mum and he sees me glancing at her. 'I came out in Drinkwater Road.'

'Drinkwater Road?'

I stare at the arm of the chair. Mum will have to make of that what she will. She didn't hear where I was. Drinkwater Road is further along this side of the railway. That would be understandable if you were afraid, wouldn't it? So long as they don't ask how I got there. 'I just panicked.'

'Do you know anyone in Drinkwater Road?'

'No. It's just where I found myself. I read the street sign.'

He puts his notepad down and sits back with his cup of tea. 'Thank you, Stephanie. You've been very helpful.' Now Mum is offering them biscuits. Chocolate bourbons. I'm embarrassed for her. He takes one, and the policewoman thanks Mum but doesn't take one. There is a silence then, broken only by the crunch of his teeth grinding on the biscuit. Then he speaks with some still in his mouth:

'One last thing, if I may. Does the name "Neil" mean anything to you?'

Now I'm stumped. Do I say? Would it matter now? Could I get Dawn's mum into any sort of trouble? My mother is looking at me intently. I'm sure she knows about Neil. Does she know his name? Under her gaze I feel hot and helpless.

'Neil?'

'Yes. In her shoulder bag was a letter. We have reason to believe that her mother knew a man called Neil.'

'Oh . . . yes.'

'Any idea who he was?'

'Dawn said . . . he was her brother.'

'Her *brother*?'

The policewoman leans towards him and whispers something in a low voice, but we can all hear it. Something about that making sense, if you think about it, from the letter. It makes sense that she wouldn't have told her husband if it wasn't . . .

Mum and I supply *his* in our heads. At least, I imagine she does.

'And have you ever seen this Neil?'

I shake my head. 'Nope. But she said he was sixteen.'

'*Sixteen?*' He gives the policewoman a meaningful look. He looks pleased with himself. He tips his head and slurps back the rest of the tea.

'Thank you, Stephanie. You've been very helpful. Very helpful indeed.' He stands up, and so does the policewoman. And my mother gets to her feet as if on a little spring.

'Thank you, Officer. I'm sure Stephanie will be more than happy to do her bit, if you need any more information.' She is all smiles. Anxious ones. Happy smiles would not be appropriate. Neither, in my opinion, are biscuits and best china. But then, they don't know yet that a girl is dead. A girl is dead, and Mum is happy to help. What have I done?

Chapter Thirty-Four

Not so Fast

'There's just one more thing.' The police officer is not finished with me. 'I wonder if we could borrow you for a little while, Stephanie? We need you to show us the exact spot where you last saw Dawn.'

He's looking at Mum now, his eyebrows raised, waiting for her agreement. I clearly don't have a choice. It occurs to me suddenly that they don't know she's dead. They think she's been kidnapped, or wandered off somewhere. I can feel my pulse thumping, gaining speed, and try ever so hard not to look terrified. Why would I be afraid to look for my friend? I would be keen as mustard.

'I'll get my coat,' I say, trying to look a suitable mixture of enthusiastic and slightly anxious. I look in the hall mirror and take in a deep breath as the policeman and the policewoman emerge from the living room, telling Mum there's no need for her to come. My hands are trembling so much I push them deep into my pockets 'What do you think has happened to her?'

'Don't worry. Nine times out of ten children who disappear turn up within twenty-four hours. It was too dark to do a proper search last night, but we intend to leave no stone unturned today. She's probably at a friend's, though.'

Mum looks relieved. I follow them out of the front door and she says, 'Take as long as you need. And you're welcome to come back for another cup of tea afterwards.'

I feel sick now. I'm going to have to take them to her, and then I will have to see her again, laid out, maybe with blood pooling around her head. What if she's been eaten by maggots or some-thing? When does that happen?

They follow me down to the bottom of Napier Road, past Dawn's house, past the net-curtained window, past Lisa Warwick and Nina Elliott, who are playing a subdued game of French skipping in the street. They stop as we go by, and stare at me. It's as if they are accusing me of knowing something they don't. Which, of course, I do. We turn left at the bottom, through the rickety kissing gate and onto the path that leads, eventually, to the footbridge. The policewoman tries to make friendly conversation with me as we make our way down through the woods, which both horrifies me and fills me with gratitude. 'That's a pretty dress under your coat – I always love blue,' or, 'Just look at the moss on these tree trunks – it's like emerald!' or, 'You must be pleased the summer holidays are here! I can remember how much I used to look forward to them,' and so on.

As we get to the last stretch of path before the clearing, I can feel my stomach clenched up like a fist and taste a bitterness in my throat. I think I might really be sick. My heart is galloping now. I mustn't let them see. They mustn't know. I enter the clearing and they follow close behind. *Catung-catung-catung* goes my heart. There is the stream. My breath heaves in and out. There is the slab of stone beside the stream, and the other slab. I stand, wordless, trying to shut out the crashing of my heart and breath, and I point.

The body is gone.

Chapter Thirty-Five

I Am a Poppet

I have to rescue Trevor from the shed before Mum goes out there for some tools to build another cupboard or erect a fence or something. She looks in the mood for some DIY, like she might fancy bashing out some emotions she can't speak to anyone about. I don't blame her.

When I manage to smuggle him back upstairs, I make the mistake of assuming that Jonathan is outside playing. It's the school summer holidays, and that's where he usually is. But not today. He's been far too intrigued by real live policemen to play with his friends in the street. He's still lurking when I'm in my room.

He calls from behind my bedroom door, 'Shall we play The Man from Uncle?'

'Go away.' I'm still shaking.

'Please, Steph.'

'No, I'm busy.' I pull Trevor towards my face, hoping he will soothe me.

'What did the police say?'

'Nothing.'

'If you don't tell me, I'm coming in.' He begins to open the door and I rush towards it. 'What are you doing?'

'Nothing. Just playing with my Sindy doll.'

'Can I play?'

There is a distinct mewling sound. 'No.'

'What's that?'

'Nothing.'

'You've got a *cat* in there!'

Too late. He's pushed past me and seen the kitten. 'A kitten! A kitten!'

'Shush! Shut up! It's a secret!' I hiss. 'You must *promise* not to tell Mum or Dad or they won't let me – us – keep it.'

'Cross my heart and hope to die.'

That's how Jonathan gets in on the secret, which is just as well, since it would be hard to keep Trevor upstairs without someone knowing. And it does give me an extra ally when it comes to finding food. I worry, though, that Jonathan, who is still only seven, might give the game away, stuffing meat paste down his t-shirt or something.

I'm wrong. It's not Jonathan who reveals Trevor's residence in our house, but something else. We are just having tea, the day after the police visit, when Mum pops upstairs to fetch a cardigan. I look at Jonathan and swallow. He looks at me like a Russian spy, or how I imagine a Russian spy might look. Dad pours the last dregs of tea into his cup. There is a sound like *ooph!* from upstairs. Then it comes louder, much louder. 'Oh! GOOD GRIEF!'

'You all right, Kath?' calls our father, without moving from his chair. She might have been confronted by an intruder with a knife or an axe, but Dad sips his tea. I close my eyes. Jonathan chews his cheek. I run to the bottom of the stairs, and so does Jonathan.

'What is it, Mum?'

'Ugh! What a stench!' She stands at the top of the landing glaring down at us. Well, at me, actually. 'Don't what-is-it-Mum *me*! You know full well what you've got in your bedroom and it's going OUT! NOW!'

'But—'

'First off, you're going to get rid of that cat shit. It stinks the place out. Even with your door shut I could smell it!'

She instructs me on newspaper and rubber gloves. I am not

allowed to touch the undesirable object with the gloves, but must pick it up with newspaper and put it at the bottom of the garden on the compost heap, wrapped in the paper. Then I must wash my hands and the rubber gloves and hang them on the line with two separate pegs.

When I've followed her instructions to the letter, I see her douse the rubber gloves in Dettol and peg them up again. I run upstairs to where Jonathan is playing with Trevor in my room, but Mum is soon behind me. She strides over to the kitten, picks him up by the scruff and plonks him in the box.

'This creature is going off to the RSPCA, right now.'

'*Nooo!*' we both wail.

'You know full well you can't have pets. I'm not having it in the house.'

'But he could live outside.'

'Where outside?'

'He'll do his business outside if he isn't locked up.'

'Where did you get him?'

Dad has followed us upstairs now, and stands by the bedroom door.

'I found him.'

'Tell the truth,' says Dad. 'Did someone give you this? A man, or someone?'

'No! I found him, I swear.' I am indignant that Dad should think I'm lying, even if I am about to tell a porky. I try to think quickly. The embankment. No, that will lead a trail back to Dawn and Mr Man. 'I found him in Drinkwater Road.'

'And it didn't occur to you that he belonged to someone?'

'No ... he was miaowing like mad, like he was lost. And he's got no collar on.'

'Some little girl somewhere may be crying tonight because she's lost her kitten,' he says, with his especially holy look.

'Yes – ME!'

'And me!' says Jonathan, supportively.

'Well, you can cry away,' says Mum, heartlessly. 'You know we don't have pets in the house, and he's going now.'

And that's that. She puts on her cardigan and marches up the road with the box, a lid clamped firmly on top of it. We can hear Trevor crying all the way up the garden path.

No one wants me to go out any more. I have to sit inside on lovely sunny days and I feel like a trapped animal. Everything is falling apart. I was convinced Dawn was dead; now I'm not so sure. I am scared to open my mouth in case the wrong thing comes out, Jonathan watches silently from the staircase as policemen come and go in our quiet house, Mum deals with everything, and Dad has folded in on himself. Honestly, I think Mum could knit herself a more useful husband at the moment.

I imagine everyone is looking at me, everyone is talking. *She* was her friend, she was the last one to see her alive, she must know something. The way people turn their gaze away from me and tilt their heads together, I feel so guilty I am even suspicious of myself. I am so determined to stick to my story, that I begin to question what really happened. I am so terrified of the truth that I'm hoping it will fade away completely if I keep on doggedly telling my version of it. But what if I get the details wrong? What did I actually tell Hilary? And who saw me coming back? I can't trust myself to speak to anyone. I prefer to let them think that I am almost mute with shock, which is not entirely untrue.

Eventually Mum says I might as well get out from under her feet, but I'm not to go anywhere near the railway. I must stay in the crescent and Napier Road. She gives me my bead tin and a couple of KitKats and suggests I go and find someone to play with. Huh! KitKats. A sad attempt to make up for what she's done. I mope out of the house, determined that nothing in the world will make me eat these chocolate biscuits. Blood money.

I spot the motorbike straight away, propped against the kerb opposite Hilary's house. A few lads are admiring it again, and Abe is leaning against the wall with another, slightly older, teenager.

'Hey, Stephanie!' Abe calls out to me. 'Come here a mo'.'

I walk over to them coyly, trying not to drag my foot too obviously. 'Hi.'

'*You're* Stephanie,' says the older boy, as if he's solved a mystery.

'Yes,' I say.

'I'm Dawn's brother.' He holds his hand out formally for me to shake, and I do.

'You're Neil?'

He frowns. 'No. Rob.' He puts his head on one side. 'Did she say I was called Neil?'

'I . . .' I can't imagine what to say. I sense it would be insulting to say yes. To be hidden for years must feel like a major injury; to be called by a different name would surely feel like another rejection, although I can't work it all out quickly enough for an answer. 'I'm sorry, I was thinking of someone else.' I take in the short-back-and-sides haircut, the leather pilot's jacket, the jeans and scuffed ankle boots. He looks very normal and pleasant. A bit like Sindy's Paul in an outfit we've made for him. 'She was very excited about meeting you. And I . . .'

'Well, looks like I'm too late.'

I stare at him, and he stares right back with a face so full of sorrow I am pinned to the spot. For the first time I am struck by the real tragedy of what has happened, and it's as if someone has put me in an old corset and suddenly pulled the strings very tight. I can feel the tears spilling down my cheeks, and he steps away from the wall and comes towards me, putting his arm around my shoulders. His eyes are so kind. It's too much. I start to sob relentlessly.

'Hey, come on,' he says gently. 'Let's you and me go for a walk and you can tell me all about her.'

Right at this moment, I would walk anywhere with him – anywhere but the woods beyond the railway. I would let him abduct me, tie me up, starve me, punish me in any way he likes. I hate myself, and I am in love with his compassion. As it is, we walk to the end of Napier Road, turn the corner and sit on the bench by the phone box. I give him my spare KitKat.

'You're her . . . her best friend, aren't you?'

I nod, not entirely sure if this is true, but I suppose it is.

'Well, the truth is, Stephanie, Dawn *did* know me.'

I stare at him, speechless. How many secrets did Dawn have? I can't imagine Dawn would have been able to keep this from me. There must be some mistake. He takes a deep breath, like someone about to dive underwater. He inspects my face carefully now, as if assessing whether I'm grown up enough for the next bit of information. 'You mustn't tell anyone this, okay?'

I don't know if I can handle any more secrets, if I can trust myself with so much information that I have to keep buried, but no one can resist a secret. To be told there is a mystery and not to want to unravel it is unthinkable. 'Okay,' I say solemnly. 'I promise.'

'Dawn's mum – my *real* mum, had me when she was fifteen, and she was too young to look after me. So, her oldest sister – who was twenty-five and couldn't have children – she brought me up as her own.' He brushes some imaginary bits off his jeans. 'So . . . I'm Dawn's cousin Rob – or that's how she's always known me.'

'Oh.' I frown, trying to understand this. 'And Dawn didn't know?'

'No. Neither did I until a few weeks ago. That's when I came to find my real mum. Dawn was out at ballet or something. It didn't go down too well with Dawn's dad, I can tell you.'

'He does get quite angry about things, doesn't he?'

'You're telling me. I'm glad he's not *my* father.'

'Who is your father?'

Another deep breath. He fixes on the door of the telephone box, as if the phone might ring and provide him with the answer. 'They think he was just a schoolboy. Another fifteen-year-old.'

My KitKat is starting to melt as I'm holding it poised in my fingers. 'Well, you have a nice mum.'

'Oh, yes. She's great, isn't she? I always liked her, "Aunty Dot", as I thought she was. Yes, she always was especially nice to me. I know why now, but still . . .'

'Oh, no, she *is* nice. She's lovely. I've often wished she was . . .'

He waits. 'Your mum?'

I smile at him, sadly. We have both loved the same woman. And now, this lovely woman is devastated. She is bloodless and thin and may never smile again. What a misfortune to find her at this moment in time, ready for all the motherly love you were looking for, only to discover she's grieving for another lost child. I want to put my arms around Rob, but instead I shove the KitKat in my mouth and lick the chocolate off my fingers. 'Why did she call you Neil in a letter?'

'That was their code name for me. I just found that out, too. So my nan and mum and real mum could write about me in secret, and if anyone found any letters they wouldn't know.'

I try to chew silently. 'She had a letter in her bag. The police asked me who Neil was. I said it could be her brother, but I didn't know. I haven't got you into trouble, have I?'

'No. Don't you worry. I hope she wouldn't have been disappointed. You know, discovering that Neil was just her cousin Rob.'

'Oh, no. She really liked you. She was always talking about her cousin called Rob.' This isn't true at all. I'm not sure she ever mentioned him more than once, and only to say that he was a spoilt only child. 'She thought you were the bee's knees.'

I don't realise until it's too late that I'm talking about her in the past tense, but he doesn't seem to notice. A solitary tear flops off the edge of his jaw and leaves a dark spot on his denim.

She smells of lily of the valley and washing powder, and she takes my two hands in her warm, pink ones and bends in to me, on her knees before the sofa, with her smiling, imploring face. It's the second time she's been round. She wants me to tell her something – anything – about Dawn and about that day. She hopes that through my hands she will make a direct connection with her missing daughter. She doesn't know Dawn is dead.

'Please, Stephie, poppet. *Please*. Anything you can remember. Why did she go down there? What did she say to you?'

I am her poppet. Now I have Mrs Webster all to myself. But I don't want to remember what Dawn said, or why she went there. I can't trust myself to say anything. My mouth is full of lies knotted up with truth. If I open it there is no knowing what could slip out.

'Do you know anything about it, anything at all? Think back, think back, Stephanie. Anything. You two were together, weren't you? You were, you were together, so you must know something, anything, anything, please, poppet, please—'

'Dot—' says Mum.

'Was it that man, Mr Lugg, with his dog? I know you girls love to take it for a walk sometimes – is that what you did? Did you take his dog for a walk? Was he with you? Did he join you? Did he follow you? Did he come up behind you, maybe . . .?'

'Dot, please—'

'Did he invite you back to his house to see the kittens again? I wouldn't blame you, poppet, none of us would, I came to see them with you, remember? They were so sweet, so I wouldn't blame you one bit. But the thing is, the thing is . . . is . . . is if he's harmed one hair on her head, *one hair on her head*, I will . . . I will . . .'

'Stephanie has said all she can.'

'Did you have an argument with her? I wouldn't blame you, poppet, I wouldn't, these things happen between friends, I wouldn't blame you if you hit her even, accidents happen, I just need to know, Stephie, please—'

'Come on, let's get you—'

'Did you pass another man – a boy – anyone, *anyone*, did you pass anyone or meet anyone when you were with Dawn? Stephie? Please?'

Her face is pink and raw. I know the contours of grief now. I've seen, with Dad, how it hides itself in the folded-in lips and the sudden intakes of breath, the cording of the neck, the grabbing onto ordinary things to stop the hands from shaking. I gently take my hands away, breaking the connection, as if I'm unplugging something electrical from its socket. I look at her and my eyes fill with tears. So do hers. My mouth draws down against my will and the tears come rocketing down my cheeks, hot and shocking. I have all the poppety-ness I want, but no amount of it now will ever make things better.

Chapter Thirty-Six

Item: **Child's lullaby teddy bear mobile.** ~~Chuck~~. ~~Keep~~. Chuck.

We've stopped again. Someone has a window open in one of the train doors. This is dangerous. I am ambushed by the smells of railway cuttings. Even now, all these years later, I have to be alert to the dangers of scent and colour. Red campion, wild lilac and clinging, climbing goosegrass; blackthorn and hawthorn and sweet yellow gorse. Woodlands are worse still, their smells linked like a long, unbroken paper chain to memories both sweet and bitter. It's impossible to trace one without pulling up another, unwished-for terror, like shallow underground roots that make pathways through the earth. Bright mossy tree trunks and secret badger paths, curled-up ferns, reeking wild garlic and mists of bluebells; vetches, trefoils, knapweed, herb Robert and rotting beechnut husks: these things trail back to my flattered ego, my first-ever compliments, my Pre-Raphaelite, raffled, ruffled hair, my early sense of mattering to the world. And the Dingle. Dragonflies and butterflies and water boatmen, leaf-dappled sunshine and wood pigeons singing deep love songs. There I must not go. For all I want to see her again, just to work it out once and for all, I have to stop this trail right here. Stop, stop it. Don't laugh about him panting by the stream, don't tell me about Neil, don't let's stroke our skin and make up stories about Mr Spruce or who we'll marry. And don't take your clothes off. Stop it. Stop it now.

*

I thought life was pretty sweet after Matt was born. There were plenty of obstacles to get over, but we had each other, work was interesting, and I felt I had carved out a sort of identity for myself at last. For once in my life, I wasn't trailing around after someone else, trying to get them to like me. I was Stephanie Townsend: psychologist, mother, spinster. I may not have got married in Rome in pink chiffon as Dawn would have done, but I was happily making my own decisions.

Strangely, though, I sometimes felt Dawn looking over my shoulder. *Don't take this the wrong way or anything . . .* Sometimes I imagined her trying to snatch Matt away from me out of some kind of revenge, and every now and then I thought I saw her. Once in a shopping mall in Bristol, ducking behind a pillar after seeing us, and another time at a conference in Birmingham. Both times she had short dark hair – once with reddish highlights – but she could have been anyone.

When Katie was born, the thoughts started coming again. I was looking at children's clothes one day when Katie was just a toddler. She had wandered just metres away to inspect a musical ride inside the door of the shop. I looked up to see her sitting in the little yellow car, hopeful that I would put some money in the slot. The shop opened out on to a shopping arcade, so I wasn't going to take my eye off her. Nonetheless, I did, just long enough to put the tiny dungarees in my hand back on the rack: Katie would really need the next size up if they were to last, and I could see they didn't have them in. And then she was gone. The car was empty. I rushed around the displays calling her name. I ran out into the arcade and shouted her name. I hyperventilated. People gave me a wide berth. Some women stopped and asked what she looked like. I ran back into the shop, interrupted a sale and begged the shop assistant at the counter for news of a lost toddler. Had she spotted her? I ran back out again. I ran back in, hopelessly. 'Katie! Katie!'

What if Dawn really was still about and she had taken her? I was in such a turmoil, I didn't know what was real any more.

Soon, one shop assistant and three shoppers were helping me look. The arcade security guard turned up and offered to put out an announcement. He asked me what clothes Katie had been wearing. I was barely able to breathe as I wailed it out, high-pitched and desperate.

I heard a child say, 'Ted-dy,' in a sing-song voice, and hopelessly I ran towards the sound at the back of the shop. There was no one. I had imagined it. Then the shop assistant poked her head round a rack of tiny leggings and beamed at me. She indicated a display cot, and there was Katie, lying flat in it and grinning at a mobile hanging above it.

There was another terrifying occasion at a bus stop, when Katie was about three. Two other people were waiting with me: a young woman of my age and an elderly woman who was sitting on the bench provided. All of a sudden, a black car pulled up at the kerb about twenty feet away. I saw the man's face before he got out. It was angry and purposeful. He was looking straight at me as he flung open the car door and barrelled towards me. I think I let out a groan as I snatched Katie up in my arms in slow motion. My feet seemed glued in place, and I shall never forget the horror of that moment as he came at me like a bullet, eyes full of hate.

I thought he would shoot me. I thought, she's hired a hitman. I closed my eyes and held Katie tight.

And then that moment of hell was over and replaced by another. I heard a grotesque scream behind me, and imagined Dawn coming at me too, in a pincer movement. Then I realised, painfully slowly, it seemed, that it wasn't me at all the man was making for, but the young woman behind me. He flew at her and landed her such a blow that she dropped to the ground. Then he was kicking her and kicking her, and the old woman on the bench let out an 'Oh, Lord! Oh . . .' and I trembled in my boots before I could dash off to the nearest house and ask to ring 999. I think it was the fact that I was carrying Katie that made the owner let me in and use her phone.

It turned out that the poor young woman had jilted this animal of a man just days before the incident. But I was shaken for days afterwards. And selfishly, not just about the woman. What if Dawn was, unbelievably, still at large? The idea haunted me. It was ridiculous.

Chapter Thirty-Seven

Lioness

Although there is less to do, sometimes it feels easier and safer to stay indoors on these summer evenings. Jonathan and I are upstairs playing our own game of *The Man from U.N.C.L.E.* I have made us little folding identity cards out of cardboard, each with its own photograph. I am Illya Kuryakin (because I fancy him) and Jonathan is Napoleon Solo (because he is the hero). In our version of the game we can communicate with each other with our identity cards because they have a button inside them (a circle coloured in red crayon) which turns the card into a walkie-talkie. We mostly report on suspicious events, and say 'over and out' a good deal.

A sharp knock on the front door gives a sense of excitement.

'Suspect at front door,' says Jonathan. 'Move carefully to top of stairs. Over and out.'

'In position, Solo. Over and out.'

It's my mother who opens the door. We can see the zip on her blue linen shift dress and the backs of her calves as she holds the door ajar.

'Kath! Could I have a word with Stephanie, please?'

It's Mr Webster, Dawn's dad.

'I'm sorry, Geoff. She's had a lot of questioning lately, and I don't think she's up to any more right now. Can I help you?'

His tone becomes decidedly cross. 'Yes, well, she may have been questioned, but as far as I can see, she hasn't *said* anything, has she? Hmm? I mean, she was the last person to see Dawn alive. I want to speak to her.'

'I'm sorry, Geoff. Not now.'

'I don't think you're hearing me, Kath. I'm not *asking* to speak to Stephanie now, I'm *telling* you. WHERE IS SHE?'

I slink back from the top of the stairs and hide behind the bannister. Jonathan picks up his walkie-talkie and whispers, 'Where's Dad? Over and out.'

Dad has taken a few days off work, since all the police interest in me. We can't see him, but it becomes clear later that Dad has decided to stay in the dining room as Mum is 'better at handling this kind of thing'.

'Please leave.'

'Get out of my way, woman!'

That's torn it. There's a scuffle now, as Mum tries to shut the door on him and he seems hell-bent on keeping it open. 'STOP IT!' she yells, in a way that Mum never yells. There's a strange silence. 'Leave my daughter alone. She's been through enough. You are not going to speak to her in this state. I'm sorry about Dawn, Geoff. I am so sorry, but you can't come round here shouting at *my* daughter. It's not her fault. And it won't bring Dawn back.'

There is the booming sound of a fist banging on the door frame. 'She knows something! That little ... She knows something and she's keeping it quiet! Believe you me, she knows *something*!' Another slam on the door frame, and it seems to shake the whole house. Jonathan raises his eyebrows at me. Mum stands her ground fearlessly. I'm so proud of her. She is glorious. She is a lioness. Where *is* Dad?

'Go home, Geoff. We'll talk about it when you're calmer,' she says. 'Go home now.'

The door closes quietly. I wonder if my mother has just shown that she loves me. I can't be sure, but it feels how I imagine that might feel.

*

179

I slink out of the house early the following day, wearing my teddy bear shoulder bag in which is half a crown's worth of pocket money. I am going to Woolworths to buy something for Mum. I don't know what yet. Maybe it will just be some Turkish Delight, because she likes that. I know she'll say that I've been wasting my money, but short of making her something – and I remember too well what happened the last time I attempted that – I don't know what else I can do to show her I appreciate how she defended me to Mr Webster.

The High Street is just coming to life. None of my friends will be here. It's a glorious day, and they'll soon be out squirting water pistols at each other, feeding ducks in the park or lounging about on swings waiting for something to happen. As I pass the electrical shop I turn my head slightly to see if Mr Man is in there, but a 'CLOSED' sign hangs at a reckless angle inside the door. Part of me is longing to go and see Mr Man and find out how he's feeling – and what he knows; I want to reassure him I had nothing to do with Dawn's horrible plan, that I really never wanted him to be involved. But another part of me wants to put everything to do with Dawn and Mr Man on that day in a box and close the lid. I am struck by a strange sense of freedom. I can stroll like this down the High Street in the sunshine and stop at any shop I like, without Dawn telling me what we're going to do next. I know that's a terrible thing to think, but the thought just sort of crawls into my head anyway. After Woolworths I shall cross over and come back down the other side of the street, which we don't usually go down. I might even visit the pet shop and see how much hamsters cost. Maybe Mum would let us have a hamster.

The Turkish Delight costs three shillings. I ask the lady behind the counter what I can get for half a crown. She points out all sorts of pick-and-mix-type sweets, and I say it's got to be a bit special. 'It's a present,' I say. 'For my mum.'

'Oh, well, love. You'll want something pretty, won't you?' She beams at me. She seems delighted to be able to help. I imagine she doesn't get much chance to give advice on the sweet counter. 'Something wrapped up nice. How about this butterscotch in a tin?'

'Dad likes butterscotch . . .'

'That's no good then. She won't get a look-in, will she? I know! Wait here, my love. I've got just the thing.' She walks to the far end of the counter and rifles about. 'Here!' She shows me the most delicate pastel-coloured pebbles wrapped in cellophane with a little mauve ribbon.

'What are they?'

'Sugared almonds. I don't know a woman alive who doesn't love sugared almonds.'

I take them, and she winks at me. 'Your mum is going to love you!'

I feel a slight spring in my step as I cross the road, already picturing Mum's face after her initial exasperation at my spending. At least she will know I thought about her. At least she'll know that.

When I reach the pet shop, I pause a moment to look in the window. There are four rabbits asleep in a large cage, next to three small kittens. In the far corner of the window, a fudge-coloured hamster runs around on a wheel but never gets anywhere. He must be so hacked off. I push open the door and a little bell rings. The shop assistant is a young pimply woman in a blue nylon overall. She asks if she can help me. I'm a bit thrown, because, of course, she can't. In the long term, because of what I've done, and in the short term, because I have no money.

I look around me. 'How much are hamsters?'

'We've got a new litter down here,' she says, walking to the bottom end of the shop. It smells stuffy and dusty. The hamsters' sawdust is covered in droppings. 'They're two bob each, but you'll need a cage. The cheapest cage we have is ten bob.'

'Two bob each,' says a parrot, who has flown up from further down the shop and now perches on a tall stack of dog food.

I'm trying not to screw up my nose with the stench. 'I quite like the one in the window,' I lie. I can't afford a hamster or a cage, but I'd like to see the kittens.

She gets Gerald out of his wheel and hands him to me. He wriggles all over the place, sensing freedom, and she takes him back.

'Oh,' I say. 'Are those kittens? Can I see them?'

They are snuggled together like the petals of a bud. She peels one away and holds it by the scruff. Its closed eyes begin to open very slightly. She plonks it in the crook of my arm. 'Ginger.' Then she picks off another one. 'This is Cliff, his brother.' She holds up a tabby for me to see, and she can see I am smitten. She thinks she can sell me a cat, no problem. I let her carry on thinking it. She lifts the ginger kitten away from me and puts it back in the window, handing me the tabby. Finally, she replaces him and offers me the third kitten. 'He's not from the same litter. He's called Minstrel.'

Minstrel has his eyes open in a flash and starts to mewl. He pushes his head into me.

'Oh, I think you've made a friend there.'

'This isn't Minstrel,' I say. 'It's Trevor. He's my kitten!'

She frowns at me. 'No, I think you've made a mistake.'

'He's mine! Look, he has a little white tip on his tail. He's mine. He's Trevor.'

The woman, who never seemed warm, now seems positively chilly. Her thin, straight mouth just looks like someone has underlined her nose with a ruler. She grabs the kitten by the scruff and practically hurls him back into the cage in the window. 'Sorry, love. We don't steal people's pets. That one's ours and it's for sale. If you want to buy it, fine. They're ten bob each. Can't say fairer than that, can I?'

'Ten bob each,' echoes the parrot.

I can't argue with this woman. I stand there for a few seconds, wondering if there's anything I can do, but she locks the cage and puts her hands on her hips. I walk out of the shop, breathing deeply. Trevor hasn't gone back to the other kittens. He is on his hind legs in the window, trying to paw at the glass through the cage. He is crying and reaching for me. I crouch down by the shopfront and rest my face on the glass. 'Trevor!' I whisper. 'Trevor!'

After a few minutes I start to run. I run down the High Street, over the road, down past Cavendish Road and Fairvale Street and Drinkwater Road and the post office, over the humpback bridge and down to Napier Road. I run to Greenfield Crescent and burst in through the back door.

'You didn't take him to the RSPCA!' I scream, to anyone listening. 'You didn't! You've taken him to the pet shop!'

'What on earth—'

'You lied! You lied!'

'Stop this!' says my father. 'Stop it right now!'

Jonathan has bounded in from the garden, and Mum comes down the stairs carrying a basket of laundry (sheepishly, I feel).

'No, I won't! I won't stop it! *She* lied! She lied! It's bad to lie! How come you get to lie but when we do it, we get punished?'

'What are you talking about?'

'I saw Trevor in the pet shop window!' I wail, not caring about being manipulative now. I *want* to manipulate. 'He was pawing the window at me and crying! He was ... *crying* for me. And ... and ... she put him in there! Anyone could ... could buy him!'

'Calm down, now.'

'NO! No, I bloody well won't! I love him! I *love* him! She threw out my bear and now she's thrown out my kitten, and he was all I had to love, and my best friend's d-disappeared and ... it's not fair! She gave him away and he was mine! And ... and she's a WITCH!'

I push past them all and run up the stairs, the sugared almonds still in my bag. I slam my door and put a pillow in front of it and sit on it. I can't contain my fury. I know I've gone too far with 'witch'. I've gone too far. What was I thinking? But I can't be sorry.

I'm angry, angry, angry. I want to break something. Maybe I've broken my mother.

There's a soft voice at the door.

'Go away!'

'It's me. The suspects are downstairs in the dining room. Over.'

I say nothing.

'Kuryakin. Napoleon Solo here. Both suspects talking in the dining room. Over.'

'What are they saying?'

'I don't know. Shall I go and listen? Over.'

'Yes.' I'm shaking. I have never spoken to my parents like that before. There will be consequences, but I find I'm not scared. 'Over.'

'On my way. Over and out.'

Five minutes later Napoleon Solo knocks on my door again, and I let him in.

'Suspect One has told Dad – Suspect Two – to *go*! And he's gone!'

'Where to?'

'Dunno. Out the front door.'

I feel a sharp pang of guilt. Perhaps I have broken up their marriage.

'Where is Suspect Mum – One?'

'She went over to the Hoopers' – I saw her from the front window. But she went out of the back door.'

'The Hoopers'? Are you sure?'

'Yes.'

Whatever is going on? I had been considering packing a little bag and running away, but now I'm not so sure. I wonder if I run fast enough, whether I could find Dad and see where he's going, and maybe join him. I don't know, though. Maybe I should get to the bottom of this, and find out if my parents are really splitting up and if it's my fault. I could go and ask Gareth if he wants to come to the park with me or something, and then I might catch sight of Mum sobbing on their sofa between Mr and Mrs Hooper. No, Mum would never cry. I'm not sure what she'd do. And also, I'd absolutely *die* if Gareth said no thanks.

Jonathan and I decide to set up a watching post at his bedroom window, which faces the front. The Hoopers' front door is half hidden by a lilac bush, but we'll see if it opens, and if the traitor walks out.

Nothing happens. After a while Jonathan goes to the kitchen and raids the biscuit tin. He seems insufficiently concerned that we have been deserted by our parents.

Chapter Thirty-Eight

We Can Work It Out

The sound of hammering in the back garden raises me from my bed, where I have been gazing at the ceiling and wondering which parent I would live with, if pushed. I dash to the window. There is my mum, wearing overalls and with nails in her teeth, placing a nail on some wooden contraption and banging it smartly with a hammer. Now she has disappeared into the shed. This is what she does.

I call Jonathan. We both lean on my bedroom windowsill and watch the shed. Here she is, brandishing a saw and a drill.

'That's called a "jigsaw",' says Jonathan. 'It's for little fiddly things.' He's seven, and already he knows this stuff.

She turns this giant wooden box on its end, so that it's almost as tall as her, and pushes it up against the shed, where she secures it with her feet. She draws something on the top surface with a pencil and ruler. Then she takes the drill and drills into it. She goes for it again and again until she's made a line. Then, satisfied, she slides in the jigsaw and starts to saw. The sound is strangely satisfying, although it doesn't answer any questions for us. Eventually, a rectangle of wood falls inwards with a pleasant *thlock*. She disappears into the shed and comes out with a small tin of paint, a screwdriver and a jam jar lid full of screws and stuff. She disappears behind the box and retrieves a strip of cardboard, which she rests on the box and starts to draw on with a pencil from behind her ear. Then she starts to cut out shapes in the card with a craft knife.

We hear the front door open and we freeze. We both look at each other with our most concerned spy faces. But even as we decide what to do, we hear the back door rattle open. There is Dad, walking across the garden towards her. She looks up at him and points at the house. We hear Dad come back in.

'Anyone at home?' he calls up the stairs. 'Anyone want to watch some television?'

We both go to the top of the stairs and look down on our father, who looks up at us with a slightly embarrassing degree of hope.

'Okay,' I concede, and follow Jonathan as slowly and regally as I can.

I sit watching some trashy cowboy film with the most sulky face I can muster. It isn't difficult. I'm still angry, although that has been tempered by the jolt of fear earlier. I'm not sure I can just snap out of this, though. My parents have to understand that I am not happy. They have robbed me twice of a loved one and there will be consequences. I don't know what, yet, but there will be.

After nearly an hour, Mum pops her head round the living room door and says something to Dad. Tea in half an hour, or something. I don't turn to look at her. Why should I?

'Let's go and take a look at what Mum's made,' says Dad, getting up and turning off the television.

I narrow my eyes at him. 'I was watching that.'

'Come on – I think you'll be impressed.'

I won't. I wouldn't be impressed if Mum climbed on the roof and took all her clothes off. She will never impress me again. Nevertheless, curiosity has got the better of Jonathan, so I follow them outside to the back garden.

There, at the end of the lawn, stands an impressive construction. I recognise it as being partially made up of the Hoopers' rabbit hutch. Mum has been standing modestly to the side, but now comes forward to show us a rectangular opening she has made on the end.

'You might want to look inside,' says Dad.

I open the hinged flap of the hutch, and there is Trevor. He steps tentatively outside.

I rush towards him and so does Jonathan. I squeal with joy, and then my voice is stoppered by the black paw prints painted carefully around the front door, with the name 'Trevor' stencilled in red over the top of it. I look up to see the creator of this little house of marvels, but she has gone inside to make tea.

Chapter Thirty-Nine

Rumours

People find themselves appalled by the news of Dawn's disappearance and probable death, and also inexplicably hungry for every detail. They start to thrive on it, wringing out every conversation with a neighbour for a drop of new horror. They are both attracted to and afraid of Mrs Webster and the strong whiff of drama that follows her around everywhere. She looks like an ill, older relative of herself. They whisper warnings behind their hands when they see her coming, but they thirst for any news she might have. Her house has become a thing of fascination. What is going on behind the pale blue front door? Are there people beyond the net curtains of the front window? What are they saying? I find myself caught up in the same intrigue, although I don't wonder what Mr Webster is saying. I know he thinks I have something to do with it. He knows I know something. He will be jabbing his stubby finger at his wife and going red in the face. Mrs Webster will be weeping, or sitting quietly, folded in on herself, because there is nothing else you can do with an angry man.

Rumour has it (and the local paper) that a dog walker reported a girl's body. It was his dog, he said, who found her. Would Mr Man really have reported that? I hope, I hope it wasn't Steven Willis walking Furrow, which he sometimes does, because he could've seen me, although if he had I would've heard about it by now. The police would've told me. And also, rumour has it (and the local paper), that when the police tried to find the body in the dark, it had vanished. But they found her clothes. So – and this is too terrifying to think about – either she wasn't dead, or someone moved the naked body. Both possibilities send shivers down people's spines – and down mine. Both possibilities offer juicy gossip that can be sucked on for years to come.

Their blame is slippery, sliding around different people before you can catch a hold of it. I hear them mostly in shops and by garden gates and on street corners. Mum doesn't want to go shopping any more, because she can't bear the things they say. She orders groceries through the delivery boy, who comes on his bike. But when she needs other stuff, she sends me off to the shops with a list, with Jonathan by my side for safety.

You have to wonder. Well, I don't like to knock someone when they're down, but what sort of parents let their child go wandering off all the time like that? I've always known where mine were. Always.

She was like a wild thing, that girl. And the language off her! I've never heard anything like it. You can always tell the sort of family who don't keep a good enough eye on their children.

And that Townsend girl. I've always thought there was something odd about her. Her father's weird. It's those religious nutters you've got to watch.

Shhh! She's . . .

Ooops. Well, I'm just saying. A pound of Granny Smiths, please.

Our Dave says it's going to rain this afternoon.

I heard there's a brother. An illegitimate one.

Get away! And that he was jealous of Dawn. So, he might have . . .

What, Dotty Webster . . . ?

Oh yes. Tried to hide him. The new potatoes, please.

Well, now I've heard it all.

She paints her toenails. So . . .

There you go.

But there's plenty of people about who do unnatural things to little girls. Look at those Moors murderers. Monsters.

Our Maggie said there's a man up Clearwell Lane who showed her and Sally his you-know-what.

You should tell the police.

It's spitting already, and I haven't brought my rain hat.

Now don't go repeating this, but I heard there was . . . blood. These tomatoes are too soft. I'll wait till there's new ones in.

So, they're looking for a body?

I'm just saying . . .

They don't want her found, not yet anyway. They're having far too much fun. If someone – like a shopkeeper – reminds them that no one knows what has happened to her yet, it's as if they've been cheated. He's not playing to the rules. They want a death. They want wicked deeds. The worst. The thrill of it is what makes life worth living. When a journalist comes sniffing around, Mum says I am absolutely not to talk to him. She sends him away from our door. But the neighbours are clamouring, falling over themselves in the rush to tell him how well they knew Dawn, how she was best friends with their son or daughter, how they often had tea with Mrs Webster, how they helped babysit from time to time, how they knew a very odd man at number twenty-seven, who was always seen lurking around the little girls, and he had a sneaky way of looking at you, and a strange walk, a sinister way of speaking – probably foreign. And unmarried. So, there you are. *And the parents. No offence, Lord help them, but the parents should've known better. And as for the father, well, you've got to wonder, you have, because she wasn't without the odd mysterious bruise, that poor woman. Always falling down the stairs and walking into doors, if you get my meaning. Wouldn't want to cast aspergens, or anything, but you think you know someone . . .*

Mrs Hooper said that Mr Man took Karen Webster a grey and white kitten as a present to cheer her up. Some people say what a kind thing to do, what a thoughtful gesture. And his name isn't Mr Man but Tony Lugg. Tony Lugg doesn't know I have his other kitten yet, but when he finds out, I don't think he'll say anything.

I certainly won't. I try not to think about that day. I can't concentrate on anything, and I can't even eat. I just push food around on my plate.

I come to know the guilt deep in the bones of me, something I can never get at or wash off. I have come to know death, which before was a fox by the side of the road or a crushed butterfly. Now I see it is everywhere, and we're all in for it. Now I see what it does to people who care, its long tail of grief. And nothing, nothing will ever be the same again. Number forty-nine Napier Road will always be a house of death, whatever colour successive occupants paint the front door or the gate; the World Cup will always be smudged with death, England's win the Websters' loss.

Chapter Forty

Item: **List in my own writing**. *Chuck.*

The little girl now opposite me is getting fidgety. She's bored with looking out of the train window. The mother fishes a picture book out of her bag and begins to read quietly, shooting me an apologetic look. I smile. It's clearly a story the girl knows very well. Every now and then the mother misses out a word or a phrase and waits for her daughter to supply it. 'Good girl!' she says then, with glorious enthusiasm, or 'Clever girl!' or 'Well done, sweetheart!' The little girl is brimming with pleasure, and keen to keep going. 'Again, again!' she says when they're finished. The mother looks at me and I smile to show it's okay by me. The third time round, the mother asks her daughter to read the story to her. Although the child can't read, she starts to tell the story, turning the pages at the right places. She is thrilled to be doing it, surprised at her own skill.

The mother has no idea how hard I am trying to hold back tears. I look determinedly out of the window. Even as I do, another child – a boy – follows his mother down the aisle towards the buffet, asking for an ice cream. 'Don't be stupid!' she fires at him. 'They don't sell ice cream.' I don't get a chance to see his face, but I can imagine how crushed he feels. He thinks he is stupid, just as another child once thought she was dirty. I wonder how many times he will be told he's stupid in the same misguided way, and how the layers will build up until he cannot ever imagine being clever or good at anything.

I remember a session with Paula when she was talking about the long reach of our relationship with our mother, how we often choose partners who are unavailable in the same way our mother was not available to us, how we then make ourselves miserable trying to extract from them the things we never got from our mother. I know all this, of course, but hearing it related to me was salutary.

She told me that when I was a child, it didn't feel safe to express my anger, because I needed the mother love too much. But now, if I wanted to release my inner child from all that hurt, it was important to express my anger and frustration freely. She asked me to write down the words 'I am angry that . . .' and quickly produce ten sentences about my mother without thinking too much.

I was, for a time, a counsellor myself, and I knew this free-flow method could work well, so I started writing. When she asked me to read them out, I couldn't find my voice. It was stuck somewhere in my throat. Paula just waited. I started, and stopped. I breathed in and out deeply. 'I'm sorry,' I said. She waited.

I am angry that you never cuddled me,
. . . that you never called me pet names,
. . . that you were never proud of me,
. . . that you never read me a story,
. . . that you never congratulated me,
. . . that you never took my part,
. . . that you never consoled me,
. . . that you never encouraged me,
. . . that you never found out who I was, or showed me who you were.

She waits again. I think of how Mum confronted Mr Webster. She did take my part once.

'Why do you think you found that hard to read out?'

'Because it feels like trashing her. I don't want to trash her. I love her. I love my mum. And it feels like I'm blaming her, and I'm not. There's no point in blaming parents. I know that.'

She nods. 'You feel guilty. That's understandable. What other feelings are you having?'

'I feel sorry for her,' I say. 'I feel sorry for me. I feel sad at the poor mothering she must have had. I feel sad at her ignorance. I just feel so . . . *sad.*'

'Guilt is a self-centred thing. You can't work through much if you're feeling overwhelmed with guilt. You can't look outwards.'

'I know.'

'But yearning to be nurtured is healthy,' she said. 'It's a human thing, not something shameful.'

'I just want to move on. Oh God, I hate that expression. But you know what I mean. I don't want to drown in self-pity. I just want to let go of all this . . . *stuff* about Mum. I don't want you to say I'm insecurely attached.'

'You had your father's love.'

'Ambiguously attached, then.'

'Let's let go of labels for now. You need to understand the limitations of your mother's emotional development. Whatever happened in her own nurturing hasn't been worked through with counselling, and is most likely fixed. You can't simply expect her love to flow out if you press the right button.'

'But am I stuck with this? Is the damage done? Am I destined to be yearningly needy for the rest of my life?'

'Of course not. You know that. That's why you're here.'

'But where do I start?'

'Here. We only let go of the past when we're done with it.'

Chapter Forty-One

A Secret Access

They're back.

'Do you recognise this?' asks the policeman. He holds out the small notebook with the otter on the front in which I write my special words.

'It's mine,' I say, in a panic. I hope he hasn't read it. Not that he would understand any of it. 'Where did you get it?'

He looks at me then, a studied look, with his chin right up, as if he is looking down his nose, as if he needs to distance himself from me now to get a better look at me and see me in a different way. 'We found it in Dawn's bag.' They found her bag, then. Of course. That's where the letter had been, too. Does that mean they found her clothes? 'Her mother says it's not her writing.'

'It's not,' I say. 'What was it doing in . . .? She stole it!'

'Why would she do that?'

I don't know what to say. Because she looked in my new bag and asked what it was, and I said it was for my special words, and it was secret. She had scoffed at that, but she wanted my secrets. Dawn always had to have what she wanted. I try to think of a way to say this, but he stops me, by saying:

'But you and Dawn were friends, weren't you? Best friends? That doesn't sound like something a friend would do.'

I stare at the notebook in his hand. He has it open, and seems to be flicking through it aimlessly. A chill runs through me. He asks Mum if there is any chance of a cuppa, which means she is out of the room for the next, terrifying bit.

'Let's see: *Free raffle light hair* . . . Did you write that, Stephanie?'

I nod, slowly, not sure what other option there is.

'And *Stone has ion ox hide?*'

'Yes.' My voice is meek, almost inaudible to myself.

He goes on relentlessly with my precious list.

'*Goldie is in smell heaven.*

'*Old factory cells.*

'*You must know your buetiful.*

'*Your going to knock there socks off.*'

Here, he looks up at me. Sternly, I feel.

'*Ro dear.*

'*Monk Jack dear.*

'*Wensday is yellow for both of us.*

'*We are both sinners seats.*

'*Good cumpany.*'

Silence. He is good at this. It's like a teacher who is cross, but who knows how to make you quake before they tell you why.

'There are roe deer and muntjac deer in the woods past the railway track, I think.'

'Me and Dawn saw them once. We weren't sure . . . which type they were, but . . . that's what we thought.'

He taps the end of his pencil in the notebook.

'So, who is "us"? Wednesday is yellow for both of us. What does that mean?'

I feel the bile in my throat. I'm dizzy. He must see that I'm nervous. I'm sure he already knows something and he's not telling me. He's testing me.

'Who is "us", Stephanie?'

I swallow. 'It's me and Dawn. We . . . discovered that we both thought the days of the week had colours, and we both thought Wednesday was yellow.'

'*Thought?*'

I don't know what he means, so I say nothing.

'And what's a "sinner's seat"?'

'It's what you call someone who does that. Who sees a colour for a day or a number or a word or something.' He narrows his eyes at me, dubiously. 'I may have spelt it wrong. Our teacher told us.'

I'm venturing into dangerous waters here, I know, but I don't like the way he looks at me, the crushing weight of guilt and blame in the room. The policewoman scribbles something in her notebook and shows it to him. I imagine it's the correct spelling, or something to say it's a real thing, because he looks a bit peeved.

'And "You must know you're beautiful". Who said that?'

'It's just ... we were just playing. It's what we wanted someone to say to us one day.' And then, with an inspired flourish, I add: 'It's what we imagined Paul would say to Sindy.'

'Paul?'

'A teenage doll,' says the policewoman.

'I see. And Pre-Raphaelite hair? Is that something Paul would say to Sindy too?'

I try not to leave a long gap. I have to think quickly. Gaps make him suspicious and I know it. 'That's just something we heard.'

'I see.'

He waits.

'And Goldie. Who's Goldie?'

'A ... um ... a dog.'

'A dog. In "smell heaven"?'

'Yes. You see, dogs have two hundred and twenty million smell cells ... things ... and we only have five million, and when they put their noses down to the ground, they can smell everything, and if they're walking through a wood or something, they're in smell heaven.'

I'm pleased with my explanation.

'Walking through a wood?'

'Or anywhere. Anywhere, they just smell more than we do.'

'And whose dog is Goldie?'

At this point, Mum comes in. I clam up. She puts the tray of tea things on a small table and says, 'Oh, Goldie is Mr Lugg's golden retriever.'

I want to close my eyes, cover my face, run out of the room.

'I *see!*' he says, as if he's getting somewhere at last. 'And do you know Mr Lugg?'

I gulp at the air.

'They walk his dog sometimes, don't you, Stephanie? You and Dawn?'

'Yes. Sometimes.'

He takes in a deep breath and tilts his head back. 'Now I want you to think very carefully about this, Stephanie. Did Mr Lugg ever touch you?'

'No!' I don't have to think carefully about it at all. I touched the stains on his fingertips once and he drew away. Apart from that, and the time he briefly put his hand on mine, our skin never touched.

'He didn't hold your hand, at all? Or maybe put an arm around you?'

'No.' I can feel my cheeks flush with humiliation.

'Is this really necessary?' asks Mum.

He ignores her. 'And Dawn? Did he ever touch her?'

'No. She would've told me. No.' I'm angry with the policeman now. How dare he think Mr Man would fancy Dawn. I can't look at my mother.

He shuts the notebook, then hands it to me, not taking his eyes off me. I'm relieved as he takes a digestive biscuit and dunks it in the tea Mum has poured. Biscuits distract him. He's in taste heaven. The policewoman takes a biscuit this time as well. I think she deserves one more than he does. I think she secretly knows it.

Mum offers me a biscuit too, but I don't take one. Nothing tastes good any more.

*

It's not long before I, too, become the focus of gossip. Neil/Rob has been taken in for questioning, and I have been seen with him 'on a bench'. I daren't go walking with Mr Man (I still can't bring myself to call him Tony or Mr Lugg) because I'm afraid people are talking about him, too. There was one day when he had to go in a police car, and people said he was being questioned. I know Mr Man wouldn't do anything to Dawn, but Dad says I'm not to take his dog for a walk any more, and I'm not to speak to him. Mum says, 'Mr Lugg wouldn't hurt a fly,' but Dad is having none of it. 'No one ever suspects these sorts of men,' says Dad. It makes me want to cry. I want to go to him and tell him I don't suspect him.

Mr Webster has made it clear to all his mates at the pub that 'that Townsend girl knows something, mark my words'. I know this because Lorna tells me. She heard her father tell her mother, and her father didn't like it. He said Mr Webster just wanted someone to blame and he should pick on someone his own size. Lorna Frisket-Lock lives in a big house on Bridge Street, just as it turns into Napier Road. Although she's from a posh house, I often see her playing in the road with Hilary and one or two of the other, quieter girls. Hilary brought me a bunch of sweet peas and asked me what had happened with Dawn, and I said I didn't know. She asked me in a whisper about the trick Dawn was going to play on her, and I brushed it away, saying I never got to find out. But her dad has told her to be careful about playing with me because of journalists hanging around, so I haven't really seen much of her since. Not properly.

One day I see a picture of myself in the newspaper at the local shop. It stares out at me from the stand beside the till. I try not to look as if I'm staring at it, and go home determined to find the paper, which is delivered to our house every evening.

It's a strange thing, but Dad, who usually sits behind his newspaper after tea, seems to read it folded now. And when I wait at the top of the stairs for it to drop on the front mat the following evening, I see Mum swoop on it before I can make it halfway down the stairs. They are in on it together, preventing me from reading it. There's clearly something bad about me they don't want me to see. In the end I can bear it no longer, and I ask Mum if I can have the paper as I need it for schoolwork.

'What schoolwork?'

'I just want to . . . We need to make papier mâché.'

'I'll get you some.'

She goes out to the dustbin and brings in a limp copy of the *Guardian*. I try to look delighted, and put it by the front door to take to school. Obviously, when everyone's watching television I sneak out of the back door and rifle around in the dustbin. I pull out two newspapers covered in ash, one bleeding with tomato ketchup.

There is the picture of me, on the front page. I don't recognise it at first. It's one of me when I'm about eight, so it must've been taken last year. Then I recognise the curtains of Dawn's front window behind me. This was a picture of both of us taken outside her house last summer, and they've chopped Dawn off and made me bigger. I hate it. I realise it must have been the Websters who provided the newspaper with this photo, because we don't have it. I imagine Mr Webster handing it to the police and saying, '*That's* the one you should be questioning. *She* knows something, you mark my words,' and jabbing his stubby fingers at me.

But my ugly mug isn't the worst of it. I don't read the print because it's a bit too small and squashed up, but I see my name in larger print underneath the photograph. 'Stephanie Townsend, the crippled schoolfriend who was the last person to see Dawn Webster alive'. I feel sick. The paper is cold and stinky in my hands. I chuck it back in the bin and look at the second paper. This one has a picture of Hilary on the front. *Hilary*. That's not fair. Poor Hilary. She's clearly walking up Napier Road, and someone must've caught her by surprise because she's turning her head to look into the shot. She's wearing a pretty shift dress with a frill on the bottom, which her mother made. The caption just gives her name, but alongside it is a paragraph in larger print at the beginning of the rest: 'Hilary Gibson, who admitted to knowing that Dawn was planning to "play a trick" on her on the afternoon Dawn disappeared, denies knowing anything about what happened'. This is horrible. It makes it sound like Hilary knows something. I unfold the paper and see a picture of the Gibsons' house: 'The Gibsons only moved to the neighbourhood recently ...'

The back door opens behind me. 'What on earth ...? I knew you were up to something!'

No sooner have I turned to see her than my mother is on me. She grabs the paper and clangs the lid down on top.

'Sorry,' I say.

'Look, Stephanie, we don't want you looking at the local papers. There's rubbish printed in them and it would only upset you.'

'What do they say about me?'

'Oh, nothing much. But it's all total rubbish. You must promise me, Stephanie, never to speak to a journalist, okay? If a man comes up to you in the street and asks you anything about Dawn's disappearance, you say nothing, okay? Nothing. Just ignore them.'

'But wouldn't that be rude?'

'No. In this instance, not at all. They are sharks. They'll try anything to get you talking and then they'll twist what you say. They're gossipmongers, the lot of them.'

'How do I know if it's one of them?'

She crouches down and holds my shoulders gently. It's a good feeling.

'It doesn't matter. What do you say if *anyone* asks you about Dawn?'

'Nothing.'

'Good. Now come on in and wash those hands.'

*

Lorna's parents don't warn her off me, though. I like Lorna, and I think she likes me, because she has often smiled at me before. When Lorna tells me about this comment of Mr Webster's, I am flooded with a new feeling. It is bolstered by the women gossiping in the shop. I'm used to being openly mocked ('oi, cripple', 'leper girl'), but it is the first time in my life that I realise people really do talk about you behind your back. Really and truly. And they might be saying anything and you don't know. I feel swept backward by a wave of gossip. I have spent most of my life being invisible or pitied, and the thought of people suspecting me, of talking behind their hands, of calling me 'that Townsend girl' just knocks me for six. I'm glad she's told me, though, and I feel warmly wrapped in the support of the Frisket-Locks; so much so, that I go to play with Lorna as often as I can.

Lorna's house was made for giants. It has high ceilings, so high you couldn't reach them with a stepladder, and with big clumps of white plaster flowers and leaves around the light bulbs and along the tops of the walls. It has a basement *and* a cellar below that. You have to go up some grand steps to reach the front door, and the level above that is the bedrooms, and even above that there are more bedrooms under the roof. All the doorknobs are made of diamonds (although Lorna says they are just cut glass, but you could've fooled me), and all the rooms have old-fashioned furniture and exotic rugs. The best thing about Lorna's house is the garden. It stretches down behind the back gardens of half of Napier Road. That's how long it is. There is a 'potting shed', a greenhouse, a toolshed and a little orchard. There is a fish pond with goldfish in it, a hammock, a 'summer house', a statue of a naked lady and a real dog called Crinkle, who is a lollopy spaniel.

What is lovely about playing with Lorna is that she makes me feel equal, a bit like Hilary, only more so. Hilary is good at everything, but generous. Lorna is very good at some things, like drawing, and she is always modest about everything. She is a little timid, I think. One day Lorna says to me: 'I always wanted to play with you, but none of us could get near you, because of . . .' Her voice trails off, and I feel confused.

'Because of what?'

She folds her lips together, then smiles shyly. 'You know, because of Dawn.' She looks at me warily, like she may have crossed a line.

'Oh.'

'Not that I'm not really sorry about what's happened. It's terrible. It really is so . . .' She looks terrified, as if she has to justify her contentment at our new relationship.

'It's okay,' I say. 'I feel sometimes like I've been . . .' I want to say 'released'. Now it's my turn to feel wobbly. Everyone is talking about me, lots of people think I have something to do with Dawn's disappearance, and here I am feeling set free. Almost free. I still have a chilling feeling that Dawn is watching me.

'Let's play pirates,' she says.

'But who can be "it"?'

'Crinkle!'

I laugh.

'Or Hilary,' she says. 'Let's get Hilary. Her parents needn't know you're here. You won't have to climb any ropes. We can get some rugs out from the summer house.'

I'm expecting us to go out of the front of the house, around the corner and down Napier Road. But she goes down the long garden, and I follow her. About two thirds of the way down is a little tree with rungs nailed into it, so you can climb up onto the perimeter wall of the garden. It's easy, even for me. We sit on the top of the crumbly red brick.

What I see from this perch is amazing. I have to sit very still for a while in order to take it in.

Beneath us is a narrow pathway, separating Lorna's garden from the backs of the Napier Road houses. Set in the back of each tall garden fence is a wooden gate. There is the gate into Hilary's garden. I never knew where it led before, when I played at Hilary's. I never thought about it. And there is Hilary up in her bedroom. She waves at us, and we wave back. Lorna beckons her over to join us.

But I have seen something else. There, a couple of doors down, is a gate into Mr Man's back garden. And there, deadheading some roses, is Mr Man.

Chapter Forty-Two

A Groovy Kind Of Love

The following day, after tea, I tell Mum that I'm going to see Lorna.

'Well, be back no later than seven,' she says. 'There are some funny people about. You just don't know.'

'You mean kidnappers?'

Mum is silent. She chews her lip.

'Just go straight there and come straight back. Don't speak to *anyone.*'

We haven't heard any news of Dawn for seven days now. They have been seven long days. When I go into the hallway, I hear my parents discussing it. The people in Napier Road are getting impatient for something to happen. They want a man to 'swing' for this. People think there are murderers around here like the 'Moors' murderers in Yorkshire, and they're on the lookout for shifty-looking people who may be monsters. Some have even suggested it's Mr Webster himself, who may have got into a temper about something, hit his daughter and accidentally killed her. But if that's the case, where is the body? Others think it's the mysterious brother, who wanted her out of the way because he was jealous. Some say it's Mr Hewlett with his dachshund, because there's something odd about him, now they come to think of it, and he never joins in with anything in the street, or gives to the jumble sales. Others say it's obviously Mr Lugg. All the children love to stroke his dog and they often hang around his gate. Some people have seen children tagging along on his walks. And he's not married. He lives alone with animals. You have to wonder about men like that. They're not normal. But Mum is convinced it's not Mr Lugg.

'Tony Lugg is such a gentle man. Just because he lives alone, doesn't make him a suspect. He's just quiet, that's all.'

'They're the ones you have to watch,' says Dad. 'I've told you, Kath, you can't trust anyone just because they're quiet.'

'He's kind, too. When I couldn't get anyone to fix my washing machine, he offered to come and take a look. And he did, but I'd fixed it myself by then. He said, "You've done an excellent job on that motor, Mrs Townsend." Said I should become a professional.'

'Which proves what, exactly? Do you want to become a professional plumber?'

'I wouldn't mind, actually. We could do with the extra cash.'

'Don't be ridiculous! No wife of mine will ever go out to work. *I* can provide for my family, thank you very much.'

'I could be part-time.'

My father looks up from his newspaper (I imagine, as I am behind the door, listening, and hear a rustle – he's probably giving it an irritated shake). 'You don't want a job. And none of this has anything to do with men who snatch little girls. This doesn't prove anything. I want my children to keep away from that man.' It's because Dad says this that Jonathan and I will keep a secret with Mum later.

I slip out through the back door and walk up Napier Road. I slow down near number twelve and keep my eyes open. There it is, in between number two and number four, a little alleyway you could easily miss as it's so covered with ivy. I turn right into it. It's sunless and smells of rotting leaves. It quickly takes a sharp turn right again, and runs down the backs of the houses as far as a little orchard, where it halts. This must be the orchard at the back of Dawn's house. So, only the first half of the road is blessed with this back alley access. I keep myself close in to the fence, which is so covered in ivy it seems more like a tall hedge. I don't want anyone to see me through their bedroom window – like Hilary, for example.

I reach the place where Lorna and I sat on the wall of her garden the day before. There is Hilary's gate. I count two gates down. There is Mr Man's.

The tall gate is painted dark green, but the paint is peeling, and underneath are layers of cream and pale blue. I like the dark green. It is mysterious and clever. I knew Mr Man would have a dark green gate. Honeysuckle reaches over his tall fence like a promise. The smell is delicious. I feel a rushing thrill as I open the latch slowly. I realise, as soon as I open it, that some of Napier Road's back windows now face me like dark eyes. Fortunately, Hilary's windows are blocked off by a full-leaved apple tree. I scurry quickly down the garden path towards the back door, also painted green. I knock.

Instantly, there is barking, and it makes me jump. I can hear Goldie's claws skittering across the kitchen floor. I'm so excited, I think I might wet myself. A dark shape appears behind the frosted glass panes in the door. The door handle rattles.

'Stephanie?'

He looks ... horrified. His eyes dart out to the garden, from side to side.

'What do you want?'

I feel sick. I can't think of anything to say. I thought it would be easy, that we would just fall into conversation the way we do on our walks. Goldie, at least, is pleased to see me, and I hide my sinking feeling with vigorous dog-stroking.

'You'd better come in.'

With the door closed behind us he seems to relax a little, but only a fraction. 'Are you okay?' he asks.

'Yes. Well ... Actually, I was wondering how you were. I don't want you to think I'm ignoring you or anything. But I'm not allowed out so much.'

'No, of course. Parents are worried. It's not surprising after . . .'

The words slip away across the room. There are the twisting coils of flypaper covered with shiny bluebottle flies stuck on their feet, motionless and dead. There is the kitten box under a small table against the wall, empty of kittens but still lined with a hairy blue blanket. There, on the tacky worktop, is the tartan shopping bag that he brought the kitten in, brought it to show us because he thought we'd be there. But we weren't, not as such.

'I just wanted you to know that I'm not listening to anyone. I don't believe what people say about you.'

'And what's that?'

'You know.' Surely, he must know. What can I say? 'That you're a kidnapper.'

'Oh, God.' He rakes his thin hair. I feel so sorry for him. I suddenly notice a small saucepan with scrambled eggs stuck to its sides, and I want to hug him. He needs someone to look after him. I could do that. I know you have to soak a scrambled egg pan straight after cooking.

'I don't believe any of it. I really don't. They don't know you like I do.'

He looks at me then with such tenderness that I know I was right to come.

'Stephanie . . . oh, Stephanie, sweetheart . . . you can't be here. You have to go. You can't be here.'

He holds the back door handle. When I make no move towards the door, he wanders into his living room, his hands in his hair. I follow him.

'No one saw me. And anyway, you've done nothing wrong. I *know* it wasn't you.'

He turns. 'How do you know? I could be anyone. Your parents are right to worry. And if anyone sees you come here, anyone at all, they'll put two and two together. Don't you see?'

'How do you mean?'

'They'll think I *invite* girls into my house, and what sort of man does that, unless he's up to no good? It's the sort of man the p-police are looking for.'

I wonder if he's forgotten that he invited us in for ice cream once. He sits down on the arm of a chair and I sit on the sofa. Outside the front window, the people of Napier Road don't know that here we sit beyond the thick veil of dusty net curtains. Me and Mr Man. Possibly up to no good.

'Stephanie, what do you think happened to Dawn?'

'Don't you know?'

Our eyes meet in a wild confusion.

'What do you mean? Stephanie? What have you told the police?'

'I didn't mention you at all. I said Dawn had this idea that we'd all strip off and then she and I would run away with Hilary's clothes, but Hilary didn't come. And I didn't like the idea, so I ran away.'

He takes a deep breath. 'I see.' He rubs at the knees of his trousers. He would look cool in some jeans, like Sindy's Paul. I might suggest it when we get to know each other better. 'So you were there.'

'I . . .' I can feel myself frowning. It's all too complicated. What a tangled web we weave, says Mum, when first we practise to deceive. 'I left, like I said. But . . . I did find Trevor. You know, your kitten? I knew it was Trevor from the white tip on his tail, and you did say once I could have him, and you don't mind me calling him Trevor, do you? Nobody knows it's yours, and even if they did it wouldn't matter, because—'

'But the police—'

'I told them I found him in Drinkwater Road. So, he could have just wandered off from here, from the house. Hilary won't remember him in detail, and Dawn's mum and Karen won't. Even Dawn, if she were al—'

We stare at each other, and then look away. I look down at the sofa cushion. I keep looking at it.

He sighs and puts his head in his hands. Then he lifts his head. 'Do you think Hilary—?'

'She was at home. I told her not to come, that it was a trick.'

He closes his eyes and his face looks contorted, like he might cry or something.

There is a whitish thing poking out from the sofa cushion. I tug at it aimlessly, and then stare. It is a pair of white socks with a little red heart on the ankles. The soles of the socks are grubby, but they have been folded neatly together and placed under a cushion. I feel suddenly dizzy.

He looks up. He sees me holding Dawn's socks. 'I ... um. I thought they were yours,' he says. 'With the little hearts and everything. Like your red shoes. Goldie had them in her mouth when we got home. I was going to give them back the next time I saw you. Are they yours?'

I shake my head. Something runs through me like a cheese wire, keeping me exactly the same, but severed in two. I can't look at him. I chew at the inside of my cheek and just hope that I don't start to cry.

So how come the police don't know where the body is? Did he move it? What's going on? Then my skin prickles all over. What if Dawn is still alive?

'I thought they were yours,' he says.

I blink at him. We wait.

'But where *is* she?'

He shoots me a look, startled and intense, and then looks away. I find I have done the same. We are two tightrope walkers who have trodden carefully to the centre of the rope, only to meet in the middle. We don't know where to go from here. We wobble. The next step could send one of us tumbling down, down.

'So, you're the man who went to the police?'

He nods.

'They don't think it's you, then? You reported it. Why would you do that if you had anything to do with killing her?'

'Killing her?'

'Or anything – whatever they think. *I* don't think that. I know you didn't do anything wrong.'

'They took me in for questioning.'

'But they let you go. So, it's okay.'

'Not if I get visits from you, it's not. Can't you see how it looks? I fit the bill. I'm a lonely man who lives on his own. Little girls come to visit. I let them play with my dog and I give them kittens ... Oh, Stephanie, Stephanie! We can't see each other like this. We can't see each other *at all*.'

The tears begin to blur my eyes. I won't be manipulative. I won't. I won't.

'But you don't need to be lonely, Mr Man. I can come and live with you. In four years, I'll be a teenager, and then I can marry you and look after you.'

He lets out a little laugh, but it's not unfriendly. It's a laugh of delight, I think. I expect he's thinking how lovely that would be: just the two of us. There are tears in his eyes now too, I'm sure of it. He shakes his head. 'No, Stephie, sweetheart. No, no, no. I can't be seen with you. This has to stop right now.'

He stands up and wipes his hand over his face, as if he might produce a white dove or a coin from it, like magic. There are tears coursing down my cheeks now, sore and childish. I can't bear it. He doesn't want me. He called me sweetheart but he doesn't want me.

There's a knock on the front door, loud and urgent. He opens the back door for me and signals for me to get out quick.

'But I love you! And I can make you scrambled egg without it sticking to the pan, and I know how to make clothes and everything. And when you come home from work, I could play you music on the record player and we could dance. And we can go for walks every day with Goldie and learn more about poetry and be in smell heaven. Don't you see? I love you!'

Chapter Forty-Three

Fuckit

I can't go home. I can't take this home with me, this sickening, raging torment bubbling through me. I have to ... I have to ... to keep moving. I run, in my pathetic way, up to Bridge Street, past the telephone box, all the way down to Plum Lane, my feet falling heavily on the pavement, pounding my shame right up through my bones. I keep running, past the school, past the church, down the lane into the park. There are a few teenagers flirting by the swings, a couple of boys kicking a ball around by the pond. I find the most secluded bench I can, part hidden by an overhanging tree, and I pull my knees up to my chest and hug them.

I cry and cry and cry. He doesn't want me and he says we must never see each other again, and he kept a pair of Dawn's socks – *Dawn's* – but he did say he thought they were mine, so maybe he takes them out and strokes them, although her feet are smelly, so I hope he doesn't. And I know in a few years' time – just a few – I'll be a woman and he'll still be a man and it will all be okay. Then we'll be together and I know I can make him happy, I just know it, I do. It's not fair, it's not fair, I want him to like me again, I want him to love me and say I have raffley hair and lie back with our lambination and sinners' seats and roe deer and William Blake and Gloucestershire under the sea and iron ox-hide. I want him to look at me like he used to – like he did even today, so maybe he does still love me, and he's the only person who ever loved me and doesn't care about my leg but just loves me how I am. And

I hate you God, I *hate* you for giving me this rotten leg because everything would be different if I didn't have it, and I don't believe I did something wrong to deserve it when people like Dawn get to have normal legs, and what made *her* any better, just tell me that! I hate you and I don't believe in you and you just care about turning bread into wine and things that don't matter, so go on! Strike me down with a bolt of lightning, I don't care! Do it! I might as well die! It's the sort of thing you'd do because you're just mean, mean. *Mean!* If Dawn was here now, I know what she'd say. She'd say *fuckit.*

'Fuckit!' I say. 'FUCKIT!' But there's no one nearby to hear, and I wouldn't care if they did.

I know something is wrong as soon as I get home. For a start, I thought I'd be able to slip in through the back door, but the front door opens as soon as I turn into Napier Road. There, at the mouth of the crescent, are Lorna and Mrs Hooper, and my father. It's Mum who opens the front door and bolts out of it up towards me.

'Where the hell have you *been?*'

Mum never swears. I only ever heard her say 'ruddy heck' once or twice when she got some chip fat on herself. Now she's said hell in front of Dad and Mrs Hooper, and he doesn't even tell her off, so I know I'm in for it. Her arms are on my shoulders and she pulls me briefly towards her. I think she might hug me, but she shakes me. 'Where? *Where?*'

I can see they know I didn't go to Lorna's. Lorna is looking at me with relief, but holding back because of my mother's rage.

'Let's go inside,' says Dad.

'We're so glad you're safe, Stephanie,' says Mrs Hooper, crossing her hands over her chest. 'So glad! We were all so worried, sweetheart!'

'Yes,' says Lorna meekly, and I feel she may be trying to convey to me that she didn't deliberately dob me in. To my shame, I'm too shaken to smile at her as Mum marches me into the house. I hear my father thanking people behind me for helping.

They are all there, Jonathan, Mum and Dad, all looking at me and wanting an answer.

'I went to the park,' I say, not quite able to tell a total lie, and hoping there is enough of the truth there to be plausible.

'You went to the park!' hisses my mother, as if I have insulted her. 'We searched the park. We've searched everywhere. We've knocked on doors all up Napier Road. That was after Lorna came round asking if she could play with you. So don't lie to me, Stephanie Townsend.'

I can't bear it. Each bitter word stings like acid. 'I was at the park. I was on a bench that was hidden.'

'And why, if you don't mind me asking, were you at the park?'

'I was upset. I wanted to cry. I just wanted to cry, and I know you don't like me crying because it's manipulative, but I just couldn't help it.' There is a manipulative whine to my voice as I say this.

'But why the park, for goodness' sake? Of all places? Now! When there may be a dangerous kidnapper on the loose?'

'He's not on the loose. He's been arrested,' says Dad.

'He isn't a kidnapper!' hisses Mum. 'He's just a quiet, lonely man.'

I can hardly breathe. I take in a deep breath. 'Arrested? Who?'

'It's not him. Whoever's done it is still out there!'

'Kath . . .'

'Don't Kath me!' She doesn't even look at my father.

'For God's sake, Kath! Can't you see she's been crying? She's upset. She's lost her best friend.'

'Roy, leave this to me. I haven't finished with you, madam! What was the last thing you promised me when you went out? Hmm? That you would go *straight* to Lorna's and *speak to no one!*'

'I didn't speak to anyone.'

'And you didn't go to Lorna's either! We've been worried sick. Worried *sick*! Thanks to you!' At the word 'sick' she sends a bit of

215

spittle into my face. I don't dare to wipe it off. Dad is cross too, I know, but he opens his arms and pulls me into him. I cling on and wrap my arms around him tightly, crying into his shoulder, shocked that there are yet more violent tears to come.

'Oh, that's right! She's got you wrapped around her little finger, hasn't she?'

I feel the full force of this remark, but it will take me years – decades – to understand the significance of it.

Chapter Forty-Four

Item: **Old rope washing line**. *Chuck.*

At last we're making good progress through the countryside. Farms and hedges and sheep spin by, as the train picks up some real speed.

I can still feel the cold terror of my mother shaking me, still remember the startling fleck of spittle landing on my cheek. Of course, I was consoled by the arms of my father, but I think it may have been the first time I sensed something out of kilter in the dynamics of this. I wasn't fully comfortable about the refuge of his embrace, where I had been before. Or maybe it had been building up for a while, layer upon layer, the sense that my mother's anger at me was increased by my father's tenderness towards me. Her anger at his always being good cop to her bad cop had nowhere else to go but towards me. I lay in bed that night and tried to catch something that kept wriggling away: the significance of her clenched jaw as she regularly spat out the phrase to my father, *Ooh, you let her twist you round her little finger!* So much spite in it.

I see now how that phrase, directed at my father, carrying the full weight of her fury at him for her disappointing life, actually managed to hold me accountable for his weakness. It allowed her to vent her anger at him while blaming me. He is kind of let off the hook. And I see now the piece of the puzzle I didn't have then: that she was, like so many women of her generation, trying to hold the fantasy together, trying to stop the little bits that had broken off over the years from leaving nothing but a stump of the story. They had all bought into the fairy tale: the handsome prince who would sweep in and make everything okay. All they had to do was believe in him, stand by him no matter what, big him up, protect him from mockery and failure. They had to do this, because if they didn't, they had let go of college degrees and any hint of personal ambition for nothing. Nothing. They had all done it: they had sacrificed their lives for a male ego, for a made-up story. Occasionally it worked; mostly it staggered on, or they were cast adrift, bailing out resentment over the side of a boat filling up with it as fast as they could pour it overboard. Some, like my mother, found scapegoats, and I think I grew up caught between them and their silent battle. They loved each other. I knew that because they said it. Mummy and Daddy love each other very much. We were a 'close-knit' family. And yet, I still don't know if my father knew what he did to my mother with those hugs he gave me. She was always jealous of her little sister – claimed Wendy had always been her father's favourite. Dad knew this. When he put his arms around his little girl in front of her, especially when Mum was angry, was he always looking out for me? Or was he deliberately tweaking her jealousy? I will never know. But somehow, on that day when they thought I'd disappeared – when she must have felt the terror that every mother feels at that moment – I caught a glimpse of the battle between them and my unwitting role in it. There was something in the air that had nothing to do with me, and yet everything to do with me in terms of its impact.

I think of that rope sometimes, to which she was tethered. How mostly it was loose as she ministered to her husband's needs, the centre of her world. And I think how often she pulled on it, past her children, past her shed, her ladder, her drill, even past her sewing machine, pulling on it tight, as tight as she dared, reaching out to her dreams.

Chapter Forty-Five

The Writing on the Wall

I'm woken that night by the most terrible sounds. There is dog-barking, as though every dog in the street is going mad. Listening more carefully, there is chanting. Like a football match, like celebrations after the World Cup. That's it. It's more celebration. But it's coming from the street. I'm scared. It's dark outside. I can see nothing through my bedroom window. I go into my parents' room.

'Mummy?' I haven't called her that in a long time. Jonathan joins me.

'Go back to bed, you two,' she says, but she is up and in her nightie. Something is clearly wrong. Where is Dad?

'Come on,' she says, 'back to bed.'

But I hear the front door closing, and footsteps on the stairs. Dad stands at the bedroom door.

'Mr Hooper's already called the police. There's nothing more I can do. I've told them to go home.'

Mum pulls a cardigan on and parts a few inches of curtain. 'This is awful. Did Dave say when they'd come? *Will* they come?'

Dad shakes his head. He's wearing his outdoor coat over his pyjamas. There's no point either of our parents telling us it's 'nothing', so Jonathan and I don't budge.

'Bed, now, you two,' says Dad. 'There's nothing to see.'

But there is. We have both come to look out of the front window with Mum, and in Napier Street a great crowd of people has gathered. They are chanting something I can't make out, but it's angry and loud and frightening. It sounds like 'RING HIM UP!', but it could be 'STRING HIM UP!', which makes no sense either. All the dogs in the street have woken up too. A flashing blue light appears at the top of the street, and Dad pulls us gently away. 'Drama over. Bed now.'

'But can't I see the police car?' says Jonathan. 'Please, Dad?'

My parents usher us back to our rooms, then go back to theirs and murmur long into the night. The chanting stops. I have nightmares about all the inhabitants of Napier Road throwing stones at my bedroom window and calling me a murderer.

In the morning, Jonathan beckons me out of the back door after breakfast. I follow him up the garden path and out into the road. We stand in front of Mr Man's house and look at the pale blue paint daubed on the front door: 'PERVERT', and on the red brick of his house: 'MONSTER'. All of his roses lie in front of the garden wall, decapitated. His honeysuckle has been uprooted, and clumps and crumbs of earth lie along the pavement. The terracotta window box has been smashed, and all his pretty flowers have been thrown in the street, too. The front window has been broken, and the closed curtains behind move in the breeze. I feel sick.

We look at it for what seems a long time, in silence. A pebble grows in my throat.

'What does it mean?' asks Jonathan.

'I don't know.'

I want to run and knock on his door. I want to say I'm sorry. I want to tell him I had nothing to do with this. *Nothing*. But, as the seconds pass, and little fragments of what has happened glue together, I'm pretty sure I do have something to do with it. I lean into the next-door neighbour's privet hedge and retch.

As long as I live, I will see nothing as shameful as the front of that house. The spite and the fury and the silence. I will know after a short reflection who has done it, because there is only one house in the street with a pale blue-painted door, and one man in particular guaranteed to be full of rage. I wonder if our house is next.

'Should we see if he's all right?' says Jonathan.

I shake my head. 'No, it might make things worse.'

'Why?'

I sympathise with my brother. It's a dreadful thing not to understand stuff. Like I didn't take it in yesterday that Mr Man must be the person arrested. There is so much I don't understand, but I know more than him, and his ignorance hurts. He just wants to be kind.

'What about Goldie?' he says.

The tears are coming now, and I try to stop them. 'She'll be fine. She's a tough old thing.'

I put my arm around my brother and lead him back to our house, to its silence and relative safety.

As soon as Dad leaves for work, Mum is out in her shed, busying herself with something. She comes out armed with various tools, and asks us to help her carry some things. To my surprise, she heads straight over to Mr Man's house. We follow her with a purpose, then sit on his short front path and watch her.

She takes out a tape and measures the broken pane in the front window, jotting down the measurements on a piece of plywood, then sticking the pencil behind her ear. I have carried two small sawhorses over from the shed, and she sets them up now with the plywood across it. Jonathan hands her the saw, which she takes out of a protective cardboard cover she has made for it. We watch as she draws lines with a ruler onto the wood, measures the windowpane again, and then starts to saw. The noise is loud, and I'm afraid people will come out of their houses and look, but no one seems to be around.

Soon, she has cut the wood into the exact size of the pane, and when the sawing stops, I hear something.

'Listen!'

We can all hear it: it's Goldie, whining.

'Oh, good grief!' says Mum. 'They haven't even thought about that poor dog.'

'Who?' I say, although I'm pretty sure I know the answer now. Still, I need to be sure.

Mum sighs. 'The police have just taken Mr Lugg in for some more questioning, and they've clearly kept him in overnight, but it looks like they've forgotten about his dog.'

'Goldie!' I sob, through the letter box. 'Goldie, it's all right!'

Mum is squirting some filler glue around the edge of the broken pane. She doesn't clear the fragmented glass, but leaves it in place. She wipes her hands and places the rectangle of wood on top neatly, then presses. 'Hold this for a moment,' she says to Jonathan, who is keen to help. 'Well, there's nothing much we can do without a key. But if I'd had a key, I could've done a much better job of this windowpane.'

'You've done a good job there, Kath!'

It's Mr Hooper. He leaves a little bit later for work than my dad because he drives. He's stopped the car outside Mr Man's, and is speaking through his rolled-down window.

'I could've done a better job if I'd had access to the inside,' says Mum. 'I'd have put some batons across inside and bolted the wood through into the batons, without damaging the window frames.'

'But you haven't damaged the frame,' says Mr Hooper, full of genuine admiration. 'That's a perfect temporary protection. Stops the glass splintering any more, too. Good work!'

'Oh, well,' says Mum, looking a bit shy, 'thank you.'

When he drives off, I make a decision. Something has to be done about Goldie. I know how to get into the house, but if I tell Mum, she might think I go in there, or something, which isn't true. Or she might think that Mr Man has told me how to get in, which might be bad for him, and also isn't true.

Goldie continues to whine as Mum is clearing up her things.

'Mum,' I whisper. 'I know where there's a key. I've seen him move the flowerpot when he comes home from his walks with Goldie.'

Most of the pots are broken, shards of terracotta strewn along the path and in the street. But Mum lifts the edge of a heavy pot by the front door, from which some red geraniums have been uprooted. She pulls out a key.

Chapter Forty-Six

Tenderness

As soon as the door is open, Goldie spills out into the tiny patch of front garden and does her business in a flower bed, as if she has been holding onto it for ever, then she jumps up at me and follows us into the hallway. Mum picks up a bunch of letters and stuff on the mat, and goes through to the kitchen. She stands and looks around, letting out a sigh. 'Poor man!'

There's a terrible smell, and Goldie's bowl is empty but for the dried-up bits of food she has left. Mum opens the back door to let some air in, and Goldie shoots out into the garden behind. Jonathan follows, sniffing around and exploring as if he'd been given a new playground. Mum stares at the curling flypapers. She stands on a chair, unhooks them and takes them out to the dustbin. I can see that my mother is troubled by the perceived dirt (although I think Mr Man is quite clean, and does his best), but also rising to the challenge of cleaning with barely concealed excitement.

'Right,' she says, decisively. 'You stay here with Jonathan and Goldie. I'll be back in two shakes of a lamb's tail.'

I can hear Jonathan playing with Goldie outside. I slip into the front room and search for the socks. I don't want Mum finding them. I don't want the police finding them. They would draw conclusions. I can't see them. I check around the edges of the sofa cushions. Nothing, except a squeaky dog toy.

Back in the kitchen, I wonder if I dare to go upstairs and look in Mr Man's bedroom. I want to, but don't quite have the courage. And then I see the sheaf of letters and stuff that Mum brought through from the front doormat. I pick one up. It's not sealed, so I open it.

'YOU ARE NOT WELCOME IN THIS STREET. SCUM.'

I fold it up quickly and stick it back in the envelope. There is a piece of cardboard from a cornflake packet, and on it is scribbled: 'DON'T SHOW YOUR FACE HERE AGEN. IF YOU DO YOUR A DEAD MAN. WE'LL TARE YOU LIM FROM LIM.' And another piece of paper is scrawled with 'YOU SICK BASTARD. I'LL KILL YOUR DOG.'

'Oh, good grief!' says Mum, coming through the front door. 'How did I miss this?' She comes into the kitchen with her mop and bucket in one hand, and a large brown envelope held at arm's length in the other. 'Oh!' she says. 'Oh, no!'

Putting down her cleaning things, she peers inside the envelope and takes it straight outside.

'What is it?' I ask, not really wanting to hear.

'Never mind,' says Mum. 'Something cruel, posted to Mr Lugg, that's all.'

I show her the letters and notes. She sits down and puts her head in her hands. She calls Jonathan in. 'Listen,' she says. 'There are some people in this world who are unkind. When something bad happens, they rush to blame the easiest person they can think of, and it's not fair. And sometimes the real baddie gets away with it, because everyone's looking in the wrong direction.' She looks at us pointedly, to see if we're concentrating. 'There are people in this road who think Mr Lugg has done a bad thing. But I don't think he has. It's for the police to decide, not for neighbours. I hope neither of you will listen to anything cruel said about Mr Lugg.'

'I won't, Mummy,' says Jonathan, looking very serious.

'Me neither,' I say.

'Right,' she says. 'Let's get to work.'

First, she gives me and Jonathan an old toothbrush each, and shows us how to scrub around the base of the kitchen taps with soap. Every trace of black gunk must go. While we are doing that, she finds a tin of dog food for Goldie, she wipes down the kitchen surfaces with disinfectant and mops the floor. She inspects our progress with the taps, and says, 'Well done, you two! You've done a really good job there.' It's probably the first time that Mum has shown she's proud of me, and I feel tingly all over.

She finds a broom under the stairs and goes out to the front of the house to sweep up all the soil from the pavement outside, and from the road in each direction. Jonathan and I try to gather all the little flowers that still have roots attached. Then Mum brings a pile of empty pots from our house and we try to replant as many of the flowers as we can. Next, she takes a rag and douses it in white spirit, then carefully attacks the 'PERVERT' on the front door. It starts to shift and smudge, until there is a cloud of pale blue across the red door instead of a word. She wipes it off with another rag, but it isn't good enough. She gives us each a rag soaked in white spirit to have a go at 'MONSTER', which is on the brickwork itself, and while we set to work, she does the best she can on the front door. 'I'd like to repaint it for him, if he's got any of the original red paint left in his shed.' She looks at her watch. 'But not today.' She helps us with the brickwork, and then we go and wash our hands in the sink. 'You've worked hard there, you two,' she says.

She goes into the back garden and I follow her out, with re-newed confidence in her company now that she is proud of me. The garden is much as it was, and hasn't been trashed. On the washing line, little versions of Mr Man swing in the breeze: a white shirt with the wind-filled arms tilting forward, occasionally swinging about to left or right, as if he is twirling back and forth doing the Twist; a pair of trousers that, inflated with air, make him look like a sturdy man without a torso; a series of tatty vests that make me feel unbelievably sad. We help Mum bring it all in and fold it up. She holds up a shirt and puts her head anxiously to one side. 'Poor man,' she says again. 'He's missing a button here. Two buttons. That's no good.'

With renewed purpose, she asks me to find Goldie's lead and says we'll take her for a walk into town to get some more dog food in a bit. Meanwhile, she writes a note on a paper bag she finds in a drawer:

Dear Mr Lugg,
    I hope you don't mind, but we came to see to Goldie and found your key under the pot. I've brought your washing in and patched up the window. Hope that's OK. All is well.
    Best wishes,
    Your neighbour,
      Kath Townsend

When she goes to vacuum in the front room, and to clear up the shards of glass, I take a look at the note. I feel a bit put out that my name isn't there as part of the 'we'. She has left the biro next to the note, so I carefully add '+ *Stephanie*'. I don't bother with Jonathan because he's irrelevant.

Mum comes back into the hallway, admiring the vacuum cleaner, which she returns carefully to its cupboard under the stairs. 'Of course, he would have a good one. He sells them in his shop. I must ask him about this one.'

'What's this?' asks Jonathan, examining a plastic funnel-shaped object.

'Oh. Put that down. It looks like an inhaler. I'm not surprised. All this cat and dog hair is enough to give *anyone* asthma. And the smoking, of course. Don't you two ever go smoking.'

Jonathan tries to smoke it before putting it down, and I make a mental note to ask about asthma later, but I forget.

We are to take back all her tools and rags, her mop, the laundry and the dog. She stuffs the poisonous mail under her arm, and we make our way back over the road to the crescent and our clean, sweet-smelling house. While we fuss over Goldie, giving her a bowl of water, throwing sticks for her in our back garden, Mum irons Mr Man's clothes. She sits on the sofa and sews his buttons back on. She mends holes in his vests and gets out her sewing machine to fix a trouser zip which has become unstitched. The waistband of his trousers has lost one of its hooks, and she replaces it. His cuffs and collar have become frayed on one shirt, and she replaces them with ones from a torn white shirt of my father's. There is a pride in the way she performs these tasks, and a tenderness.

Although I'm feeling churned up and confused, afraid that Mr Man might go to prison, this day is one of the best days I remember from my childhood. It sits alongside the little-lamb-who-made-thee incident, when she once warmed my cold hands.

Before we set off on our walk with Goldie, there is a ring at the door. We all go quiet and look at each other. I don't know why the others are looking so scared, but I know why I am, and I fear it's the police or something. It is. Mum goes to answer the door, and it's a policewoman we haven't seen before. Mum hesitates, then asks her into the hallway.

'Mrs Townsend?'

'Yes?'

'You may or may not know that we have Mr Lugg with us at the police station at the moment.'

'I heard. I hope he's all right?'

The policewoman sees me lurking in the hall, my back flat against the wall like someone hiding from a gunman. She has fiercely short black hair, peppered with grey.

'He's extremely worried about his dog. He's named you as a neighbour who might be prepared to take the dog in and feed it until he comes home.'

'Well . . .' My mother sounds hesitant. Jonathan and I wait for her answer. Goldie pants in the kitchen.

'Only I was just about to go and let the dog out, but I wanted to check with you first. He's given us a key.'

'Oh, there's no need,' says Mum quickly. 'In fact, we've got Goldie already.' She opens the kitchen door to show Goldie, who runs up and down the hallway, excited about the lead she can see Jonathan holding.

'How did you—?'

'Oh . . . I, um . . . I have a key.' I study Mum, watching her tread ever more dangerously close to telling a lie. Jonathan is interested too. I hope he doesn't interrupt. 'Yes, I sometimes water his flowers or feed Goldie if he's away.'

A porker! A real porky-pie.

'Oh . . . oh, well. I'll let him know.'

'Thank you. There's no need to go round. We have everything for the dog.' And I suddenly see, right there, a possible streak of cunning in my mother. She doesn't want the police to go to Mr Man's house any more than I do. She doesn't want them to see that she's left a note for him, that she's tidied up; she doesn't want them thinking that she may have tried to help him hide anything that could be seen as 'evidence'. Could that be it? 'Please tell him not to worry. Goldie is being well cared for.'

The policewoman smiles and nods. She is making her way to the door when Mum says, 'Wait!' and runs into the front room to retrieve the pile of horrible notes and letters. 'I found these on the doormat – and worse! An envelope containing you-know-what.'

'What?'

Mum pulls a face of disgust, and whispers something we are not supposed to hear.

'Oh, I see.'

'I'd like you to show these to your superiors. No one should be subjected to this kind of hate mail. If he got to read them, he'd never choose to come home. He'd be terrified. Please make sure they are seen – but not by him. He must be protected, you see? The police need to look out for him.'

I can see that the woman is flicking her eyes across the message on the piece of cornflake packet. She looks very serious. 'Thank you, Mrs Townsend. I'll see to it that this is dealt with.'

'And please tell Mr Lugg not to worry about Goldie, won't you?'

'I shall.'

The three of us go into town, Goldie pulling at the lead as Jonathan and I take turns with her. It feels strangely as if we are all doing something a bit naughty, something we wouldn't want Dad to find out about. In fact, when we've bought some dog food and tins of corned beef and chicken supreme for Mr Man, Mum says, 'There's no need to tell Dad about this.'

We walk back, but instead of going down Napier Road, we head straight over the bridge towards the park. Goldie is in smell heaven, and Mum gives us some bread she has brought in her handbag so that we can feed the ducks.

'Is Mr Lugg in prison?' asks Jonathan, to my horror.

'No,' says Mum.

I keep wondering what Mr Man thinks of me now. Does he blame me for all this? Maybe the police searched his house and found the socks. Do they think he moved the body? But he didn't take the dress and the bag, did he? The police found those.

'But has he been arrested?' I ask, certain now that he has.

'Well, he . . . I think the police have taken him in to question him, yes. But he'll be home soon, you'll see.'

'So, he hasn't done anything wrong then?' asks Jonathan, trying to get a mallard to walk towards him for his bread.

'No,' says Mum. 'If he has, I'll eat my hat.'

Jonathan stops what he's doing and looks at her. 'Why?' He holds out his hand. 'You can have some of my bread if you're hungry.'

Mum and I laugh. She throws some bread to the ducks herself, and there is a great fluttering and rushing and splashing as they all crowd around her. 'Okay, okay,' she laughs. 'Keep your hair on!' Jonathan and I burst into giggles.

'Keep your hair on!' he shouts at the ducks, delighted.

Once again, I'm struck by that strange mix of joy and terror that surely shouldn't ride together. I have never been happier in Mum's company. I have never been more worried about something terrible happening to Mr Man. And it is all my fault.

Chapter Forty-Seven

Item: **Sindy's wardrobe and clothes.** *Chuck.*

Jonathan stayed over in the end, to help me declutter. I don't think he trusted me to carry on with it on my own. He thought I might go through all the things I'd agreed to throw out and retrieve half of them. He waded through my spare room, bringing down larger items to put in his car and take to the council tip: small rolls of lino, cut-offs of carpet and underlay, tins of paint with surfaces like rubber, unused picture frames, spaghetti heaps of wires that connected to appliances I no longer owned, moth-eaten picnic rugs, an old plastic tricycle.

'Wait! I might have grandchildren . . .'

'And will you want to give them this?' He held up the tiny vehicle by its faded handlebars. A few fluffy clusters of spider eggs were visible underneath the saddle.

'Okay. No.'

When he came back from the car he helped me with my sentimental pile. It was less of a pile and more of a hallway. But everything in it seemed to matter. There was my old autograph book, for example, that everyone signed when we all left primary school. The pages were coloured, and covered in childish hand-writing. There is one from Hilary:

> *When you get old and ugly*
> *As people often do*
> *Remember that you have a friend*
> *Who's old and ugly too!*

This makes me well up. Dear Hilary. She, Lorna and I had kept in touch at university and went interrailing one Easter, but then when she wrote a cheery card suggesting she came to see me in Oxford, I didn't reply. She'd made some comment or other once about girls we'd known who'd become pregnant, and I couldn't help thinking she'd disapprove of my status as a single mother. I had no real reason to think that, except that her family seemed to have quite strict views about things. I was too ashamed for her to see me with Matt, and then became ashamed that I hadn't replied.

Leafing through the little album I saw one from Lorna, too:

> By hook or by crook
> I'll be last in your book.

But Gareth had squeezed in after it:

> By eggs or by bacon
> You are mistaken.

I had been so pleased when he wrote that in my book. Flicking through the pages, I spot something else in his slightly more mature hand, when he was twelve and moved away:

> If you ask me to write
> What shall it be?
> Just two little words
> Remember me.

I had completely forgotten about it – perhaps too busy thinking about older boys at the time. I would keep the autograph book. I'd been rubbish at keeping my friends, and now I didn't want to lose the evidence of them. But there were so many other things. So many. I couldn't explain to Jonathan that letting go of things was like losing my footing. Putting something in the 'chuck' bin bag was terrifying; a bit like losing altitude, like going down suddenly in a lift, or that sensation you have in a dream when you just drop. I needed to hang on. I needed to feel safe. It was as though losing any of these objects was like losing a bit of myself or my children.

'The thing you have to do, Steph, is ask yourself when you last looked at something.' He picked something at random from the top of a box. 'This, for example.'

It was Sindy's wardrobe. 'But Mum made that.'

'Yes, but when did you last look at it?'

I opened it up. Inside were Sindy and Paul and all their clothes. Or some of them. We were both aware why I had kept this, and Jonathan looked a little sad that he had picked it out. I removed the dolls, and looked at the handmade outfits and dozens of little slippers. I inspected Paul: he was wearing his needlecord donkey jacket with fur trim, made from the faux fur of my mother's Astraka coat hem. She had sewn poppers onto the front to do it up, and there was not a stitch out of place. I tried not to choke. He could see that the decision was too much for me. I couldn't face all these decisions about losing things for ever.

'Why don't you photograph it?' he suggested. 'If you want to remember it. It'll take up less space that way.'

'Okay. Chuck. But I'm keeping Paul's jacket, though. And I'll keep it on Paul.' I stick Paul under my arm as if Jonathan might try and take him from me.

He blew air into his cheeks and slung the wardrobe into the 'chuck' bin liner, along with all our years of wet Saturday sewing and dreams of our teenage selves.

Funny how there was nothing to remind me of Mr Man: no photos of him or Goldie, and no press cuttings. Mum had made sure any newspaper articles about the incident were binned. Mr Man had moved away not long after the graffiti incident, but I was so preoccupied with keeping out of trouble that I barely noticed. I pushed thoughts of it all away, because thinking about it would've meant confronting a tangle of emotions too knotted up to unravel. One day there had been a pale blue car outside his house, and a cocker spaniel appeared along with two small children. They stayed and grew and the curtains changed and the gate was painted white and Mr Man no longer appeared, and Goldie no longer pattered along the street towards the railway cutting.

We were about to call it a day and get a takeaway when my brother stood very still. I could feel his stillness behind me. 'Christ, Stephanie. What the f ... Look at this.' I turned, and he held a small box, about the size of a chocolate box, open in his hand.

The sight of it made my heart miss a beat. I remembered quite vividly the day this came about. I was ten.

Chapter Forty-Eight

Samson not Delilah

The girls are all looking at Hilary's nipples, which are growing. 'It's called budding,' she says, very matter-of-factly. 'It's how we begin to grow breasts.'

We are ten years old, in the changing rooms after a swim at the local baths. I have managed, despite my leg, to swim a width, and I'm triumphant. I'm put in 'B' team, where no one seems to stay long. Everyone else I know is in the 'A' team, for length-swimmers, and now just two poor souls are left in 'C' team, where I have languished for over a year with these other unfortunates, one with sinus trouble who hates chlorine and one with a terror of being seen in her swimming costume (and I sympathise).

When Hilary talks about budding, everyone looks at their own nipples and I look at mine. To my shock, these are beginning to swell a little too. I hadn't noticed before, but now I realise what it is, I do seem to remember a few aches and pains.

This is bad news. This is terrible. A girl in our class called Jill Cricklewood, who almost has proper breasts already, comes over and confirms Hilary's diagnosis. Hilary is pleased. Why? I am filled with such a sense of terror that I can barely understand it. This cannot happen. Today has been a good day. I am in 'B' team, which means I can swim. But today is also the day that I realise I am changing into a woman, and I can't stop it, however slowly it happens. And I know that not so long ago I couldn't wait to be a teenager, so I don't fully understand this feeling inside me;

but I do know that one thing my mother doesn't want is another woman in our house.

When I get home, I tear upstairs and scour my *Famous Five* books. I have three. In them, Georgina calls herself George and wears her hair short like a boy. There are pictures. She wears boys' clothes and does boys' things, like have opinions and ideas and make important decisions. Anne, who wears girls' clothes, has no ideas at all. She just goes along for the ride and to provide a sort of boy–girl balance to the stories and to say wimpy things that George can make fun of. Okay, I'm going to be a boy. If George can do it, so can I. I'll cut my hair really, really short and call myself Steve. I've got some shorts. I can borrow my brother's grey socks. I've got a stripy t-shirt. I try it all on and come down to look at myself in the hall mirror. Not bad. I don't have a gang or a dog, but it's a start.

At teatime I announce my plan.

'I'm going to be a tomboy,' I say. 'From now on I'd like you all to call me Steve.'

'Ergh! Like Steven Willis?' asks Jonathan.

'No. I'll be Steve, not Steven.'

'That's what his brother calls him.'

'How about Steffan?' says Dad, helpfully.

'Or Steff?' suggests Mum.

'That's what I'm called already: Steff.'

'Steffan is exotic,' says Mum.

'Okay. Steffan. From now on, I'm Steffan.'

When the tea things have been cleared away and I've offered to dry the washing-up, I make my request.

'Will you cut my hair, Mum?'

She goes to fetch her hair scissors from the drawer. 'I'll do it now, if you like. I need to clean the kitchen floor anyway.'

Dad hovers in the doorway, looking anxious. 'You're not serious are you, Stephanie?'

'*Steffan.*'

'Sorry,' he half-smiles. 'Steffan.'

'Of course. I want it cut like a boy.'

'Are you sure this is a good idea, Kath?'

Mum clicks her scissors open and shut (with a little too much enthusiasm, perhaps). 'Whatever madam wants.'

'But Kath—'

'If she wants it short, she can have it short. I'm the one who has to get a hairbrush through it every morning. Anyway, hair grows out.'

Even as she says this, she is putting her home-made hairdresser's shawl on me, which has a drawstring neck and is made out of an old striped sheet. I didn't like it when she called me 'madam', but now I see she was just pretending to be a hairdresser. She divides my hair into four sections, and ties each with an elastic band. Then she says, 'Sure?'

'Absolutely.'

She snips off the four bunches of hair and they flop to the floor. She picks them up and lays them flat on the worktop, then she continues to cut my hair with gusto. When she is finished, she brushes my neck with a soft baby brush, just as she does when she cuts Dad's or Jonathan's hair.

'Can I have the razor on it?' I ask. Mum has an electric razor which she uses on their necks.

Dad shouts from the living room, '*No!* No, Kath. No razors. That's too much.'

She raises her eyebrows at me, as if to say, 'The master has spoken', and shakes out the hair from the shawl. 'How's that?'

I go to look in the hall mirror. 'I like it.'

'Good.' She picks up the four long bunches of chestnut hair and holds them over the waste bin. 'Shall I throw these out? Or do you want to hang onto them?'

She doesn't want to hang onto them, obviously. I watch her hand hovering, ready to drop them into potato peelings. 'I'll keep them,' I say. 'They might come in handy for dressing up.'

I take them upstairs and find an old chocolate box I have under the bed. I lay the tresses in it, remembering how Mr Man used to love my hair. My free-raffle-light hair. Who cares now? I put the lid on the box and bury it in my bottom drawer.

Chapter Forty-Nine

Tomboy

With my new tomboy persona, I have given myself a sense of freedom along with a new identity. I'm determined to get this right, to be the sort of tomboy the Famous Five would be proud of, so I need to watch the ways of boys. I start by tagging along with Jonathan when he plays, and as he mostly plays with Paul, Gareth's brother, I often find myself playing with all of them. Paul isn't allowed to go to the park or the railway cutting without his older brother. That suits me just fine.

Before I know it, I'm the crucial fourth player in a regular two-aside football game. Jonathan and Paul against me and Gareth. And because Gareth, aged ten like me, is a far better player than the two eight-year-old boys, he doesn't object to having me as a handicap on his team. Gareth and I nearly always win, unless I score an own goal, or unless Gareth takes pity on them and lets them score. Clearly, football is never going to be a great strength of mine. Even though I can shoot with my left foot, my weak right foot is not a reliable support. I'm so keen to improve that I get Jonathan to be goalie and let me practise shots in the back garden. Over and over until I can make a half-decent kick. He seems happy with my new interest, and shows me how to do press-ups to improve my biceps (and his). If I really want to be a boy, I have to build up my muscles.

I can't say that Mum shows any obvious signs of loving me more as a boy, but I feel hopeful. She isn't at all bothered by my new masculinity. She even buys me a pair of canvas lace-ups to knock about in. I do at least feel that I no longer disgust her sometimes. I feel I have found my niche (although I'm not very good at any of the skills required).

Sometimes, when we're playing football in the park, a dog will come ambling over and cock his leg up on one of our goalposts. As they're our pullovers, this is not funny. The boys think it's hilarious, so I have to pretend to as well. Occasionally, Steven Willis joins us, and when that happens, I have to play on the side of the little ones. It's Gareth and Steven against the rest of us, and of course, despite our side having three players, we always lose. When they score they say, 'Nice one, Hooper!' or 'Nice one, Willis!' I become known as 'Townsend', Jonathan calls himself 'Solo' and Paul goes with 'Best – George Best'.

I try not to notice how hopeless I am, how uncoordinated, how uselessly unfitted to sport. Some small voice inside me tells me I have to make a go of this new role, that everything depends on it. Somehow, my mother seems happier with things now, and I can't risk losing the possible new ground I have made.

One day, when Steven Willis is playing, we are one–nil down. I keep my hopes up. I've practised my dribbling, and Jonathan is pretty good himself. We can afford to have one person in goal, given that there are three of us, and Paul volunteers. He's good at saving balls, so we stay one–nil for twenty minutes. Then, to my amazement, Jonathan dribbles the ball all the way down the 'pitch' and is close enough to their goal to shoot. I don't know whether out of kindness or stupidity, or simply fear of the ultimate responsibility of failure, but Jonathan takes a notion to pass the ball to me. Tackled by Steven, he misfires and sends the ball into the air. It hits my head – hard – and flies straight into the goal.

'Nice header, Townsend!' shouts Gareth.

'Yeah, nice one, Townsend!' shout Jonathan and Paul.

I feel myself blush. I want to put my hands in the air and do a lap of honour. I have arrived. I'm one of them. But I smile and shrug. I secretly decide to practise headers from now on. I don't need two good kicking feet for headers. I just need to be in the right place at the right time.

The other place we go to play is the railway. For some time after Dawn's disappearance I avoided the cutting. It was a strange experience when I first went back to it, revisiting the exact spot by the Dingle on my own one Saturday. It was full of oddity. I hadn't expected the trees to have turned orange and gold, hadn't expected the blank white sky, the lack of birdsong or the pungent smell of fungus and damp earth. But now, going back with Gareth and the boys, it is a magical place all over again.

We play there all through the seasons, watching the snowdrops poke through the woodland floor, then the dog's mercury and the primroses and the garlic flowers and the bluebells. On the railway bank itself we hide behind bushes of wild lilac, gorse and hawthorn. We stride through the willowherb, scattering butter-flies, looking out for badgers and foxes and watching slow-worms wriggle carefully out of their old skins, leaving behind what look like the crinkled cellophane wrappers from sticks of rock.

Gareth and I join in the games of cowboys and Indians that Jonathan and Paul want to play, pretending we're humouring them in a grown-up sort of way. In fact, these games are brilliant. For one thing, the younger boys always want to be the Indians, and this involves making wigwams and tying up their enemies: me and Gareth. They have an old piece of washing line, which they use regularly to bind me to a young hazel sapling. Some-times, we pretend to tie each other to the train track itself, and although this is more dramatic, involving the potential flattening of a body by an imaginary train, it isn't as much fun since we can't easily secure the rope to anything. Little Paul, in particular, enjoys a good roping to a tree. He goes to Cub Scouts (Jonathan isn't allowed because it is a bourgeois invasion of the Anglican church) and can tie really convincing knots. They enjoy watching me struggle (I have to make a big show of the struggling) as they dance around me doing a war cry.

The best thing about being tied up is being rescued by Gareth. He ducks and dives behind the bushes, holding an imaginary gun, and eventually, when the Indians are having a break, he will untie me. Even when he gets the knot sorted, there follows a serious unravelling (the rope is the length of a washing line), and while he's unravelling me, Gareth will say, in character, 'It's okay, Townsend, I've got you,' and I will say, 'Thanks, Hooper. I owe you one.'

If I turn my head, I can smell his hair and the warm skin on his neck. When my hands are free, I imagine reaching out and touching his neck, or his sun-warmed arms or the veins in his wrists.

Obviously, we have to tie them up sometimes, but nothing is as much fun as being unravelled by Gareth. Sometimes, in bed at night, I rejig the scene. I'll be lying tied up somewhere – behind a curtain of ivy, perhaps – and Gareth will whisper in my ear, 'It's okay, Townsend. I've got you!'

It has well and truly replaced the Sunday school conveyor belt dream with Steven Willis and others. That is all dead to me now.

There are three occasions that make me uncomfortable about being a boy. The first is playing kiss-tag in the school playground. It's the last year of primary school and the girls gather in great groups, provoking the boys to kiss them. The boys themselves form a great gang, ready to oblige as forcefully as they can. The girls mean business, and so do the boys. In this strange and potent mix of boy–girl longings, I find myself – as usual – in the boys' gang. This is where I have grown to belong. But however hard I try, I cannot make myself feel part of it now. There are talks of tactics. I can't tell if the boys are leaving me out of this, or if, in fact, I am distancing myself from it. There's a thought I try to ignore, but it keeps popping back into my head: I want to be with my friends, Hilary and Lorna; I don't want to chase the girls and kiss them. I want to *be* chased, and *be* kissed. By the boys. By Gareth.

It's all far too complicated. I can't lose my male status. So I gallop limply around the playground, half-heartedly pretending to take part in the chase, but I don't catch anyone. And of course, no one catches me. At least I have an excuse. I can just imagine what Dawn would have said if she were here and I was the only girl not to be kissed. But she isn't. And anyway, maybe if I were in the girls' team now, I would be kissed. Maybe.

The second occasion is when I'm playing with the boys on the hill. Right on the top, past the sheep grazing on the slopes, is a piece of land flat enough for the local golf course. Sometimes in the summer months we go up there and play in the sandy bunkers. Usually, we're told to clear off when we're caught, and we don't mind because the man who shouts at us says 'Clear orf!' just like the men in the *Famous Five* tales, and it makes us splutter with laughter.

On this particular day, we are having a right old laugh, hiding when we see him coming.

'Hey, you lads! Clear orf! This is a golf course for private use. I've told you lads before, clear orf!'

Jonathan and Paul and Gareth are giggling, and I try to as well, but inside I feel a sinking, a folding in of myself. A few months ago, I would have been thrilled to hear myself called a 'lad', to be mistaken for one. It would've made George in the Famous Five leap with glee. But something isn't right about it. It's almost as though I'm disappointed by my own success, but I can't face what that actually means just yet.

And then the oddest incident of all.

Chapter Fifty

Excluded

It's nearly a year later. I'm at secondary school, but still friends with Lorna and Hilary, who are both in my class. One day, when the three of us are on the way home from school, I invite them round on Saturday afternoon. Hilary says she can't come. I don't ask why not, but she looks so awkward that it makes me curious.

'Maybe Sunday, then. Or next Saturday?' We always get together at some point over the weekend, either at mine or at hers or Lorna's. But Hilary shakes her head.

'Sorry, Steph, I can't.'

I catch a glance she shoots at Lorna, and I feel a sharp shock of exclusion.

'Look,' says Hilary, hugging her satchel close, 'I've been meaning to tell you this, but I don't really know how.'

I freeze. I look sideways at her and then down at the pavement. I try to prepare myself with a deep breath, but it comes in shallow. They both know something, and they haven't told me.

'The thing is, my dad has forbidden me from seeing you.' (It's been nearly two years since Mr Gibson advised Hilary against playing with me during the aftermath of what happened, and that was only for a few weeks while the police and press were sniffing around Napier Road.) 'He says I should mix with different girls. I'm really sorry.'

A woman passes us slowly on a bicycle. Her brown brogues push laboriously at the pedals, and we can hear her breathing. I want to run after her and jump on the handlebars. I want her to take me anywhere but here, right now.

'But . . . why doesn't he like me?'

'It's not that he doesn't like you. He thinks it's . . . unhealthy for me to spend so much time with you, that's all.'

'Unhealthy?' I look down at my droopy foot. I hear a fuzzy sound in my ears, like a television that's lost its signal. 'It's not catching. Does he know that? I had polio when I was little. Tell him you can't catch it from me now.' Even as I say this, I'm so horrified that Mr Gibson has thought to forbid friendship with me, that I'm not sure I want him told; I'm not sure I can ever look him in the face again and feel the same.

I knew it was too good to be true. All this time I've had two friends who like me and respect me without making me perform tasks for them, but I've always known I was unworthy of this sort of friendship somehow. I've always felt a bit like an imposter, and that at some point they would see it. I should never have imagined it could be this easy. I should've stayed away. Who did I think I was?

'Tell you what,' says Lorna. 'Let's meet at mine. You can both come over on Saturday. I've found some amazing old magazines in one of the sheds, and you've got to see them.' Hilary seems keen. I agree tentatively, and she doesn't change her mind. 'We can *always* meet at mine, if you like. Then your dad doesn't need to know.'

This appears to solve the problem for Hilary and Lorna, but it doesn't resolve anything real for me. I know the Gibsons cooled off a bit after Dawn's death and all the gossip, but they've never stopped us seeing each other since. I wonder if this is Hilary's way of seeing less of me. Or perhaps she and Lorna are sharing some secret information about me. When Saturday comes round, I rush to change after lunch and head round to Lorna's before Hilary gets there. I need to know the truth.

We are sitting on Lorna's bed listening to Radio Luxembourg

208. 'Let's Spend The Night Together' is playing; we can hardly believe the words, they're so exciting. But I mustn't get distracted.

'Why doesn't Mr Gibson want me playing with Hilary now, all of a sudden? He never used to mind my gammy leg.'

She traces a rose on her bedspread with her finger. 'It's not your illness, Stephanie. It's got nothing to do with your leg.'

I swallow. I may be about to hear a horrible truth. I may not want to hear it. It may be a rejection, an ending of something, a pushing away.

'What, then?'

The lyrics from the radio are heady and dangerous and fill me with a wild sense that things are about to change; and I'm amazed that the person who is most likely going to bring about this change is me.

'When he says he doesn't think it's healthy to spend so much time with you, he means like . . . like he thinks you're . . . you know, well, like the woman bus conductor on the number six.'

'What? The one who . . .?' The bus conductress looks like a man, except she isn't because she has breasts, which even the wide straps from her heavy coin bag and ticket machine don't manage to hide. But we wouldn't mind her looking like a man if she didn't chat up the girls. We're all embarrassed by her calling us 'Darlin'' in a fake cockney accent, and asking some girls what they like to do at the weekend. Sometimes she props herself against a hand pole by the prettiest girl on the bus and just flirts openly, and asks her out. It makes us all cringe as we listen to the chosen girl's excuses. We look at our satchels or our tickets and pretend we can't hear, but she doesn't let up. She keeps on asking until the poor girl in question gets off the bus. 'But I'm not like that,' I say. 'I don't want to go out with Hilary. Not like that.'

'I know.'

'Does Hilary know that?'

'Of course!'

We all three play together as usual that afternoon, although we have stopped calling it playing. We go down into the garden and feast on piles of fusty old magazines in the shed, laughing ourselves breathless over the daft fashion pictures and the dotty expressions of the knitwear models, the ancient advertisements and wild claims of upholstered underwear or certain brands of cigarette.

After the magazines, we dress up in disguises. Lorna has a whole chest full of old clothes, and we spend our pocket money in the joke shop on plastic protruding teeth, fake moustaches and glasses. Jonathan often goes in there to buy itching powder, artificial dog turds or stink bombs. We all love nothing better than inventing a character, practising different voices and turning up on our parents' doorsteps pretending to be a gypsy ('Buy my sprig of thyme, my love, and you'll have seven years' good luck'), or a long-lost relative with goofy teeth and a headscarf ('You don't remember me, do you? Cousin Edith from Dursley. All right if I stay over a few nights? I've only one bag and the five poodles …'). We love the split second when our parents frown, confused, before they realise it's us. We still continue the charade for all it's worth, until they grin wryly and say, 'Not today, thank you,' and shut the door.

We all agree now that we'll only do our own parents' houses, if at all, and that it's best if we don't sit on the wall at the end of the garden, in case Hilary's father sees us together from the Gibsons' back window. Hilary explains that her father is from Antigua, and they have strict laws about 'things like that', so it's not his fault.

'It's okay with me, though, Steph. I know you only dress like a boy because you want to be like George, and you want all the freedoms that boys have.'

I smile and nod. But I'm not certain, when she says it, that it has ever really been about the same freedoms as boys at all. It's been more like a disguise, and I'm not at all sure I want to wear it any more.

Chapter Fifty-One

And so it Begins

Gareth moved away not long after we started secondary school. I felt a great sense of loss. I know I probably didn't mean so much to him, but I remember him helping me down the rope when I got stuck, playing pirates, and unravelling me and calling me 'wife' in a den we had made in the Forest of Dean. Tender moments of friendship that shone out in my childhood, moments that helped me to move away from fear. But everything is changing, and there are more things to look forward to.

When my period starts, I am twelve. I'm ready for it. Girls in my class have started already, and I'm joining a motley band who mostly speak positively about the event. *Just think*, Cathy and Claire tell a girl who has written in to the problem page of *Jackie* magazine, worried about menstruation, *what this means is that one day, you'll be able to have a baby of your own.*

When I whisper to my mother, before church on Sunday, that my period has started, she whisks me upstairs. She seems cross.

'Are you sure?'

'Yes.' I show her the bloodied pants I have stuffed in a drawer, with wads of toilet tissue stuck to them. She sighs and takes me to the bathroom.

'I don't see why you have to start now. I was thirteen when I started.' She says this as if I have been wilfully inconsiderate.

'Sorry.'

She huffs and puffs. She opens a linen bin, and from underneath a pile of towels she brings forth a sanitary belt and some pads. It is the oddest contraption, and I simply can't picture my mother wearing something like this. When I put it on, it barely covers my pubic hair. It's like the tiniest of teeny-weeny bikini bottoms. There are plastic straps with poppers on them, which click shut around holes in the top end of the pad. On top of all of it, I am to wear a clean pair of pants. I stare down at myself, feeling vaguely kinky. Again, the image of Mum wearing this is a bewildering one. She tells me that I must change the pad at least four times a day, and always before bedtime. I am to take them around with me in a paper bag, and when I have used one, I tear it into four pieces and put it down the toilet. I must always tear it first, or it will block the system. I must on no account place the offending article in a bin – even if there is a public bin in the toilet for this purpose.

'Why not?'

Foolish question. She pulls her most extreme face of disgust. 'A bloodied sanitary towel, that's been ... down there ... festering away in a bin!'

I nod.

'I just can't believe you've started a whole year earlier than I did.' I am clearly a disappointment to her. She tuts and shakes her head. She sighs some more.

'Just think, though, Mum ...' I am determined to cheer her up, to look on the bright side. 'This means that one day I'll be able to have a baby of my own.'

'Don't go getting any bright ideas.'

'No, I mean, I'll be able to have children *one* day.'

She rolls her eyes. 'I wouldn't be too pleased with yourself if I were you! You're stuck with this curse now until you're fifty.'

Crushed, I don't feel at all pleased with myself. But I refuse to be ashamed. This is a natural thing, the other girls have said – *Jackie* magazine has said – this is just growing into a woman. I can't stop it now. Cutting my hair short like a boy can't stop this. Nothing my mother can say, no amount of objections or expressions of disgust, nothing can stand in the way of my relentless journey into womanhood. And I suddenly know, with more certainty than I've had about anything, that I don't want it to. I am becoming a woman. I like it.

I give it one more shot as I leave for church with Jonathan and Dad. She stays behind lately to get the dinner ready and do chores, and he lets her. I lag a little behind my father and brother, and on the doorstep I turn. I'm so desperate to establish a mother–daughter bond that I smile at my mum and wink. 'Our secret.'

In all the many ways I will try to know my mother, I can't forget her response to my attempt at complicity: she scowls and rolls her eyes. I attempt to adjust my features to a look of nonchalance, and turn to walk casually away. This is quite hard to pull off with a dragging foot and a small mattress between my legs.

A few days later, Mum says something to me that fills me with horror and shame. She needs to tell me about washing more often, as I'm growing up. Until then, we have only been allowed one bath a week, on a Sunday. That's how my parents have been brought up, and it's no different in our family. If I had wanted more baths, I would have been refused them. But on this particular day she decides to tell me how to wash my private parts every day with a shower hose attached to the bath taps. Instead of approaching the matter delicately, she chooses to put it like this: 'Dad says you smell. You'd better start washing more often.' She screws up her nose. 'I'll tell you how.' Suddenly, this reference to my father speaks volumes about how she sees me: not as a daughter who needs some cherishing by her mother, but as a rival. I am, of course, mortified.

I grow my hair out, I wear skirts and dresses, I make myself clothes that Mum won't let me buy. My friends all have a 'clothes allowance', but my parents are avidly against this. Or rather, Mum is avidly against it, and Dad doesn't want to get involved. One thing I can't make is a bra, and Mum says I can't have one. By the time I turn thirteen, all my friends are wearing a bra. I beg her to let me have one. But she holds the purse strings. I don't have a clothes allowance. I cannot have a bra.

I become increasingly humiliated, changing for games and wearing a sleeveless vest under my shirt. Some of the girls smirk. Most are not unkind. We understand each other's anxieties at this time of great change. I feel a sort of sisterhood around me, cushioning me from the worst outrages. It is the one thing I won't let go of at home. I beg Mum for a bra, but she is adamant: 'I didn't have a bra until I was sixteen.'

The arguments spill over into family mealtimes, and one day Dad says, 'Can't you just let her have one?'

To which Mum retorts, appalled: 'She's only got a couple of pimples!'

She lets me have one, begrudgingly, about six months later. I am thrilled. I'm becoming a woman. This is who I am, and she can't stop me any more. I embrace my womanhood, and life just keeps on getting better.

The last thing I expect is for Dawn Webster to turn up.

Chapter Fifty-Two

Filled In

They start building on the railway cutting in 1971. It is filled in with rubble ready to be turned into one of the many housing estates with uninspired designs and identical streets named after flowers or birds or famous men. Not famous women. There are no famous women yet. Not enough for a housing estate, anyway.

She hasn't been buried or anything. She was found at the bottom of an old well. It seems that Mr Man was right about that side of the railway having been the grounds of a grand house. Some of the land was sold off to make the railway a century before, and there was a well that has been covered over with two slabs of limestone. As the years have passed, the stone has become eroded and covered in undergrowth, and one initial theory was that a girl had stepped onto the centre of it and the slabs had caved in, sending her to the bottom of the deep shaft. Another theory is that someone dumped her there, already dead. Some people even speculate that the slabs have been upended for years, and that it may have been a childish prank gone wrong. Another child may have pushed her and failed to report it. Of course, I am interviewed again, but no new light can be shed on it.

I can't help wondering (although I try not to) what the body of a nine-year-old girl looks like after five years down a well. Has she been under nine feet of water – as they think – all that time? Or was the well dried up when she was dumped there? I know they've identified her as Dawn from a shoe, and from a remnant of cloth from her underwear. But what if it isn't her? What if it's another girl with Woolworths shoes and pants? Clearly, it's not a place much frequented by anyone. It wasn't until the diggers came in to level out the railway cutting that the well was even discovered.

I am just fourteen years old, bubbling with hormones and desire. It's a warm afternoon in April as I trail down Napier Road with my home-made denim school bag over one shoulder. So cool. I am at that age where I watch myself. I tread self-consciously with my trendy, centre-parted hair, slouching down the road in my over-short skirt, my collar unbuttoned and my tie loose. I affect a nonchalant look, although no one is watching or cares. And nonchalant is tricky with a trailing foot. Except that on this particular day, someone *is* watching. I'm not aware of him until I'm halfway down the road, when I suddenly see him standing outside our gate in the crescent. He is pacing back and forth, as if he's waiting for someone. Obviously not for me. Even from a hundred feet I can see he's gorgeous. He has dark curly hair and a beard, like Cat Stevens. He's wearing a purple corduroy jacket and black loons. He has his hands in his pockets, and he slouches. By fifty feet I am in love with him. At thirty feet he looks up at me and watches my approach. He leans back on our garden wall and our eyes meet. I will have to walk right up close to him to get through our gate.

'Excuse me,' he says. His eyes are a startlingly lovely blue. I am going to let him whisk me away to live in sin in his bedsit. We'll write novels together and go on marches for peace. He'll play the guitar and put a romantic picture of the two of us on his album cover. 'Do you know where I might find Stephanie Townsend?'

'That's me!' Too eager. Too eager by far.

'Well, Stephanie, perhaps you can help me?'

Of course I can help him. I'll do anything to help him. He sits down on the wall. Fortunately, it is the small bit of wall to the left of the gate, which has the privet hedge behind it, blocking out any view Mum and Dad might have of him.

'How's that?' I'm pleased with this. A little less eager.

He pats the wall beside him, and I sit down like a shot. I can smell the cigarette smoke from him, I'm that close now. His purple sleeve brushes up against my school shirt.

'The thing is, Stephanie, I'm just starting out in a new job and – oh' – he looks across at me – 'oh God, what amazing hair you have!' Then he *touches* it. He *strokes* my hair. We'll make love every night under the stars all summer. He'll read *Lady Chatterley* to me and poetry he's written, inspired by my hair. 'Anyway, as I was saying, I've started this new job, working for the *Gloucestershire Echo*, and they've sent me out to get a story on the Webster girl. Now, obviously, I know you probably won't be dead keen to talk about this' (he sees my expression change), 'but I just need to come up with something – something that hasn't been said before, you know?'

I look at his dreamy blue eyes and feel so disappointed. I will remember those eyes. I can smell the sweet sweat off him now. He wants to look good in his jacket even though it's far too hot for it. Maybe he is for real. Maybe he can be on my side. But Mum has told me so many times, 'Don't say anything to journalists. Not even one word. Journalists twist things. If anyone comes round asking questions, say you're sorry but you have nothing to say.'

'I'm sorry,' I say. I slide reluctantly off the wall.

'Wait! Look . . . just, you know, did you have any idea where she was?'

'No.'

He puts his hand on my arm. Tenderly, it seems. I dare to hope. But then he says, 'Stephanie, come on, did you have a fight five years ago? Did you accidentally push her?'

'*No!*'

I shake him off and shove open our gate, tears pricking my eyes as I run up the path.

Well, Mum was right, of course. The next day the headline to the local newspaper reads:
'STEPHANIE TOWNSEND DENIES MURDERING SCHOOLFRIEND'.
I'll never trust a journalist again.

About six months after that, I bump into Mr Man.

It's on Cheltenham Promenade, and I'm still fourteen. A cold, bright day in autumn, the impressive tree-lined walkway is dappled in sunlight. I am bending down to pick up a conker. It has just fallen; the prickly shell has split open and the conker has bounced out onto the pavement, shiny and new. I'm vaguely aware of someone sitting on a bench, set back from the wide pavement, and when I stand up, I see that he's looking at me. His hair has receded a little more, but otherwise he looks the same.

I smile.

'Stephanie?' His face breaks into pleasure, then. 'I would hardly have recognised you. You've got rid of your long hair.'

'Yes. It's growing out, though. It was very short before.'

I walk over to him and perch on the bench. There are plenty of people around, but no one knows either of us. It doesn't seem to bother him. We sit like that for a few seconds in sunlit silence.

'You look . . . so grown up,' he says.

'I'm fourteen.'

I might have said, years ago, that I was a teenager now. This was how I imagined it would be one day, one day when we would be a proper couple. It doesn't seem important any more. He is just a middle-aged man, sitting on a bench in the sunshine.

'You're a proper young woman.' He feasts his eyes on me, then looks down at his shoes. 'Are you still in Shepford?'

'Yes. I go to the grammar school nearby. I was just here meeting some friends.'

'Of course.'

'You live here now?'

'Nearby.' He doesn't want to tell me. Does he think I would pester him? I do have lots of questions for him, but they're not the sort I can ask him. He puts the tips of his stained fingers together. 'I couldn't stay there. Not after . . .'

'No. I understand. I felt terrible. I wished you'd said goodbye. I understand that you couldn't, though.'

'No . . . They interviewed me again, you know. A few months ago. When they found Dawn.'

'Yes. Me too.'

'It's okay, though. There's no new evidence.'

'No.' I pick at the paint on the bench. What does he mean? Both of his sentences are fine, but together they seem suggestive. Do I want to know what they suggest? Perhaps I do. But perhaps I don't. 'So . . . what are you doing now?'

'I work as a plumber.'

'I see. Good.' I want to go. I want to meet my friends, but I don't want to hurt his feelings. It's hard to believe I was in love with this man once, that I was devastated when he didn't see a future for us together. 'How's Goldie?'

'I'm afraid she passed away in February. She was twelve. It's not bad for a dog.'

'Oh, I'm sorry. I'm so sorry—' I don't know how to do grief. It terrifies me. I see my father's twisted face while polishing shoes, Mrs Webster's hands wringing mine.

'Here.' I hand him my horse chestnut. 'A lucky conker.'

'For me?'

I have to take his hand. It's like holding a bunch of bendy carrots. I place the conker in the palm, which is cool, and trembles slightly. He studies it. 'It's the same colour as your hair.' Then he looks at me directly. I think he might reach out and touch my hair, but he simply turns the conker over in his fingers, gently stroking it. 'Your Pre-Raphaelite hair.'

The words hang softly in the air, and his fingers might as well be stroking mine, for the memory of his skin is seconds away.

The moment stretches away into the past and into the woods where wood pigeons once sang to each other by a burbling stream, where I once felt I mattered to someone, where I was special.

'*There* you are!'

Two of my schoolfriends are walking up the Prom towards me. I fly off the bench, too suddenly by far. I turn. 'Goodbye,' I say, hurriedly.

'Goodbye, Stephanie. It was lovely to see you again.'

And I feel he means it. Really means it. I don't ask myself why that matters to me. I am off down the Prom with the girls, only embarrassed that he most definitely would have heard one of them saying to me, with mock horror, as we walked away, 'Who was *that*?'

Chapter Fifty-Three

Fine Words

I suppose it is inevitable that I should choose to study psychology for my degree, when I look back now. And Simon is the first man I really notice at university. It's during my second year, in an Experimental Psychology lecture. His eyes catch mine and rest on me long enough that I have to look down at my notes. Every time I look up, he seems to catch the movement and looks at me again, so directly that I can't pretend it's nothing. In the end, I only trust myself to look up when I can hear the squeak of his pen on the whiteboard. With his back turned, I can observe his full head of dark, shaggy hair, his slender wrists, his long shoulder blades moving beneath a navy-blue shirt, and a corduroy jacket – also navy – slung over the back of his chair.

When the hour is up, he says, 'I have one or two useful books on this subject, if anyone would like some further reading material in preparation for the essay.' And, as he says it, he looks directly at me.

I'm not sure why I go to his office. I suppose he seemed to be inviting me specifically, and no one has ever paid me quite so much special attention before. Well, only one. He is my very own Mr Man, but I am nineteen and free as a bird, and he is twenty-seven and appears to want me.

'Oh,' he says, when I knock and he has called me in. 'It's you.'

He puts his pen down and sits back in his chair, putting his hands behind his head.

'I came about the books. Is there one still available?'

'Of course. Take a seat.'

He reaches for a shiny-covered book and talks animatedly about it for five minutes, giving me advice on what chapters are the most useful and how I should structure my essay. It is interesting. Everything he says, it's articulate and inspiring and, above all, it's aimed at me. I find I can engage with him and it's exciting.

'Look,' he says, leaning forward and snapping his ballpoint pen closed, 'it's been a long day and I feel like a drink . . .' At first I think he's bored with me now, but he adds, 'Do you fancy continuing this conversation at the student bar?'

Of course I do. Only when we get there, it's so packed that he reaches into his pocket for his car keys. 'How about we drive out to a pub somewhere? That okay with you?'

I have never been driven out to a pub somewhere. It turns out to be an idyllic village pub, and he has clearly been several times before. I ask for a half of cider because it's all I can think of. 'Dry or sweet?' I have no idea, so he buys me a dry one. After two halves my head seems a little adrift from my body, but only slightly. We talk and talk, and everything he says is so fascinating, and everything I say is so fascinating to him, too.

We sit next to each other on an old oak settle, and beyond our table is a log fire. Our arms touch. He puts his hand on my shoulder when he asks if I'd like another drink, and when he goes to the bar, I miss him. I can't wait for him to come back and talk some more about cognitive dissonance.

We go back to his house and make love in his cold bed. We soon warm it up. We spend much of the next year in that bed, and in my third year I move in and become his non-paying lodger. We are living together. *Living in sin*, as my mother would say. If she knew.

He is intending to marry me, of course. Although now I think of it, he just talks about 'our future together', which is not the same thing. Which reminds me of another of my mother's sayings: 'Fine words butter no parsnips'. I didn't have a clue what this meant at the time. At the time being what age? From about eight or so and all through my teens. I think it was intended mostly for my father, whose impressive way with words had long ceased to be sufficient to butter any of her parsnips.

I cannot imagine what the impact of meeting Simon will be, how dramatically it will change the course of my life. I say Simon is the first man I meet at university, but that is not strictly true. I slept with three students before him, but they were more like boys. Certainly, they had no style. Decades later it would be called rape, but then it was just called a one-night stand (or, if you were unlucky, a two- or three-night stand). The first one I was too polite to say no to. The second one I was too polite to say no more than once to. The third one I stopped being polite and it ended in a scuffle, which I didn't win. With Simon, I manage to fall in love with him about half an hour before the issue of consent arises.

Chapter Fifty-Four

Slut

In the Psychology Department we have a set of undergraduate pigeonholes, with a box for each letter of the alphabet. They aren't used a great deal, except for students passing messages to each other, or letters from old friends who don't know your student address. Nonetheless, we are encouraged to check them every day, in case there's something urgent from the department or from one of our tutors. I begin to get small, functional-looking brown envelopes from Simon, and inside is always a piece of A4 with his familiar scrawl, suggesting assignations for the evening, or 'meetings' in his office. The notes are always witty and full of clever innuendo (or perhaps I just think they're clever). We spend most of my second year in this way, even after I've moved in with him. It's one of the most exciting moments of the day, checking to see if there's a little brown envelope. Then one day, while I'm busy with June exams, things go horribly wrong.

There's quite a lot in the pigeonhole this particular day, and I fish out the envelope with his familiar writing and go to get myself a coffee from the vending machine in the foyer. There's a comfy chair by the window, so I sit myself down and yield to the pleasure of this small gift. It goes something like this:

Dear Gorgeous,
I haven't been able to stop thinking of your elegant backhand since yesterday afternoon. (And your elegant backside.) I think

*you could teach me a thing or two. I'm frantic for the 'lesson'
you promised. We should meet up soon to practise this and other
moves. I think you'll enjoy my forehand. Let me know if you're
free this afternoon, about 2 p.m. The ball is in your court.*
    Advantage: Towers,
        Your anxious server XXX

I've tried many sports in my time, but tennis has always defeated me. There seems little point in dragging my foot across the hard court to duck and dive for a ball that I'm destined never to reach, let alone hit. I look at the envelope again. It's his writing. But it doesn't say 'S. Townsend', it says, 'S. Towers', who, as far as I know, is a psychology student in her final year. Sarah Towers. Blonde, tall, tanned, athletic. (Advantage: Towers.)

I fold the sheet of paper and make my way through a blur of liquid vision to the bus stop, and then home to the house I share with him. He isn't there. I sit down on one of the swivel chairs (he doesn't even have a sofa, but three swivel chairs his father got cheap from an office sale) and yield to a shuddering grief, trying not to rotate. It's my first broken heart. Although it isn't the heart, really, is it? The pain is felt there too, across the chest, but it's the stomach that seizes up first. The heaving, hollow stomach. The inability to eat anything or keep anything down. His sports shorts are slung over the back of one of the swivel chairs, waiting. My face aches with tears. My brain is in a total fug. For three hours I pack my clothes; I wail; I pace about; I swivel.

At last he comes home.

'What are you doing here?' He looks as shocked as I'd hoped he would.

'I thought I'd save you the bother of changing into your tennis shorts. Gorgeous won't be there.'

He looks trapped then, but it doesn't give me the satisfaction I'd thought it would. Instead I feel wounded all over again because he's unable to convince me it isn't true. Nothing he can say will convince me, of course, but I was holding out for the sort of mis-understanding that only ever happens in a Thomas Hardy novel. That shred of hope gone, I feel numb. I let him witter on about how it meant nothing and nothing happened and how I know how much he loves tennis (he has never played it as far as I know) and it was just a bit of a laugh. Can't I loosen up a bit? I must know he loves me, and only me.

I reveal that I have packed my bags and I'm moving into an empty room on campus (I know there is one: a girl on my course has moved in with her boyfriend in town but has paid for the room until the end of term). He does all the melodrama to my satis-faction, I suppose. The head in his hands, the pretend tears that I know he can squeeze out when he thinks of his grandfather eating his own belt in the trenches. He must be conjuring up his grandad now, because he does quite a good job with the damp eyes. It only increases my contempt for him. He even offers to drive me up to the campus, and I accept. As he helps me with my bags, I notice his sports shorts sticking out of his briefcase in the boot.

He tries to woo me back so hard, and the weather is so delight-ful, that a week later, I'm ashamed to say, I head off on a picnic with him. It's idyllic. We make love. (That's what they call it: love.) Basically, we have bad sex. His prize is an orgasm, mine is getting him back; although, as it turns out, that is no prize at all.

In the car on the way home I reach into the glove compartment for some mints I know he keeps there. I pull out a pretty object: some plaited lavender. I turn it over in my hand. It is the work of a woman.

'What's her name?' I say, handing him a Polo. I know Sarah Towers isn't the sort to plait lavender.

To give him his due, he puts on quite a convincing act with his 'Who?' but he can't maintain it. Especially when further investi-gation produces a dried-up daisy chain. I say investigation, I'm not investigating anything: it falls out of the glove compartment when I put the mints back in.

Within a week, he has confessed to one more undergraduate, one female history lecturer, a Belgian exchange student and two postgraduate research students. All while we were living together. *How?*

It barely matters now. I arrange for a room on campus for my final year. I shuck him off, and ignore his passionate pleas to have me back (I am apparently the only woman for him, he has just been sowing a few wild oats before we tie the knot). Even so, even then, I want to believe him, but I am just too humiliated to take him back again. I spend half of the summer teaching English as a foreign language to a few dozen disgruntled, crisp-munching French teenagers who practise their English swear words in museums and shopping arcades, and the other half spending the hard-earned money interrailing around France and Italy on my own. I take up with a Eurocommunist, wear Gramsci badges, go on demos in Florence and Avignon and come back covered in blistering mosquito bites, happy and liberated.

The following autumn, I am off the pill and determined to get a first in my degree. I have my room on campus and manage to have nothing whatsoever to do with Simon. I have been flattered by men throughout Europe; I am not going to fall for his slithery ways.

He visits my room in mid-October, one week into term, with a bottle of wine and begs me to marry him. *Marry?* Whatever next? I tell him I wouldn't marry him if he got down on bended knee with a massive diamond. He had his chance and he blew it.

It does briefly cross my mind how restorative it might feel to be sporting a ring among all those women he has seduced, but the image is quickly replaced by one of me turning into my mother. I see my sleep-deprived self, welcoming him home in the evenings with baby sick on my shoulder, a toddler on my hip poking its porridge-encrusted fingers into my hair as I prepare an evening meal one-handed. I can already feel contempt for myself at how hard I would try to stay attractive, can already count the infidelities I would be dealing with.

Although ... I also see my mother looking at the ring, and I think it would please her. This would be what my mother wants for me, and marriage to a university lecturer would definitely meet her approval. And I used to dream of a wedding. I picture myself in chiffon that would out-chiffon Dawn's ballet class tutus and Sindy's most elegant evening wear. But then I remind myself that Simon is no Sindy's Paul. He wouldn't hang about pleasantly in his trendy donkey jacket while I went to parties and chose between my umpteen outfits, pairs of shoes and skates. And also unlike Paul, more importantly, Simon has a willy. There would be other dolls on his list. No, it can't happen. I don't want to repeat my mother's life, however much it might make her proud of me. I refuse to be tethered.

I never want to be married, anyhow. Not any more. Not if I can't be a steamroller driver as well.

We sip the wine and I tell him about my summer. He tells me about his, how lonely he's been without me, what a massive mistake he's made. Maybe I enjoy it a bit, I don't know. Then he really does get down on one knee and produces a diamond ring in a little box. I feel sorry for him. I don't say yes. I really and truly have decided by now that I will never marry. I want more of the summers I've just had; I want to decide where I go, how I spend my money. And I want my own money, since I've seen what's happened to a generation of women without it. I want to get a good degree and earn for myself. Simon insists I can do that with him, and actually, I think he means it. He has always been a bit tight with money, and would've been happy with an extra income. And I know he would provide me with stimulating conversation, but somehow the whole thought of marriage is a massive great trap. I've had my own ball and chain with my dragging foot, and I'm only too aware that my dragging foot is itself the result of a husband's decision taking precedence over a wife's.

But Simon's disappointment seems genuine. And I do believe that in this moment – even though he would never be capable of fidelity or committed fatherhood – he wants me to say yes; he wants an imaginary happy future with me.

Perhaps because I feel bad about making him so sad, perhaps because we've both had too much wine (two glasses are enough to cloud my judgement), we have sex. It's probably the most tender sex I have ever had with Simon, and it results in the conception of Matthew.

My cycle is all over the place after coming off the pill, so I don't learn that I'm pregnant until it's too late to get an abortion. I don't know the first two weeks aren't real, that four weeks after conception you're already 'six weeks' pregnant. At eleven weeks I go to the doctor's for a test. I take a week to pluck up courage to make a decision. I'm not ready for a baby. I don't want Simon telling me he wants me to have it, and I don't want him to think I've got pregnant deliberately either. I don't want a baby, which could arrive right in the middle of my finals, but probably would come just after. I decide not to have it, and not to tell Simon. I'm pleased with my decision. I go back to the doctor to announce it. I'm twelve weeks and one day, approximately. Twelve weeks is the cut-off point.

I tell Simon. He says I've done it deliberately so that he'll marry me. (By this time, he's dating a research student who is stunningly beautiful.) I tell him I haven't.

'You knew you weren't on the pill!'

'I can't remember you asking!'

'Well, I'm not being a father to it. You can forget that. You had your chance with me, Stephanie. You're on your own, now.'

It's harsh, but I would've been more worried if he'd used it as a way to marry me.

A couple of days later he apologises, although his apology is worse.

'I'm sorry I gave the impression that … you know … that I

don't care. I do care, Steph, but the thing is, well ... Don't take this the wrong way or anything, but the truth is, I don't love you any more.'

I fold my lips in and nod slowly, closing my eyes like someone in a dentist's chair trying to pretend it doesn't hurt.

'I *did* love you. I mean, I really did ...'

(*Stop!*)

'But I just *don't* now. It would be dishonest of me to pretend that I did.'

I see then that the offer to marry him earlier had merely been a way to hook me in, because he thought he was losing me. He isn't used to losing. Instead he makes me feel like the loser. And that really isn't hard.

At Christmas, I see my parents and don't tell them, there being little in the way of a bump. At Easter, my mother looks at me when I take my coat off, glances at my left hand and calls me a slut. Her face is distorted with disgust. No one does disgust like my mother. Both parents ask who the father is, and I say it doesn't matter; I won't be marrying him. They ply me with questions, and Dad even asks if I've been raped, which makes Mum roll her eyes and tut, as if he's just finding a way, typically, to let me off the hook.

'If I'd come home from college like *that*,' she says, her face screwed up as if I were crawling with maggots, 'my parents would've thrown me out.'

I leave the next day. I don't go back until after Matt is born.

Chapter Fifty-Five

Item: **Conger eel made out of stuffed, knotted stocking.** ~~Keep~~. *Chuck.*

Fancy still having the daft old conger eel. I made it for Matt one wet afternoon when he was very small and he giggled his head off. Years later he made Katie giggle with it too. It's just a black stocking stuffed with soft material and knotted at one end. The big white eyes I sewed on with a black dot in the middle still look slightly mad. With little thought and a lot of assertiveness, Matt called him Congy. I wonder if, when I made it, another incident of knotting a stocking crossed my mind. Probably not, as I was far too happy to go rifling around in the past.

I'm still haunted by an incident that took place the year before that summer of Dawn's disappearance.

Dawn's father had put up a new garden shed himself (perhaps inspired by my mother) and the old shed now stood empty. It had a leaky roof, a crack in the windowpane, and some of the wooden slats were rotting; Dawn wanted to use it as a play house, and Mr Webster cleaned it out for her so she could.

This shed was heaven for me and Dawn. It was our cottage in the woods, a witches' den, a kidnapper's house, a castle for a princess. A moth-eaten blanket covered an old chest full of dressing-up clothes and became a bed; there was an upended tea chest for a table; a faded deckchair and a paint-spattered kitchen chair. We added pots and cups and potions, jam jars full of flowers and jam jars for drinking out of. I see now that this was my attraction to

Dawn. We shared a fantasy world, and within it – and only within it – my ideas counted as much as hers. It was an exciting, boundless world of passion, love, death and risk-taking. Plots were rambling and endless and alarming. It was an unspoken bond we had: when we met, anything could happen.

We had so much fun inventing stories around this shed, it was inevitable that Dawn's sister would want to join in.

'Can I play?'

'Get lost, Karen. This is *our* den.'

I liked the 'our', but I didn't like the way Dawn spoke to her sister, who at that point was only about three years old. I could see her tears welling.

'Can't she join in? She could be a dwarf.'

Dawn considered this, sensing the beginning of a long, whining wail about to reach her mother's ears. 'Okay. You can come and sit here.' Karen did as she was told. 'Drink this magic potion.' She offered Karen an empty jam jar, and Karen played along. 'Now you fall asleep.'

As soon as Karen closed her eyes, Dawn tied her to the chair with a skipping rope. 'We're wicked witches and you're our prisoner.'

Karen opened her eyes and looked alarmed. 'I don't want to be a prisoner!'

'You're a *princess*,' said Dawn, cunningly. Karen looked pleased. 'You're a princess, and the handsome prince is going to come and rescue you. But first, we are the wicked witches and we've captured you. Okay?' She said it so sweetly, any child would have been convinced.

As soon as Karen closed her eyes again, Dawn grabbed her arm and twisted her skin fiercely, giving her a Chinese burn.

'OW!'

'Don't worry. I torture you until the prince comes to rescue you.'

She gave her another horrible burn, and another and another, leaving her with bright red streaks on her soft arm. Karen started to shriek. Dawn clamped her hand over her sister's mouth, telling her to shut up. But I could see she was blocking Karen's nostrils off with the edge of her hand.

'She can't breathe!'

Dawn looked down at her sister with interest, and rammed her hand closer against her nostrils so that they were blocked off completely.

'Dawn!'

'You do it then!' She let go and glared at me. 'Quick, before she starts again.'

Karen was gasping for air, and then filled her lungs to start bawling. I bent down and told her the prince would be here soon, but she howled anyway. Dawn fished a stocking out of the chest, and handed it to me.

'Tie it round her mouth!' she commanded.

I stood there, afraid to disobey, as usual.

'Do it!' She clenched her jaw, and I did as I was told.

Of course, it was at that moment, as I was tying the knot in a stocking around her mouth, that Mr Webster, drawn by the howling, flung open the shed door to find his three-year-old daughter tied to a chair and being gagged – by me.

'What the hell are you doing?'

He pushed me roughly out of the way. 'Untie her!' he shouted at Dawn, and pointed his stumpy finger at me again. 'You! It's always you, isn't it? What's wrong with you?'

I could see Dawn releasing her sister and bending down to whisper something in her ear. My pulse was galloping and my face was hot. By the time he had finished with me, Mrs Webster was outside, asking what on earth was going on. For a moment I really thought she might take me in her arms and poppet me. But seeing her little one sobbing, she rushed at Karen and wrapped her arms around her on the lawn. 'What is it, poppet? What's the matter?'

'This girl here,' snarled Mr Webster, 'this *friend* of Dawn's, tied her to a chair and gagged her! Can you believe it? The daughter of a preacher! It's that weird God Squad you have to watch.'

'Geoff, please!' Mrs Webster held out Karen's red arm. 'Who did this to you, my poor poppet?'

Karen snivelled. She snivelled and hiccoughed and snivelled some more. Dawn and I held our breath. Karen folded her lips together and looked down at the grass. Then she raised her arm and pointed. She pointed at me, as I knew she would.

I was halfway up the road, sitting on someone's wall, too afraid to arrive home crying, when Dawn caught up with me.

'I'm sorry,' she said. 'I had to do it. Dad would've killed me if he'd known it was me.'

'He wasn't very nice to *me*.' Injustice had found my tongue.

'Yes, but he really would've *killed* me! You don't know my dad.'

I did, actually.

'I *had* to make her say it was you. I had to do it!'

'You didn't have to hurt her in the first place.'

Dawn wasn't used to me challenging her. I could see her nostrils flaring; she was straining to control herself. Then I spotted Mrs Webster standing at their gate, looking up the road at us. And I knew, from her anxious face, that she wasn't angry with me at all, that she was checking on Dawn's apology. This was my weakness. There was an unspoken tie between me and Dawn's mum. She didn't quite know how to deal with her either. Maybe I sensed that if her husband hadn't been there at the shed, she would've knelt down on the lawn and said, 'I'm sorry, poppet. I know that wasn't your idea.'

I must have glanced too long and too longingly at Mrs Webster, because Dawn saw that I'd seen her. There was an almost imperceptible sigh. And then the charm: 'Friends?' She held out a packet of Spangles for me. A whole packet.

'For me?'

Dawn smiled at me, winningly, and chewed the inside of her cheek. A bewildered moment passed, while I took in whose idea this was. She was still proffering the sweets. I took them.

To this day I can see the look of excitement in her eyes as she twisted her little sister's skin so tight. There was an opportunity and she took it. Dawn reacted to things quickly, angrily and without reflection.

Even so, when she fell that summer, getting out of the stream to tell me off, when her head hit the wet slab, when he came and . . . I should not have run away like I did.

Then again, maybe I had waited all my short life for Dawn's terrible death, for that definitive proof that I did not have to be the underdog, that I did not have to beg for crumbs.

I could have no idea of the price I would pay.

Chapter Fifty-Six

All is Forgiven

I am over eight months pregnant when I take my finals. The last paper is on Quantitative Research Methods, and I remember being desperate to empty my bladder for two thirds of it.

At some point during my pregnancy I learn that I might have trouble with delivery because of my history of polio. Apparently, as my mother informs me by letter, there is a risk that the disease and my subsequent gait means that my pelvic bones (especially my sacroiliac joint) might not have developed sufficiently, and that I might have an asymmetric birth canal, or one too narrow for normal delivery. She has researched it in detail, like she might research the construction of a shed. Caesarean section also poses dangers, because an epidural could lead to a recurrence of muscle weakness from which I might or might not recover. Post-polio syndrome has always worried my mother, it seems, but she has never mentioned it to me before. I am suddenly struck with fear for the future. Perhaps she's worried that she will have to bring up this child herself; perhaps she thinks it's my just punishment for being a slut. On reflection, though – and because it's so rare for her to write me a letter – I think it's her way of making sure I am prepared, and that I warn whoever is delivering the baby to take all possible precautions.

I have a normal delivery, although it takes twenty-three hours. I'm so afraid of setting off any new nerve or muscle damage that I refuse all pain relief. There are three shifts of midwives, and when the last shift changes, I am left alone for a few minutes. I don't even realise I'm alone, until suddenly I'm not, but the company is little Matthew, gazing up at me from the messy sheets. We take to each other straight away.

When I'm stitched and bathed, I lie on the bed facing Matthew and we study each other happily. My eyes keep blurring over with tearful, joyous love for him. We're interrupted by an announcement that I have visitors, and suddenly Mum and Dad are there, sitting either side of the bed. I have no idea how they'd heard. Perhaps they'd rung and rung and come to the obvious conclusion, but in any case, they have travelled up by train to see their new grandchild. As soon as Mum picks him up, her face fills with love, and all my fears of being shut out for ever for being a slut evaporate. My mother is pleased. I can't stop smiling.

From that moment, my parents dote on Matthew. Nothing is too good for him, they visit regularly, I visit them, they babysit whenever they can, they want all the news about him, and I love them for loving my boy.

Simon turns up at the hospital the day after the birth with his camera, and asks a nurse to take a few photographs of him posing with his son. 'My son! My son!' he wails, with tears in his eyes (is he thinking about his grandad in the trenches? Or is this a new source of tear production?) and picks him up high like a trophy. After that he shows no interest in him, and forgets all his birthdays apart from his second one, for some reason, when he buys him a pedal car.

When I tell my parents I've won a scholarship to study for a DPhil at Oxford, they are not supportive. 'You're going to be a perpetual student,' Dad says. 'Who's going to pay for it?'

'I'm funded. I've won a scholarship. It has money attached.'

'That'll soon run out. Get yourself a proper job. Look after your child.'

The exhortation to look after Matt is a low blow. It nearly

works. Then Mum comes out with the desperate – and almost comical – 'No one will marry you!' This is a given, because, 'Men don't like clever women.' She may well be right.

'Perhaps I don't want to get married,' I venture.

'Of course you want to get married. Who's going to look after you?'

'Is that what you've been, Mum? "Looked after"?'

I shouldn't have said it. I wish instantly I could take it back. She sneers. She grinds her teeth. 'You think you know it all, don't you? Well, I'm a darned sight better off than you'll ever be. There's not many men want to bring up someone else's child. You've narrowed your field, there, for certain.'

It feels curiously like the bra incident all over again. *You'll have what I had.* And also reminds me starkly of Dawn: *No one's going to want you! Look at you.*

I so nearly topple. This generation of women may have had a completely different set of choices to their daughters, but they have successfully passed on many of the values. The sense of being unfulfilled without marriage – not sex, but marriage – runs deep. We all struggle with it. I think of me and Dawn plotting our futures with Gareth and marriage and children and his job and our *own* exotic jobs. Somehow, higgledy-piggledy, it worked. We didn't see how it couldn't. How we might have to drop our own dreams in favour of the main breadwinner. But then again, if no one is going to want me, I might as well do my own thing.

I change my mind several times before I accept the scholarship, which I have fought off forty-two other candidates to win. I apply to a postgraduate college, find outside accommodation, and manage to get my doctorate within three years. I am paid a little extra as a research assistant on various projects that I can do from home, and manage to afford babysitting twice a week. Matt hardly ever leaves my side. We spend a lot of time feeding ducks or looking at ancient skeletons and stuffed animals in the Pitt Rivers Museum.

When he is very small, I read all the books I can find on good mothering. I compile a list of things to remind myself how to be a good mother and stick it on the fridge, but it's too long; also, my parents will see it when they come to visit, and I don't want them to think I am having to try so hard. So I whittle it down to five things, and write them on a piece of card with his footprint on it that I use as a bookmark in my diary:

I love you
I see you
I am here for you
I will keep you safe
I delight in you (I'm glad you're here)

I look at it every day. I memorize it like a student sitting an exam.

It's a piece of cake: I read him stories, I encourage him, I get down on the floor with him and join in his games, I hug him, I tell him I love him, I listen to him, I giggle with him, I console him, I cherish him. It isn't difficult. It's a joy. But once, when he's still very small, he grabs my arm and I spill a glass of water all over an academic paper I'm writing, and I find myself saying, 'Shit! Look what you made me do!'

'Soy,' he says, a look of terror in his eyes. 'Maddy spill a water – soy, soy.'

'Sorry isn't …' I am appalled with myself. I apologise for frightening him. We clean it up together with kitchen towel and I thank him. I thank him for saying sorry, too. 'Well done, Matty.' He gives me a hug.

Mum was right, to an extent. A lot of the clever men prefer dumb-but-pretty women. Those men that are too smart for that are also too smart for my neediness, or else just see me coming. I have a lot of sex: mostly bad, some good. It seems that many of them have learnt their sexual prowess through rugby club songs and girls too afraid to say '*Ow!*'. I have a few relationships that follow a predictable pattern of my being a pleaser and making excuses for bad behaviour. There is one wonderful man who seems to truly love me, and likes Matt too. His name is Knut and he specialises in the study of seaweed and its properties. He is shy and kind. Not unlike Mr Man, only younger. He even says once – because he's Norwegian and enjoys collecting English idioms – that I knock his socks off. But thinking of Mr Man suddenly only makes me think of relationships that are destined not to work.

I picture Knut living in a little pink or yellow shiplap house by the side of a harbour; his mother knits him chunky sweaters in a rocking chair and his father throws wood on the log-burning stove and cooks up some of the fish he's caught that day in his trawler. In fact, Knut told me, his father works at a meat-packing factory and his mother works in a supermarket. But still, there is a log-fire-chunky-knit homeliness to Knut that can't be spoilt. I take to wearing a fur-hooded parka; in the fantasy in which he takes me home to meet them, I want to fit in. I want them to like me.

But of course I sabotage the relationship. I tell myself it's because he's going back to Norway soon, and I'll only get hurt, but I know there's a more complex thing going on. He actually asks me to marry him, and I say no.

'You know what I think, Stephanie?'

'No. What do you think?'

'I think you can't bear to be a member of a club that actually wants you as a member.'

Maybe he's right. Maybe I have become so comfortable with the feeling of longing for something I can't have that it has become preferable to having it. I know all about Bowlby's attachment theory, and 'the self-perpetuating quality of our internal world'. Why, having studied behaviour so intently, I can't see this pattern in myself, will baffle me in years to come.

Not long after that, I move back to my old university town in the West Country to look for a potential school for Matt, and find myself a part-time job in clinical psychology. It will have to do for now, but I keep looking for something more full-time. My parents do not congratulate me on becoming Dr Townsend.

Chapter Fifty-Seven

An Independent Woman

The flat I find is a picture of neglect. The sofa is balding, the radiators temperamental and the stringy carpets held together by dust and dead woodlice. The place seems like an old person in need of care: every bit of it thinning, spluttering, leaking and prone to the cold.

Even so, I feel I have everything I want. I enjoy my work, and I love spending time with Matt. But as soon as he starts school, I find myself bereft. The part-time job doesn't lend itself to friendships. There is no 'happy hour' after work, or if there is, I have to go and pick up Matt. There are occasional social events which I find hard to attend, as they require a babysitter. Eventually I hire a babysitter every Friday, and start to go out on my own. I go to the cinema and find I can't cry at the sad bits or laugh at the funny stuff in front of people. I imagine I would look like a madwoman laughing to myself. I go to the theatre, milling around in the interval, trying to look as though I'm searching for my friend.

Sometimes I look out of the window of my flat at the other houses in the street. All along it rectangles of amber light glow warmly and announce other lives being lived just yards from my own. I imagine sitting on the sofa of the family at number nine, and listening to their chaotic family dialogues; or else I shadow the beautiful young woman at number eleven, follow her clicking up the steps in her heels and watch her prepare her couscous while chatting on a phone propped in the crook of her neck. I imagine the dinner parties thrown by the chiropodist and his wife at number thirteen, and see myself making interesting conversation with some of the guests; I picture a man with dark hair called Jerome or Angus or Geraint offering me a lift home (ignoring the fact that I would have to get out after a few yards). Sometimes I'm so lonely I have romantic fantasies about the man who sells ice cream to Matt from his van on Sundays, or the carpenter who replaced the rotten wood in my window frames, or Matt's head-master with suede elbow patches. And there are days when I want to grab hold of my neighbour – a single man who works in town planning and who occasionally smiles at me on the stairs – and beg him to take me away with him. Anywhere.

Eventually I write to Knut to see how he's doing, and say I may be coming out to Norway for academic purposes. He writes back a cheery letter, and hidden in the friendly news is one line telling me he is engaged to a Swedish endocrinologist now, and she is expecting his baby.

There, I have allowed myself to get hurt anyway. I cry myself to sleep for three nights in a row. I find an old jumper of his and wear it round the flat, arms swinging below my wrists (he had long arms). One night I stuff two pillows into it and hug his large, chunky-knit torso, hurt by the fact that his arms don't hug me back, but merely flop about limply. After a week or two I admit to myself that it would have been hopeless anyhow. I wouldn't take to short dark days and long sunny nights; my parents – who have to steel themselves for a journey by train – would never fly over to see us and they would miss Matt; and despite my initial envy of the Swedish endocrinologist, who I imagine in a shiplap house leaning her head on Knut's firm woolly chest, I know she will soon feel held down, pinned in place by the dazzling paperweight of motherhood. I try not to tell myself that at least she will have someone to share it with.

I do make friends: I get to know some of the women at the

school gates. Five of us go on little excursions to parks and farms and on day trips to the seaside. They all have husbands or partners, but we all have each other. We exchange funny anecdotes and recipes and intimacies. We roar with laughter and sympathise with hugs. Whatever our different backgrounds and qualifications, we sit on a beach, looking out at our children, and know that we are all held in a quiet orbit around them, wherever they are, whatever they are doing.

It's so easy to love Matt. And the more I love him, the more it hurts that Mum has found it so difficult to show me affection. What has helped me to push that thought aside is the pleasure I feel in seeing her with him. She is a wonderful grandmother, although she still isn't quite finished with me.

My flat is sparsely furnished but neat – apart from Matt's scattered toys – and I am house-proud. Before their visits I vacuum thoroughly, scrub the countertops and put Matt's toys away in toy boxes. But she will flick the pad of her index finger over my windowsills, examine the thinnest grey film of dust left on her skin and give an exasperated shrug. When I put the kettle on for a tea or a coffee, she'll pick up the chosen mugs and wash them, as if they aren't already clean.

'Mum,' I protest, on more than one occasion, 'my mugs and cups are clean. I've washed them.'

'Oh yes, they're *your* idea of clean.'

'Kath,' my father says, helplessly; and she'll clean them anyway, scrubbing as hard as she can with washing-up liquid and a sponge scourer she will have brought with her. She won't use my washing-up brush, but dunks it in bleach and insists on leaving it there overnight. Whenever she comes, she leaves me a set of clean scourers. When I put a meal in front of her, she frowns at it as if she is about to summon a waiter to say she's got the wrong order. Once she brought me a new duster. It's a bizarre bunch of acrylic strands on a stick, and looks a bit like a mauve party wig. I have used it a few times, under her supervision, to remove cobwebs from the corners of the rooms. I really don't give a toss. Spiders have to live somewhere. They're welcome to my corners. But it makes Mum happy – or triumphant. Either is okay.

Chapter Fifty-Eight

Item: **Faux-velvet cat collar, red.** *Chuck.*

Not long after Matt starts school, our old cat dies. Trevor is fifteen, and has to be put down after a squirrel bite became infected. We have no garden with the flat, but the neighbour downstairs lets us use his. So I dig a deep grave for him under a blossom tree, and make a headstone on which Matt paints his name. He solemnly sprinkles rose petals on top of the furry corpse, and we play 'What's New, Pussycat?' on the cassette player, because it's the only cat song Matt can think of, and he likes it.

Back in the flat, we put his collar and name tag on the mantelpiece, and have a takeaway. A wake, snuggled on the sofa with pizza.

'Would you like another kitten soon?'

Matt squishes his mouth to one side. 'Perhaps.' He munches on his pizza and swallows hard, his face full of concentration. 'But I'd rather have a brother or sister.'

'A brother or sister?'

'Yes. Is that okay? Can I have one?'

'Well . . . that's a little more complicated.'

'You just need a man's seed, don't you?' (I had told him as early as possible about the facts of life.)

'I suppose so. But the thing is, I don't really know any men who would give me their seed.'

He reaches for another piece of pizza. 'What about Grandad?'

'That wouldn't be a good idea.' On so many levels. (I haven't done genetics with him.) 'It has to be someone outside the family – for it to work.'

He sighs heavily. 'Well, we'll find a man.'

'Do you want a daddy, then?'

He looks thoughtfully at his pizza crust. 'No. Just you and me and a brother or sister – and a kitten maybe.'

I must look daunted, because he adds helpfully: 'I don't mind if it's a boy or a girl. We can have whatever you like.'

We cannot possibly guess at what a joy and a punishment she will be.

Matt doesn't give up. It's the one thing he wants that I can't give him. I've even considered sleeping with a random, pleasant man a few times and not telling him he's going to be the father of my child, but that seems too underhand to contemplate. There is an obvious candidate: a man I work with called Chris, who seems intermittently besotted with me – perhaps only when he can't find anyone else. He's a good egg, by and large. But when I try to picture a combination of my genes and his in the shape of a child, I find myself pulling faces and frowning so hard that my eyebrows ache. (I'm a great believer in subliminal messages.) Anyway, I imagine how I would feel, in that man's shoes, years later, stumbling upon a son or daughter I never knew I had – and might even have very much wanted.

One day when Matthew's five, and I'm picking him up from school, I bump into Simon. Although actually, it is Simon who bumps into me. He has been trying to find me at my flat because a friend of a friend said I was moving to Abergavenny. This is true. I have been offered a job at the hospital there, and I'll be properly using my psychology degrees for the first time. He joshes around with Matthew on the way home from school – who is amused to know that this is his father – and he takes us both out for a burger. Later, back at my flat, after Matthew's gone to sleep,

Simon explains his decision that I should not go to Abergavenny. It isn't fair of me to take his son away from him.

I should probably have laughed, but the more he talks, the more maudlin he becomes, until I almost believe he believes he cares. He has just been dumped by his latest girlfriend, and he seems to be looking for meaning in his life. We go to bed and make love. Well, we do it. We repeat the mistake the following week. The next month I move to Abergavenny with Matthew, newly pregnant.

I have a growing sense of unease with the next pregnancy. What if it's a girl? Will I be able to love her in the same way as I have loved Matthew? Although I know in my bones that I will, I am plagued with nightmares about unwittingly making her feel unloved. What if, with the best will in the world, I find myself parroting my mother's *Sorry isn't good enough* or *Crying is manipulative?* or *Look what you've done now?* or worse, *Don't be so filthy?* I'll have to make a determined effort not to be like my mother, while all the time respecting the way she loves Matthew. But most of all I'm afraid, if I have a girl, that Mum will treat her the way she has treated me.

Mum falls in love with her from the very first moment. I name her Katherine after her, but she'll be called Katie. Katie can do no wrong. My mother calls her 'sweetheart' and 'love' and 'little sausage'. She will never be a poppet-user, but Katie doesn't lack adoration from either of my parents. Gone is the prickliness around a little girl; coldness and jealousy and rivalry are totally absent. I begin to wonder if I imagined it all in my own childhood.

What we know, as psychologists, is still fairly limited, but there are accepted patterns. Small children are such tender little animals that they will attach themselves to the nearest available object that can provide comfort, relief or warmth; even if the object in question is hostile, if the solace is imaginary. If that's all there is, then it will have to do.

The tragedy with a cold, emotionally absent mother is that it provides the child's blueprint for all later close relationships. Many is the young woman (or man) who unconsciously seeks out and attaches herself to the unloving, careless friend or lover. Yes. Friend. Or lover. Or both.

I have to get it right with Katie. And it seems I do. It is easy. And Mum and Dad and Matthew love her too. What can possibly go wrong?

Chapter Fifty-Nine

My Girl

Although my greatest fear has been that I will somehow, unaccountably, not be able to love Katie in the way I love Matthew, it disappears the moment I hold her; but there is still a nagging anxiety that I won't know how to love her well as she grows up. I consult my list again: *I love you; I see you; I am here for you; I will keep you safe; I delight in you.* I become so worried that I mention it to a work colleague, a child psychologist of some standing.

'The crucial thing is that you know how you *don't* want to mother. That's as important as having the path all mapped out in detail. It's your path to choose, but you know which one you are definitely *not* taking.'

It all makes a lot of sense. And there is no husband to spoil Katie or vie for her loyalty. But still, sometimes, when I'm exhausted and she whines for attention, a little voice pulls at my sleeve and says '*I* would never have got away with that', and the drive to ignore my daughter will battle with the desire to pick her up and hold her close. Sometimes I resent her ever so slightly for reducing my time with Matthew. This is my quiet time reading to Matthew; how can she want feeding now? This is when I play with Matthew; why is she squawking? How can I possibly give him all the attention he needs with another child to consider? What if this hardness in me grows? I see it like an indoor plant, spilling over the mantelpiece and sending out its leathery leaves on winding

288

stems to every part of our house, putting down suckers, growing thick and woody until it is impossible to cut back.

But Matthew is my ally. He never seems to be jealous of Katie, and – perhaps mindful of his desperation to have a sibling – he is always very attentive to her. As soon as she can sit up on the carpet, he gets down with her and helps her build towers, makes her stuffed animals talk, or shows her how to stroke our new cat who, as soon as she can talk, she will name Gavin Baguette. She has the most infectious giggle, and I can't help cuddling her. She loves cuddles, and I buy her a bear to hold at night. She calls him Peter, when she can talk, and she loves him with the same fervour I loved Trevor. I often hear her chuntering away to him after the light's out. I make him little outfits and we make up stories about him together. She is an inventive storyteller. Peter can do almost anything, and she draws alarmingly funny pictures of his adventures with a dolphin that Mum made for her. The love I feel for Katie and Matt is boundless. I know it's going to be okay. It will all be okay.

And it is the oddest thing, and perhaps the most wonderful of all: how my mother dotes on her grandchildren. On both of them equally. It's as if her affection – like the crockery she has been saving for 'best' in the cupboard – is unlocked at last for her grandchildren. Now it's allowed to be manhandled, chipped, cracked and covered in cake and jam for the sheer joy of using it.

She still draws her finger across my mantelpiece for dust, re-washes my coffee mugs and inspects my cutlery for smears, but I have never seen her show the slightest slither of disgust or contempt or anger towards Katie. I do try to keep an eye on them when they're together, hovering for any sign of repulsion or mention of germs, but it seems that her granddaughter doesn't trigger the same strange fury that her daughter did. She makes her pretty outfits and toy animals with endearing faces (the furry dolphin is a special favourite); she makes her a cot out of pinewood, and builds her a doll's house with roses stencilled around the door; she loves to brush her hair, and as soon as she can stand on a chair, she has Katie's hands in a bowl of flour and butter, 'helping' her to make cakes. Dad is the one who reads to her and tells her stories. But he never mentions Jesus or God or David or Goliath. He is content to read from the picture books we have, and to make appropriate animal noises, which makes her squeal with joy. He will bounce her on his knees and throw her down between them until she's hot with laughter, her fat peal of giggles ringing out through every room in the house. On these occasions, Mum will laugh too. There isn't a trace of a sneer, no thought of winding round little fingers.

They come to visit one weekend in June, and I pick them up from Abergavenny station. We all go on a picnic, squashed into my Mini with Katie in her car seat in the front. (Dad still doesn't drive, and Mum still does what she's told, too exhausted to dig up old arguments.) We drive through the luscious country lanes, which are swollen with leafy trees and wild flowers. We pull up on a grassy patch of land across a cattle grid onto an open common, where sheep and wild horses are grazing. I say 'wild', but they're probably simply roaming free, like the sheep.

We lay out our rug and all the picnic things. The hedgerows are a frenzy of birdsong. Katie, at nineteen months old, toddles around the picnic rug, stopping to listen to the magical sounds, then starting up again, trying to locate them, a look of wonder on her sweet face. I feel so relaxed. I know Mum will be watching out for the children, and it gives me a rare moment of total peace. I lie back in the grass and savour it. There are no cars on the quiet country road. There is a stream nearby, and the sound of it is like the Dingle, burbling happily under the mating dragonflies.

When we've finished our food, we wander over to see the animals. The sheep are indifferent, nibbling away earnestly, and only bolting off if we come too close. The horses are more interested, especially as Mum has brought the remains of a loaf of bread to feed them. There are two foals, and about three or four horses. Katie is overwhelmed by the foals. 'Baby horsey!' she says, pointing her small, soft finger. 'Baby!'

Mum explains that we have to be careful, because mummy horses don't want anyone touching their babies. We can feed the mummies, but not the babies. 'Like this.' She holds out her hand flat for the horse to eat from. Katie is delighted when it peels back its hairy lip and snaffles up the bread. She reaches out her hand and Mum shows her how to softly stroke the side of its face. Katie offers her hand with bread on it, nervously pulling away when the horse breathes its hot breath on her palm. She tries again, and looks about at us all with a big grin when she's successful. 'I feeded horsey! I feeded it!'

She had started speaking at thirteen months. Not counting 'Mama', her first words were 'Matt' and 'cat', both applied to the correct individuals. By fifteen months, she could knock out a few expressions, like 'Oh, God!' and 'Shit!', for which I must take full responsibility. 'I feeded horsey' is a wonder. A proper sentence. Use of a past tense. What stories she will tell and write one day. We are all enthralled.

And I am happy. I am happy they love her so utterly, and happy they come to visit often. Mum will always bring a pointed gift for me, like a bottle of bleach or antibacterial spray. At this stage, my house is still clean and tidy, by anyone else's standards, but she'll tell me I need to clean my telephone or my photograph frames, and the next time she comes she'll make a show of doing it for me. My housekeeping skills may have been hammered, but my sluttishness is never mentioned. Nor do they ever say they are proud of me. But I know they're pleased with the grandchildren I have provided, despite the disgusting life of sin that has engendered them. I feel this is now considered to be merely the error of my ways, which no doubt God will forgive, if I ever find it in myself to repent. I never do find that need, despite what happens next.

*

We return to that picnic spot each summer, when the weather is fine enough. More often than not, the horses aren't there. They seem to appear about the same time every year, in June, for a few weeks, which makes Mum suggest they probably belong to travellers. And it's in June, when Katie is four and Matt ten, that we see them again for the last time.

Once more, Mum takes Katie's hand and walks her over to them with Matt. She gives the children half an apple each to feed to them, which they hold out in the flat palms of their hands.

'It tickles,' says Katie, delighted as ever, and then makes up a story about the horses, which she tells us throughout the picnic. They have names like Mrs Conker, David Longjohn and Richard Chomper, and they gallop throughout the country, putting things right, rescuing people and having adventures. There are all sorts of romances, births and marriages – in that order, although Mum doesn't flinch – and the odd death, from which the horse in question is revived and lives to have another escapade. Plot twists abound, endings never come. She chunters away with her mouth half-full as we munch on our sandwiches. Mum doesn't tell her not to talk with her mouth full. The sun is hot, but quite a strong wind blows up and we start to put things away.

'What do you want to be when you grow up?' Dad asks Matt.

'A builder,' he says, decisively.

'And what about you, young lady?' he asks Katie.

'A farmer. I'll have lots of sheep and horses and bears and dolphins.'

'That might not be very nice for the dolphins,' says Matt. 'They need the sea to live in. It's cruel otherwise, because they need lots of space.'

Katie frowns. 'My farm will be by the sea. And all the fields for the animals will be very, very, very big. *Huge*. And they'll have lots to eat.'

I wrap my arms around her. 'That sounds like the best farm in the world,' I say. 'Can I come and visit?'

'You can live there too. And Matt and Gran and Grandad.'

I feel the soft skin of her cheek against mine, the firm, wriggly, perfect body in her red cotton dungarees. I feel blessed that I can live with her on her wacky farm.

The horses wander over towards us as we put things in the car. Matthew grabs a remaining sandwich to feed them, and Katie goes with him to watch. I reflect on how far we've come, the five of us. The fact that we should be sitting here, with my parents doting on their two illegitimate grandchildren, would have been unimaginable when I was younger. At this moment, on this June day, I couldn't be happier. There is the strangest stillness and silence around us, cushioning us from the rest of the world. The next thing I remember is Katie hurtling through the air towards the road. She is like a very small acrobat doing a backward somersault, but she spins around several times, then bounces back up in the air like a rag doll. She has hit the bonnet of a car, and after the bounce she comes down with the most terrifying sound I shall ever hear: a resounding crack. On the tarmac of the road.

There have been no cars! What are the chances of a horse kicking her and a car coming along at that precise moment? It isn't my car. It's the car of a young doctor out on call. He flings open his door and is distraught. But we are deaf to his apologies, to his hair-wrenching, to his offers of help. We only see the dark red blood pooling around Katie's head, some thirty feet away.

It is a massive haemorrhage. She dies thirty-six hours later. All the stories she would tell us one day still germinating inside her.

Chapter Sixty

Hold Me

I should have all the tools available to me, the tools for grieving I talk about so much in my job. But what do I know of any of it, when it has to be put into practice? I go from huge surges of emotion to total numbness. I am good at the numb bit. I'm practised at shielding myself from pain, even though I know it's just parked somewhere else for now. Sometimes, it is all I can do to feed the cat and cook something for Matt. I have nothing left to give. I know how hard it is to be both the comforted and the comforter; I know all the theory by heart. And poor Matt gets such a raw deal when Katie dies. He has, after all, lost a little sister he had longed for, and has to tread carefully around a grief-stricken mother, his only source of solace. He must feel guilty at being the surviving child – he probably doesn't feel he is enough for me, despite everything I try to tell him.

I experience an overwhelming sense of failure, not being able to care for and protect the little girl I had expected to look after for years to come. I feel cheated of the chance to prove to myself that I could be a good mother to a daughter, and guilty that I should even care about that, and certain that it's a punishment for all I have done and not done. I keep thinking, if only I had suggested a different place to picnic, if only I had held her hand the whole time, if only she had landed on the grass. And those who would comfort me, Mum and Dad, both feel the same guilt – Mum especially. She is certain it was her fault for suggesting we feed the horses in the first place, and Matt thinks it was his fault for taking them the sandwiches on the day it happened, but I keep saying that nothing would have stopped Katie wanting to stroke them. It was just an accident. I knew that. She might have reached the age of ten and been run over by a bus; she might have been brutally attacked and raped as a teenager; she might have been stabbed by an aggressive lover or dealt a fatal, slow-wasting disease. But she flew into the air at the age of four, taking all her ungiggled laughter and surprising possibilities with her.

I keep bargaining with a god I don't believe in, to give me one more hour with her. One more cuddle. Oh, oh. One more cuddle in her little red all-in-one pyjamas. One more bedtime story. One more kiss on her fat, soft cheek. The things I bargain for with that god, but he doesn't listen. I keep thinking of Mrs Webster – and try not to think of her – on her knees, swollen-faced and pleading before me. *Please, Stephie, please! Anything, anything, please!*

From everything I have learnt in my work, I know how important it is not to neglect the remaining child. I do my best in those early years after her death, but I know it's a poor show: unable to throw out anything she has ever touched, unable to let go of the protection I feel I have failed in, and therefore ladling it on too much for poor Matt. He must feel suffocated. And occasionally, invisible. What a nightmare for a child. And later, for a teenager.

The relationship between Mum, Dad and me is now non-negotiable. It is as if someone has moved our pieces around on a giant board game and we are now in the same team. We do what we can for Matt and each other, and I drive back to Gloucestershire every weekend to start with. On the journey, I pass the turning we took that led to the picnic spot. I try other ways to go home, but they are always longer. And somehow, I allow myself to withstand it. I inflict it on myself. But what I become increasingly sensitive to is a pub on the corner. It's called The Blacksmith's Arms, and has a whole wall painted with 'WELCOME TO THE BLACKSMITH'S ARMS'. Every time I drive past it, my eyes are red with tears. I start imagining what it would be like to stop the car and run into the arms of a sturdy blacksmith with biceps like hams and a warm embrace. I feel what it would be like to be held close by such a man and allowed to weep openly, to sob my heart out and be told it's okay. He strokes my hair. He makes me a hot drink. He gets a cushion and puts my feet up by the fire. He plays with Matt.

One day it is too much. I do stop the car, and Matt and I go in. There is a giant television in the corner showing live football, and one noisy slot machine against the wall. Two men sit on stools at the bar eating pork scratchings, one with a purple nose and the other with brown teeth and a large, smelly dog. There is no sign of the blacksmith. Miserably cheated of comfort, I ask lamely for directions and leave, with Matt trailing me asking if he can have a drink of Coke.

There's a little time bomb ticking on the kitchen table. I see it every day after Katie's death, and on the seventh day I pick it up. I lift the small lever on the top of the camera and rewind the roll of film. I stand looking at the camera, afraid to open it in case I've made a mistake. What if I've failed to rewind it correctly? What if I let in some light when I open it now, and destroy the last pictures I have of my daughter? I brace myself, take in a deep breath and ping open the little door of the camera. There's the roll of film, intact, waiting to be developed. I slip the treasure into my pocket and set off for the shops.

At the chemist's, I ask how quickly they can develop it. After waiting seven days without action, I now want it as fast as possible. I watch the chemist plop it into an envelope and put it aside. How can he be so careless? I feel affronted that I am expected to walk away and leave this precious item with such a reckless man.

'We can do it the same day for an extra pound, madam.'

'Can't you do it any sooner?'

'Well . . .'

'It's urgent. It's very, very precious. I don't want to ... It's important that it doesn't get lost. I need to ...'

He looks at his watch. 'We do have a bit of a backlog, I'm afraid. I could get it done for you in two hours at the earliest, but that would be an extra three pounds.'

'I'll do it.' I feel like sitting down in the shop and waiting. He's going to take this envelope casually into a developing room somewhere and anything could happen. I may never see it again. 'Could I have two copies of each?'

When I pick them up, I am a bag of nerves. He insists on showing me the top photograph to check they're mine, but I don't want to see them yet. I take the two packets home with me and put them on the kitchen table. I wipe the surface down carefully. I make myself a cup of tea. I watch the packets of photographs uneasily. Then I open one envelope and look at each picture in turn.

There, captured for ever, the glorious, golden-sunned day of the picnic. There is Katie reaching for a sandwich, Katie holding her teddy bear, Katie rolling in the grass with Matt, Katie on my dad's shoulders, Katie with my mum's arm around her, Katie feeding bread to the horses ... Which one, which one of those horses was the one who ...? Does it matter? Then four pictures from another time: Katie on a swing, Katie and Matt watching television with Matt's arm around her, and two of a den he helped her build with both of them peeking out.

I set them all out on the table. For two days I walk around them, glancing at them from the corner of my eye, studying them when I dare. Matt looks at them every day, picking up each one and inspecting it closely, like a map-reader. After the second day he asks if he can have one or two for his bedroom. I say of course, and that I have copies. He takes three, each with him and Katie, and Blu-Tacks them to the wall by the side of his bed. Every time I make his bed I see them, the two of them peeking out at me from a den, grinning their heads off, and rolling around in the grass. I can hear Katie's shrieks of laughter. But not well enough.

Soon they may be lost for ever, those shrieks, those giggles, the sound of her voice. Every time I go into Matt's room, I feel a pain in my chest, and I hope that the time will come when the pictures are just squares of coloured paper on the wall, like his Ninja Turtles and his maps of the solar system, and I won't have to register them.

Katie's bear, Peter, is almost bald on his chest and arms. I take him to bed with me, and Matt has her beloved dolphin – also balding – called Finnegan. She loved all animals, but dolphins were her favourite. Still, sometimes, at night, I think I hear her cry out 'Mama!'; I often hear her in supermarket aisles or playgrounds. Her *exact* voice, her exact inflection. Surely it is her, I think. There has been some mistake. The five-year-old on the swings, that six-year-old walking to school, that adolescent with the school bag wearing make-up – they are all versions of her, of Katie at the age she would have been, of Katie come back to me, miraculously. A miracle. That's the sort I need, Jesus, if you're listening. Not your water-into-wine trick.

I send some copies of the photographs off to my parents, then bundle all the others together and put them in my bedside drawer. It will be six months later before I can get two enlargements and put them in frames. But if I am almost terrified of remembering her at times, I am even more afraid of forgetting her. Unwittingly, I hoard her things like treasure. I am afraid that time will close over the memory of her like seawater, so that all that remains of her castle will be a swirling eddy on the surface, a thin ripple, and then nothing.

Chapter Sixty-One

Strange Bedfellow

When Katie died, something inconceivable happened. Something which, at any other time, would have been wonderful, but which I can only really dare to savour now.

It's just days since the accident. I am in that numb state, not present in the world but too present in my head, unable to escape an onslaught of memories and feelings rushing along the pathways of my mind. Mum comes to stay for two nights. Dad wants her to go back with him, but she is adamant: Matt and I need someone around, for the practical things. She will only be a couple of nights. And although I don't care what happens, I soon realise I'm glad of her.

During her stay she manages to repaper Matt's bedroom, with him sploshing the wallpaper paste on for her as she cuts and hangs the pieces. While she's at it she replaces the skirting boards, which are about half an inch above the floor, and he measures the lengths for her with a tape measure and pencil. She wants to put in a new worktop for me in the kitchen, as there's a saucepan-sized burn mark which has been there since I moved in, but I stop her. (Two weeks later when she comes to visit again, she arrives on Abergavenny station with a five-foot piece of wood-effect Formica. She fits it, and replaces the washer on the dripping kitchen tap.)

But that first stay, in between DIY, she potters around, shopping, making small meals, taking Matt out to the park, making dens with him in the garden. At night, she cuddles him until he's asleep, and then prepares to sleep on the couch. I won't let her, of course, but she won't let me sleep there. I want to sleep with Matt, to put my arms around him, but she says, 'Let him sleep.' So we sleep back-to-back in my bed, my mother and I. The first time we've shared a bed since I was violently sick one night in my childhood.

I can't sleep, of course. My mind is full of these speeding thoughts, taking corners too fast and coming off the road. I am so tired, but there they all are on a chaotic racing track: my mother's back, a warm slab behind me; Katie's warm body through her little all-in-ones, the soft, waistless feel of her, the little jelly arms around me; Mummy, Mummy, Mummy; read me, read me!; you smell nice; I feeded it, I feeded the horsey; pools of blood around heads; heads on hard stone; stones with shells and bones in wells; Jesus bids us shine; sorry isn't good enough; Dumpling has had kittens; twenty-two is more curly; in and out the dusty bluebells; reek of wild garlic in clouds of snowy white; crying is manipulative; rose petals in the waste bin; you'll make a lovely dress out of that; Let's face it, no one will want you; Have a break, have a KitKat; fox cubs in the sunlight; World Cup Willie; I don't love you; chiffchaff, chiffchaff; you must know you're beautiful; magical roe deer; scrubbing out 'Monster'; Don't be so disgusting; a rabbit hutch with stencils; Look what you've done now; Mama, Mama, Mama!

I can hear my breathing, loud and gasping over my thoughts. My face aches with the tears that won't come, my pulse races and pounds. If I could just hold her one more time, one more cuddle. She had still been warm when we left the hospital bed. Perhaps she wasn't dead. Maybe they made a mistake. I must go back. I can't leave my little girl there in the cold vault of a hospital, or wherever they put her. No! I need to hold her. My baby. My poor baby.

I let out a sound that doesn't seem to come from me. A deep, visceral groan, a release of air and grief and tears, a giant sob to wake the dead. And then I feel my shoulders shaking, the wailing coming from my mouth, my lungs, my stomach. I don't even try to stop it now. It is unstoppable. I howl, I snort, I sob. I say 'Katie!' and 'No!' in a high-pitched voice, as if I can stop something. I know my mother can hear, but she says nothing, does nothing, just keeps her back to me.

Eventually it subsides. Some part of my body has had enough – for now, at least. The sobbing becomes whimpering, the whimpering becomes great breaths sucked in and let out chaotically. There is a rustling of the sheets, and behind me my mother turns. An arm reaches over me and a hand lays itself on mine. Slowly, she unpicks my fingers from my clenched fists. She holds my hand in hers. She strokes my arms. She says nothing. I can feel her face and lap pressed firmly against me, and her hand caressing my skin, like someone who loves me. And even though I long to turn over now, I stay like that, and she keeps her arm over me all night, her body warm and close as a limpet. Mummy, Mummy, Mummy.

Chapter Sixty-Two

*Item: **Fluffy dolphin**. Keep.*

I'm not quite sure how I managed to leave the little house in Abergavenny that had so many memories of Katie, but I did. I couldn't bear driving past that turning any more. I moved to Cheltenham – back to Gloucestershire, but not to Shepford. I was just fifteen minutes away from Mum and Dad, but I had my own place with Matt. We brought a lot of boxes with us, some of which I didn't open until Jonathan's visit earlier this year.

That's when I started up The Dolphin Project in Gloucestershire. It's meant for children and young people who need something different to counselling, something easier and less threatening. Children like Matt, bereaved and confused; children like me, who didn't know where they fitted in. All sorts of children with anxieties.

The idea was to have a programme of creative activities – writing, painting, designing, debating new ways of doing things in the world – and giving young people freedom and encouragement. It is all on a voluntary basis, with teachers and parents able to suggest and support certain individuals who might be in particular need. The key features of the project are empathy and encouragement. I've never been a fan of jargon. It abounds in education, and slips in and out of fashion like an eel. What's important is that the students feel they matter.

The tutors for the project all have to make sure that their

constructive criticism is based on encouragement. Not that anyone would be happy with endless cries of 'That's super!' or 'Wow, that's amazing!', but more that there should always be an attempt, as a guiding principle, to find something positive and home in on it. Something as simple as 'That's a really intelligent question' can make someone feel good about themselves, can increase their motivation. It's astonishing how a remark such as 'good question' can give us a little lift, whereas 'I already explained that' can privately crush us.

Now the project has started to produce anthologies of poetry, short stories (some of which have been published in local and then national papers and magazines); art exhibitions; design exhibitions and debating societies. News of its success seems to have spread, and the conference today was about setting it up in five major regions of the UK, going as far afield as the Highlands of Scotland and the west of Wales. It's received major funding, and I can hardly believe that I set it up in the first place.

I'm convinced this man who seems to be stalking me was at The Dolphin Project conference. I'm pretty sure he was the man who asked a question at the end. The lighting on the low podium was a bit fierce, and it was hard to make out faces, but it could have been him.

It threw me, actually, that question. But now I think of it, it wasn't hostile. Maybe he wasn't anything to do with the journalist at all. I thought I was all done, but the woman who introduced me – who had just saved me from the journalist – seemed to think there was just time for one more question, and he asked, 'Out of interest, why did you call it "The Dolphin Project"?'

Why had I called it The Dolphin Project? I thought he must know something about Katie. I panicked. Put on the spot like that, I didn't know what to say, so I tried to think on my feet.

'Well ... okay ... so, dolphins are known for their empathy, and empathy is – as I've discussed – one of the key facets of this project: that is, to encourage young people to put themselves in someone else's shoes, to see the world from someone else's view-point. They can do that through creative writing, painting, debate – any number of creative endeavours. And secondly' (*come on, there must be a second thing*) 'dolphins are known for . . . they're known for . . . leaping. Leaping out of the water.' (*What the . . .?*) 'There's all sorts of speculation about why they do this, but . . . but the most popular reason is that they do it for fun. They leap out of one element into another. It seems to be an act of pure joy. They seem to be shouting, "Look at me! *See* me!" and . . . well, I think we want our young people to be *seen*. We want them to break the surface and *leap*.' I felt a total idiot.

The room had gone quiet, and I could feel myself flush.

'Thank you,' said the questioner. Was it him? That would explain why he knew my name on the station. Or he read my lanyard. Perhaps he knew about me losing a daughter, and wanted to talk about something similar in his life. That would make sense. But the way he grabbed my arm, I'm still wary.

I think of Katie's dolphin, Finnegan, still on Matt's bed. Some trees outside the train window begin to move. We've started up again, and I try to relax into the comforting sounds of the track. Finnegan, they say. Finnegan, Finnegan.

Chapter Sixty-Three

The Missing Piece

One Friday when Matt is eleven, I get home from work and the phone is ringing. We bundle through the door together with shopping bags and school bags and a model house Matt has made in class. We are heading off to visit my parents, and he's going to show it to Gran to impress her. The phone is Dad ringing me to say that Mum has had a heart attack and died on the way to hospital. She was fifty-four. The best grandmother in the world.

The funeral was always going to be heart-wrenching. There are so many factors at play. Quite apart from the loss of a wife, mother and grandmother, there is the revisiting of religion, the decision about burial (Mum had wanted to be cremated, but Dad is determined to 'do it properly' after the church's rejection of his sister), the coming together of family members who have never managed to meet, the sudden revelation of family secrets. That last bit I am not expecting.

Me and Jonathan have kept in touch infrequently, but we are both in agreement over the funeral. Mum wanted to be cremated. We should follow her wish. Dad is adamant: a coffin, a proper burial. He gets his way. Jonathan says it's as if he's making her agree with him, yet again, from beyond the grave. I smile at that. It never occurred to me that Jonathan had noticed all these things too, has been quietly enraged by them all his life. These days he's a busy man – a design engineer, as it happens – and he has a successful job in Bristol. Lots of girlfriends, but none he ever commits to. Mum was very proud of him – justifiably – and I had probably been blinded by unacknowledged sibling jealousy.

Two women from the church come up to help me make the sandwiches. The kitchen is quite small, so after we've got going, I take the vacuum cleaner from under the stairs and give the house a good vacuum. I can't help noticing that the vacuum cleaner is the same make as the one Mum admired at Mr Man's that time. I remember how she whipped round his house, cleaning everything in sight, and making it bearable for him to come home to.

The front room is a mess. Dad has made no effort to tidy. There are empty coffee mugs and biscuit crumbs and apple cores lying around, along with discarded newspapers. I plump up the cushions and push the chairs back, then switch on Mum's pride and joy and glide it over the carpet, feeling sad that she will never perform this task again. Before I put the furniture back in place, I attach the hose and go round the edges of the carpet. The two weeks since Mum died have not produced a lot of long-term debris. No dead woodlice or bits of toys from another era. But when I poke the hose behind the television, it catches on something sharp. I imagine it's a prong from the carpet treads, although I'm surprised. Mum laid all her own carpets, and she was meticulous. I pull out the television table and run the nozzle along the edge of the carpet, right into the corner. There it is again. I try to suck it up, by holding the nozzle over the top of it and wiggling it about. It won't budge. So I turn off the machine and get down on my hands and knees. I find it with my fingers, but it's sharp. I can see a small point of something white. I go to get a knife and start to dig at it. Within seconds it flies up and hits the skirting board. I pick it up and examine it. It is a small chip of china. A piece that is black on one side, and which belongs in the chest of a beautiful galloping horse. I slip it in my pocket and move the television back in place, take the vacuum cleaner back to the understairs cupboard and go to fetch some glue.

The horse is still there on the mantelpiece. It is a strange sight now, seamed with veins of glue around its neck and torso. I turn the little chip over in my hand. I kiss it. Then I carefully apply a thin layer of glue and push it back into the heart of the animal, between its front legs. For all its wounds, it is a wild, leaping horse, full of life and energy. I forgive it for any unwanted kicks it might have made.

But of all the surprises at the funeral, it is Aunty Wendy, my mother's younger sister, who shines a light for me on so many things.

Mum's father died some years earlier (also of a heart attack) and her mother, Wendy says, is too poorly to come. Her leg is 'playing up'. She's seventy-three, apparently, and in quite good health, according to Wendy. I'm determined to catch my aunt at the small wake back at Greenfield Crescent, but there are far more guests than any of us expected, and I know I will have to make a concerted effort to greet every one of them before I can take my time over Wendy. Fortunately, Wendy has some children not far off Matt's age and they go to sit on the garden wall and throw bits of sausage roll to the neighbour's spaniel. Jonathan is fully engaged with a younger brother of Mum's, with whom he's discovered he has a lot in common. They're talking load-bearing in concrete structures when I walk past. Dad is deep in conversation with his Great-Aunty Vera, who is enthroned on the settee, unable to get herself up and down without someone to 'winch' her these days.

'So,' I say to Aunty Wendy, offering her some shrivelled quiche I made earlier, 'tell me about Mum. Why was she so distant from her family? We always wondered.'

Wendy has an appetite for gossip. She is slim, like our mother, and very beautiful. She must be forty-nine. I know so little about her, except that Mum couldn't stand her. It is clear almost immediately that Mum has been intensely jealous of her. 'Bubbly',

Mum called her, whenever asked about her, and 'A complete flirt'; 'Our dad's favourite – spoilt'. Here she is, at last, this much-reviled younger sister.

'Well, she hated me for a start,' she says, smirking. 'She never forgave me for borrowing her new red shoes without asking and getting them drenched in the rain.'

'Well, that would explain it,' I say drily.

'I was only thirteen, mind, but I had fatter feet than her, so they got stretched as well as splotched.'

'Red shoes?'

She nods. I think of the red shoes she bought me every summer. Always red, even if I might've preferred blue. I was never to let anyone try them on. She bought them for me with a sort of tenderness, and I saw suddenly that in that small act she identified with me.

'No, but really. Why did she stay away so . . . resolutely?'

Wendy stuffs a triangle of egg sandwich into her sensuous mouth. 'Oh, God. Our family. Where to start? We have the world's coldest mother. She was one of twelve, so Lord knows what she learnt about motherhood. Kath thought I was Dad's favourite, so that didn't help. And I probably was, until Valerie was born. And then Kenneth. He was besotted with Ken. And Mam and Dad were both cross with her when she got into college and then packed it in for your father. And, well, they didn't much take to him, of course, what with being teetotal and goddish and a bit doolally, if you don't mind me saying. All that stuff about not letting you get vaccinated because it wasn't God's way. And look how *that* turned out for you! Mind you, I don't think your mum ever forgave him for that. Not that she said anything to him. God forbid she should be angry with him. But she was livid! She got furious with the doctors, and when she saw the painful stretching and whatnot they did to your little legs in physiotherapy, she took you straight out of there. And they gave you a leg iron. You remember wearing that leg iron? Well, she gave it a couple of weeks then she took it off, said it made you cry and she wasn't having it, she'd make you a pair of boots herself, and I'll tell you what, I wouldn't put it past her. She went hunting for a pair of support shoes for you when I was up here once, I remember. The medical people said they had to be lace-up boots, so we went round all the shops, but they only had lace-up boots in brown or black, and she wasn't having that, so she bought some little skater boots in white. Goodness knows what she did with them. Can you remember wearing white boots?'

I shake my head, a little taken aback by this mine of forthright information. 'You were saying about why she didn't have much contact with her parents . . .?'

'Oh, yes. I was saying, well, they didn't like her leaving college, that's right. They didn't like him – your dad – I'm afraid. They thought she'd been brainwashed. But anyway, it wasn't really any of that. I don't think that stopped her. It wasn't that. If you ask me . . .'

I find I'm staring at her, trying to take it all in, what she is saying and the broad but chiselled contours of her face, the big white teeth, the wide, doll-like blue eyes. I wait as she shovels two cocktail sausages into her mouth.

'No, if you ask me, it was the uncles. See, Mam had several brothers, but two of them used to hang about the house, always on the sponge from her, if you know what I mean. Always trying to borrow money and never quite paying it back, or else, you know, arriving when Mam had just cooked a nice meal. You know the sort. Well, those two made themselves so much a part of the family, that when our dad was away working – he worked shifts, you know, so they were often "the men of the house" – they took it upon themselves to punish your mother and me when we'd been naughty.'

'Punish?'

'You know, give us the belt.'

'Two little girls?'

309

'Oh, yes. I remember Uncle Alf used to tie Kath to a chair and take his belt off. The slightest thing. He couldn't wait.'

I realise that my mouth is open.

'And me,' she said. 'But not very often, because I was so much younger. And she never cried. I think he wanted to make her cry, you know. And also . . .' she lowered her voice and looked around a little, 'and also, I think he, you know . . .'

'What?'

'You know.'

'No. What?'

'Tampered with her.'

I let out a long breath. I shake my head slowly. She isn't finished, though. She seems unaware or unconcerned at the effect she's having on me.

'*I* think, if you ask me, anyway, it may have had something to do with why she was, you know, a bit . . . puritanical. Always wanting everything to be clean. She was obsessed with germs.'

'Yes . . .' It is the only little word that can find its way out of my mouth.

'And I remember vividly – like it was yesterday – I remember Kath standing in the parlour and scratching herself like mad, because we both had ringworm, and the uncles were there (when weren't they?) and Mam said, "Look at her, playing with herself! Filthy bugger!" I remember that clear as day, and the look of shame on Kath's poor face. They laughed, those uncles. They roared with laughter. I was about four, I think. So, she was about . . .'

'Nine.'

'Yes, but I reckon they'd got to her earlier than that. Dreadful, they were. Merciless bastards. They're both dead now, thank God.'

'Does she . . . did she know that?'

Wendy takes a breath. 'Dunno. Don't suppose she did. Doubt she cared, really.'

'I wouldn't blame her.'

'Nor me. So, tell me. What are you doing? You married? I see you've got a son. Your husband here, is he?'

'No, I'm a single mum.'

'Oh, ho, ho! And what did my sister make of that, I wonder?'

I want to say 'not much', but I feel protective of my mother. I am furious on her behalf, and although I don't want to shoot the messenger, metaphorically speaking, I find I do, actually, want to shoot the messenger.

Chapter Sixty-Four

These Boots Are Made For Walking

After everyone has gone, the two ladies from the church start trying to tidy up, and I ask them as politely as possible to leave it all, but they keep on going as if I haven't spoken. I can't face their chatter in the kitchen. *What a good turnout. She was a good woman. What a lovely service. What a marvellous send-off. She would've loved it. Everyone loved the ham.*

Dad is kicking a ball around in the back garden with Matt. I go into the front garden and sit on the wall overlooking the road. How different it seems now. There are no longer any groups of children playing, no rhythmic skipping, pounding on the pavement to *I showed my knickers to the football team*; there are no boys crouching, playing marbles dangerously close to the drains; no girls sitting in huddles swapping beads; no hopscotch or tag or people walking up the road with their different walks. No, the road is full of cars now. They are parked all down one side of the street. And Napier Road is no longer a dead end, bounded by the railway cutting. Instead, it leads into Churchill Avenue, Einstein Close and Brunel Approach. I look across at Mr Man's old house. I remember the day Mum set about taking the graffiti off and mending the window. The door is painted a dark blue now, with a shiny brass letter box. There is a hanging basket by a new porch, trailing blue, red and white flowers.

I go back into the house, but the women are still drying plates. I go to the understairs cupboard and take out the vacuum cleaner, just to be alone. There are plenty of crumbs on the carpets now, and orders of service, folded in two and forgotten about. Seeing Mum's face folded in half on the floor and on windowsills makes me feel strangely hurt. After one room I realise the vacuum bag is full, so I switch off the machine and go under the stairs to find a new one. There would be no point asking Dad where Mum used to keep them. He wouldn't have a clue, and anyway, he is spending some precious time with Matthew. I unhook the torch from the wall and shine it into the corners of the tall diagonal cupboard.

All along the back wall are shoes, arranged neatly. Dad did nothing practical, but back then, shoes were a man's business. As long as I remember he sought out shoes to clean and polish. It was an act of tenderness towards the family. And although he made little other domestic contribution, these shoes are well-cared-for and stand in an orderly fashion. Above them are shelves Mum put up. On the lowest shelf are more shoes and stacks of shoe polish. Above that, Mum's open tins of spare plugs, curtain hooks, batteries and screwdrivers. My heart gives a little leap. How will he manage to change a plug without her?

Once, when I was on a train as a student, I sat opposite a middle-aged man in one of those old compartments. We soon found out that we didn't speak each other's language, which was a pity, as it was a long journey and there was, most of the time, just the two of us there. I remember that the ticket collector was so pompous that when he'd left, we both smiled. And then we giggled. It was an extraordinary moment of contact. I was reminded of that, looking at my mother's shelves of DIY products. We didn't speak the same language, she and I; that was our problem. But once, on a hot, sleepless night in June, we had our own extraordinary moment of contact.

On the floor, right up underneath the lowest part of the sloping wall, are two big cardboard boxes. I get down on my hands and knees and pull them out. One contains an old tartan shopping bag, the small garden sieve she once used to find Jonathan's plastic stag, and the vacuum cleaner bags. The other is full of older shoes: Mum's 1960s crocodile skin stilettos, Marks and Spencer sandals, Dr Scholl wooden slip-ons. And there, too, is a little red lace-up ankle boot. It is tiny, perhaps for a two- or three-year-old. I have the vaguest memory of wearing it. I rummage about in the box to find its partner, and there it is, only different. I shine my torch onto it. The heel is about an inch taller than the flat heel of the left shoe. The sole, also, is raised. Inside is an extra insole, which I recognise as made out of carpet underlay, the same underlay that stands leaning in a roll at the side of the cupboard. I can just make out the ragged edge of shoe dye inside the top edge of the shoe. These have been dyed red. I hold one little boot in each hand. There is a teddy bear motif stuck on the front of each. My mother adapted these for me.

What will we do? What will we do now you are not here?

Chapter Sixty-Five

Rituals

When Mum dies, Dad goes to pieces. The devastation after the death of his sister is magnified many times over. He is used to being the centre of Mum's world, and suddenly, without any warning, he is the centre of no one's world. We love him, of course, but both Jonathan and I have busy lives. Neither of us lives in Shepford any more, and although we both visit frequently to begin with, it is impossible to keep it up indefinitely.

He becomes very miserable and self-pitying, batting away all our suggestions for ways of getting out more and meeting people. But the truth is, he never bought my mother pretty things; he never took her anywhere romantic; he certainly never bought her flowers. As far as he was concerned, the marriage meant 'job done'. He had a way of reinforcing his wishes in this respect by telling my mother what she wanted – or more precisely, what she didn't want. You don't want a Christmas present; you don't want to waste money on a foreign holiday; you don't want to go getting a job/learning to drive/go ballroom dancing, and so on. And then he worked the same process with me: you don't want a pet; you don't want to go to discos; you don't want to go to university; you don't want to do psychology; you don't want to learn to drive. It can be strangely compelling, in a deeply frustrating way.

I can't help thinking about how unsettled I felt when Paula asked me to jot down and read out why I was angry with my mother. And I see now why that was: the truth is, I wasn't angry with my mother. I was angry *about* my mother. And I still am. I'm angry about that whole generation of women tasked with restoring a sense of male pride after the war, with building a home fit for heroes, and who in doing so were denied the very freedoms they had started to enjoy by taking on men's jobs while they were off fighting. Newly educated women who left college in droves, sold a romantic dream of happy-ever-after with pretty aprons and stand-up vacuum cleaners. Women who handed power wholesale to their husbands, and then watched ruefully as they inexpertly wielded it over them. All these women, many of whom never enjoyed sex, who watched their daughters grow up with freedoms – or at least, opportunities for freedoms – they themselves would never have. Women whose childhood traumas were never resolved, and which played out with the next generation.

Whether or not my father reflects on any of these things, I can't say. He becomes very withdrawn for a year or so. Then Lorna's dad, of all people, takes him out to play badminton one evening, and that's that. He starts getting involved in the fixtures, joins the club, buys all the right gear, is pernickety about size and weight of racket and even starts courting one of the women players. He draws up charts of team scores on card with a ruler and coloured stickers, he catches the bus into Cheltenham or Gloucester to visit sports shops, and will spend hours looking for the right shorts or sports shoes or racket covers. In other words, he becomes obsessed. I realise that his life revolves around badminton in exactly the same way it once revolved around the church. Religion suited him so well because it was full of rules and rituals. It told him what to do, and he just had to do it right. Here are a new set of rules, much easier to follow, and he soon becomes the person in charge of fixtures. He doesn't have to prepare sermons, but he prepares strategies and gives pep talks to his team members when they play in a tournament, and colour-codes them on his grids afterwards.

Nobody challenges his self-appointed leadership, as nobody else can be arsed to organise as meticulously as he does.

I become resentful that Dad has so easily let go of his religion, when he made it the bane of our lives for so long. I know now the angst Mum would have felt, having to go along with his important whims. And her grief at one in particular. What a strange mix of relief and bubbling anger she would have grappled with when Jonathan was born, when he changed his mind about medical science. How dumbfounded by his limitations. His fear of heights, driving, working women, car traffic and foreign holidays. His fondness for weak tea. The uncomfortable creep of understanding, realising she had filled in his blanks all wrong. But he was to be protected at all costs, along with the myth she had bought into. It hurts to think of all the adapting she did to achieve that. His religion was like a made-to-measure suit. Even though he would grow out of it one day, it fitted him perfectly at the time. For my mother, it was more like a second-hand dress to which she had added sleeves and let down the hem, but which managed to look brand new because she was so skilled at adjustments.

When my mother was first out on our street to mend Mr Man's broken window, when she ironed and mended his clothes and protected him from all the poisonous notes through his door, she was showing kindness. She was a kind, decent woman. I have known many religious people who are kind and decent, but I think they would have been kind and decent with or without religion. What my mother did for Mr Man that day in August 1966 will always stand out for me and Jonathan as the purest act of kindness. A gesture my father never knew about, or wouldn't have approved of if he had. Jonathan and I kept her secret because we sensed it was her one wilful act of liberation. She did something instinctively, without his permission, and it was good.

It becomes clear to me then, when Mum dies, that our father has not been touched by God all these years. It was about his

317

personality, his need for fervour, for rules and rituals. When he exchanged religion for badminton, he merely replaced one obsession with a more convenient one. Well blow me down. What a waste of God anxiety my childhood was.

Chapter Sixty-Six

*Final count: 53 full bin liners (biodegradable),
17 full cardboard boxes of clutter. Chuck.*

The tannoy is announcing that we will shortly be arriving in Swindon. Change here for Gloucester and Cheltenham. I know this man will not be going to Cheltenham, like me. What are the chances? Unless, of course, he's following me. At any rate, I decide to be the first off so that he can't see where I go. With any luck, he'll be staying on the train to South Wales. If he does get off here, then I'll just lose him. And if I don't, well, it was meant to be. But I can tell from my suddenly thumping heart that I am not ready to surrender.

Swindon, this is Swindon. Change here for services to Stroud, Gloucester and Cheltenham Spa. Please remember to take all baggage items with you. There appears to be an item of baggage in seat C64: she has sprained her ankle by trying to look cool in heels at a conference, she has hardly any friends, has hopeless parenting skills and has not had sex in five years – no, wait – six years.

I'm ahead of the game. I'm opening the door as soon as the train has stopped. I'm 'minding the step' in one clumsy leap and I'm running to Platform Five, which is where the ticket collector said the connection would go from. I gaze up at the screen to check the time of arrival: *Approximately 40 minutes late.* This can't be right. But even as I have this thought, the tannoy announces it, along with the availability of a range of hot beverages, bacon rolls and sandwiches in the waiting area.

I rush to the waiting area, not wanting any food, but a seat somewhere quiet and out of sight. The few tables by the buffet are already full, and even the long, transparent shelter is filling up fast. I venture in. It's warm, at least, and I can't sit in the ladies' toilets for forty minutes. I sit myself down between two people and take out my novel. I'm sweating already. I pretend to read, but it's no use. I keep looking up, searching furtively for the man. He's nowhere to be seen. It's okay. I look back at the book and remember the young journalist who waited for me outside our front gate all those years ago. What would he look like now, with his Cat Stevens beard shaved off and his hair flecked with grey?

The air inside the waiting room is muggy. Every now and then the tannoy goes and we cock our ears for information. But it's for other arrivals, other departures. We seem to hear a kindly voice, not unlike that of someone reading a bedtime story, saying 'Please mind the gap' on a loop. I begin to imagine us all trooping out onto the platform and looking after the gap, making sure its needs are met. Maybe giving it a rusk.

I'm going mad. This was meant to be a journey of two hours and twenty minutes. It's already been three hours, and no sign of a homeward-bound train yet.

A woman who plonks herself down opposite puts her hand on her heart and lets out a huge sigh of relief. I think of Dad. My father died last month. A heart attack, like my mother. I should watch out for my heart. The metaphor is not lost on me. I have wondered these last few weeks if I broke his heart, if I was responsible.

Ever since I left home – maybe even a bit before, as a teenager – I haven't been able to resist taking some small pleasure in baiting him. A taunt about religion here, a sneer there, I watched him squirm. I was like a child poking an old bear with a stick through the bars of a cage. I slyly fed him versions of himself that shocked him and shamed him. Not all in one go, but in little amuse-bouche portions, enough to make him wonder, but not enough to be certain of my cruel game. More recently I would rile him about his badminton mania, about the similarities to his religion in terms of ritual.

'I've challenged Jonathan to a game,' he said. 'A father–son contest.'

'What about the Holy Ghost – does he get to be umpire?'

'You may laugh, Stephanie, but I gave you a strong set of rules to grow up with. The church gave you a sound set of moral values, a good start in life.'

'Quite right. A single mum with sound moral fibre.' Which was true, as far as I was concerned, but I knew the single mother idea jarred with any thoughts of morality for him.

'We did our best,' he said.

It wasn't the religious rules I felt cheated by, it was the family rules. No one explained to me what was going on, perhaps because they didn't know themselves. My harshness was my clumsy way of telling him this now, demanding an explanation. I feel bad about this. I knew I was being cruel, because he had been so loving, but I was intensely disappointed that he hadn't lived up to my view of him as superhero. This wasn't fair of me, and I feel bad now, as he had never claimed to be anything better than he was. It was only Mum who had done that, on his behalf.

This was the man who had prevented my vaccination against a disease that left me lame, who made us go to church twice on Sundays, who told my mother what she did and didn't want. But he was also the man who taught me tenderness, who cleaned and polished our shoes every night, who loved his sister, whose keys jangled in his pocket as he ran nimbly up the stairs, bringing us the comfort of his arms when we couldn't sleep.

I was tormented that I couldn't make things add up. I kept looking for a solution to this conundrum, but I know there is none, except perhaps that we are all flawed, limited by the springs and coils behind our short trajectories.

*

I was surprised how many people there were at his funeral. It was hard to tell the religious friends from the badminton friends. I went by girth, largely, although there were one or two skinny men in shiny suits who knew the hymns without reference to the hymn books. In fairness, so did me and Jonathan. I couldn't sing, though, because I was unaccountably crying all the way through. I don't know why I say that. He was my father, after all, and the man whose arms were always there for me. Always. Perhaps it was because I felt I had broken his heart, in an attempt to mend mine.

I look down at my novel. It's hopeless. I look inside the jacket at the list of quotations. 'You won't be able to put it down' – *The Guardian*. And 'A compelling read' – *The Times*. Not compelling enough for Swindon station with a weird man looking at you. He's here now, the man, hovering outside the waiting room, staring at me through the Plexiglas, an indecisive frown on his face. Jesus. I find that I'm taking deep breaths. I'm trying not to pant. I will have to get on the train last, when it arrives, so that I can sit anywhere but near him.

Unfortunately, when the connection arrives there is a mad rush. Everyone spills out of the waiting room and surges onto the train like a stream of ants. Nobody minds the gap. The gap can look after itself. By the time I get on, ambling along at the end of the swarm, there is standing room only, and only just. The gangways and luggage areas are packed with passengers. I close my eyes and sigh. Forty minutes of standing up, squashed between hot, tired people, groping for something to hold onto. I find an overhead rail to grasp and clutch my bag close to my side. Doors snap shut with their familiar train station echo. A whistle blows. The train lurches forward.

My face is jammed against the ripe armpit of a man with a pink shirt. He is reaching up to hold onto the handrail above us. Behind me, a woman leans back hard on the wall of the train, hoping to steady herself, and on either side two students chat endlessly about a party they went to and how much they drank. The quantities of lager and beer and whisky chasers make me feel sick. I realise I haven't had any liquid for hours – not since lunchtime maybe. I begin to dream of a large glass of water, so cool that the glass is misted. I swivel my head to see if the stranger is anywhere near, but I can't see him.

I try to think about nice things. The glass of water I'll drink when I get home; the ripe avocado in the fruit bowl that I can put in my salad; the butternut squash soup I can defrost; the two Florentine biscuits I have left in a packet; Matt. Matthew. I can get to love his girlfriend, Alex. I'm sure I can. If she isn't hostile to me. If I don't come over as too 'needy'. Perhaps I could buy a flat out there in Australia? I will come into a little money now that Dad has died, although I should use it first to help pay off the mortgage. Maybe just a bedsit? Maybe I could rent a bedsit for a month at a time, and then I wouldn't ever be under their feet. I could just take a holiday in Australia. A few times a year. Who am I kidding? How could I pay for it without this job, and how could I do this job and go off for months at a time?

SMACK! 'I'm so sorry!' The man with the armpit has fallen up against me as the train rocks violently. I smile and say it's fine, and try to look out at the passing countryside under his arm, but it is mostly blocked by a man in front of the door. I think there are sheep, but I couldn't bank on it. They could be marks on the window.

My arm is aching now. I swap arms. Maybe she, Alex, will come to England on holiday and fall in love with it. Still, her parents will always be in Australia and she won't want to deprive them of their grandchildren. Maybe they won't have any grandchildren. Maybe she's a career girl. What did Matt say she did? Was it working in a bar? Working *at* the bar? Was she training to be a barrister? No, she was taking a year off before uni. That was it. So, who knows? Maybe she can't have children. Maybe he can't. Maybe . . . maybe he won't want children, after what happened to

Katie. I hope that's not the case. I mean, I don't mind if he chooses not to have children, if that's what he wants, but I hope it's not because of Katie.

I should've done more for Matt when Katie died. Instead I let everything build up around us: not just Katie's clothes, toys and drawings, but every scrap of paper she had ever so much as doodled upon. And then the same for Matt, so that it all stayed growing up around us like a forest. Jonathan made me see that I may have been replicating some weird comfort zone of mine – life with obstacles – but it wasn't fair to impose this on Matt. Now I have only one pair of her little shoes. Just like my mother, who kept my boots.

I wish I'd done more for Matt. Perhaps I should have contacted his father. And that's another thing. I had thought about telling Simon, but what could I say? By the way, you had a lovely daughter, but anyway, she died. So ...

He knew he had another child, or at least, he could have guessed. We bumped into each other at a conference in Bristol when I was heavily pregnant with Katie. He would have done the maths. He said I looked great. He flirted with me. He invited me for a drink in Clifton, and we sat outside, reminiscing and overlooking the gorge and the suspension bridge.

'I miss you,' he said. 'I miss our conversation.'

'Huh.'

'I do. You know I always cared for you, don't you, Steph? Always.'

'Cared for me?'

'Yes. I did. And I know I let you down – badly – with Matt and things, but at the end of the day, I was just trying to be honest.'

'Of course.'

'I assume the father of that ... bump ... is doing a better job?'

'He's not involved.'

He looked at me then, full of suspicion and fear. I took a sip of my non-alcoholic fizzy drink, which made my stomach churn.

'I mean, the thing is, Steph, I really care about you. I want you to be happy, but if that baby's mine, you need to know something . . .'

'It's okay. You don't need to say anything.'

'But I do. I care about you, you know that, don't you? But I never *loved* you.'

A demotion, then. Last time he talked about love it was to tell me he had stopped loving me. Now he'd never loved me. I didn't give a toss. Really.

'It's fine, please—'

'I used to think I did, but I didn't. Since I met Angelique, I realise, I really didn't have a clue before, and—'

'Angelique.' I looked out at the bridge lighting up like something in a fairy tale. 'Look, please don't worry. I'm happy as I am. Too much water under the bridge. Please.'

I finished my drink. *I never loved you.* I knew that. So, what was new? Just that feeling again. That unlovability. Don't take this the wrong way, but . . .

Oh Matthew, what a useless mother I've been. I should've paid more attention. I let grief swallow me whole, and barely had time for yours: the loss of your sister and the loss until-further-notice of your only parent. I should've done so much more.

I could've done more.

I could've done more.

I should've done more.

The sound of the wheels on the tracks vibrates through the carriage. I nod and sway with my fellow passengers, each of us locked in our own private agonies, trying to stand upright, longing for home.

Chapter Sixty-Seven

Hot Pursuit

When the train pulls in to Gloucester, quite a few people get off. I look around warily. There is one aisle seat free just behind me. Hesitantly, I take it. There are no other free seats around me, so I should be safe.

Then I spot him.

Further down the same carriage, taking a newly empty seat that faces towards me. I look down. He's seen me.

I don't care, I'm looking down. I shan't make eye contact. This is my journey, and I'm making it alone. I shall look at *A compelling read* and I *won't be able to put it down* until Cheltenham.

The air in the compartment has been momentarily renewed at Gloucester station, but smells gassy. I need some fresh air, a cool drink. When I get home, I'll change into something comfortable, grab some food and put my feet up in front of the telly. There's a drama on at nine. I should catch it. Then the news. Then bed. I can't wait. The promise of these delights makes me dream, and the act of reflection raises my eyes. I gaze out of the window beyond the passenger next to me. The backs of houses. Green fields now. More houses. Fields. Green. Take me home, little shuttle train. Take me home. If I can just get through that front door, I'll be safe.

At last we pull into Cheltenham.

Mind the gap.

I run down the platform, rush up the steps and onto the little footbridge that crosses the tracks.

'STOP!'

I turn my head enough to see him rushing up the steps behind me. He's trying to catch up. I dash as fast as I can to the end of the footbridge and past the ticket man until I am outside the station. Panting, I scan the taxis. The third one is free, and I take it, my panic contrasting with the calm of the taxi driver. 'Where to, love?'

I breathe deeply. Then, in the wing mirror, I spot him – the stranger – getting into the taxi behind. Surely not. I close my eyes. This is ridiculous. He has every right to catch a cab. He's unlikely to live anywhere near me.

The taxi driver is chatty and wants to know where I've been. What took me to London? Do I go there often? I'm so busy looking in the wing mirror I can't concentrate. When we pull up at some traffic lights, I see that there is a taxi right behind us. It probably isn't him. It's hard to tell as the headlights are on now, the sun having begun to sink behind the houses. Nonetheless, my heart does an extra beat.

'I had a lady yesterday, and she'd been up to London on a demonstration. Now they normally take coaches for demonstrations, but she was going up on her own with her two kids, to demonstrate outside the Houses of Parliament. Gun control, I think. Banning of handguns, or something. After that school massacre a couple of months ago. You had to hand it to her ...'

'That was terrible.' I can't think. I can't think straight.

'It was. You want to know your children are safe, don't you?'

'You do.' You can't always. You can't always know your children will be safe. But you have to do what you can.

I look in the wing mirror again. It's still there, taking the same right turn we take, the same left turn. If it follows us around The Park, I'm going to say something. Here we go. I don't believe it.

'Is that taxi following us?'

'Huh?'

'It's going everywhere we go.'

'Pity you hadn't known. You could've saved yourself a taxi fare!'

I say nothing, but keep my eye on it.

'That's Eddie,' says my driver. 'He does seem to be going the same way.'

As we get closer to the street where I live, I feel a real panic. If I get out outside my house, I might as well tell my pursuer where I live, invite him to knock on my door. I don't know what to do. If we take the next turn, there is no going back. I swallow hard.

Whoever he is, he is definitely following us.

Chapter Sixty-Eight

Run to Ground

'Go straight on here!' I say, urgently.

'You sure? That won't get you to—'

'Change of plan.' I direct him straight on up the road: 'Turn right at the little war memorial, down into Church Road.' He does as he's told. We'll be heading back out into the countryside soon. 'Drop me here.'

'What, here?'

'By the church'll do.'

He must hear the anxiety in my voice. He takes my ten-pound note and starts to rummage for change, but I thank him and slam the door. I'm about to make for the church entrance when I realise that my pursuer will assume that's where I've gone. I'll be trapped. I head instead for the field next to the church, the one with cows and a gate in the far corner. As I climb the stile, I hear another car door slam. No!

I'm rushing now, as fast as I can with my wretched foot, heading diagonally across the field to the far corner, towards the last ribbon of sunset. The grass is long and lush and clumpy, and I stagger across it. I turn briefly. He is getting over the stile too. He's following me! I can hear my pulse in my head. This can't be happening. I reach the next stile, my breath jagged, and I spot the old oak tree in the middle of the next field. Once I'm over the stile, he can't see me. I'm still hidden by the tall hawthorn bushes between the fields. I step away from the path across the field and hide behind the great oak tree. I'm panting now. I can go no further. The path across the field is open. He'll catch up with me in no time. My only hope is to sidle round this tree and wait for him to pass, and hope he doesn't look back.

I lean in against the corrugated bark. The base is too wide and spreading for me to get in close without standing on the roots. I press my face into the oak. If he doesn't turn around, if he doesn't turn around . . . please don't let him turn around. I hear the rustle of his busy footsteps through the grass.

They stop.

Catung-catung-catung.

'Hello,' he says, putting his head around the trunk of the oak.

God!

'I saw you go behind the tree. Are you avoiding me?'

Well spotted, mister.

'Um.'

'You don't remember me, do you?'

I dare to look at his face properly. Could it be . . .?

'It's Gareth. Gareth Hooper.'

'*Gareth!* Gareth!' I let out such a sigh. My hand flies to my chest. I have to lean forward to get my breath back and restore some composure. 'Why didn't you say?'

'You didn't give me much chance.'

I sink down onto the wide roots of the tree, which form a seat. He sits beside me. I study him. He really is a fine-looking man. Dark hair, greying very slightly around the temples. Eyes alarmingly blue, as ever. To think that I've been running away from him.

'I can see it now. Yes. I can see it.'

We sit there chatting, catching up. He tells me how he's often wondered what happened to everyone in Napier Road and Greenfield Crescent. He heard about Dawn's body being found, but since then there's been nothing.

'I went back, about fifteen years ago, to see if you were there, but you'd gone. Everyone had gone. Families had moved away, you know. No one answered your door.'

He was looking for me. He rang our doorbell.

'Oh. They must've been out. They were still there, then. Mum's died since. And Dad.'

'I'm sorry.'

'How are your parents?'

'Alive and kicking.'

We gaze out across the fields towards the western sky. Gareth Hooper has been looking for me. The sun is the colour of barley sugar, the edges of the clouds taking on a lemony tinge. There are the dark shapes of cows grazing gently on the far side of this field, and in the next one. Gareth Hooper has been looking for me. Me.

'I'm sorry I didn't recognise you at the station,' I say.

'You didn't recognise me earlier, either.'

'Earlier?'

'I was at the meeting for The Dolphin Project.'

'You *were*? Are you part of it?'

'No. I was interested in it, that's all. I'm in educational psychology.'

'You are?' Not zookeeping, then.

He nods. 'And when I saw your name in the programme, I wasn't really expecting it to be you, somehow. I kind of assumed you'd have changed your name. That you'd be married by now or ... you know, just because of what happened. All that dreadful newspaper stuff.'

'Oh, God! That!' I roll my eyes and try to make light of it. 'You saw it, then?'

'It was hard to miss.'

I sigh and try to change the subject. 'Hey, can you remember the trips to the Forest of Dean?'

'Of course. They were the highlight of our summer.'

'Cook this rabbit, wife!'

He laughs. I adore him all over again. He rests his elbow on one bent knee, the other leg out in front of him, so that he is turned slightly towards me. 'Are you married now?'

'No. You?'

'I . . . I was. Not now.'

'Do you have children?'

'One girl – Gemma. She's three.'

'Oh. How lovely. That's a lovely age.'

'Do you? Have children?'

'Two – one. Matt. He's nineteen.'

'Oh, did something . . .?'

I wave the air, as if I'm waving Katie away. But I don't want to unlock that box right now.

'It's a long story.' Except it isn't. Her whole life is a short story. She was beautiful, she was gorgeous, she was kicked into the road by a wild horse and died.

He looks at me as if I have something more to tell him. When I don't, he says:

'I'm sorry if I gave you a fright earlier.'

'Oh, no. Not at all . . .'

'The thing is, Stephanie, I've been looking for you for ages.'

I'm in such a state. My nerves are only just beginning to settle after the discovery that this is not some determined journalist or undercover cop, but now they are jittery again.

'There's something I've been meaning to tell you,' he says, 'for a long time.' I can hardly contain myself. The cows seem to blur, I am almost levitating with joy. 'It's about Dawn.'

Chapter Sixty-Nine

The Truth about that Summer

I close my eyes. I don't want to hear this.

'Everything in my life changed that summer,' he says. 'I've been haunted by it ever since. I haven't been able to live with myself. Not really. Not since . . .' He takes a deep breath. 'They interviewed me. The police. Did you know that?'

'I'm sorry.'

'No, *I'm* sorry. That's the thing, Stephanie. I knew stuff, and I didn't tell them.'

I turn to look at him abruptly. 'What stuff?'

He's going to tell me he moved the body. Please, please don't tell me that. What does he know? I don't want to know what he knows.

And yet, I do.

He looks at me earnestly, and then starts to pluck at some grass, which is thin, underneath the oak tree, where the cows have sheltered and nibbled all year.

'The truth is, if I'd spoken out earlier, I could've made it so much easier for poor Mrs Webster. She would've at least . . . maybe they could've . . .' His breathing is laboured.

I take his hand. 'Stop. You don't need to say anything. None of it was your fault.'

'But it was.'

'No. Listen,' I say. 'I'll tell you what happened.' He tries to speak again but I stop him. 'I was there.' I expect him to be stunned by this, because I've never told it to a living soul, but he just looks in front of him, across the dusk-dark field. 'I was there when she died. Okay? She wanted to play a terrible trick on Hilary. To be honest, she really wanted to kill Hilary. She was so jealous of her, and Dawn always got what she wanted. She made this plan to poison her with hemlock. She made a drink out of it, and gave it to her.'

'Hemlock?'

'Yes! And the thing is, it would've killed her, except that I knew it was common hogweed, and wouldn't hurt a fly. *But she intended to kill her.* That's the thing. So, when she had this plan to trick her, well, I stopped it. I warned Hilary.'

'I know.'

'How?'

'I was there too. We were going home from school, and Dawn went off to her house, and you stopped and told Hilary not to go on Saturday to the Dingle. You said it was a trick. Me and Steven both heard. I certainly did, anyway.'

'Oh.' I frown. I never knew that. 'Did Hilary ever tell you what Dawn said to her?'

'No. I never asked. But she probably told the police. They questioned her too.'

'Well, Dawn told her that she and I were going for a dip in the Dingle, and having a picnic, and that there was going to be a wonderful surprise treat for us all. It was never going to work, but she was so mad with rage at Hilary – you know, winning the cup, being held up by all the boys, and going down the field with Steven. God, she was furious. And then she had this plan, that if we both took all our clothes off, then Hilary would too. We'd go for a naked swim, and then she and I would run off with Hilary's clothes.'

'So that's what it was.'

'Yes, only it was worse than that. She'd told Mr Ma— Mr Lugg, she'd told him that we'd be there, and that we wanted him

334

to come, and to bring his kittens. Well, Hilary had just been given the two grey ones, but I don't think Dawn realised she had them yet. What she thought was, when we ran away, Hilary would be left naked with Mr Lugg and he'd . . . he'd have his wicked way with her.' I pause, a little awkward. 'Can you believe that?'

'Dawn was cruel. I didn't know what you were doing being her friend. But the thing is—'

'Wait. I have to tell you what happened.'

'No—'

'Yes. I didn't want to take my clothes off. I didn't want her to either, but she got cross waiting. I hid and pretended to take them off, just to kill time, but I didn't. And when she saw I hadn't, she kept telling me to take them off. She kept on, and on, and . . . Anyway, she stomped off and got in the water, and I . . . I said again that I didn't want to . . . to undress, and she got so furious with me, she got out of the stream and she went flying. She slipped. She cracked her head hard on a slab of stone. Jesus, there seemed to be blood . . .' For years I have tried not to synchronise that image with the one of Katie, lying on the tarmac of a Welsh road. 'And the thing is, Gareth . . . the thing is, I ran away.' I find that my voice is wobbling, and I have to give in to tears. 'I ran away. *I ran away*, and I didn't tell anyone that she was dead, I didn't tell the police and I didn't tell Dawn's poor mother, and now I know what that poor, poor woman went through, not knowing, not knowing if her daughter was alive or dead. Oh, God! What I did to that poor woman. What I did to her!'

Gareth leans in and strokes my arm. I look up at him and there are tears on his face too.

'Oh, Stephanie! Jesus. What have I done!'

'What have *you* done?'

His hand, which was stroking my arm, goes limp. He stares out across the meadows. 'I did something far worse.'

I wait. I can't think of anything he can possibly have done that was worse. Still, I wait for him to speak.

'I was there,' he says, swallowing hard.

'What?'

'I was there. All the time. When you told Hilary that Dawn was going to play a trick, that the "surprise" was a trick, me and Steve thought we'd go and see what it was. You know, undercover. It sort of appealed to us. Seemed like a bit of an adventure. But then Steve's dad said he had to do various chores, including walking the dog, because he'd been "allowed" to watch the World Cup with fish and chips, for goodness' sake. So I went on my own. And I saw it all. I saw you both. I was in some bushes opposite yours, a bit further away. I mean, I should've come out, but then Dawn took her clothes off – and what could I do? I was stuck. And I think I wanted you to take yours off, too. Jesus, what a twat I was.'

He shakes his head and plucks frantically at the grass again.

'There was a deer. I remember, there was a beautiful deer. It seemed to come out from where you were hidden and I ...' he laughs slightly, 'I kind of almost thought it was you, turned into a deer.'

'You saw the deer?' My pulse races. That deer!

'Yes. Anyway, I stayed put. I heard Dawn being mean to you. I saw her fall. And I saw you go. And I stayed because ... because someone else came.'

I can hardly breathe. 'Mr Lugg.'

'Yes.'

'What happened?'

He is silent.

'What happened?'

Gareth starts plucking frantically again at the sparse blades of grass. He sighs.

'Well, he looked upset. He looked ... curious. He went over to her. He looked up and around, and he called your name.'

'My name?' I knew this. I was there. There, holding my breath, holding the kitten, trying not to look.

'Yes. And then . . . he sort of bent over her. He could've been . . . I don't know. I couldn't see very well.'

'You think he . . .?'

'I don't know.'

I'm panicking now. I don't want this to be true. I saw his strange movements myself, but he had had his back to me. 'Do you think he fiddled with her? Or . . . with himself?'

'I don't know. That's the thing. I was only nine. I've tried, since, to think back, but . . . I thought he was kissing her.'

I gasp.

'But now I'm pretty sure he was giving her mouth-to-mouth resuscitation. I didn't know about that then. I didn't have a great view. I really couldn't see well enough, anyway. But it was him that rang for an ambulance and told the police, so I don't think he hurt her.'

I cover my face with my hands. He can't possibly know what this means to me. Of course, it should mean nothing now. But strangely, I still want to believe in Mr Man. I need to believe he would do no harm, despite what everyone else thought. Gareth must think I'm upset about Dawn.

'Look, Steph, I'm sorry. But that's not all.'

Dear God, please. No. I had waited for Mr Man to go before I left. Surely he didn't come back?

'It's what happened next you need to hear.'

No. No, no. I don't. Please don't tell me. I look at him, pleadingly.

'He went away. I stayed where I was. I waited because . . . I don't know why I waited. I don't know. I think I was just traumatised. There was someone rustling. I thought it was him – or you – but it can't have been. I wanted to wait long enough that I wouldn't bump into him in the woods or anything. And then something happened. I still can't quite explain it.'

'What?'

I'm terrified now.

'She got up.'

337

'*What?*'

'She sort of stirred and sat up. I thought she was dead. It made no sense. But she got to her feet – really wobbly, she was. Then she took a pace or two. She nearly slipped again, and she came back to shove on her shoes. She didn't buckle them up. Or maybe they were already buckled. I don't know, but she started to walk. She walked down by the side of the stream, and then she sort of slipped in and walked down it. All the time she was swaying. I thought she'd fall. And then she was out of sight.'

'Where did she go?' My knee is wobbling up and down.

'Well, I started to follow her. I came out of hiding and watched her climb out of the stream, then, I don't know, she went up that grassy slope towards the ruined garden ... She stood at the top with her arms out, looking down at me, half-naked. I swear she said, "Come and get me".'

I could see Dawn doing that. That's just the sort of thing she would do, even in her dazed state.

'But then she just *disappeared*. Literally. One minute she was there and then ... I mean, she just vanished before my eyes. So, I climbed to the top of the bank after her, and I saw this hole in the ground. It wasn't very big. I mean, I had no idea it was a well. I called down the hole, but there was nothing. And then I got scared. I didn't want anyone to see me there, in case they thought I'd pushed her in. And if she was found with no clothes on ... I mean ... I was scared.'

He puts his hands over his face for a while. 'You were nine,' I say. I put my hand on his shoulder. He places a hand on it, as if to keep it there.

'She was all over the place – like she was drunk or something. But I swear there was blood on her arm. I just thought, you know ... I didn't want to be accused of anything. For years I wondered if she could have been rescued – if I'd gone for help. I thought I'd left her there to die.'

'*I* could've gone for help earlier,' I say gently. 'But she couldn't

338

have been saved after she fell. She was eighty feet down in nine feet of water.'

'But I didn't know that then . . . I was afraid. I was a bit afraid of *her*, to be honest. She was always a bit of a loose cannon. Oh, God, Stephanie. It's haunted me all these years. I've never told anyone what I saw. I was such a coward! I just ran home.'

'You were a child,' I say.

Chapter Seventy

A Letter

He walks back to my house with me, and I offer him a lift back to his. He has come miles out of his way to catch me. His home is on the other side of town.

'Can I see you again?' he asks, before getting out of the car. 'I mean, we don't have to talk about the past and stuff. Well – the good bits.'

'The good bits.'

'Yeah. We used to have fun. I always liked it best when you were playing with us. You were inventive. Good company.'

'Good company? Me?'

'Yes, you, Townsend.' He grins. 'Tomorrow? Come round tomorrow and I'll cook you dinner. And you can meet Gemma.'

'Oh, I don't think—'

'Come on, she'd love to meet you. And she goes to bed at seven. We can talk some more. I think we've got a lot of catching up to do. I'd really like to talk this through.'

'But what about . . .?' I nod towards his front door, which has been opened by an attractive young woman with dark hair, and she seems to be hovering there.

'Oh. Oh, Sally, she won't be there. I said I'd be home an hour ago, so she's probably a bit hacked off. Will you come? Say, six thirty?'

Tomorrow is Saturday. Why not?

'I'd love to.'

We exchange telephone numbers, and I drive home, churned up and exhausted.

I keep humming a Joni Mitchell song. I know why this is. My subconscious is so transparent. I've looked at Mr Man from both sides now. Actually, I've looked at him from all the angles I can think of, and I can't bring myself to see our friendship as an illusion.

Of course, I can't bear to think that he might have harboured sexual feelings for me or Dawn, but I really don't believe he had any bad intentions. I don't like to think of the panting that time at the Dingle, but maybe I exaggerated it for Dawn. Probably it was his asthma. Maybe I imagined it. Or maybe it happened, and it meant everything she wanted it to mean. I don't like to think about that.

What I do know about Mr Man is this: for one whole spring and summer, he made me feel good about myself. He made me feel that I wasn't a freak. He shared his synaesthesia with me, and smell memories and William Blake and birdsong and foxes and deer and belladonna and bluebells. He had a small speech impediment, ironed his own clothes, kept an untidy house and loved his dog. And this gentle man had his windows smashed, his walls daubed and all the flowers in his window box strewn down the street. On the face of it we were an unlikely pairing, but we were two lonely people. We recognised each other. And whatever people thought, for four glorious months of 1966 we saw each other, we made each other matter.

What a day this has been, I think, as I put my key in the door. But it's not over yet.

There's a sheaf of letters from this morning's post on the mat. I take it through to the kitchen, plonk it on the table, fill a mug with tap water and glug it down. I go upstairs to change into some comfortable old dungarees, then I prepare a quick meal and lie back in front of the television with the bowl on my lap. I scan the post: a pamphlet about reclining chairs; a thin news-sheet from the local council – housing plans and public toilet facilities in the shopping arcade; an envelope about offers on roller blinds (it might come in handy to read if I'm desperate later); and I open a telephone bill and an invitation to have my oven cleaned. There is one brown envelope left, and when I turn it over and see the address on the front, I'm seized with shock. It's Matt's handwriting. This ridiculously plain brown envelope is a letter from Australia.

I stare at the envelope, laid out before me like saffron or caviar or white truffles. I breathe deeply. I'll eat my food and save it for later. I take a mouthful or two of my avocado salad, without taking my eyes off the envelope. I watch it, as if it might get up and walk away. I'm saving it. I breathe. I chew. I open it. It is two sheets of lined A4 paper written on both sides in his loopy scrawl, and decorated in the margins with biro illustrations:

2nd May 1997
Hi Mum,

Yes, a letter from me. Don't fall off your chair. I thought I'd write to you because some things are easier to write.

Oh, God! They're getting married! She's pregnant!

Well, to cut a long story short, I've split up with Alex. Actually, Alex split up with me, for someone else. And actually, I'm devastated. I'm writing to you because I was thinking of coming home. I'd like to come home.

I don't mean I'm coming back to live with you (no offence) – I mean back to Blighty. I was thinking I might apply to uni. I've been thinking about it a lot.

I feel I've got all this adventuring stuff mostly out of my system now. It's been a great year, and I keep reminding myself of that, and in some ways the split may be for the best. It's made

*me ask myself what I'd really like to do, if I don't have to align
myself with someone else's needs. And what I'd really like to
do is something like Uncle Jon, you know, a design engineer or
something. I've asked him a bit about it on the phone, and he
says he'll fill me in on some stuff when I get back.*

    *Anyway, here's the thing. I didn't tell you because I didn't
know how, but Alex is a man. You just kept referring to 'her',
so it seemed easier to let you carry on. But he's a man, and I'm
gay. Telling you over the phone didn't seem as easy as I thought
it would be, and I'm sorry, but I just kept chickening out. I was
afraid you'd tell me it was just a phase or something. The thing
is, Mum, it isn't.*

    *I think I've known since I was really young. I've been out
with a couple of girls, and honestly, I felt NOTHING. And that
wouldn't matter, it shouldn't stand in the way of friendship,
except that it did, because the nothing I felt was so strong it kind
of acted like a barrier to anything – humour, companionship, all
the other things you can have going on if it's not The One.*

Oh, darling boy! I don't mind if you're gay. I hope you've been
careful about AIDS, though. But I don't mind who you partner up
with. There will never be any children, of course, and you've always
loved children. But then, if Alex is your first experience, you never
know . . .

*Alex wasn't my first, by the way. Just my first really meaningful
relationship with a man. Although now it feels like it wasn't
really meaningful at all. Even so, you know what I mean. It
was different. I can't stay here and bump into him all over the
place in Sydney with his new man. I'm not going to do that to
myself.*

    *Mum, do you mind? Do you mind if I stay with you for a
bit before I get a job and a flat-share or something? I know I'm
not in a position to call the shots here, but you would have to*

promise not to try and convert me or lament the prospect of no grandchildren or warn me about AIDS or set me up with a gay man you know or get me counselling.

I know this probably seems cowardly, writing to you, but the thing is, this will give you time to digest it all, and decide if you're okay with it, and me coming back, and not trying to talk me out of it (not that I think you will or anything, just if you did, I'd feel such a disappointment to you, and I want you to be proud of me). What you think matters to me more than anything.

Anyhow, that's me done. That's me news. Hey-ho.

Ring me one evening (from 7 p.m. here is okay). I'm in most evenings now.

Love you, Mum.

Matt XXX
  P.S.
  Actually, I won't mind if you set me up with a really fit guy. Just so you know.

He's coming home! He loves me! Matt! My little Matty!

My heart is all over the place, skipping beats, adding beats, whatever it's doing, it's not steady. I'm dizzy with excitement. What sort of mother have I been that he was afraid to tell me? It reminds me of when Katie died and he didn't want to upset me any more, so he didn't tell me he'd grazed the whole side of his hip and ribs in a fall. He was pushed. He was bullied a lot when he was young. Now that makes more sense. Or maybe the whole Katie thing changed him. He always wanted a sister so much. Maybe he thought I was disappointed that he wasn't a girl after she died? That he wasn't enough? Stop it, I tell myself. He's gay because he's gay. I should have picked it up, but I didn't. It makes sense now. I can see how it all fits into place.

I read the letter again, seeing how difficult it has been for him in every line, spotting my own terrible inadequacies and presumptions as a mother. I need to clear away some more baggage, but I'll keep trying. I finish my food, the fork trembling in my hand. Then I read it again. *What you think matters to me more than anything.*

Matthew!

I have a surprise for you, too. You wait until you see your old room. You won't recognise it.

I delight in you.

Chapter Seventy-One

Unravelled

Gareth's house is ordinary-looking. A semi-detached with a front garden that needs some tending. There are some pretty, fragrant roses around the door, but they clearly haven't been pruned for a few years, and the row of standing pots along the paths are full of weeds and clumps of dried grass.

When he answers the door with smiling eyes, I step into a hallway smelling of delicious food.

'Something smells yummy,' I say, handing him a bottle and a bunch of sweet peas from my garden. He takes them from me and puts them in a jam jar, like the ones Mr Spruce used to have on his desk, and fills it with water.

'Must be your flowers! By the way,' he says, 'I forgot to ask you – is there anything you don't eat?'

'No,' I say. 'I eat anything.'

'Of course you do.' He holds my eye for a while. He's analysing me again, I know. A pleaser, he is thinking. 'I'd like to say I'm experimenting, but this is a safe favourite. Chicken Bourguignon. Or "Chicken Boggy None", as Gemma calls it.'

'Chicken Boggy None!' comes an excited voice from the kitchen doorway. There, standing in a little red all-in-one pyjama suit, is a small girl with a big grin and a mass of brown curls, not unlike Katie's head of hair when she was . . . I catch my breath.

'Well, hello!' I manage. I crouch down next to her. 'I like these pussycats on your pyjamas.'

She bows her head to look at them too, and to point out her favourite. Then her second favourite. Then her third.

'Are you the special guest tonight, Gemma?'

She nods happily.

'The special sleeping guest,' says Gareth, putting some pepper into his pot on the stove. 'This is my friend Stephanie, Gemma. And you're supposed to be in bed.'

'I want a stooo-ry.'

'Well, you go up to bed, and I'll come up in a minute.'

Suddenly, without warning, she takes my hand and leans her cheek against it. 'I want Seffany to read me.' She smiles up at me, and I look over at Gareth, hoping he can see my desperation. I can't do this. Surely he can read my angst, but he doesn't. He continues to stir his casserole dish, smiling, and says, 'I think Stephanie likes to read to little girls who are already in bed.'

Gemma does an excited little run on the spot. Then she lets go of my hand and rushes to clamber up the stairs.

Gareth turns to face me and smiles. I smile back, to show him my appreciation of his charming daughter. 'I assume her mum has curly hair?'

'She does.'

'Was that her, yesterday?'

'No. Sarah has her two days every fortnight – when she can. That was Sally, the childminder.' I must look confused, because he adds, 'Sarah left me for another man, and he's not keen on fathering, and she's very career-driven, very successful, and if I'm honest, I was the one who pushed for children. So . . .'

'How old was she?'

'Thirty-seven.'

'No, I mean Gemma – when you split up.'

'Oh, she was only about eighteen months when her mum left. She's three now.'

I feel the blood drain from me, and I sink down on a chair.

'Yes, it was terrible. Gemma didn't understand, but she missed her so badly, because she didn't see her for about three months – she was in New York. She sees her every couple of weeks now, of course, but she still latches onto women who are kind to her.' Oh, no you don't, Gareth Hooper. Don't think I'm going to slip in here and replace your wife. I have no wish to be anybody's wife. I'm quite, quite happy on my own, thank you very much. And I would be a hopeless mother to a little girl, if that's what you're thinking. Hopeless. I wouldn't have a clue how to even keep her safe. 'I have to be careful. I don't normally bring any women back. Except Sally, of course, the childminder.'

I remember the young woman at the door. I see now why she was desperate to go: because Gareth was late home and she was running late.

'So maybe it's not such a good idea if I read to her.' I don't think I can do it. The little girl not much younger than my daughter was when I lost her.

'She'll love it.' He sees my hesitation now. 'Please.'

He must know. He must have guessed. Perhaps he's forgotten my 'two' children.

'I had a little girl,' I find myself blurting out. He comes to sit next to me at the kitchen table. 'She was four. I'm sorry – I can't do it. I'm sorry.'

'No. *I'm* sorry. I shouldn't have . . . you hinted that there had been another child. It was insensitive of me. I'm so sorry, Stephanie.' He strokes my hand so gently that I want to hold him. I want him to hold me. I can feel the lid of my grief pushing open an inch or two, and I don't know if I want it to fling open completely or go back into its box. I'm straddling the possibilities. I'm afraid of what else might come out. He'll work deftly on the knots like he used to with the old washing line, and unravel me. He must stop stroking my hand. 'Look,' he says gently, 'I'll pop up and read to her. I won't be long.'

As he gets up from the table, I feel bereaved. 'No, don't go.' He looks back at me, and I get up from my chair. 'I'll go. It'll be good for me. I'll go.'

Gemma is sitting up in bed, whispering something to her fluffy penguin. She informs me that Dudley wants the one about the fish and the mermaid. It's called *Haddock*, and is about a haddock who falls in love with a mermaid, but has to compete with a fisherman for her affections. I do the voices of the sad haddock, and the lusty fisherman, and the fisherman's bullying wife. I really get into my stride, and begin to like it. Gemma falls about laughing. I'm enjoying myself.

When it's over, she asks me to read her another.

'Daddy said just one, didn't he?' I ask, weakening already.

'*Please!*'

'Well, just one more, then. A short one.'

She hands me a book about a naughty cat, and I read it with the same enthusiasm, giving the main cat a cockney accent, and another one a Cornish accent. She giggles and giggles until she's out of breath, and has to take in great gulps of air to stabilise herself. I can't quite believe that I have done this. It's been so easy. I close the book and say goodnight, and she holds her arms up to me.

It takes me just a moment to realise that she wants a cuddle, so I bend down and hug her. She squeezes me tight, seeming reluctant to let go. It's a good feeling. Then, without thinking, I kiss her on the forehead.

'Night night, poppet,' I say.

'What's "poppet"?'

I have to think. 'A poppet is actually a little doll, but it's what you call someone you care for very much. Like your penguin. It's like saying "sweetheart".'

She smiles, pleased.

'Snuggle?' she says. She wants it to be more of an instruction than a question, but there is an unmistakable note of pleading. I recognise it, hesitate, but I want nothing more than to lie down next to her for a bit, like I used to with Katie, like I did with Matthew before her.

I lie down with an arm around her, and she holds on tight, breathing out a giant sigh of contentment. 'Just for a moment,' I say. I feel her head nodding, and she pulls closer to me. Soon, I will go downstairs and Gareth and I will talk about what binds us. Our grief, for a start; our years of keeping damaging secrets. I knew, for all those years, that Dawn was dead (or thought I knew) and told no one. He knew for all those years that Dawn was alive (or thought she might be) and told no one. Both of us have borne the guilt of keeping something back from Dawn's parents, information that might have helped to find her – perhaps before she fell to her death. But I wonder about that.

I think about what Paula said once, about only being able to truly put the past behind us when we're done with it. First, we have to patiently sieve through it, examining all the stones and lumps. I think I can do that now, the way my mother found the toy stag. The soil is slipping through the mesh. I can make enough sense now of what clogged my mother, my father. Even, to some extent, Dawn. There's only myself, and I have a feeling that Gareth is going to find that remaining stone before the night is out.

On Gemma's curtains are woodland creatures: squirrels, foxes, deer and badgers. I gaze at the deer. Gareth saw that deer. He saw the deer that I saw when I went to pretend to undress behind the bushes the terrible evening of that summer.

I was just crouching there, frustrated and fed up with Dawn. She was always pushing me around. None of it was meant to happen. I thought I was in control, but I wasn't. You could never be in control when Dawn was around. I'd like to think I would've gone out from behind that bush and said I was off home, I'd had enough. I'll never know, though, because something stopped me.

It was the deer. I saw her as I turned my head; her nose was down level with me, as if she was eating. My movement made her bolt. She skipped away as light as air, but I felt she'd been

350

watching me. I remember how she stilled me, how I couldn't move then, for a while. And that's when I saw it, poking out through the leaves: dark and shiny, it was a berry like the one Mr Man had warned me about. I stretched out my hand to pluck it, so that the deer would not come back and eat it, but I spotted another . . . and another. I had to gather them all. If the deer came back, she would surely be tempted by the luscious fruit. I opened my shoulder bag to put them in, and found a screwed-up paper bag that had held some pear drops. I put them inside. There must've been a dozen or so. Maybe twenty. Too many to hold comfortably in one hand. I would go straight home and flush them down the toilet. I didn't care about Dawn any more. What was the worst she could do? Be there when Mr Man came? But he wouldn't come, because it was the World Cup. Except I didn't realise that the final, on that last Saturday of July, was at three o'clock in the afternoon, and was already over. The other matches had seemed to me to take place in the evening, but I had a loose understanding of football matches. Dawn knew.

'I'm going home,' I said, as defiant as I had ever been with her.

'You haven't done it! You haven't undressed. You're pathetic! What's that in your bag?'

'Nothing.'

She came over and snatched at my shoulder bag. I pulled it away, but too late. She reached her hand in and took out my note-book of special words. She was flicking through the pages, reading aloud from it: '*You must know you're . . . beautiful.* What? *You're going to . . . knock their socks off.* Oh, Stephanie! Honestly, is this what you think someone will say to you one day?' She laughed, as if it was the funniest notion anyone could ever come up with. Mr Man's beautiful words were all spoilt coming from her mouth. 'Oh dear. Do you really think someone will *ever* say this to you?' I turned to go, furious with her, but she held my arm. 'What else have you got in your bag?'

'Berries,' I said. 'They're old. Don't eat them.'

351

She grabbed the bag of berries.

'Is this all you brought with you to eat?'

She picked one out and put it in her mouth. Then, with the psychological skill you could only get from spending so much time with someone like Dawn, I said, 'Don't eat them *all*.'

Did that 'all' get tacked on the end as a flash of genius? An afterthought? Or a mistake that I didn't bother to correct? I knew she would eat them if I told her not to. That was how Dawn operated.

Of course, I have tried to find out about the effects of such berries since. It's not clear that deer even eat them, or if they do, whether they suffer any ill effects. It's not certain whether one or two can kill a child, or whether whole handfuls can cause no more than dizziness or hallucinations. Nothing is certain, even now.

I have always felt that Katie's death was some sort of punishment for Dawn's. I, who consider myself a staunch atheist. Maybe I'm poisonous around children. I look at Gemma's soft, sleeping face as I ease away from her out of the bed. It is the gentlest, most peaceful vision in all the world. The cheeks so flawless and tender, the lips so full and parted, the eyes closed on the cruel world. A picture of such innocence and trust. I stand and tiptoe quietly towards the door.

'Seffany . . .' she murmurs. I tiptoe back to her. 'Say it again.'

'What?' I whisper.

'The nice word.'

I stroke her soft hair, I swallow, I gulp at the air. It matters so much to her. 'Night night, poppet.'

She snuggles down and I go to the bathroom to wipe my face, which is wet with silly tears. Then I go downstairs, with a strange feeling of weightlessness.

Acknowledgements

I would like to thank my agent, Alice Lutyens, for all her magnificent support and careful guidance; my lovely editor Francesca Pathak for so firmly believing in this book and helping me get it up to scratch; everyone at Orion who championed this work.

Thank you to my walking companion, Helen Smith, for thoughtful conversation and support; to my wonderful Gloucestershire women writer friends: you know who you are.

I would like to pay tribute to Shirley and Frank Bailey (whose deaths bookended the writing of this novel: Mum at the beginning and Dad at the end) for being such loving parents and grandparents and for giving me the space to write over the years.

Thanks also to the Royal Literary Fund, for helping me to keep on writing.

The children's book mentioned, *Haddock*, is by the late Jan Mark, who was a kind 'godmother' to my daughters.

Ah, most importantly! For their endless support in good times and in bad, for their hilarious banter and their very good company, my daughters: Anna – a writer herself now – who read the first ever draft, and gave invaluable comments, and Lucy, whose illustrations and insights leave me in awe; and finally, John Bicknell, always, for his support, calm, wisdom and love.

Illustration of bear: Lucy Bailey
www.lucyelliebailey.com
Instagram: @lucyelliebailey

Credits

Jane Bailey and Orion Fiction would like to thank everyone at Orion who worked on the publication of *Sorry Isn't Good Enough* in the UK.

Editorial
Francesca Pathak
Lucy Brem

Copy editor
Jenny Page

Proof reader
Linda Joyce

Audio
Paul Stark
Jake Alderson

Contracts
Anne Goddard
Humayra Ahmed
Ellie Bowker

Design
Rachael Lancaster
Joanna Ridley
Nick May

Editorial Management
Charlie Panayiotou
Jane Hughes
Bartley Shaw
Tamara Morriss

Finance
Jasdip Nandra
Afeera Ahmed
Elizabeth Beaumont
Sue Baker

Marketing
Lynsey Sutherland